Copyri

All rights reserved

The characters and events portrayed in this book are fictitious. Any similarity to real persons, living, dead or undead, is coincidental and not intended by the author.

No part of this book may be reproduced, or stored in a retrieval system, or transmitted in any form or by any means, electronic, mechanical, photocopying, recording, or otherwise, without express written permission of the publisher.

ISBN: 9798778457416

Cover design by: Asya Kazafanli
Printed in the United States of America

THE KILLSMITH OF ETHERDEIGN

D. Ertug

Amazon Publishing

CONTENTS

Copyright

Title Page

Prologue: LET'S TALK DRAGON

Chapter 1: Whereupon the Killsmith and Her Spoils Go Head to Rear — 1

Chapter 2: A Bit of Resurrection Never Hurt Anyone — 52

Chapter 3: A Time to Be Undead and Other Embarrassments — 75

Chapter 4: The Awesome Power of Communication — 99

Chapter 5: The Nature of Time and a Time for Nature — 140

Chapter 6: Leaving the Past Behind and Other Gardening Tips — 175

Chapter 7: When In Doubt, the Goddess Will Fund You — 205

Chapter 8: Of Bondage, Bindings and Birthrights — 242

Chapter 9: It's All Relative — 276

Chapter 10: The Mountains of Kharkharen — 313

Chapter 11: The Killsmith of Etherdeign — 343

Epilogue: A KINGDOM WITHOUT A KING — 379

About The Author — 391

PROLOGUE: LET'S TALK DRAGON

How do you know a dragon when you see one? The answer may not be so obvious. Firstly, a dragon must never be confused with a *wyrm*, for the latter is almost always smaller and cannot fly. Wyrms choose to spend their days guarding the seas and seldom meddle in the affairs of their greater brethren. As it is in their nature to dwell in the watery depths, rarely surfacing, they have evolved to become the most passive of the drakes and hardly pose a threat when unprovoked; but as humans venture further in their quest to conquer the waterworlds they risk forfeiting the forgiving nature of the beasts. Not unlike their serpentine kin, wyrms must also display an assortment of colors and patterns on their tightly woven scales; however, the majority remains a deep shade of turquoise so as to blend seamlessly with the salty plains. In fact, the creatures have shown such a preference for the hue of late that several noteworthy wizards and serpent-enthusiasts have noted a significant decline in showier colors-to the point where oranges and reds have become a true rarity. Since wyrms have progressed their evolutionary cycle in the waterworlds their scales tend to be sleeker, much akin to the other aquatic life that populates saltwater. They are lengthy in body such as that of an eel, only much grander in stature and even quicker to move, despite their size. And when they have not yet finished their growth cycle it is possible to find that a wyrm has usurped the mind of a larger creature, usurping its host from the inside while manipulating its basic functions. Scholarly wizards have argued that this may be one possible explanation for the rate at which kraken are known to take down ships, for in truth the kraken are nothing but gentle giants who wish only to be ignored by the outside world.

Nor must a proper dragon ever be mistaken for its cousin the *wyvern*, as a wyvern is more compact in structure, practically feline in its agility and easily distinguishable by its poisonous nature, which no other member of the drake family is known to possess as a general rule. A few exceptions may be made for dragons but that is another subject for another time. Antidotes for wyvern venom are difficult to procure so it is best, upon encounter with such a creature, to look it straight in the eyes and bow as low as one can go without ever breaking eye contact. If the wyvern is unable to transfix you with its gaze within one minute then you are free to make a hasty and respectful exit and should get as far away as possible. A traditional dragon has little need for such gimmicks or charms but the extent of their mercy is far less predictable.

Wyverns are known to be the least civil of the drakes. Indeed they boast the greatest potential for fatality, for their minds have not sharpened to the level of a drake's and their speech is often a bungled mish-mash of grunts and shrieks. Their animal instinct still claims a greater hold over their intellect and they protect their habitats fiercely against intrusion. They are deadly in that they are lithe, swift and a greenish almost-sickly yellow in color that camouflages easily in a lush forest. But the wyvern has expanded its territories since the ceasefire between the humans and dragons and its evolution seems to be progressing at an alarming rate, producing multi-patterned serpents that are smaller yet have greater wing spans and are swifter on the swoop.

While other forms of serpentine species and subspecies are known to the world of Ethra in plenty and bear no lesser significance, the aforementioned pertain more closely to our story. All serpents vary in size and even in configuration but it is unlikely to find a wyrm, wyvern or other such creature that will be larger than a pure drake. As such, we are come to dragons at last.

What must be noted first and foremost is that a dragon's eyes are always golden. It is said that all other eye colors gradually faded out through thousands of years of evolution and the dragon's eternal obsession with gold is what has kept the greatest hold over the drake's physiology. Very little can stand between a dragon and its hoard for when the eyes of the serpent are fixed upon treasure, almost nothing can break the animal connection. One would do best not to intervene.

One must also be aware that the frail ceasefire between humans and dragons was dearly bought. Much bloodshed on both sides has led at long last to a begrudging truce, though it is a sad fact that both mortals and dragons have been known to stray from their promise of peace. It is rare for a human to provoke a skirmish with a dragon for the former almost always becomes prey and such incidents are not infrequent. Contrarily, should the human come out the victor, dragon parts have been known to fetch handsome rewards in shadowy markets due to their rarity and rate of deterioration. But the elitist nature of dragons and the commonly held belief that they sit atop the food chain makes them altogether difficult to communicate with and entirely easy to aggravate. So, you see, it is a silent rule that to avoid one another's company is best for, more often than not, it is the landscape that suffers.

That much being said, chance encounters cannot be prevented so one must exercise extreme caution when dealing with drakes of any kind for even the most personable of the lot can pose a fatal threat. Fortunately, the unparalleled pride of dragons dictates that they prefer to stay within their own community and seldom inter-mingle with other species save for feeding.

    Yet all the wyrms and wyverns and strange creatures of the world of Ethra ever pale in comparison with the magnificence of the only drake who wields fire in its very gut and, in uncontrolled combat, claims victory a cool ninety percent of the time. Dragons may be any color, bear any amount of heads, whiskers, facial and/or bodily hair, long or short snouts, broad or lean figures with a slight roundness in the belly; their horns may grow even as thin tree trunks and their wings powerful enough to summon storms. In all these silhouettes a dragon may appear- but their eyes will always be golden and that is a fact no longer victim to evolution. With regards to their size we must allow dragons the fluidity and/or limitations of their genes for they possess hereditary traits on par with humans. The smallest dragon ever on record was little enough to fit inside two human palms placed together. She was named Puffpuff and though her story had an unpleasant beginning, the humans who adopted her ensured that she lived happily- as short as her life was. The largest dragon remains a mystery as there is some discrepancy between the one humans have recorded into their histories and the one that was said to have existed, as recounted by the dragons themselves. Neither source recounts a name, nor do they attach any significant detail to him except to say that he was just larger than the oldest peak of Kharkharen and also most noble of character. Such histories, if and when they are kept, are tucked well within the libraries of aging scholars but a fair amount have been lost to fire and ruin throughout the troubled ages of Ethra.

    There is one final point we must bring to light ere we

conclude our discourse on the state of species and that is the law that a dragon will not kill another dragon- if they can help it. This is not to suggest that one dragon is incapable of killing another; rather that to do so is an unthinkable crime. Even in the event of such an extreme scenario the drake collective will go to any length to avoid imposing the judgment of death upon the killer. For the most part of present day recollection no dragon has intentionally brought about the death of another- save one- but that concludes the basics of species at present, whereupon our story begins; under blazing hot sun, summertime swelter and not a single hope of rain's respite.

CHAPTER 1: WHEREUPON THE KILLSMITH AND HER SPOILS GO HEAD TO REAR

Summer is a hellish time to be alive. Laboring under the heat of an unforgiving sun makes for ill tempers and over-functioning bodily fluids from which none are safe. A simple action becomes an ordeal, grunts turn into drawn-out sighs and one wonders if other seasons even exist or were merely figments of some deluded memory. Bouts of nausea bob in the belly as rays of light bear vertically upon your unprotected head to the point where you want to fight the goddamned sun and plunge all life into eternal darkness. But enough poetry...

Killdeed complete.

Bredikai Cronunham wiped her forehead for the tenth time since the battle between her and the dragon Gomra ended. That had been twenty minutes ago. Everything in the immediate area was caked in blood and sweat. Gomra's corpse was already sprouting stone and the petrification came faster than the killsmith expected. Cleansing her faithful sword- the Sacré Hexia- of the serpent's bile was more tiring than the killdeed itself. Had her magical prowess not been at an unyieldingly subpar level, life would have been easier for the killsmith- but such was the case, she reminded herself, tearing off another piece of her raggedy garment to wipe her hands.

Bredikai sat down on a rock whose jagged edges wedged themselves into places best left unmentioned. She was close enough to the fleshy remains of the dragon's carcass so as to keep an eye on it, as rogues-gone-rogue had a tendency of showing up and claiming the spoils for their own. Still, she was distanced enough that its stench couldn't numb her nasal passages. She allowed herself five minutes of rest. Her soaked black hair had long since forfeited the tidy bun she had bunched it into and was now stuck to her face with sweat. She was not a tall woman but at that moment it seemed as though Bredikai was only a meter away from the center of the sun and it was welding what little was left of her cheap armor directly onto her skin. Flies were buzzing around her head now and she swat them away, almost stabbing herself in the face with her own sword. Fighting a dragon had not been on her list of things to do that day and she would have gladly avoided the encounter had the so-called Gomra not scorched half the countryside. The latent heat of afterburn was still wafting her way, doubling temperatures and pestilence. Everything sucked.

    She'd have to make quicker work of dicing up the beast into salvageable parts before the entire thing petrified. Under normal circumstances a serpent's flesh will decay first, then the organs will harden, until only the bones remain to endure a slower petrification. Then, if left unattended and untreated by strong enchantments, what is left of a dragon will eventually become indistinguishable from the landscape blotted with jagged rocks and peaks. To the untrained eye the remains of a deceased drake are impossible to discern from stone- not that such a skill is ever necessary.

    Now that the killdeed was over and Bredikai was alone, she took a moment to process what had transpired. Her breathing had yet to even out and not a puff of wind alleviated the heat. She could admit to herself that she was shaken up by the experience. Even in her turbulent experience with drakes, she knew that something about the deceased had been unnatural.

When peace was struck between the humans and dragons, killing drakes without provocation was declared illegal and the laws were quite clear on the matter. To that effect, Bredikai reminded herself that she had been minding her own business passing through to familiar lands, looking for a single functioning portal, when Gomra came tearing through the skies setting half the horizon aflame. There had been no reasoning with the beast, no sense to be made of his crazed urgency. She would have been pleased to let him be had he not seen it fit to try to make lunch of her. More on that in a moment.

Killsmiths, though aptly named, are not a group to be underestimated by the population at large. They are mercenaries in the loosest sense, uninterested in policing civil or political disputes. That is the job of the royal guards of the kingdoms and whatever thugs they wish to employ. Killsmiths deal with the scraps of every other nuisance- for spoils. It's your standard fare of ill-mannered beasts and no-gooders, creatures upsetting the flow of the day-to-day and being general bloodthirsty pains in everyone's asses. The turnover rate for the profession is high. As such, killsmiths often cap well before the age of thirty whereupon the law for each and every citizen to register with a guild is enforced. But the mark of the profession holds for the length of a killsmith's life, as a trained and licensed professional will have a single line inked from the top of their forehead where the hairline begins straight down to the tip of their chin- thus making killsmiths instantly recognizable. This line which divides the killsmith's face in two is said to represent the duality of life and death, kept in check by the single blade. Though the inky enchantment is simple, it is no less permanent than the act of killing. It begins with a single vertical dash, faint and barely discernible, extending and deepening in color with each killdeed completed. Bredikai's face was nearly completely divided.

Killsmithery, a profession that sits somewhere between respect and revulsion, is still idolized by young adventurers yet to earn a status and, begrudgingly, by the old whose secret regrets keep them up at night. The spoils are decent when one has them but life as a nomad is unsuitable for most. Many killsmiths are disillusioned as early as twenty and register with a guild not long after that. Now at a whopping twenty-nine-and-a-half, Bredikai was one of the last older killsmiths roaming around, having earned herself the nickname 'Carver' for her quick hand and manner of dealing with spoils. Her semi-international reputation carried with it a lot of raised eyebrows but the Carver always delivered- and she delivered well. On the other hand, this... This was going to be difficult to explain.

With her five minutes up, Bredikai sighed and stood, ready to set to task. She studied the carcass with her pale eyes and remembered that she hated this part when unwanted empathy overcame her. Gomra had been an average dragon all around. There was nothing terribly out of the ordinary about his dull grey coloring, no significant patterns across his body. How she'd managed to hook her sword into his neck and splice through was a thing of mystery but the creature had been so invested in torching her that her speed gained Bredikai the advantage. Killsmiths were notorious for taking any opportunity to overtake an enemy in their moment of distraction and Bredikai was no exception. She said a final farewell to the fallen and held her sword to her chest as a sign of respect. She'd start with the head, as she always did, for that was the softest and easiest bit to take apart. That, and it ran the risk of decaying fastest.

Bredikai sat beside the head and swat the flies away. Something was bugging her about the whole thing. She stared at the head as though waiting for it to come back to life and tell her what she was not seeing but it lay hopelessly still on one side, tongue out, seeping blood into the loose dirt with a glazed eye gazing into nothingness. A single obese mosquito braved the descent and landed just inside the dead drake's eye, where the ball and bottom of the lid met, and Bredikai was so grossed out her face almost deformed permanently. Ew. But upon second glance the killsmith had to lean in closer, for the drake's golden eye was almost entirely overpowered by a redness harkening to blood- and this was a sight most unusual. Part of her told Bredikai that this strange occurrence had been brought about by her own hand, that severing the head from the neck had caused something to burst. But this was not the first head Bredikai had sent rolling and she couldn't recall having seen such an outcome before. For the sake of clarity she used what was left of her strength to roll the head over and check the other side. Sure enough, the right eye was in a similar crimson state.

    The Killsmith took in a deep breath of rotten air and looked around as far as the sunlight would allow. Her face was in perpetual squint. She looked back at the head staring at her, almost mocking the fact that she had no idea what to do with this information, when she noticed that wedged between the creature's impressive dental foray there sat one black, deadened fang. It was about the length of her hand and slightly larger than the ones it sat between. The tooth was so out of place that it seemed to not belong to the creature at all; browned and inconsistent with the gleaming white of the others. It was such an ugly feature that Bredikai almost felt bad for leaving the dead drake with it so she carved it out, gently so as to not break it apart, and placed it in her rucksack. She looked at her busted shield, now reduced mostly to char. It had been the only one she could afford and she'd known it was cheap goods but... damn. It was tossed aside. With one more wipe of the brow and a crack of the back, the sound of her snapping bones offended Bredikai's ears and she was suddenly left annoyed by her age, her situation, her everything. Spoils were spoils but she hadn't been able to salvage more than scraps and those would have to be gotten rid of discretely.

"Fucking lizards," the killsmith grumbled with her sack on her shoulder, all the way back to town.

"Are you of your burnt brain?! You can't bring those in 'ere! I ought to report you to the guard and that'll learn you but good."

"M-master Cronunham," interrupted a meek voice belonging to a small boy in greens and browns, "I've been working on a simple spell to preserve-"

"You quiet, you," old man Cronunham warned with his thick mainland speech and thick mainland finger. "Blew up 'alf the guild last week with your damned simple spells!"

The young boy who couldn't have been more than nine years old now looked about six as he shrank into himself like a baby turtle. Bredikai rolled her eyes at him and he replied with a scared smile. The killsmith rubbed her face and tore off another piece of her shirt to wipe the sweat around her forehead. Clearly the old man had not taken her advice regarding proper ventilation.

"What part of *he* attacked *me* are you not understanding?" Bredikai asked, staring now at the hysterical old man with a deadpan expression, still covered in filth from the guts and gore of her afternoon. She abhorred dealing with elders at the best of times but they were impossible to sidestep if one wanted to accomplish any financial feat. The elders ran all the guilds, controlled every faction of commerce and owned everything from the wineries to the dineries to the fineries. Needless to say they had precious little faith in the younger generation; and if it is needless to say then one need not say it but Old Cronunham was a man of choice words and they were being catapulted the killsmith's way.

"And how'd ya propose to prove it, ah?!" the old man barked. "Ach- me! What did I do to deserve such shame upon my house?" He wiped his swollen hands on an apron covered with coppertine dust and was bemoaning his cruel fate when Bredikai noticed that, in between the theatrics and feigned sobs, his interest in the items bleeding through her rucksack had been piqued. When she caught him sneaking a glance, he upped the drama.

"No!" the man carried on and the young apprentice handed him a goblet of wine to settle his nerves. "I won't 'ave your filthy third-rate spoils in this Guild. They're probably half petrified as it is... And that stench! You mean to poison me, you do," he said and took a hefty gulp. "I'll give you five duckets for the lot and that's doing you a mighty favor."

"Five!-" began Bredikai, "How *dare* you, you gnarled up old swindler! Do you know what I went through to carve these?"

"Dragon, my backside," countered the old man and his big belly jostled with every word. "That stench reeks of wyvern rot. Or did you 'ave another scuffle with your feathery friends? Mean to pull the wings over my eyes, you do."

"Just now," Bredikai warned, "tread lightly old man."

"And what else can I expect from someone with the nickname-"

"Don't you say it-" she said through a clenched jaw.

"*Griffinbait.*"

Bredikai squealed as though a thousand nails were being dragged across all the metallic surfaces of the world and one thousand feathered nightmares ruffled through her mind. Every hair on her body stood on end right down to her crotch and she steadied herself against the mousy boy who all but crumbled under her weight.

"Zira, move or I'm going to vomit all over you, kid," she said and the boy retreated quickly.

The old man looked at his apprentice Zira with exasperation and then at Bredikai and shook his large head from side to side. His general assessment of the killsmith was as an "oafish woman-child with more balls than brains, who ought to stop chasing reptiles and register with a guild before she's no use to no one." Sadly, he was not altogether mistaken in his survey. Bredikai steadied herself against the nearest wooden pillar and slowly dragged her body upright.

"But if you're not the lousiest grandfather in the kingdom," she said and the people milling around the area who weren't even pretending to not eavesdrop began to laugh. Old Cronunham flailed his arms about before clamping a hand over Bredikai's mouth and shifting his glance hastily from left to right.

A difficult to deal with, stout and toughened old man with a head almost as round as his aproned belly, it was hard for Bredikai to remind herself that her grandfather had her best interest buried deep within his shriveled heart. The reality remained that, while the old man loved his only granddaughter, liking her was an entirely different matter. The Cronunham line had established and upheld the Coppertine Guild since the dawn of time and not the fiercest dragon of the mightiest mountains could budge the old man from that position. But there was a single creature in all the wide world of Ethra whose life choices and inked face offended him to the core and made him want to feed himself to the manticores piece by disapproving piece- and she was staring at him; tight-lipped and only semi-defeated.

"I told you a thousand times not to use that word in public," the grandfather hissed until the veins in his neck were throbbing with stretched embarrassment, and he added an awkward "carry on, carry on," to their growing audience. "It's *Guildhead* Cronunham you little... Here," he said, clicking his fingers for the boy Zira to bring him a small pouch which he plunged straight into the girl's gut. "Take this and get out of my Guild! Come back when you're decent. You're a bad one for business, you are. *Killsmith*. Ach- me! Ink on your damned face and who knows where else. Thirty comes knocking and you're off chasing monsters- and not a drop of magic! My poor, heirless, *shamed* house," he sighed, shaking his head until he turned red. Seated guild-goers ordered another round of drinks and leaned back into their wooden chairs.

"I should've taken my father's last name," Bredikai grumbled.

"Well, now, my wee huntress, that's difficult to do when you don't know who he was, now isn't it?" old Cronunham said and even Zira flinched at the impending storm. The entire nosy crowd sucked in their breath but they were surprised when the killsmith applied gentle breathing techniques and responded sweetly.

"I remind you that *you* were the one who told me to be worldly. To help those in need," she said.

"I told you to be of 'elp to me *here*!" the man barked back, not enjoying having his words twisted.

"Well, then... Agree to disagree," Bredikai smiled and gave a sisterly wink to Zira who giggled, only to be shut down by a fierce stare from his master. "Come on, gramps," Bredikai entreated as the old man dove into her rucksack and almost passed out from the smell. "What's got you so worked up, huh? Look, I'm sorry I haven't registered yet. And you know I don't run around chasing dragons for a living. Not dragons specifically, anyway. You act like my spoils haven't been good for the Guild over the years." Old Cronunham grumbled unintelligibly and shook his head again. "Let's just keep on pretending you don't hate every single one of my life choices and I'll keep pretending I'm not offended every time you tell people I died in that incident with the... *the birds*," she added ominously.

"Didn't you?" the old man asked, hastily closing the sack and looking at her. He seemed to be tearing up. For a moment Bredikai was almost taken with emotion but she snapped back to reality.

"Stop telling people that!"

"It's like... I can almost hear my granddaughter's voice-" the old man spoke wistfully into the air.

"And I need a new shield."

"Calling from within a flock of feral Griffins-"

"For fuckssake," Bredikai declared. "Keep your lousy bag of coins. Just give me a new shield and I'll head out. And I want a better one than the crap you gave me last time. Fortified coppertine. *Upgraded*." She could have sworn she heard the old man call her a *conniving little shitstain* but let it slide as he rummaged around his stock for a shield he could be parted from.

"Thank you," Bredikai said, wrangling one from him

that he was trying to hide.

"Bleed me dry and be done with it," whimpered the old man, calming down at last. He rubbed his hands clean on his apron then relieved himself of the outer garment by tossing it at Zira's head. The guild-goers had doubled in number now as had their drinks, while others leaned against pillars watching the skirmish like a traveling theatrical play.

As a structure the Coppertine Guild was large enough to host no less than three cozy taverns within the overall establishment. One did not need to belong to that particular guild in order to patronize the various businesses located within the grounds but hanging around could be expensive, for coppertine is a high-grade metal and everything pertaining to it means big business. Old Cronunham not only took pride in his work but, as far as he was concerned, he was the demi-god of coppertine and in no mood to turn it over to a girl who couldn't care less for honest business. Guild-goers were a faithful audience to the Cronunhams' verbal skirmishes whenever Bredikai descended upon her hometown without forewarning and the older the two got the more entertaining they were to watch.

The building was old and getting close enough to warrant the word *ancient* but the structure had been very well maintained. Unlike many of the newer establishments in the kingdom the Coppertine Guild could thank the nigh indestructible nature of its namesake metal for keeping it upright throughout the ages. Wood had been used internally to fortify the single-level building and equip it with modern appendages and compartments- but the bones were entirely coppertine and no expense had been spared to date. As it was the kingdom's general aesthetic to build around trees and not uproot them when it could be helped, the building was one of many to enhouse small courtyards, letting trees grow unhindered while adding a touch of serene beauty. The

Coppertine Guild was a tasteful mix of metallic oranges and browns, with hints of green popping through its multitude of connecting passageways.

But despite the trees and colors of familiarity, total serenity was not upon them yet and old Cronunham had had enough for one day. He had orders to fill for the King and was short-staffed. He ordered Zira to see to some business about that explosion the child had caused and replace his apron with a clean one at once.

"Pray, when is the heiress to return next?" he asked with fake sweetness. Bredikai was having a tough time as a staff member took one look at her filthy hands and refused to relinquish the pint she ordered.

"With all due respect, this is the last guild I'll be heiressing," the killsmith said as her grandfather dramatically clutched his heart. "Besides, I've got time. Six more glorious months. For that matter, I'd come around more often if you'd stop reporting me to the Royal Guard."

"*More* often?" the old man repeated in shock.

"Yeah, I know how popular I am in Etherdeign," she smiled and shouted for drinks to be refilled for the entire audience- on her grandfather's pay. With people rushing to place their orders and the bar staff distracted, Bredikai grabbed her pint and downed it even as applause broke and her name was cheered. Just as the final gulp ran down her throat Bredikai was shooed through the building with a broom, past the wooden halls and coppertine glory, all the way out the main entrance into the town square.

"And clean yourself up!" was the last thing she heard as the door slammed shut upon a terrified Zira's face. Several of the older townspeople laughed and shook their heads.

Bredikai sighed and dusted herself off. She knew her

stench had begun to permeate when dirty looks were cast her way. She wasn't any happier to be there than her grandfather or the general populace were to have her but it was sheer coincidence that had steered her back into the borders of the Kingdom of Etherdeign, to her home: the capital city of Riverlong. Too tired to hoof it to neighboring lands and too money-conscious for proper lodgings, her evening plan changed to making a tidy little camp near the closest water source, the River Moondegrande, away from the gossip of her townspeople and the public disapproval of her grandfather.

    A light summer drizzle was no bother and a welcome break from the mind-numbing heat. For Bredikai Cronunham, the Killsmith of Etherdeign, it had been one of those days. Everything ached- even her eyeballs- so she took a swill from her trusty flask and let the background noises of the kingdom seep into her. She was a creature of wit and means-on-demand, a lonely profiteer, an object of unassailable intrigue and a lost cause to the rest of proper society who knew well of the Cronunham line. Freedom of movement was worth every soreness from roughing it in the wild but, every so often, Bredikai wondered at the paths not taken and how it would benefit her to settle to town life, to develop other skills and live in the tranquility of stability- not that she would have a choice in six months' time. It wasn't that she loathed the notion of stability; in fact, the one thing Bredikai often regretted was not having spent more time developing her magical skills. But magic was flighty to begin with and one had to be born with a drop of talent at the very least. She had always been better with a blade and this wandering life was one she had grown accustomed to, for better or worse. The thought of relinquishing her freedom of movement to work the Coppertine Guild day in and day out was the only thing that would always bring her to tears... She sniffed, casting the inevitable aside for another day.

The rain fell harder now, pasting her hair to her head, but she was too lazy just then to bathe in the river. She let the drops wash over her while lazing beneath the leafy umbrella of a willow, completely tranquil, her eyes at rest. The soft moss she was sitting on was a better bed than most flea-ridden cots she'd burdened. Far off and faintly came the evening bustle of the pubs and taverns of Riverlong, filled to the brim with drink, tall-tales and merry-making. The orange dots of strewn living quarters were stacked atop one another, nearly inseparable from the trees they wove around. Neat little bridges of stone and wood, some intricately carved, connected the buildings riddled with flora and fauna that cared nothing for physical limitations. Every now and again a billow of smoke would follow a bang and shoot up from a chimney in hazy purples and bright blues- even green if one got lucky. They lit up the evening sky and were usually followed by a stream of obscenities from some alchemical mishap and an apprentice about to spend his night transformed into a beetroot for having mucked up his master's evening.

Riverlong had always been a most beautiful city, worthy of being the capitol, in the equally beautiful Etherdeign which boasted a sensible if not obstinate reputation for standing loud, proud and aboveground. Many mortal kingdoms had moved underground during the Draconic Wars; back when Ethra was saturated with drakes with very short tempers and a taste for man- or so the stories go. No other creatures in the world had posed a greater threat to one another than humans and dragons; perhaps that was why the wars had been so frequent and long-lasting. Eventually peace was reached through a stalemate and by then it would have been pointless for Etherdeign to relocate for it had- through some fortune- been spared the brunt of the battles. Nearly unburnable coppertine had helped, of course. In time, newer kingdoms made their way upwards and while many kingdoms had acclimated to their sub-surface existence, living above was once again being considered trendy and edgy.

Etherdeign was known for its generous metallic resources, the greatest of which being the aforementioned coppertine. But the kingdom had more to offer, for her luscious landscape was painted in older shades, her business fed nearly a quarter of the world- and she loved her alcohol. Indeed, the kingdom had signed contracts to be the sole purveyor of Coppus Ale to all the neighboring kingdoms for the next billion years and damned if that hadn't been a slick business move. *'When you're out and about, have a cup'a Coppus'.* That's how they'd been selling it. When Bredikai had noted to her grandfather that goblets were preferred to cups she had gotten herself banned from all three of the Guild's taverns for a year. Thus Etherdeign had chosen to keep aboveground, along with her guilds and houses and her breweries, with very little subsurface accommodation to speak of. With the crux of the breweries operating from the capitol, no true Riverlonger was going to forfeit them to start from scratch beneath the soil.

Bredikai's mental promenade just about led her to peaceful slumber when, suddenly, she was doused with shockingly hot water, hoisted unto her feet from her armpits, held tight at the sides and her face nose-deep in the barrel of a pistol that could make short work of her inked face.

"It wasn't my fault," she said nasally, affronted by the treatment too rude for even the Royal Guards' lax standards.

"Take the Carver's sword and any pistols," the Captain said, as bored with the task of retrieving the killsmith as the killsmith was with having a weapon shoved into her face. The man's voice was familiar but his coppertine helmet guarded his face. What it didn't guard was his muffled chuckle and it occurred to the girl that there could only be one person who took such delight in assaulting her nerves.

"I don't use pistols," Bredikai said, now fully insulted out of her snooze. "They're useless against most killdeeds and can't, as you may have guessed, *carve*. Hence the nickname. Now I'd appreciate you getting this fucking thing out of my face, Fitzburt."

"Most pleased to see you in the Kingdom again, dearest cousin," smiled the ginger-bearded captain with sharp green eyes. He removed his helmet and his smile took over half his face. She could see the smirk from under his well-trimmed orange moustache. He looked only slightly older than the detainee but as unimpressed as her grandfather and said, "you'll have to sort yourself out before meeting with the King."

"Royal favors do wonders for promotions, don't they?" Bredikai smiled sarcastically and was ignored.

Captain Fitzburt puffed up with an equally saccharine smile and began to recite. "Bredikai Cronunham-"

"Don't rub it in."

"*Bredikai Cronunham*," he repeated, "you are forthwith summoned by His Majesty, the one true King Althaean of Etherdeign, to appear before him. Immediately."

"This is your idea of 'summoned'? Are you drunk?"

"Just doing my job, cousin," he replied. "Bind her."

"Unnece-" was where it ended. Before Bredikai could begin mouthing off she was magically gagged and bound to the back of some winged creature she prayed wasn't of the Griffiny ilk. As the late evening quickly drained away into night Bredikai found herself experiencing an adrenaline rush. She hadn't had occasion to meet with the King for over a decade, when she was a less tired woman, though the leader's gates were always open to his subjects. Seeing him now would have been a pleasurable visit if not for her reluctance in registering with a guild and the dragon she had slain earlier in the day. Now what were the odds of the topic of their meeting being the former as opposed to the latter? Maybe she'd luck out and it was something entirely unrelated. She snorted.

The journey was relatively short as the castle Etheria sat just on the outer rim of Riverlong and could be seen from any point within the city. One cannot be blamed for assuming the image of a pristine white structure of stone, set upon the land like an untainted jewel whose very making reflects the purity of starlight. But not in sunny Etherdeign. The castle Etheria was the most beautiful eyesore this Eastern side of Ethra and the entire thing looked *hot* as layers upon layers of coppertine would suck up the daytime sunlight and continue to blind and radiate the general populace at night. The general joke around the kingdom was that if the sun were ever to extinguish, the castle would be enough to keep the lands lit for the next thousand years. Bredikai didn't need to see the castle because she could quite literally feel the damn thing as they drew closer and everyone started to sweat.

Their trip was silent save for the sporadic laughter the killsmith could only guess was at her expense, especially after hearing whispers of what sounded like the word *Griffinbait*. She shivered and shuddered, calling to mind monsters of the deep, bottomless swamps and any other grim consolation to take her mind off of the atrocious creatures. Just as suddenly as she had been plucked from her rest, Bredikai was standing in front of the throne, sweating her face off and apologizing to the King for having punched his captain dangerously close to his ill-armored jewels.

"Quite alright," spoke the jovial King Althaean as Fitzburt simpered. "Good to have some energy around here! We've gotten so...so..."

"Bureaucratic, Sire?"

"I was thinking *boring* but, yes, I suppose that amounts to the same thing, what!" the King chuckled. Despite his good nature, Bredikai noticed that the creases in his face had deepened. The greys in his hair and trimmed beard had taken hold and a slight slump of the shoulders indicated that something had come to weigh on the man's merry humor. He had never been one to wear his crown unless formal occasions demanded he do so and, sure enough, the coppertine crest sat on a small table beside his throne. Althaean was no less the kindly statesman he had always been in his fine purple robes and assorted metal accessories. Etherdeign was beyond fortunate to have such a leader who had never given in to powerlust, let alone greed, and was more a father figure to the people he could never bear to disappoint. Kings like Althaean were truly born once in a lifetime and Bredikai knew that from experience- having traveled extensively and come face to crown with the law even more extensively.

"Welcome again, child," spoke the King, "it is a true pleasure to have you with us. You've made a grand name for yourself, indeed."

"Thank you, Your Majesty," the killsmith bowed. "It's good to be appreciated."

"Yes, yes it is," the King smiled. "Your grandfather must be quite proud."

"Oho, proud as punch, Sire," Bredikai beamed, lying through her teeth and Fitzburt snorted at her side. "How may I be of service, Your Majesty?" she asked, smiling at the King's unchanging habit of toying with the jewels on his necklace whenever he was about to deliver uncomfortable news. Whatever the man had been at fifty he was at seventy and counting.

The King cleared his throat and pulled out a

handkerchief to dab at the beads of sweat collecting on his brow. He decided, for the third time that year, to have more windows installed and no more coppertine this time. "I do hate that I've had to disrupt your regular business, my young Killsmith," he began, "but there is a rather delicate matter to be dealt with and considering your extensive experience with dragons..."

"I can explain almost all of it," Bredikai exclaimed before she could stop herself and it caught the King by surprise.

"You were... informed as to the nature of your summons, yes?" Althaean asked, sitting upright in his throne and folding his hands in his lap. Fitzburt looked anywhere else besides the King.

"Apologies, Sire, I wasn't," answered Bredikai. "Hoped maybe it might have something to do with your Majesty's sister, Mistress Althaea." She took a shot in the dark but the King groaned loudly at that name.

"Terribly embarrassing having a necromancer in the family," he sighed. "No. Thankfully my sister is busy foregoing all morality and ethics somewhere past the Mortlands... Or so I'm told," he said, rolling his eyes. "Pray she stays there."

"Oh, OK..." Bredikai nodded innocently. "So we're just... not really concerned that she might be raising an undead army to march upon us or anything..."

The King blew on one of his jewels and rubbed it on his stole. "Another problem for another decade, my child," he said with a restored smile. "Indeed, the pressing matter does deal in death but, mercifully, not the undead. We must discuss the issue of the Dragonfather- Lord Septiannus."

The King spoke the name Bredikai had heard all of twice in her lifetime as though it was a subject they had spent decades discussing through parchment and magical transmissions. For a moment she thought to offer that the King had summoned the wrong person but, then again, better to discuss Septiannus than the recently deceased Gomra.

"Oh?" she asked, "Has he had it with our ceasefire?"

"He's dead," the King said and his flimsy grimace was instantly replaced with a new smile. But he fell into an uncharacteristic silence and his speechlessness was more difficult to read. He looked as though his thoughts were far away, beyond the horizon in unknown lands, and while his warmth never faltered, the energy in the room seemed to shift. Even the few lords, ladies and guards who were present squirmed uncomfortably. The King was a humble man of old-world decorum and diplomacy who took no delight in conveying ill news to his subjects, let alone grilling them. He often struggled with his phrasing and, attempting to say things delicately, ended up spraying the subject matter like a volcano with a vendetta.

"Regarding dragons," the man continued, "it has been brought to my attention that you've completed a killdeed today. One who came within our borders."

"Yes, Sire, that's... what I do," Bredikai said.

"You are aware that killing dragons is nigh illegal and punishable by death," the King said, his kind smile still in place even as Bredikai's own withered.

"Your Majesty," she began carefully, "as an *older*, more experienced killsmith, I know my providence better than most. My killdeed came as a natural consequence of open hostility instigated by the aforementioned dragon. Gomra was his name- and that was about the only sensible thing I could get out of him. There was some kind of... malady, a sickness about him. My reputation remains beyond reproach," she said as the King listened to her intently and nodded every other word. "I mean... There've been a *few* off-key incidents but that's really just splitting hairs. I was attacked and I defended myself, is the long and short of it." It was getting mighty balmy in that throneroom.

"I see, yes... We certainly assumed as much," the King replied, nodding to his people as Fitzburt rolled his eyes. "And you have proof of the drake's provocation? A witness?"

"I'm sorry to say that I don't, Sire," Bredikai replied. "I have my word. But the countryside's scorched so... there's that." The real question was how such a hazard had gotten so deep into the kingdom but Bredikai thought it best not to delve into the details just then.

Althaean fiddled with his grey beard then stood and paced in front of his throne. Bredikai began to fidget. She was uncomfortable in non-drinking groups and the entire day had had an air of unevenness to it. That uncanny feeling was not being helped by the silence of the throneroom's audience or the still-life of the banners hanging like cloths of mourning above their heads. Nothing was breathing in the hollow room and someone really needed to open a window. All eyes watched and waited for the King to ease himself into the real matter at hand and it was like drinking the stale bottom of the ale Bredikai hadn't had enough of.

"It pains me for our laws to be so severe," spoke the King at last, "but we must do as our rules dictate, my child. Our peace with the dragons was obtained through great strife. Oh, I know your generation doesn't enjoy historical anecdotes but we must accept our past and draw lessons from it if we are to build a better future, yes?"

"Of course, Sire."

"I don't like having to explain our deeds to dragons."

"I couldn't agree more, Majesty."

"And now there's no Dragonfather to explain it *to*."

"So... I'm to be killed?" Bredikai asked with a scrunched up face.

"No need for extreme solutions," the King said, waving his hand in the air. "Truth be told, I would strike that consequence from the law but for those rogues-gone-rogue blatantly going against the will of the kingdoms for profit. We are lucky the dragons don't hold us responsible for their recklessness. Nevertheless, we must enforce *a* consequence. You are a public figure, after all. An influencer, if you please! An example must be set."

Bredikai nodded, following the King's smile. "Just what kind of example did Your Majesty have in mind?" She rubbed her wrists wondering what foolishness this prelude to death would lead to. The King dismissed everyone from the hall save for Fitzburt and two high-ranking guards who were sniffing the air for a phantom stench that was wafting through the room and settling into their armor. Althaean sat back down and slumped so deeply into his throne until he was almost swallowed up by his furs. He sighed, mumbled something to himself that Bredikai couldn't hear and folded his hands in his lap once more.

"Tell me, child, do you possess sufficient knowledge of Draconic hierarchy?"

Bredikai was puzzled. She had never seen the King frown before, nor speak with such a grave tone. "I don't know that I'd call it sufficient, Sire," she replied. "I know that when a Dragonfather passes, it's tradition for parts of his body to be detached before the rest becomes petrified. They're spread throughout Ethra. His people are then charged with collecting those six parts; sort of like a test of fortitude and wit and worth. The one who gathers them all is, ah, not sure what the wording is here but I guess *crowned* the new Dragonfather? *Proclaimed?* Right. That's the one. There was an old poem about it, wasn't there? Dumdeedum, something something, lailalai...

"Ere the day dawns and the sun eclipses,

In the greys where the moon on high wanes and waxes,

Through whispering winds and thunderous storms,

Beyond the kingdoms and past their thrones...

"Hail to the Dragonfather's age,

Hail to the Dragonfather's name!

"When evils laugh and good men kneel,

New worlds the gods themselves unveil.

An eye, a horn, a claw, a bone,

An emerald wing no longer flown,

The sixth a heart plucked from home-

All this for the one true heir alone.

"Hail to the Dragonfather's age,

Hail to the Dragonfather's name..."

    The King listened to the nostalgic tune which called his memory to the first time his own father had hummed it. The words were set against a bittersweet melody and he was glad to not have the bards among them for fear of being moved to tears.

"I remember it being longer..." Bredikai mumbled. "Like, *really* long."

"Good gracious child, that ditty goes on for about twenty leaves of parchment. Even the bards were exhausted and could only suffer to set melody for half. Mercifully, you touched upon the important bit," said the King. And he was right. Strange that such a piece had been composed considering that it was of human-make and likely unknown to the dragons themselves.

"Thank you, Sire," Bredikai said. "So that's the road to leadership if you're a drake. I believe the poem just about sums it up. As far as Septiannus- I didn't even realize he was still alive. Last I heard his name must have been a decade ago. I don't even think anyone's seen him in my lifetime. That's all I know."

"You are correct, my child," the King said, once again drifting into his thoughts.

"But something else is troubling Your Majesty."

The King looked around at nothing for a while. He had lived honestly- as had his people- so, generally speaking, there was little reason to be unhappy in life. But there had been a few milestones in his years that had struck at the man's heart and now a killsmith stood in front of him waiting for him to reveal his intentions and it pained the King to lay the burdens of the old onto the shoulders of the younger generation. He sighed.

"That news of Septiannus' death has just reached us is an unfortunate tell of how lapsed our communication has grown with the dragons," Althaean said. "With such a break we must cautiously assume that our frail peace has a lifespan- one which may draw to a close in *my* lifespan. That will spell evil times for us all. Bearing in mind that the hunt for his remains is anyone's game, Septiannus leaves behind a fair number who will be vying for ascension. While I am not familiar with the entire brood of hopefuls, there is one who must not be the victor.

"Many years ago, there was born to Septiannus a son whose name I prayed would stay forgotten…" the King continued softly. "He was, in fact, the strongest heir apparent: the drake Borghalus. He is a creature so disturbed that I fear my description would hardly do him justice. If the reports are true- if he has not wasted away as I had hoped and returned in the wake of his father's death- he will fight monstrously to claim the throne with the backing of a veritable horde."

Both Bredikai and the King jumped as a large window swung open and crashed into the wall before an apologetic Fitzburt could control it. To the relief of everyone's noses a strong gust was sucked into the room and the temperature became bearable for a brief moment in time. The King and killsmith chuckled, unsure why their nerves should be so on edge.

"Now that you mention it, Sire, I've heard of this Borghalus…" Bredikai said thoughtfully. "Once. Yeah, only the one time. Thought he was made up, actually. Someone was telling a story, maybe? Wait, I remember! I ran into this old dragon last year and when I tell you he talked my ear off-"

Fitzburt could barely stop himself from rolling his eyes but the King loved hearing stories from young people. He hadn't left the kingdom in many years.

"Surely not in Etherdeign?"

"No, Sire. Zindahn, I think? Jaedahn? Wow my memory's gotten rough. One of the Dahns. Anyway, sweet old drake, once you got past the snobbiness. Honestly I don't even notice it anymore. You could tell he wouldn't harm a fly if he could help it. He was living his last days. Just wanted someone to talk to and I guess I was as good as anyone. So we sat for a while, shared a fire. I asked him what he was doing so far from Kharkharen and he said something about it no longer being the home he knew... That it would never be the same again now that Borghalus was back."

Althaean and Fitzburt shared a look that Bredikai didn't notice. She was lost in the memory trying to recall anything of significance that the old dragon had said.

"It was the first time I'd heard that name so I asked who that was and, of course, I got an earful of exasperated annoyance. Like I'm supposed to keep track of serpent names. Long story short, I remember him saying that this Borghalus is large, even by their standards. Highly intelligent and manipulative... Ruthless. Told me Borghalus should have been kept imprisoned in exile. Then he said I looked *just* like his third daughter if only my eyes were golden so you can understand why I took his mind to be slipping. And then... Just like that, I was sitting by myself next to a small mountain."

The King stood and motioned for Fitzburt to aid him in removing his furs. Bredikai watched, unsure as to whether or not she was meant to be averting her eyes.

"Borghalus is very much those things," said the King, "and more." When Althaean's upper body was stripped of all clothing he turned his back to the girl and Bredikai was stunned into silence. Only the bare minimum amount of flesh stretched the King's back and what thin layer remained was torn and mutilated.

"I am afraid he blames me in part for his imprisonment, though in my heart I must have known that it could not last forever. Come closer, child, the pain is gone," Althaean said. "It's important for you to understand that you, as a killsmith, are very lucky to be in one piece. Your line of work is not to be taken lightly."

Bredikai timidly walked closer to the King and with a quivering hand trailed her finger along the leathery remains. The terrain on Althaean's back was tortured and crude, bits of skin held together by extensive amounts of coppertine thread that made it look more like an undead quilt than flesh. She muttered a quick apology when the King shivered and Fitzburt quickly shooed her hand away and robed the King.

"Borghalus did this?"

The King reclaimed his seat and smiled. "Your grandfather did this," he answered kindly, "and I am ever grateful for his dexterity. You might say he saved my skin. Do not worry, my child, it was so long ago that what pain existed remains now only in memory. But Borghalus hates our kind with a depth unparalleled... It was Septiannus who stepped between us and stopped his son from bringing about my end. I am thankful for my good fortune that I got a few strikes in and marred his throat, for I was not much in the way of a fighter, you see. I leave that to the more capable youth," he smiled again and Bredikai instinctively bowed, as did Fitzburt. "He was cast away into imprisonment in exile after that incident. Septiannus was a just and fair ruler who reigned in peace- the best of the Dragonfathers, and the one who finally ended the wars his forebears began... And he was a trusted friend whose loss I mourn."

With this revelation Bredikai noticed that the King's eyes began to water and she felt a tug at her heart as the aging King chuckled and apologized for his softening nature.

"I will not have Septiannus' memory tainted by Borghalus' cruelty now that he has freed himself, nor will I have the kingdoms plunged back into endless war. Do not be fooled, for if such a war begins in my lifetime, it will most certainly spill into the remainder of yours."

Bredikai nodded but the sinking feeling in her stomach indicated that the rest of their conversation was going to take her someplace she was going to enjoy even less. That she had been summoned to handle a situation was clear but just what was lost on her. Surely the King didn't have it in mind for her to deal with Borghalus, let alone his lackeys, by herself. Althaean, having noticed the worry on her face, was quick to put her fears to rest.

"Goodness child, I should never think to throw you into such certain death. But I will ask you to seek out Septiannus' other heirs. From such a just ruler there must be one among his brood who is better fit to take his place without foregoing our peace. Do everything in your power but see to it that Borghalus is subverted else we must abandon Etherdeign and... everything. I realize what a burden I've placed on you, child, but..."

"I understand, Sire," Bredikai said. She was being watched very carefully by her cousin and knew to tread delicately. "I believe in my heart that you chose me because you know I'll do anything in my power to set things right," she said and the King nodded and if he believed that then they were both swimming in one giant heap of denial.

"There are few killsmiths to choose from and even fewer I would place our fates in," the King continued. "This news comes to us far later than I would have liked. I have learned that Septiannus passed a little over one year ago, meaning that the hunt for his remains will have already begun. Alliances will shift among the drakes. Some will use this as an opportunity to ravage our lands. Etherdeign is charged with great responsibility I would not wish upon other kingdoms for our connection with Septiannus runs deep. I place great faith in your line, my child. It was through your grandfather's arts that I lived and kept what little skin I have left. Your cousin is a trusted captain of my guards. You are undefeated- as is proven by the fact that you stand before me in one piece. To that end, you are the natural choice. Would that I could aid you but I am an aging king and an aging king belongs in his kingdom."

"I understand, Your Majesty," Bredikai said once more.

"I don't wish to sound more desperate than we are," Althaean added, "but I must emphasize the need for haste as well as discretion. We don't know which way Borghalus' campaign will swing. It is my hope that the Draconic horde will suffer neither his return nor his ascension. You must ensure this. Succeed in your quest and you will want for nothing upon your return."

Bredikai's eyebrows shot up at the gain this opportunity would provide. At that moment she thought that the fates themselves had come to dangle their teets of fortune in front of her face and it was all she could do to stop her mouth from latching on.

"Your Majesty," she began and sighed at her own stupid morality. "With my deepest respect for your intentions I ask that you consider I might not be the right one for this campaign." When Fitzburt rolled his eyes again she glared at him and made herself clear. "What I mean to say is that this crosses into the boundary of investigation and diplomacy- possibly negotiation- and I'm not sure I'm cut out for any of that. I'm not exactly a mercenary for hire. I complete killdeeds for spoils..." She thought about that for a second. "Alright so *technically* I'm a mercenary for hire but what you're asking of me is to go on a prolonged suicide-stroll and skip the scenic route."

Althaean never let his dignified stance falter. "What I am asking is for you to aid your people with the skills you have earned a reputation for. You stand strong against dragons.

Fearless and cunning! This promises to be the greatest killdeed of your career- and for your efforts you will be rewarded handsomely. You have my word." With that last sentence Bredikai heard the desperation in the King's voice.

"A handsome reward for a handsome death," the killsmith mumbled. "I hadn't realized I'd gained a reputation for gold-digging... *or* glory-mongering. Lords, I'm so misunderstood."

"Not as much as you may think, child," said the King and held his forefinger in the air. "If riches and glory are not what you seek- and I had anticipated as much- I have something of greater value. With the monetary compensation you will receive, the kingdom will also grant you something that has only been offered once in the past two centuries to a civilian."

"I'm listening," Bredikai said, eyes narrowed, her heart beating at the prize she dared not anticipate.

"*Permanent guild exemption.* Total occupational freedom as enforced by these, the King and Kingdom of Etherdeign."

"Exemption!" Bredikai repeated in awe and practically salivated at the thought.

"My word upon it."

Bredikai took a moment as Fitzburt watched her intently, inwardly congratulating himself on his character assessment of his cousin. "Your Majesty, it seems you've made me an offer I can't possibly refuse," Bredikai answered and before she could even comprehend that she had accepted, the King had the place in an uproar.

"Excellent!" Althaean jumped up and began to babble. "I don't know where you think it best to start but the Rogue Guild will outfit you with information we have been unable to gather. Those busybodies know everything. Tell them who sends you- though they will likely know long before you reach them. It is just over one day to the nearest Southern portal but we will give you whatever mode of transport you deem appropriate. It will take you to-"

"Yes, the Western exit by the Karryon border," Bredikai said and the King nodded happily, his faith in the girl having temporarily rejuvenated his zest for life.

"I am not entirely certain the portal operates as a two-way passage these days," mused the King. "It is questionable how many of them are even functional. Need to get those checked again," he said to Fitzburt.

"Well this blows. I mean," Bredikai added hastily, "that is most unfortunate."

"Portals are so unreliable and require more magic than I am willing to expend to reconfigure," the King said pensively. "You would be wise to assume them to be non-functional or lead to one-way exits so travel may prove difficult. Ill days are stretched upon the horizon!" the King prophesied but his excited smile was sending mixed messages around the room. "Will you choose a steed or some form of winged-creature?"

"I'll take my chances with a horse," the girl replied.

"Yes, I understand, of course... That *Griffinbait* business."

Bredikai shuddered from head to tit. It seemed everyone in the entire kingdom had heard that damn story. "Please don't remind me."

The King laughed and walked to the girl's side. "Come," he said, "you will spend the night in the castle before we hasten you on your journey in the morning. We shall dine and talk of happier things before the days take us into the unknown.

Captain Fitzburt, if you would be so kind." Fitzburt nodded and took the lead as the King held out his arm out for the killsmith. They kept a brisk pace through the throneroom and down a hall, followed by passageways where magic orbs lit the way and torches were used for aesthetic purposes only.

The group walked deeper into the folds of the castle where the winding paths and under-bridges twisted just enough to disorient her. The trek was more pleasant than the journey to the castle had been and the King's mood lightened so much by Bredikai's assumption of duty he seemed to have forgotten the bit where she might not be returning.

"How are your parents then?" the King asked, making merry conversation.

"Still dead, Majesty."

"One would hope, child. Can't be too certain these days," he said and they chuckled. "You and my Captain are cousins on your mother's side, are you not?"

"Like second or third, Sire. My mother, may she find peace, was a free spirit. Her dalliances have the family tree all muddled up."

"Ah yes, of course, the beautiful Brenadine! She was so full of energy and charm," the King sang and sighed a little too nostalgically. Bredikai's eyebrows sank and she glared at the King suspiciously.

Althaean laughed heartily as they walked. "Now I see you are ready for that drink!"

"Local gossip mentioned that Your Majesty had sworn off drinking," teased the killsmith.

"Indeed- much as half this kingdom swears upon it every night. And you, child? Do you not drink?"

"Hardly touch the stuff, Sire."

"CHUG! CHUG! CHUG! CHUG!"

"Pints down, hands together.... begin!" commanded the King and a booming cheer overtook the mess hall.

Bredikai and Fitzburt were in the fifth and final match of their drink-arm wrestling and the whole of the hall was in a frenzy. The cousins were hand-locked now, tied together in a two for two that was about to hail its champion for the night. Veins throbbed, sweat and copious amounts of alcohol soaked the table burdened by two strong arms, each trying to pummel the other into defeat. Fitzburt was a tall man of sound bearing but Bredikai was a formidable foe in that she was a small bundle of pure muscle. They were evenly matched as a hundred guards cheered and howled but, in the end, the only one who made damn good on his bet was the King.

"I never lose a bet," the leader smiled as he graciously accepted half the hall's gold.

"Sure, it's not insulting that you bet against me, Sire," Bredikai said, rubbing her sore arm.

"Had to be certain young Fitzburt was worth the promotion, you see," Althaean chuckled. "You've done your King proud, son! And you, young lady, stick to dragons. But don't you fret; Fitzburt will be worse for the wear with all that drink come the morrow. Something tells me you are the real winner." From anyone else that remark may have come off as condescending but with one more pat on the back Fitzburt ran to vomit in a corner and more cheers and laughter erupted. "And now this old man will retire."

Everyone stood as the King tried to steady his footing, slightly tipsy but still in top form. He paused in front of Bredikai and took her hand in his as a gesture of fatherly faith and affection which made the girl feel a blushing awkwardness.

"I thank you for doing this for us," Althaean said. "You will forgive me for not seeing you off but farewells are another one of my weaknesses. Let us part in affection and esteem," he said and Bredikai's heart swelled. "In affection and esteem," the King repeated, "and the hope of your safe return." Choked up, Bredikai smiled and nodded as the King and his retinue flowed through the halls and disappeared into more regal corners of the castle. The evening continued and they had well passed the midnight hour by the time the hall emptied. At last the cousins were left alone to a well-earned silence and it was a peaceful one in which they were both exhausted.

"You should get some sleep," Bredikai said as Fitzburt wiped another bout of grossness from his face. "I'll probably head out in an hour or so. Best get a head start since I have no idea *how* I'm going to start or *where* or literally anything." Fiztburt didn't answer. He was looking at her with a strange expression and it was so discomforting that she finally had to ask him, "*what?*"

"I want you to see something," he said mysteriously. He had been debating over-sharing with his cousin for the better part of the evening for he had not been cleared to divulge kingdom secrets. But Bredikai was family, no matter how distant they'd become in adulthood, and there was no telling when they would be seeing one another again. "Follow me."

"Ow."

"Shut your face, for the love of everything be quiet! We're not supposed to be here."

"Then why are we?" Bredikai hissed back. "Stop poking around in the dark, you're stepping all over me!"

"Here we are."

"Where we are? Are we even in the castle still?"

Fitzburt summoned lights where he walked and the further they went into the bowels of the keep the darker and cooler the atmosphere became. Bredikai's tension was on the rise with each step they advanced towards an unimpressive-looking wall adorned with nothing but a dull torch. The killsmith observed as her cousin demonstrated simple yet smooth magical prowess- so smooth it made her jealous- to reveal a door which they entered quietly. At once the air became downright cold and were it not for the comforts of alcohol they would have been shivering. After a short walk the pair stood at the entrance of a cavernous gallery inhabited by the preserved remains of creatures great and small. A wild synthesis of laboratory and museum, the killsmith stood awed by the meticulousness with which the creatures had been kept.

"Hey... hey! That's one of my killdeeds!" she yelled, unable to stop her outcry. Fitzburt stopped and glared at his cousin. "Not a problem... just pointing out..."

"The necromancers are attempting to woo us," the man

said at last and it was a curious statement to make at the time. They were drunk, breaking out in cold sweats and standing in an animalia mausoleum. What in the hells was he talking about?

"The...? Didn't think they had much wooing power left after the Bone Wars fiascos. Plural."

"No one did," Fitzburt admitted. "But the King's sister holds strongly to her position as guildhead and word is she still bears great affection for her brother, such as it is. The King won't hear of it. He blames her for something that I know nothing about. What I *do* know," he continued with an air of conspiracy, "is that she has been sending him gifts over the years. The most precious came just a week ago. Come." Bredikai kept silent as they strode through all manner of gorgons, skeletons, demons, a rather impressive wyrm that still occupied part of a giant octopus, griffins (she shuddered) and, at long last, dragon. The drake was reduced in part to bone though, for the better part, the creature was relatively intact. It took the killsmith several awe-stricken minutes to realize that her cousin was staring at her with full appreciation of her shock.

"But how..." she began, "how've you been able to preserve it? Nothing's petrified!"

"Take a closer look," Fitzburt said and Bredikai walked towards the dead beast. The creature's body was mounted, pierced through with many coppertine rods. It hovered just atop a small dune of gold which she shuffled past with difficulty. Closer she drew to the dragon and with each step Bredikai felt that familiar unnaturality about the serpent. No sooner had she gone as far as she'd dared when a rancid smell assaulted her nose. She quickly snorted it out and took a step back for fear of choking. When her foot knocked down a pile of gold, the killsmith saw the eyelid of the dragon slowly unveil and a great slit eye, no longer enhoused in the color gold but a filmy white, rolled to fix upon her. Gasping for air, Bredikai jumped back and clutched at her sword, struggling to make sense of the situation.

"That thing's still alive!"

"Close," Fitzburt stated casually. "It is undead. Didn't make the connection when I opened with that bit about the necromancers?"

Bredikai looked at him in horror, for such a thing was not known to be possible- not with dragons. Any other creature may have been susceptible to the necromancers' dark arts but to the best of her knowledge dragons were the one species that had yet to be overpowered. Not even their serpentine cousins were exempt.

"That odor is a strong combination of elements but mostly it's being kept in check by a dangerous amount of mercury," Fitzburt added.

"I thought sulfur was the way to go," said Bredikai and snorted out the vile smell from her nose.

"Apparently it's mercury when they're dead. They sent it over with a list of instructions, believe it or not."

"Huh. Who's they? And what are you supposed to do with it?" Bredikai asked, aghast as the creature's eye closed once more and it fell into a deep slumber.

"I haven't the faintest idea!" Fitzburt replied. "In all likelihood this cannot be undone. And *they* is the King's sister and her people. Really, are you not making these connections?"

"Why would you even want to do this, let alone *undo* it?" Bredikai mused. "We can barely handle the living ones. Still… Can't help but feel sorry for it. Look, it's not even doing anything. Just… lying there."

"Never mind that," interrupted Fitzburt. "I wanted you to see this for a reason."

"That would be?"

"You're going into something that none of us can guess at. Not even the King. It's likely that you won't return."

Bredikai looked her cousin straight in the eyes and smiled. "Have I ever told you that my family's undying support is the reason I get up in the morning?"

"Yes, you're the pride of the pack," Fitzburt smiled in return. "You won't be so cute when you're a human torch, I daresay. What I'm trying to tell you is that if all else fails, there may be some aid to be had from the necromancers. Althaea seems desperate for any opportunity to make amends with the King. Strange times, cousin... After seeing this, one wonders that the necromancers might even be powerful enough to stop Borghalus- should things go sour."

"Aha," chuckled Bredikai. "Ahaha. I think you need to build up your alcohol tolerance." She crossed her arms and took another survey of the area. "First of all, things are definitely going to go sour because hey, that's life. Secondly, I'd rather die than trust a necromancer even if she *is* his sister and, wouldn't you know it, she'd probably like that. Third... Do I even need a third, Fitzburt? Say we stop Borghalus; who's stopping the swarm following him? You and the grand Etherdeignian legions? Please don't make me make you cry again." Her fists were now on her hips, daring the man to make sense of himself.

Fitzburt scratched his beard and shrugged. "Don't insult the army just because you're being sent into the fire."

"Alls I'm saying is we don't *have* an army," the killsmith replied. "And as for the ones who did... Do you remember what the necromancers did to those barbarians before the Bone Wars? *So* embarrassing. Like even more international embarrassment than the actual damn wars. How do you even confuse *resurrection* with *rise, erections*?! No wonder they had to accept half the damn barbaric population into their guild. Lords on high, I'd probably kill myself. What a fucking time to be alive."

"But Althaea was not the guildhead then," Fitzburt interjected. "She is avidly trying to re-establish an amiable connection with the barbarians- and everyone else."

"Well gooooood fucking luck to her, I say. In your *extensive* experience, my dear cousin, have you ever met a barbarian? Didn't think so. They're rather large," Bredikai said, enlightening the man with a finger to his face. "I've seen them turn into bears and birds and all kinds of crazy shit. And, contrary to the beliefs of the general populace, they're quite smart as a people. Well above average, I'd say. That's right. The reputation they've gained for being brainless oafs- that's aaall Bone Wars stuff. They're still terribly upset."

"What do you know of historical politics?" Fitzburt scoffed and folded his arms. Bredikai groaned and rolled her eyes. She hated having her word questioned- which was always- and even the preserved death that surrounded them was looking at her to justify her claims.

"I know pissed off and that's all I need to know," she said and threw her hands into the air. "Lords, why do you get me going when I'm drunk? This is why I advocate travel and general life experience. You people have no idea what's been going on in the world these days. People aren't *nice* anymore, Fitzburt. Aid from the necromancers; *please.* They should join up with the alchemists and work on their erections together. Do you have *any* idea how large Borghalus is? Neither do I- and that's a problem. With every bit of hearsay the terror of his name's going to grow and so will his size. That one time I was told about him I heard him compared to a mountain. A literal fucking mountain *Fitz-burt*," she carried on, clapping her hands in front of his face so he could follow her train of thought. "But you can't say shit like that in front of a King, you know? The man's already traumatized so no sense in reopening old wounds. *Stop Borghalus*, he says. Been snorting too much mercury's what I think."

"It was merely an alternative suggestion," Fitzburt said placidly.

"Fuck it. I've lived reasonably well until now," Bredikai said, placating herself. "Please just show me to a room or a corner or something so I can gather my thoughts and get going. Have a horse ready. I'll be gone by sun-up."

"Alright, alright. Come on," Fitzburt said, ushering them out through even more secluded paths. The killsmith mentioned a change of clothing and some foodstuffs she could fit into her sack. As for armor Fitzburt could only offer her something of standard quality. It was peacetime and the kingdom had preferred to pour its metallic resources into infrastructure rather than the armory. Bredikai would be given the basics and that was enough for the start of her journey. As for the remainder of her adventure, the message was short and clear: she was on her own- as usual.

"So, will you be informing Ye Olde Guildhead of all these, ah... developments?" Fitzburt asked as they travelled through winding halls and very little stirred.

"That's a hard *no*. He'll guilt me into not going and leaving the guild heirless. Heiressless. Whatever. And how long until you retire from the guard?"

"I'm not taking over the Coppertine Guild, thank you," the captain replied. "I have my own immediate family on my ass."

"It never fucking ends, does it," Bredikai sighed. "Gramps'll find someone if it comes down to it. Maybe I'll return in one piece and have a child by then," Bredikai said and the two stopped for a moment before bursting into laughter and hushing each other up. It was a good exchange and their shared sense of salty humor reminded the cousins of how close they had been in childhood.

"Here we are," Fitzburt said as they stood in front of her chamber door. The captain suddenly turned serious. His composure stiffened and he stared into his cousin's eyes with seeming worry. "Promise me one thing, will you?" he asked and Bredikai glared at him.

"What?"

Fitzburt took such a deep breath he almost passed out. "Don't swear so much in front of dragons," he said. "They already don't like us."

Bredikai gave her cousin a sour smile and promptly shut the door in his face. It seemed no one in the castle had an appetite for drawn-out goodbyes, especially on the doorstep of impending doom. The hour dragged as Bredikai stared up at a high ceiling her eyes couldn't discern in the dark. She never really slept and for a few hours could only lie still, hoping for a wave of clarity to come to her by morning. Night melted into the first rays of dawn and the smell of early day crept through her window. Not a single bright idea had come to mind. It would make sense to swing by the Rogue Guild for information first but they were so ball-bustingly far from Etherdeign that the thought of going all that way to get the life interrogated out of her was truly unappealing.

Bredikai got up and rummaged through her sack. She pulled out the dead tooth she had salvaged from the dragon

Gomra. The brown thing looked almost wooden as it glistened under the thin shafts of daylight. But what she held now was an entirely different beast; no mere trinket from an accidental killdeed. Her instinct told her that the tooth was meant to be kept hidden until the time was right. Too late for any real sleep, Bredikai outfitted herself with what she found outside her doorstep and then deftly bore a hole through the tooth to hang around her neck. She had been wearing a thin coppertine necklace and it was unlikely that the metal would snap. She placed the tooth beneath her undershirt and put on the flimsy breastplate clearly meant for a woman with a smaller bust. Dressed and packed, Bredikai went to claim the horse waiting for her. The black beast was jittery and didn't seem too invested in following her command but the killsmith saddled up and made her way through the castle gates while day broke and the castle Etheria heated anew. Five minutes into the journey and she was already feeling sweat trickle down her back. She was telling her horse to go left while the beast refused and insisted on going right and the whole thing was already decaying into a summer nightmare. She looked at her breastplate and it was the cheapest grade of coppertine she had seen since the last shitty one her grandfather had given her. Now in the daylight the shield she had wrangled from the old man wasn't looking too spiffy either. Nevertheless, Bredikai had a job to do and she had accepted the quest- and there was no bitching out of anything now.

Indeed, everything sucked. And there were dragons.

The pale dirt road was tedious under the malicious

sunshine and Bredikai took so many breaks to seek shade that even her horse was beginning to dawdle under her infectious sluggishness. Trees were sparse in that area of open land and there was more dust than grass. She just had to tough it out a little longer before she made it to a raggedy patch of wood she knew to be just before what was, hopefully, a functioning portal.

Somehow the one-day trek that was supposed to be faster on horse was now honing in on two with precious few encounters or persons of interest to distract her along the way. When she finally got to her destination without mishap, Bredikai was all sighs, staring at a busted heap of stones, skulls and other bits of formerly enchanted rubble. Her horse she let loose into the small wooded area barely large enough to offer shade but the stubborn beast seemed content to be released from her command. There was no telling how long a reconstruction of the portal would take and she didn't need him gnawing and neighing beside her ear. Bredikai loathed using magic when she could barely muster it for it had a way of turning her into a walking target for creatures much larger than herself with even greater mood swings. Just her luck she'd have to put the thing back together. She set herself to work and the job was not as glamorous as one might think. The keystone had been gnarled by extreme weather and affixing it back into the crescent arch took no less than two hours and a delicate balancing act better left to the hands of taller people.

"Not too bad, girl, not too bad at all..." she said, admiring her shoddy work. Would it get her to where she needed to go? Only time would tell.

At the end of the reconstruction it occurred to Bredikai that she had assembled the entire thing backwards and the mess of semi-precious stones one needed to charge the portal had, unsurprisingly, been looted. There were a few lying around and may have been enough but they were either chipped or completely cracked and utterly useless. Her personal stock was a strong nill. Scratching her head, she ended her long sigh in a grunt and looked around for her horse. They'd need to take a small excursion to scavenge for stones but the deviation wouldn't hinder them for long, she hoped. Bredikai walked into the shabby wood without a second thought but the fussy creature was nowhere in sight. She whistled and scanned around the foliage but the beast of burden had vanished without a trace.

"You're going to have four nubs when I'm through with you, you inbred sack of –" she grumbled and walked through the dreary thing one could barely call a forest to where the animal was certain to be nodding off under a cool canopy. Bredikai quietly moved past the low-lying leaves, her growing anxiety pressing her forward. Even her keen instinct had no time to warn her when her eyes came upon pools of blood and gut making a messy trail towards the fiend who was finishing off chunks of her ride in several artless gulps while other undesired pieces lay about. The last bite that Bredikai saw of her horse was its stunted head making its way down the jugular of the smallest, if not strangest dragon she had seen to date.

"Fuuuuck this..." she sighed but her low-level declaration did not go unheard. The dragon who turned towards her was a blend of greens that darkened into blacks towards its lower half. The creature bore two stumps where wings should have proudly sat. It was longer yet only slightly larger than an adult elephant with a scraggly tuft of off-brown hair on its chin and above its golden eyes. The spikes on its back had been dulled and some had been reduced to half their size. It barely had horns on its head and for a moment Bredikai almost felt sorry for the dull oaf who made for a sad sort of threat. But this pathetic misshapen drake was a drake nonetheless and had to be treated as a potential hostile. Out of habit the killsmith slowly crept backwards with as much stealth as the vines and twigs would allow but the creature was onto her scent, and before she knew it they had both crept out into the open air, dancing just past the non-functional portal, each surveying the problem in front of them.

When the dragon cocked his head to the side to survey the young woman, Bredikai loosened her grip on her sword and waited for it to speak. Then the dragon shrugged and the killsmith shrugged and finally the waiting got to such an absurd level that the drake merely pulled its head back and asked,

"*What*?"

"What *what*?" Bredikai asked confusedly. "My ride."

She wasn't sure but for an instant Bredikai thought she heard the creature breathe a sigh of relief. "Oh, is *that* all," the serpent said and put his nose in the air as if readying to lecture her. Bredikai blinked and blinked again to make certain she was on the right planet. "Young lady, I have travelled far and am in no mood for skirmish. I apologize for inconveniencing you with regards to your transport but I was on the brink of starvation and am desperately lost. In any case I hear your kind is resourceful so... Well there you are. You'll be fine. On your way, if you please."

"I-I-," stammered the girl, altogether perplexed into a tizzy. She had never been dismissed by a dragon before. Attacked by- yes. Lectured by- yes again. Never dismissed. Sure they were snobs, but... When the killsmith didn't answer the creature was overcome with embarrassment and wiped the blood from his mouth.

"Oh good golden grief," declared the drake and drew close enough to lean into her face. "I. A-PO-LO-GIZE. FOR. EA-TING-"

Bredikai's shoulders began to sag. He was taking all the fun out of a potential killdeed and it was terribly difficult to fight with a beast who was so... eloquent. And apologetic. And yet dismissive all at once. The entire scenario was odd enough that Bredikai took into consideration the possibility of hallucinating from the heat. She kept her sword at the ready.

"Stop shouting for fucksake; your breath stinks of horse," she finally said, snapping back to the present. "You're awfully small for a dragon. You *are* a dragon, correct? What happened to your wings?"

"Yes, I am a dragon," the serpent replied snootily, "and never you mind what happened to my wings, you foul-tongued girl. I haven't the time or energy for stories." The dragon looked around at the atmosphere and, finding it to be far from what he had expected, knew himself to truly be lost. That sad little bit of forest had been a nice place to rest but now that his respite had ended he needed directions."Tell me, which kingdom have I crossed into?"

"Why, so you can plan your meal-stops? I don't think so, serpent. You owe me a horse. That or you're about to saddle up."

"You're a rude little thing aren't you? I've a right mind to-"

A wind so powerful it caught them in a micro-tornado rained from the sky and the rising dust obfuscated the view of a winged terror descending upon them. A brutish drake fat in its belly and haunches with putrid yellow scales and a bloodthirsty visage was now standing amongst them, seething and ready to be the permanent end of their discourse.

"To escape was unwise, Solannus," the newcomer hissed and her venomous breath was enough to wilt Bredikai's new shield. She inwardly cursed up a storm. The dragon Solannus looked at her apologetically. Bredikai was almost disappointed that she'd run into another eloquent lizard when the she-drake snarled, "What's this? You've finally found yourself a friend worthy of your insubordinate company. How fitting that it is a filthy little human," she chuckled.

That was more like it. The billowing demon was just what Bredikai was used to but she had never been caught in the crossfire between two drakes so clearly at odds. The killsmith was surprised to find herself insulted not only for her own sake but also on the so-called Solannus' behalf. Realistically, he was the nicer of the two drakes.

"A disapproving family member?" Bredikai asked the dragon Solannus. "I'll let you have her since she insulted you first. Smoke her and let's roll."

Said Solannus looked at her angrily then back to the more immediate threat. "Do not bring your bloodlust here, Karthon of the Northern Gales. I have nothing you want; Borghalus can have no use for me. I pray you leave me to my mourning."

"You dare mourn for Septiannus, you wretched excuse for a son!" Karthon barked and the bile from her crude mouth drained as pools of acid into the earth. Bredikai's ears perked up and when she looked from one drake to the other then back again, she quickly weighed her options.

This Karthon was clearly the stronger and more seasoned drake but her disposition stood firmly against humans- that much was clear- and the killsmith stood to make little headway with her before ending up as a summer snack. That the she-drake's eyes were blood red was not lost on the killsmith either, but for the moment she chalked it up to uncanny coincidence. On the other hand was this Solannus; apparently a son of the late Septiannus. He was small, a bit too round around the waistline, wingless and, Bredikai thought, a bit of a pussy. Nevertheless he was the more amiable of the two and, ugh, she cursed her luck and grumbled "fckfckfck," under her breath. Bredikai closed her eyes, exhaled deeply and strolled chest-first into the madness.

"My dear dragons," the killsmith puffed up, sword at the ready. "What seems to be the problem? You got something she wants?" she asked Solannus.

"Not as such," the drake answered politely but he was squirming so uncontrollably that Bredikai clenched her jaw and glared him into the ground.

"You're lying. Stop fidgeting for fucksake and just give her whatever it is she wants or you're going to get us both into trouble," Bredikai hissed at Solannus and signaled *'just a moment'* to Karthon who watched them in condescending amusement.

Solannus bent his head so he was in Bredikai's face but she didn't flinch even from his soured breath, so annoyed was the killsmith. "I believe her insults were aimed at the both of us," the dragon stated. "I cannot commit murder against my kin, no matter the threat, but she will try to kill us either way; for she is one of Borghalus' henchmen, though I doubt you know who-"

"I *know* who Borghalus is, thank you," Bredikai said and patted the dragon's snout. "Heard his damn name more than I've heard my own these past few days. Alright listen. I'll take care of *that* over there but don't you ditch me. Not like you can get too far like that, anyway."

"I beg your pardon!"

"Beg me later. Swear it!" demanded the killsmith.

Solannus closed his eyes and took a mental moment to orient his thoughts. Today had begun as one of his better days, he told himself. The more distance he put between himself and Borghalus, the more secure he felt. Just when he had thought the distance to be enough that he could risk a little exposure, he had the misfortune of running into this- this pest who looked like she would melt before Karthon had a chance to set them both on fire. Solannus groaned. He'd been running for so very long and he had had such high hopes for today...

"Upon my honor I would never leave a lady to face my kinsmen thus-... *thus!*" he concluded dramatically. Before the dragon and the killsmith could further their strategy, Karthon was done with their negotiation and up in the air ready to blast them with an inferno from her belly. She was too high for Bredikai to mount an attack. "Get under me!" Solannus commanded. "I can withstand her fire. She'll run herself hoarse and have to come back down."

Bredikai followed Solannus' lead and Karthon laughed monstrously from the sky. "Hah! You are not enough to save her, Solannus. No, I will not call you brother when you are barely dragon!" the beast expanded her belly, ready for the scorching. The first onslaught was so severe that even with Solannus shielding her, Bredikai could feel parts of her armor burning into her skin. It was too goddamn hot for such dragon-drama but, sure enough, the crazed brute was too much acid and too little fire. She ran herself hoarse and had to descend if she had any hope of scorching them further- just as Solannus had predicted.

When Karthon landed even more angrily than she had taken off, Bredikai said, "Quick, open your mouth!" to Solannus.

"What?!"

"Cover me in your mouth and charge her!" Before Solannus could argue Bredikai pried his jaws open and snuck in. Her command of "charge already!" was so shrill Solannus could hear her in his brain and he found himself barreling straight towards Karthon who was getting ready to unleash fire once more. "When I say *open*- Steady, steady.... Don't stray. Open!"

From inside Solannus' mouth Bredikai lunged at Karthon's throat and pierced her so deeply that her breath was ended. Blood overwhelmed the creature's mouth and she coughed and writhed in agony. She slung her large belly into Solannus with such force that, without thinking of the law, Solannus sank his teeth into the dragon's neck and tore into her jugular. Bredikai was caught off balance and Solannus barely remembered the killsmith crouched in his mouth that with the sudden closing of his jaws she lost her footing and fell backwards down Solannus' throat. Solannus hacked and choked but could do nothing except swallow else he risked suffocating. He dry-heaved and did what he could to swiftly force her down his intestines.

Karthon breathed for no more than half a minute as her poisonous blood stained the battlefield and the light left her crimson eyes. Her fall was welcome and Solannus fell on his own belly from the writhing of a foreign object. Luckily, the fall placed just enough pressure on his stomach to forcibly expel the disturbance.

Unable to move from fatigue, the dragon merely rolled his right eye sideways, staring at the intestinal stool sample sputtering up curses and hexes at everything dragon, clutching her blade to her chest, unable to stop gasping for breath.

"I-" wheezed Bredikai Cronunham, the killsmith of Etherdeign, the Carver and heiress apparent to the Coppertine Guild, "-I think I hit my head on something. Fuck that's a lot of blood. Is this all coming out of my head?"

The last thing the killsmith heard before losing

consciousness was the painful breaking of wind by her serpentine savior and a low moan as he cried, "Uuuunnngghhh... You've destroyed my anus."

CHAPTER 2: A BIT OF RESURRECTION NEVER HURT ANYONE

"Why are you drinking so much, little human?" the dragon Solannus asked, finally filled up to the scales with their tense silence. He thought it brutish and beneath him to simply up and leave the traumatized human after their...intimate moment... without attempting some sort of conversation. Late afternoon settled around them, bringing with it a midday heatwave from which they sought shelter in the flimsy forest of their meeting. And so much the better that they sat for a while, as the dragon had unintentionally ran the portal through during his charge. So that was that.

From where the two sat they had a decent view of the carnage that had petrified into an unimpressive pseudo-mountain. The heat catalysed the process and the stench of Karthon's corpse was as difficult to bear as it was slow to dissipate. Surely it was better that they rested for a spell rather than risk heatstroke, the dragon told himself, and to that effect they were now alone with no one left to fight but their own ill moods.

Seated together inside the circumference of the forests's only clearing, the dragon dared assume his counterpart's shivering derived from disgust rather than any mortal malady and he would make due effort to assuage her before parting ways. It was the gentlemanly thing to do.

"Far too much drink, indeed," he tutted and shook his

head.

"My life's a crapshoot, like the one I just passed through... And that's what we Etherdeign folk do. We drink... *Solannus*, was it?" Bredikai replied, head bandaged with the only tattered rag the dragon could find in her horrendous rucksack. At least it was a reprieve from the silence at last.

"That is correct," answered the dragon, shaking his large head as the 'little human' Bredikai swallowed her fifth gulp of brew all the while glaring at him as if she wished his scales to spontaneously char. "And what are you called, human?"

Either serpents had a different barometer for condescension or she was growing sensitive with the booze running through her system but Bredikai kept her glare fixed even as her eyelids drooped. It was sheer stubbornness which is the life-force of the female spirit as what kept her awake and semi-alert.

"I'm Bredikai Cronunham," she said. "A killsmith. The Carver from Etherdeign also seems to be popular. Makes me sound like a crazed killer, though," she finished and took a swill.

"That's desperately unflattering," Solannus noted. "Then I have crossed into Etherdeign at long last..." The dragon sat much as a human would sit in a chair. His thoughts were far away, not searching so much as paying silent gratitude for another day he lived. When his eyes began to water the alarms in Bredikai's head began to ring once more and she sought to get him talking. The threat of having to deal with an emotional dragon was too much to bear.

"You won't have more visitors from Kharkharen anytime soon, I hope," she began. "Why *are* you so far out?"

"I... I hope to be as far from Kharkharen as possible," replied the dragon. His voice betrayed more sadness than fear but Bredikai heard the underlying longing the dragon felt for his home and understood him to have been forced out. "Going back would cost more than just my own life. My father spoke most highly of Etherdeign and... Goodness, your drinking habits are most uncouth. Surely your organs must be disintegrating by now," Solannus implored with genuine concern but the killsmith ignored him and bit back a hiccup. Solannus shifted and now sat like a big demonic cat, with his appendages tucked beneath his belly and a tail that unconsciously swung from side to side, yawning every now and again from the exhaustion of their encounter.

"You're awfully articulate for a puffed up leather pouch," Bredikai retorted, shaking her drink in Solannus' general unimpressed direction.

"Excuse yourself at once, young lady," reprimanded the dragon. "That is an inexcusable way to speak of the one who saved your life." Bredikai snorted. "My, but mortal manners have depreciated since last I was among your kind." Another row of tutting, another judgment-laden silence.

"Before I drown my sorrows further and, if I'm lucky, myself in a river, tell me how you came to be in these lands, son of Septiannus."

"A gentleman does not reveal himself so willingly upon a chance encounter."

"And a wanted dragon who helped kill his kin, with no wings and no sense of direction is hardly in a position to withhold information," Bredikai replied, still unsure of whether or not she had slain the wrong serpent. "Come now, don't be shy. It just so happens that my quest involves the late Dragonfather. And I'm known to have a *special* relationship with dragons."

"Special relationship, my scales; you kill my brethren

for sport; *Carver*, was it?" Solannus said and put his right paw/hand/haunch/whatever at his side. They pursed their lips simultaneously.

"I do no such thing. Fucking gossip following me everywhere I go..." Bredikai grumbled. "My killdeeds are entirely a result of unprovoked- stop rolling your eyes, please- *unprovoked* aggression on my part. Not my fault I do my job well. Dragons don't know how to play nice with anybody these days."

A mild wind was around them, flurrying most of the loose dirt into their faces and making it rain on an already wearied killsmith whose good humour had all but gone the way of the destroyed portal. Bredikai leaned further back onto the jutting boulder upon which she rested her back, deep in thought as to how to regain control over the situation.

"Well, I certainly do not make it common practice to sit and simmer with murderers-" Solannus began.

"*Freelance survival professional.*"

"-but if you must know I have escaped my home because my brother Borghalus means to proclaim himself the next Dragonfather. He has usurped the soul of my land and I fear I am his primary target at present. But I do not suppose the affairs of dragons are of interest to one such as yourself, Madam Carver."

Bredikai perked up. Eying the dragon cautiously she felt for her sword just in case the conversation turned unpleasant. "Aha," she said, "but you suppose incorrectly, Sir, for the affairs of dragons are of great interest to me since... since this week. Particularly that of your father's. May he find peace," she added hastily. "But something's not adding up."

"Indeed?"

"Indeed."

"I do not take your meaning," Solannus said.

"How do I put this delicately? You're lying to me. There. Delicate," Bredikai said and left her sword alone for it gave no signal of warning against the drake. She crossed her arms and looked him dead in the eyes as the drake squinted at her menacingly.

"I'm *what*?"

The wind picked up, moving clouds swiftly across the encroaching nighttime canvas but this shift to a cooler temperature still held no promise of rain. The moons were clearly visible this evening; not an uncommon occurrence for the season. As the daylight hour waned neither killsmith nor dragon seemed interested in parting ways without having spoken their mind.

"No offense but you're about the last dragon to pose a threat to the hierarchy that I've seen," said the killsmith. "Daringly small in stature, no wings, a little too round around the waist. So you must have something Borghalus wants-"

"Do not *think* to comment on my diet you two-bit boozehound!" Solannus cried and would have snatched the girl in his mouth had he not been busy trying to suck his belly in as far as it could go. His emotions were getting the better of him now and he was sputtering and stammering. "So- so I'm a fat liar, am I?!"

With all that ruckus Bredikai had to reconsider her approach as the dragon's hollering was sure to draw more unwanted attention to them, so she tried to placate him before he began sobbing.

"I never called you fat-"

"You said *round* and round means fat! I have been *starved* and tortured and hunted, you unfeeling wretch!" Solannus moaned. "I inherited this figure from my father's side- brute!"

"I apologize, for fucksake calm down! Alright already, so you've been through unknown traumas and you're a little worse for the wear-"

"My heart is broken!" Solannus wailed and in between his sobs Bredikai offered him everything from Coppus ale to coppertine coins to crumbled old biscuits she had rolling around in her sack and, while the biscuits seemed to calm him down somewhat, Solannus' tears were overwhelming. She quickly tore off the cloth from her head to dry the dragon's eyes before he could cry them into an ambush.

It took a few more sniffs for Solannus to regain composure and if Bredikai could clench her jaw further she would have ground her teeth to dust. But yelling at the emotional heap seemed unkind even for her tough love sort of stance so she decided to take a more motherly tone in the hope of salvaging the remains of a broken day.

"There, there now. Talk it out. Come now, I'm sort of a friend."

"I don't know you and I don't like you," sniffed Solannus, drying his eyes. He was sitting on his rear again and making no secret of the fact that he was more than capable of crying them a river.

"Well I'm the only one you've got so start bonding because I'm running low on alcohol and patience and so help me I'll kill us both here and now," Bredikai sung through a crazed smile. Solannus sniffed his last and Bredikai sat back down, rubbing her temples. "Let's just calm ourselves, yes? Breathe in, out, in... out... Now, friend Solannus, tell me why you're here and... the way you are," she said.

The dragon sighed and laid the bloodied cloth down. "I am the most unfortunate of my father's line," he began and the killsmith sat on the boulder, fully concentrated on the drake. "My forebearer, the late Septiannus, was hailed as the greatest of Dragonfathers. They will sing of his might and fairness of hand for centuries to come. His strength came not from his physical prowess- which was not meager- but his merciful heart. He loved and respected all things and never was there a Dragonfather so esteemed as he. I mourn his loss deeply, though it has surpassed the year," the dragon said and Bredikai found herself enthralled by this depiction of a king she had never known.

"I suppose it is the fate of all great leaders; that the heirs who follow must be lesser in quality," continued the dragon sadly. "I am the last of my father's line but I was my mother's first and only child and much loved by both my parents. As you see, I am without wings and smaller than the majority of my kin. Perhaps it was love mixed with pity that led my father to show greater concern for my well-being. I do not doubt it inspired jealousy among my brothers and sisters and I am the sorrier for it. My father would not have intended for any of his children to think he loved one above the others."

"Good intentions don't always yield the results we'd want," Bredikai said softly.

"I don't suppose they do," Solannus agreed. He threw one of the moldy biscuits she had offered into his mouth and nearly gagged but it stopped his sensitivities long enough for him to continue. "You said you knew of dragons. Then you must know the tradition that follows when a Dragonfather passes. Believe me, little human, when I say that I have never had eyes upon titles. Indeed, I am happy enough to be ignored and live out my days in solitude but Borghalus..." he said and stopped. It didn't look like he wanted to finish that thought but Bredikai was in too deep to stop now.

"Solannus," Bredikai entreated.

"My father had no choice but to imprison him, you see. Even in his youth he was a threat to everything my father stood for. And after what he did-! We all knew the day would come when my brother escaped from his prison. As soon as my father passed- I had to flee!" Solannus was starting and stopping now, making little sense. His sentences were broken and half-spoken.

"He came for me, you see- And I knew he would-"

"Solannus what did you do?" Bredikai demanded.

"I- I- don't know what came over me! Borghalus is a monstrosity and will drown the world in an ocean of blood if he becomes Dragonfather. I couldn't just stand there and- and- so I took it! Yes, I took it and fled. It was the only thing I could think to do, don't you understand?!" pleaded the dragon.

"*What* did you take, Solannus?"

"My father's heart!"

The pulsating threat of Borghalus was nothing compared to the one in her head as Bredikai paced to and fro and created a neat little footpath around their makeshift camp. Once every few minutes she would stare at the dragon as if to say something but Solannus was caught in his own web of self-loathing so she resumed her pacing and strategizing. When she sat back down Bredikai took her sword and used the lower part of her shirt to clean it. What did it matter anymore when they were swimming in filth? Up and down she went over the blade and it was enough to unnerve the dragon.

"Please refrain from polishing your sword further."

"Why?"

"Because it is stressing me out," Solannus cried. "I have enough problems with anxiety without you brandishing your weapon, cheap as it may be." He had gone from sitting like a feline to sitting on his rump and back to cat-mode all within the half hour.

"Hey, you watch how you speak about the Sacré Hexia. This piece of shit hasn't failed me once. It can carve through anything- including *you*," Bredikai answered but, at this point, neither of the two had much fight left in them.

"I should think they had stopped producing coppertine swords," Solannus said, studying the orange hued toothpick. "And I can understand why. It is most garish. Is it imbued with any noteworthy enchantments?"

"As a matter of fact, it is!" the girl beamed. "It vibrates when there's danger about. Yup, anything poses a threat to me and this thing goes off like the bells of Santolini Temple when it's time to end the winter diet."

"Ridiculous," Solannus mumbled. "So it vibrates and draws you near to your victim? Does it glow? Does it *grow?*"

"No, it just...vibrates."

"What a useless attribute."

"Useless or no, it hasn't so much as twitched since we dealt with that Karthon character. What does that say about *you?*" asked the killsmith.

"I am entirely capable of posing a threat when I have rested and fed, thank you."

"Alright, well, you'll see what this bad girl's capable of when next we're in action. Looking at you I can't imagine that there was only one dragon you've annoyed," Bredikai surmised, swinging the Hexia about. Solannus twitched every time the blade swung past his face. "Anyway," the killsmith continued, "I've been thinking that this doesn't have to be a melodrama just yet. I have to reconfigure a few things but it seems to me that we have a common goal here: stop Borghalus so that literally anyone else becomes the new Dragonfather. Am I right so far?" The alcohol was flowing through Bredikai now and she was stretching her legs by walking around faster with each word.

"... I wouldn't say *literally* anyone. Volantus isn't exactly a beacon of morality either and Breannus has no appetite for leadership. Xacharus, on the other hand, I could see-"

"Solannus please, we don't have time to go through the entirety of the Draconic dynasty and its intricate politics right now. Borghalus poses the greatest threat and must be stopped. The one who brings together all your father's bits can claim the throne." The dragon nodded as she whizzed around like an agitated moth.

"Correct, as such," Solannus said. "But he will not suffer my escape much longer. I have travelled this far to seek the aid of one King Althaean. I cannot recall that I have ever met him though father always told me to seek his aid should I come to trouble. I thought to find refuge with him."

Bredikai pointed the Hexia straight into Solannus' face and the dragon pulled back. "And you're in luck, Sir Serpent, because I'm going to help you do just that!" Bredikai was on such a hot streak she was practically jogging around. Solannus' head swerved this way and that trying to keep up with her. Before the dragon could get too excited the killsmith was making rapid decisions so that she could swing this fortuitous meeting to their advantage. "It just so happens that I have great rapport with the King," she declared. "Apparently my mother did too; may she find peace. But that's neither here nor there and as far as I'm concerned he owes me one. I will do everything in my power to gain you the refuge you seek."

"You speak for the Kingdom of Etherdeign, do you?"

"I... I'm *from* Etherdeign, if that's what you're asking."

"That is decidedly not what I am asking, little human."

"Nevermind the technicalities," Bredikai said and sat on the rock but was up again in less than a minute. "I'm thinking you help me resolve this Dragonfather business. The sooner we have it handled the sooner you'll have refuge. Fuck it, you probably won't even need refuge once we get this business sorted out- and you can get back to doing whatever it is that dragons do. And since you have no deluded aspirations of ruling- for which I am eternally grateful- we can gather all the bits, you can help appoint the Dragonfather you deem fit and there; everyone's happy."

"If you would but stand still for a moment; just why are *you* facilitating all this?" Solannus asked with a claw pointed her way.

"Well, firstly, you don't know a damn thing about fighting dragons," the killsmith pointed out.

"I humbly call your attention to the fact that I *am* a dragon."

"And when was the last time you *killed* one?" Bredikai asked.

"Sadly just a while ago. But I am blaming you for

that as it is the most heinous of crimes in my culture and unforgivable. It is the last thing I need weighing on my heart right now."

Bredikai rolled her eyes. "Sure, blame me for it. I promise you that Karthon wouldn't be wracked with regret had she come out the victor. In any case that puts you at a grand total of zero. Care to assess my score?"

"*Score?*" Solannus barked, "I do not care for that term you heartless girl, nor am I amused by your unaffected tone as you boast of slaying my majestic kin."

"Your *majestic kin* has made it regular practice to devour mine and we have the motherload to deal with before the entire world is up to its neck in dragon. That'll fuck with the eco-system, no mistake." Solannus thought about what the girl was saying and couldn't argue with the reality they were facing. But when Bredikai asked about where he had hidden the stolen heart he thought it better to keep that information to himself for the time being. Suffice it to say that it was buried deep in the heart of a mountain, beyond Borghalus' reach. Though she was not entirely reassured, Bredikai regained a moment of clarity and she agreed that, for now, she was better off not knowing the exact location until they had to retrieve it. Solannus was proving difficult to sway so she played her strongest hand and knew her intuition to be correct for when the dragon saw the dead tooth around her neck, he knew it to have been his father's, and they were now in possession of two of the six pieces.

"I've got an eye for these things," the killsmith said proudly and even the dragon was impressed, though he chose to follow that up with a concise lecture regarding the slaying of his kin and the dangers of relying on dumb luck, upon which Bredikai's eyes rolled so far back into her head she felt another headache coming on.

"Therefore, at the expense of sounding like your captive- which I most certainly am not- I will agree to be your travel companion until I am guaranteed refuge," Solannus concluded. "I feel it is fair compensation for relieving you of your transport. But know this: I will not return to Kharkharen while Borghalus lives," he added. Neither had noticed that during their scheming a cloudless and refreshing nightscape had settled around them and they were below the star-filled canopy of a summer's eve; a dragon and a killsmith who was rubbing her chin as if to say *hold on, dragon*.

"Hold on, dragon. We can't stay in Etherdeign; I just left the damn kingdom and we've got bits to find. Refuge is going to have to wait but I'll protect you- you have my word. Also, we can't discount ending up at Kharkharen at some point. Don't worry, it'll likely be our last stop."

The way she spoke the word *last* rubbed Solannus the wrong way. "You're a ghoulish one, you are. Just why do you covet death so?"

"I don't covet death," replied the killsmith, "I just have very little delusions about surviving such a campaign. Not going to lie to you; I'll protect you until I can't. Do you know how big your brother is?"

"Yes, as a matter of fact. Do *you*?" the dragon retorted.

"I can't worry about that now," Bredikai said dismissively. "We should aim to get more information about these bits first. Here's hoping they haven't all been found yet. Killdeeds have gone through the roof in this shitty economy and with these portals all busted up... I don't even know which ones work anymore. Now that I think about it, how the blazes are we going to feed you? I can't afford to keep you." If Solannus had any feathers they would have been primed for the ruffling. But the killsmith got a neat little fire going in the midst of her vocal stream of consciousness and resumed her pacing. The evenings were prone to be much too dark and temperatures were known to drop drastically when one was out of the city proper.

"I am not some pet to be kept, you ingrate-"

"It's a legitimate concern!"

"You keep your concerns and your foul biscuits and do not think to offer me anything that has creatures writhing in it ever again," Solannus huffed.

"Why of all the ungrateful, spoiled lizards-" began Bredikai, stomping on the ground.

Suddenly the soil beneath her feet began breaking but not in such a manner as to suggest a quake or other natural disaster. Rather, the oddly widening gaps in the loose dirt made way for what the duo assumed to be a group of annoyed gophers. They should have been so lucky. Bredikai, stick in hand, was less attack-ready and more curiosity-ridden as several skeletal arms busted through the ground and groped upwards, propping up the rest of their languorous remains to reveal three very disoriented skeletons, two of which were still seeking their miscellaneous parts lost somewhere in their holes.

Solannus glared at Bredikai who simply sighed and said, "Ugh, I don't know, I deal with drakes," upon which the dragon squinted and focused on his new potential chew-toys.

"Why the devils be you makin' such a ruckus for, you two? Stompin' and bangin' above my head!" The voice was gruff and masculine, betraying no age.

Bredikai blinked away the booze as best she could. Everything ached. "I... what?"

"Can't a lad get some peace anywheres?" With that the

speaker turned to the other two skeletons who were still dusting themselves off. "I be tellin' yas this wasn't no way to stay dead."

"We *really* don't have time for this," the killsmith muttered as the odd three clumsily tried to regroup. They exchanged a few bones among them until everyone was adequately re-situated. Not only were they not hostile in the least, they appeared to be as confused as the killsmith and the dragon regarding their sudden reanimation in the dead of night.

The second skeleton made another attempt at walking only to crumple back onto the ground. When it laughed, the voice was more melodic than the one who had initially spoken and, what had once been a female, was now a cackling skull so obviously used to her state she could barely finish collecting herself.

"Fine business, death be," she managed to get out.

"I be tellin' you two not to pick these shallow grounds an' here we are again. Next times I choose the hole," declared the third, who was also male.

"But it be *my* turn to choose, brother. I'm not wantin' to end up in another one of your swamps with all your mosquitos just because you be likin' the ambiance," said the she-skeleton.

Bredikai's eyes narrowed as she studied these creatures of dubious intellect and she whirled on Solannus. "*You*," she said accusingly.

"I beg your pardon," Solannus responded, already affronted without even having heard the killsmith's accusation.

"You summoned them," hissed Bredikai. "Just to annoy me. Because having a dragon in tow wouldn't cramp me enough."

"Preposterous. I'm a dragon not a necromancer," Solannus snorted and Bredikai whirled back upon the three but they had no eyeballs so she didn't know what or where or whom to look at. So she looked at everything and everyone all at once.

"Alright folks, resurrection's over, back in the ground you go! Nothing to see here but a girl and her dragon."

"Oy, ease off the Scales, lass, we not be undead for our likin', you know. An' it be your doin', not his. Woke us up, you did, with all this prancin' around," said the first skeleton on behalf of the trio.

Bredikai had never seen such a proud smirk on a dragon's face before and it was all she could do to not carve it off and hand it to him. It seemed as though the very campfire was taunting her.

"Not that simple, lassie," added the other skeleton and it was already becoming difficult to tell them apart. The one who had spoken just then had something crawling happily through his ribcage and the she-skeleton was decidedly shorter than the other two. The first had a skeletal parrot on his shoulder and all three came equipped with their own rusted swords. "It be another gold moon 'tils we can get back under an' you've woken us up with all your stompin'."

"There's no such thing as a gold fucking moon. Literally neither of the moons operate that way-" said Bredikai and was duly silenced by a very well-mannered dragon who decided to take the lead.

"Madam, language! Now, my dear, ah, fellows. How have you come about to…erm… how have you come about? Surely it was not the lady's intention to summon you, despite her gross thomping." She was going to hand feed that smirk to him.

"Aye, but summons she did, Scales. We be at your service 'tils we die, so to speak," the she-skeleton stated as a matter of fact. "An' there be nothin' you can do about it. Where you go, we shall follow," she finished right proudly.

"Indeed," Solannus answered, pondering the pros and cons of their group's inflation. The skeletons thought nothing of seating themselves comfortably around the fire though there was no logical reason as to why since they couldn't feel anything. But they held their boned hands up to the flame and Bredikai went to stand by her dragon for sheer lack of anything better to do.

"We was cursed," spoke the first who settled his undead parrot closer to the fire.

"By?" asked Bredikai, eyebrows roofed on her forehead.

"Dragon gold," he answered. The killsmith immediately resumed her disapproval of Solannus.

"Madam," the dragon sighed, "if I had any gold to speak of, would I be cavorting with the likes of you?"

"Fair enough," she admitted. It was the first thing he'd said that made sense all day.

"Nah-," drawled the other male, "this be moons ago. We didn't know you," he said as he broke off his foot to shake away the dust. "Greed got the better of us, methinks. Gold'll do that to pirates." Solannus nodded understandingly like a know-it-all mother hen.

"You're awfully land-based for pirates," Bredikai muttered. "Nearest ocean's at least half a week away, as the dragon flies."

"Shiver me saltwaters- can't go near the stuff!" the first pirate exclaimed. "We'll be done in if we touches it. Stuck like this fore'er. Part of the curse!"

Bredikai plastered on a fake smile and nodded angelically as if she were the very picture of sympathy. "I'd like to suggest that my be-scaled counterpart here do some curse-lifting for you but in his state I don't even think he thinks he's much of a dragon anymore." Who knew dragons could growl? She gave herself a mental pat on the back.

"Think nothin' of it, lass," replied the first. "We be happy to help yas regardless. Bored out me skull lyin' in the dirt!"

"Aye…"

"Aye!"

"Well," Solannus exhaled, lost as to how one dealt with animated mortal remains. "You will make a merry addition to our little group, I should think. Goodness knows we could do with some *pleasant* company," he finished but Bredikai was on him like a tumor and the fire illuminated her face menacingly.

"Excuse me, Solannus? This isn't an open forum. I hold the sword, I make the decisions," she declared and was, regretfully, shoved aside.

"I am Solannus, last son of the recently deceased Dragonfather, the illustrious Septiannus," began the dragon and cleared his throat of all the dust. "And this noisy, feral little human is Madam Bredikai Cronunham- a killsmith who otherwise makes her living by preying on my brethren for killdeeds. We seek six items to declare a new Dragonfather before my bloodthirsty brother plunges us all into war. My partner and I were just caught in a minor disagreement which was certain to resolve itself before someone got *re*-digested."

"Charmed, to be sure," the she-skeleton chirped daftly.

The first skeleton took it upon himself to make the necessary introductions. Clearly the chosen leader, his word held about as much weight as Bredikai's sobriety right then but they listened politely.

"I be *Ashley the Tooth* on account of me not havin' any. Eldest of' these scamps by eight minutes," he said and his declaration was met with a jovial *aye!* by his brethren. "This wee scoundrel here be Fluffers, though he ain't got much of the fluff left on him," he continued and Fluffers the undead skeletal parrot made such a desperate sound that both Bredikai and Solannus screwed up their expressions. "Me brother here be *Lesley Crawbelly* on account of some minor misidentification- hah! The lass be *Melonshank Murray* but you be knowin' that for yourselves if she had any skin on her."

Bredikai crossed her arms and snorted. "Really? The girl gets the guy-name?"

"Murrayannah," drawled the skeleton, pronouncing her name is if it had an *r* at the end. "But they be callin' me Murray for short."

"Hah!" laughed Ashley, "kept cuttin' her hair to play with the boys. Mother, bless her twisted black heart, could'na tell us apart 'tils we was old enough to be trimmin'' sails. Triplets, we are- most fearsome threesome to plunder the Morduanas Seas!"

"Should've stuck to the open waters, lads," Murray said, shaking her skull.

"Now you be sayin' that, what's your idea to go after the blazin' dragon gold in the first place, ya silly lass," Ashley laughed.

"And yas ne'er be sayin' no to a gift for Mother!" Murray replied and the three came together to cry *Mother!* in unison.

Bredikai surveyed the triplets. When she cast her eyes on Solannus, who seemed to be enjoying the scene despite their linguistic handicaps, she sensed that the argument to return the newcomers to the grave was a battle already lost. Then, the thing that had been crawling in Lesley's ribcage- which turned out to be a snake- decided that it had had enough of captivity and gleefully slithered out of the bones to Solannus' side.

"Hullo there, little one," the dragon said and damned if that stupid snake didn't have the most darling smile and a patch of black on its forehead that looked almost like a heart if you squinted the right way. Just like that, the pale snake wrapped itself this way and that around Solannus and the two played around as though they had been friends for years. The dragon twisted and giggled while the snake wriggled and snuggled all the while the skeletons cheered and *aaaw*'d and Bredikai lifted her emptied flask to her mouth without ever taking her eyes off the lunacy.

"I'm going to sleep," she declared sharply and everyone stopped to look at her. "We're leaving this fucking forest at dawn. Solannus!"

"Hmmm?" the dragon asked, nuzzling his new pet.

"Keep it down or so help me I'll have that thing for breakfast. I've eaten worse." With that she lay hunched up against her rock and made every attempt to tune the crazy out.

A quick glare at the fire and clearly the elements were making sport of her plight. The last words she heard Solannus mumble were along the lines of *ignore her, she's drunk*, while the shapeless figures of her dreams danced across the memory of blissful solitude. The night passed uneventfully and Bredikai was just in the dead of sleep before she realized that they had left a perfectly good dragon carcass to petrify without relieving it of its useful parts. But she was too tired to care and it seemed that there would be much more dragon to reckon with on their horizon. The fire died down to lazy embers. It appeared that nothing would jump out to ambush them that evening. Bredikai Cronunham found herself drifting to the lull of a jovial sea shanty coming from behind her. When it ended, she had just enough energy to open her left eye as the deep voice of Solannus began to hum something akin to a lullaby.

"There now goes the lady of dreams,

Sleep, sleep... she says to thee.

She is a mother to all who see

Her nightshade cloak of fantasy...

"Now she comes to lead me away,

Out the garden of song where I dance and play.

Oh, my lady, I'm meant to stay

"*So sleep, sleep...*" I hear her say..."

Slowly Bredikai's lid drooped and her heart began to beat in the same rhythm as the song. It was a melody she'd known from childhood though she could not recall who had sung it to her. Nostalgia wrapped itself around her shoulders and the killsmith slept as comfortably as she would have in a feather-filled bed, snoring lightly from her twisted position.

"That was a beaut, Scales," the pirate Ashley said.

Solannus all but blushed. "My mother used to sing it to me when I was very little," he said and the group sighed. "It sounds better in the Draconic tongue but, then again, dragons did create the common speech of Ethra- as you are aware of, no doubt..."

Only Bredikai gave in to sleep that night for the triplets

had no need of it and Solannus could operate on little as his body was used to staying alert. Years into the future, that ruddy excuse of a forest would become home to a delightful little tavern where creatures both magical and non-magical alike could enjoy drink and company in merriment; it would be named *Barebones Birth* but there remained many adventures before that came about.

Having a skeleton shake the sleep out of you while a wicked hangover takes hold was not one of Bredikai's chosen methods for arising, even as she ripped the arm off Lesley and bashed the rude awakening into his skull. Lesley remained undaunted in his task to revive the killsmith who yelled more obscenities than even his piratic vocabulary allowed.

"What, WHAT, throw me to the harpies but I hate you people!" Bredikai yelled, trying to prevent her impending heart attack.

"Master Bredikai- you're needed, lass! Scales tried to eat a wraith an' now she's havin' a right go at him!" Lesley cried.

"He *what*?" she demanded, head throbbing as every vein in her forehead pulsed its presence. And just like that, Bredikai was no longer where she had fallen asleep but in a grander, denser forest overlooking a coastline which very much did not belong to Etherdeign. The disorientation was about to melt her brain but Bredikai had no time to question the bones off Lesley's ass when suddenly Murray was with them and pulling her in another direction.

"Come quickly, lass!" urged Murray, "it be scarin' the life out of him!"

"Where the hell is Ashley?!"

"Who?"

"The Tooth, curse you- your brother!"

"Aye! He be tryn' to parlay with the wraith-lass but methinks he be annoyin' her even more," Murray said.

Bredikai closed her eyes and inhaled, exhaled, once more, there we go... With the help of her new crew she was able to get moving and suffered only a few minor sways before realigning herself. Sword in hand, she swallowed back her nausea and sped after them but it was difficult to keep up with their necrotic speed.

What the killsmith found was more discomforting than what she had thought to see and nothing made sense in Bredikai's world anymore as she happened upon a sitting dragon and wraith fully engrossed in a set of beautifully piled up stones and leaves, and a snake trying to nuzzle the empty specter. Solannus was stroking his thinly bearded chin as the wraith, arms folded, studied the fortunes that lay before them with extreme concern.

"But the tower can represent change and higher learning, can it not? It doesn't necessarily have to spell doom, surely?" pleaded the dragon. "Tell me this is open to interpretation!"

CHAPTER 3: A TIME TO BE UNDEAD AND OTHER EMBARRASSMENTS

Bredikai rubbed her eyes and they teared up adjusting to the morning mayhem. She put the Hexia back in her sheath for there was nothing truly amiss so much as it was... strange. Rain clouds crept over them and the general green-brown charm of the scenery waned to a sunken drear ready for the soaking. Yet the sullen weather lingered with no hint of release except an even duller wind too lazy to move the useless leaves dangling above their heads. They provided no shade from the daylight sun obstinately piercing through the clouds and no shelter from impending weather conditions; just sort of there, spotting the landscape above bushes of inedible berries and other toxic flora. In the dismal clearing she had been led into was where Bredikai wheezed air back into her lungs.

"There you are," spoke the wraith and Bredikai had questions, so many questions...

"Where we are? Who are you? Solannus, why is she telling your fortune? And yes, you susceptible serpent, the tower can symbolize higher learning so stop being so gullible for the love of-"

"Madam," interrupted the wraith, "I am Lamure; soothsayer and student of sorcery, at your service," she bowed. "I was sent by your grandfather and his young charge, the boy Zira, to aid you."

"You look... like a wraith," the killsmith drank the air

hungrily. "Thought you had to be dead to be a wraith."

Lamure's spectral face smiled grimly but there was no malice in her milky eyes. She was robed from head to floating foot, really living the vision of a wraith, so to speak. "Yes, I am very much both those things," she answered. "The boy got into a mishap which I do not wish to relive at present, if you'll excuse the wordplay, and let us just say that your family ward owes me a life." The annoyed smile never left Lamure's face. "As it is he was able to salvage my spirit. I agreed to be of service until he can find a way to undo this."

"Can this be undone?" Solannus asked.

"Not very likely, no," the wraith answered, seemingly unperturbed. "And just how *I* am indebted to the boy still remains fuzzy but apparently I have nothing better to do with my time."

"Gramps put you up to this," stated the killsmith but Lamure waved all that business away.

"I'd really rather not get into all that just yet," the wraith said. "My memory continues to fail me."

"Uh-huh," nodded Bredikai and moved her jaw around, thinking. "Well aren't we just a delightful band of freaks." Ever in a foul mood, the killsmith sent a silent prayer to the ancients for a meteor blast to end the morning merry-making for every creature within her circle.

"Is it getting musty out here?" Solannus asked, settling his stout underbelly in such a way that made it appear as though he was sitting on a throne, like an older brother lording over a tidy troupe of insanity. He was fanning himself so hard with a leaf he almost summoned up a gale but alas, this was not to be a morning of miracles. One by one the skeletal trio that had reassembled by his side crashed down with an *oomph-oomphoomph* and they fell straight through Lamure into a bonepile. Fluffers squawked most dreadfully and the snake, which Solannus had lovingly named Sir Hiss-a-lot, slithered to his big brother's side.

"Where in the hells are we, Solannus," Bredikai asked but her tone was more demand than inquiry.

The dragon apologized to the triplets for having sent them sprawling and explained to Bredikai how she had been snoring so peacefully; and since none of them could bear to wake her- nor did they wish to be verbally assaulted- they decided to relocate for fear of staying in one location too long. Sitting pretty would have eventually attracted unwanted attention and someone may or may not have suggested the scenic route, so they packed up their leader and ran, if you please, out of that mangy wood and into the borders of the Kingdom of Termia. They were ninety percent sure it was Termia. The coast was charming so long as no one got too close to the water.

That was all well and good but Bredikai had had enough of random encounters and willy-nilly hangers-on. They needed to stick to a plan if they were to make any substantial progress else she'd soon have an entire town on her hands. As they were now, they stood to weird the life out of Borghalus. Bredikai took inventory of her group.

She was the leader and that title remained unchallenged. There was her begrudging partner, the wingless dragon Solannus and his pet snake- she couldn't bring herself to reiterate his idiotic name. There were the skeletal pirate triplets who would be attached to them until the next gold moon- not that such a thing existed- but couldn't touch saltwater. There was nothing to say about poor Fluffers. And, finally, there was the wraith Lamure, who seemed neither here nor there with regards to their campaign. But, Bredikai thought, it might yet prove helpful to have a wraith in their group if the gift of fright was with her.

So lost in her thoughts was the killsmith that she didn't notice the dragon walk up next to her. He scared the shit out of her when he broke her concentration and asked, "Might we speak for a moment?"

"Ah! Don't do that," she cried. Her palpitations just weren't going to get a break today. "Yes, walk."

They ventured away from the group, just far enough to be out of earshot but close enough to intervene quickly should any shenanigans arise. The smell of saltwater was too close and why they had thought that venturing there was a good idea she would never know. Bredikai could hardly tell what time of day it was but she was silently thankful for the rest and the fact that her head had stopped bleeding.

"Bredikai-"

"Look, wait," the killsmith interrupted and took a deep breath. "I'm sorry, Solannus."

"Goodness, are you ill?"

"A little hungover but I'll get over it," the killsmith said, stretching her back. "I'm sorry for being so irate but the truth is I've been going at it alone for... pretty much my whole life. My whole professional life, anyway. I prefer it that way but I'm also not stupid enough to think that you and I can make a go at Borghalus on our own. And now I've got to be responsible for more than myself. I guess every bit of help counts but I won't lie to you; I have no real plan, bare-minimum magical ability-"

"Bare minimum?"

"Alright none. All we really have is two out of the six of your father's... bits- sorry, I don't know how to be sensitive about that- and a group with very questionable capabilities," she said. Bredikai turned back to see that the triplets had somehow managed to lure a wild boar from somewhere beyond the forest, no doubt to feed the thing to Solannus. For the dragon's part, Solannus was in no mood to sass the girl and knew their situation to be growing stranger by the day. She had spoken honestly and with sincerity, so he thought about her words and looked at her with due sympathy.

"Young lady," he said, "I do not know what stake you have in this campaign but you are not alone. Much as you would have it that way, we are now a company and… and you have already given me more hope than I had yesterday," he smiled. "We will follow your lead, that much I promise, but if you are at a loss as to whither we proceed let us take the matter up with the group. Then, perhaps, we may form a strategy. There is no ill in asking for help," he said and Bredikai was touched by the dragon's temperate approach. It must have taken a lot for him to admit as much. He had that look in his eyes again; the one that said his thoughts were beyond anyone's reach. In that moment Bredikai realized that, in a world where she had fought to have her voice heard and succeeded, there stood a creature before her who had begged for a helping hand and received nothing in return.

The dragon could not bear to keep her gaze but when Bredikai turned back to their company, she saw one of the triplets waving happily as the other two masterfully hacked up Solannus' meal. Bredikai winced at the fountain of blood they were enjoying a little too much and rubbed her temples. They made their way back and a long discourse ensued as the killsmith tried to ignore the guzzling of a boar next to her.

They had been at it for the better part of the day. Dumb idea after dumb idea came reeling in. Sir Hiss-a-lot had wandered off with Fluffers on his back, not a hair remained of the boar and the triplets were making busy chatter amongst themselves, utterly uninterested with the unfolding logistics of their non-existent scheme. As the hours dragged on they, too, went into the thick of the wood in search of their pets.

"I'm just saying we might entertain the idea of asking the necromancers for help," Lamure suggested for the third time. "I *think*- and I may be wrong as my memory has yet to return- I may have studied with them for some time before this happened," she said pointing at herself. "I feel like I want to say they weren't that bad."

"You're certain they weren't the ones responsible for your current situation?" asked the killsmith.

"No."

"Then why does everyone keep telling me to try the necromancers?" Bredikai asked, frustrated with their standstill. "Like why not the wizards or the rangers or even the fucking barbarians? Look, I'm not being racist or specist or whatever Solannus likes to call it; it's just that *maybe* they have a shitty reputation because they've earned it," Bredikai said. "They're the entire reason why elephants went extinct, you know. Random knowledge, I grant you, but this is a thing that happened and a thing I know."

"I wouldn't know about all that," Solannus interjected, picking at the hairs wedged in his teeth, "but perhaps said elephants should have fought harder to stay alive."

Bredikai snorted. "Easy to say when you're at the top of the food chain."

"I am merely stating that I sense we are not far from the Mortlands," Lamure said before they could waste another half hour arguing dietary evolutions.

"Don't get me started," Bredikai said and held up a hand. "You can't know that we're not far because no one knows where the Mortlands are. They keep relocating them. That's why the fucking maps have to be redrawn every five years. And they do it on purpose, you know, so innocents can just walk in unknowingly and then it's all *hello, welcome to the Necro-kingdom* and boom! you're dead. Ish."

"Boom?" Solannus asked, blinking innocently.

"Death, Sonny. The cold hand," the killsmith said in an ominous voice. "More skeletons than you can shake a claw at." She leaned in and then they leaned in and she whispered, "*they eat people.*"

"Absurd," Solannus spat and settled back into position. "Utter lunacy! Never in all my years have I *ever* heard of necromancers being... being *cannibals*. Wild stories," he grumbled and Bredikai threw her hands in the air. "You are fabricating this nonsense and poorly, might I add. Didn't you mention that the Guildhead was your King Althaean's estranged wife?"

"Sister, Sonny. She's his sister. Do you even listen?"

"Less as the hours wax and wane."

"I wish to add that I feel the necrotic pull," Lamure said.

"Hence why I feel the Mortlands are not far. I could hasten ahead and check."

"Well, we can't afford to stay here for much longer," Bredikai conceded. The skyline rumbled, calling to their attention just how grey and musty the atmosphere had become. Breathing was no different than chugging water and both the killsmith and dragon were having frizz issues.

"Let's not split up, though," Bredikai ordered. "Not yet. Forget the necromancers for now and let's focus on other goals. We have your father's tooth so that's technically the bone, right?" she thought out loud, bringing the poem to mind and checking off the items. "And you have the heart but won't tell us where. Nevermind; the less we know for now... We need the claw, the eye, the wing and the horn- and that's assuming no one else has gotten to them yet. And there's only one guild that has a prayer of having such information." She looked at the dragon and the wraith who practically fell into her face with curiosity.

"Oh, come on people, where does one go to get information, no matter the subject?"

"Where?" they asked breathlessly and Bredikai was about to answer when there came a rustling through the trees and out popped Sir Hiss-a-lot and Fluffers holding a-

"What the fuck is that? Oh, oh no- p-put that thing down. Sir Hiss-a-Lot! Down!"

"What in the good golden grief is the matter with you?" Solannus asked. "It is merely a baby!"

"A g-g-g-riffin baby! Down you stupid snake, put that thing back where you found it!" hissed the killsmith, slowly edging away from the group. But the snake merely stuck its forked tongue out at her and Fluffers was no help- as expected. Lamure began to laugh as something to do with the nickname *Griffinbait* came to her but then they saw the triplets approaching, all playing with a baby griffin of their own. Altogether there were too many griffins among them and one frazzled killsmith shouting nonsense. Then, like the roar of an incoming tide of destruction, there came screeches from beyond the clouds, followed closely by the encroaching stench of feathers, beak and death by fowl.

"Move it people, MOVE!" barked Bredikai. "Leave those things behind- the swarm's coming!"

As the wilderness of the skies gained ground towards them, everyone hurled themselves onto Solannus' back- all save Lady Lamure who couldn't really understand what all the panic was about for she was in no real danger herself- and they charged towards what Solannus deemed to be the coastline. It was a shame that in his panic the dragon barrelled over the edge of a cliff he had mistaken for the horizon and before the triplets could even scream about saltwater they were all dangling from the edge, each holding on to the other as they all held on to Solannus' tail. The dragon sunk his claws into the face of the cliff but his weight was proving difficult to manage and the brine-bellied grave roared below them.

"There are easier ways to kill us, Solannus!" Bredikai cried as Ashley's boney fingers dug into her calf. Griffins almost as large as the dragon whirled above their heads as the babies they left behind cantered to the edge and looked at the desperate group.

"Shoo! Shoo, you feathery devils!" the killsmith shouted but the babes merely cocked their heads and continued to stare.

"They look like they're about to swoop," Lamure observed thoughtfully as she floated beside the dragon.

"Caves! Right yonder!" Murray yelled and sure enough,

even as the feathery terrors of the skies descended upon them and Bredikai shrieked in abject horror, Solanus swung them down into a plunge of faith and through the mouth of an open cave. With great difficulty he latched on and nearly tore his claws out of their roots but the company managed to fling themselves in. Solannus scurried to gain a proper footing and he had just about entered but he was as large as the cave's mouth itself and squeezing in posed a new problem.

"Help me!" he cried, with more than half his behind plugging up the cave's entrance. "They're gnawing my ass!"

"Will you stop screaming!" Bredikai hissed and the group held the dragon in place like a plug as the sound of squawking dissipated all the while Solannus bit on his lower lip. They were left breathless in the darkness. "Lamure, float outside and see if they've gone," the leader bid and the wraith did as she was told. She was gone only a moment and when she returned to the group she calmly waited as they tried en masse to un-squish Solannus' rear out of the entrance. His jiggly bits (of which he was sensitive) were jammed in so tightly that the entirety of the focus was on his moaning and Bredikai's cursing when Lamure faked a cough and they were all bid to look behind them.

As small or tight as cave mouths had a tendency of being, it was commonplace for the entryways to disguise a large cavern or a string of cavernous hives beyond them. Bredikai hoped that to be the case here or they would have a tough time trying to squeeze through with a dragon. The cave was too dark and said dragon all too distracted by his own plight to make sense of what loomed ahead. The killsmith slowly turned around. The cave was suddenly illuminated by torches and Bredikai wished that they had stayed in the dark.

"Funny story," the killsmith began with a charming smile that would have withered the tits off anyone living, "but we were just discussing whether or not we were due for a visit to your gracious... kingdom... queendom..." The sentence fell short. A veritable horde of the armed undead stood, stretching as deeply into the large tunnel as they could see. They were silent; frozen in place, breathless and leering with what intent none could discern. Solannus chose that moment to relieve his backside of the cave and with a *plonk* he was whole once more and ready to take action.

"Madam!" he cried, "take cover!"

Bredikai didn't have a single moment to announce that there was nothing to take cover under and she was knocked down to kiss the floor. Within seconds the entire tunnel ahead of them was up in flames as the dragon's torrent blazed straight over her. But Solannus was too frazzled by the plunge and ran out of firepower quickly. When he stopped wheezing and the smoke cleared, he was greeted by the scalding death-gaze of an equally scalding killsmith with a molten pile of armor fallen at her feet and not a one of the skeletal horde had budged. Several of the zombies melted apart yet the swarm stood its ground unperturbed.

"You about done?" Bredikai asked, glaring sharp lethal objects at Solannus.

"Your armor is rather poor," stated the dragon. "Did you think to face my brother in such a flimsy state?"

"Rather underwhelming display," came a smooth, deep voice before the killsmith could reply to the dragon. The speaker was somewhere within the horde and now the group's attention was diverted back to the silent sentinels.

"Who goes?!" Bredikai demanded and the skeletons began to part. A shadow- a fragment of the very darkness itself- moved towards them, slowly manifesting into a tall, brooding beauty with silver hair, a face that seemed to be chiselled by the gods themselves, his piercing blue eyes penetrating into their very souls as his robes swayed flawlessly-

"Is it getting hot in here again?" Bredikai whispered and Solannus nudged her with a claw.

"What *is* that gorgeous creature?" the dragon whispered. As the gorgeous creature drew closer there was no mistaking the vampire that this mystery man was. In a matter of seconds his blue eyes muddied and settled upon the deepest red at the sight of the living human- but Bredikai was too appreciative to notice.

"Mm-mm but the gods are cruel to me today," the killsmith said. The Hexia didn't so much as twitch so, in a display of good faith, Bredikai handed the sword to Solannus and walked to face the undead beauty unarmed.

"You must be the Mistress Griffinbait," the vampire said and Bredikai flinched at the moniker. "Your reputation follows you most literally," he said with mild amusement and bowed, never releasing the killsmith from his gaze. Even Solannus was ready to swoon but Lamure was busy trying to stop the triplets from annoying their boney brethren into an attack.

"It's Bredikai, actually. The..ah... Carver, something. I apologize for barging in-"

"Quite the contrary, Madam. We've been awaiting your visit. Why else would we be standing in a cave?"

"Why, indeed?" giggled the killsmith and even Solannus began twirling his chin hairs.

"I am Florian Cilvantean, one of Mistress Althaea's head attendants. She is most keen to intercept your company. Do not worry," said the vampire regarding the triplets' antics, "they will only attack upon my Mistress' word."

"Who's worried?" Bredikai smiled lamely. "We love us some skeletons in our little band." Solannus snorted and shoved the girl aside.

"Abject apologies for our intrusion, Master Florian," spoke the drake, "it was very much *not* our intention to trespass. We seem to attract misfortune of late, though, if you'll excuse me for saying, perhaps our luck has turned... One of ours, at least," he mumbled the last bit quickly. "You say that we are expected?"

Florian bowed once more and spoke with such dark and soothing magic that the group hardly noticed him turn and resume walking back into the cave. They followed him, hypnotized by the tranquility of his treble. Only the tip-tap of the wordless army behind them bounced around the vampire's words as he explained to the group that Mistress Althaea had perceived rumors of their quest and wished to hold council with the killsmith of Etherdeign and her company. In truth, the vampire could have talked them into the pits of any hell he wanted for there was no telling who was more entranced by his words; the killsmith, the dragon, Lesley or Ashley. His necrotic appeal was somehow lost on Murray and Lamure.

"Are we near the Mortlands, Master Florian?" the dragon asked and was told that their journey to the Necro-kingdom would involve passage through a discrete portal and out into a muted land of dusk, fog, crags and fortification past a washed-out forest that spanned even beyond Solannus' eyesight. They followed the vampire without further question and before long the group was transported to the heart of the Mortlands, on a lifeless road to meet with the Mistress Althaea. What little Bredikai knew about necromancers came primarily from a steady stream of Etherdeignian gossip passed around the taverns but, so far, they had spoken true about the lay of the land; it was most uninspiring. She had also heard that the Necromancy Guild was physically situated in a castle built upon the edge of a cliff- yeay!- whose towers overlooked an endless night. The only thing that looked endless to the killsmith was the road they were on and the fog was doing a wonderful job of disguising their path. She was thankful for the horde's torches.

"Not that I am worried for my own sake because, thus far, this place is absolutely charming," Lamure said as she sidled up to Bredikai, "but do you think it wise to march our group into death incarnate? You're so... *alive*."

Bredikai's head had gone fuzzy. They had been on a dark dank road mere moments ago- of that she was certain- and then all at once it appeared that they were on different terrain altogether. She felt like she was having an experience outside of her body, watching her legs step lightly into a land that was, actually, much more decorated and -dare she admit- festive than what she had been expecting. They were walking through a city now; one paved with cobblestones with the odd bone here or there where stones had been plucked. The fog was lifted from around them and hung in the sky so as to not impede the remainder of their journey.

There were candles and torches and other fire hazards *everywhere*- so many, in fact, that the entire city was aglow with warmth. Grey was the predominant colour scheme but it's coldness was tempered by oranges and reds and yellows with hints of green, all belonging to the old-world structures populating this undead city. Towers of all size and girth stood like rocky spikes in places one would have little use for them, proudly burdening the infertile soil. Fell birds of prey fluttered through the sky like noisy butterflies. Laughter and song could be heard at regular intervals and the very air was pregnant with enchantment. The magic was dense enough that even the magically-handicapped could feel it. Lamure and the triplets had never looked more alive. Sure there were bones and other bodily scraps littered around the streets but the decrepit structures were also adorned with gold, tattered fineries and wooden signs that swung against a light breeze. It was the liveliest death that Bredikai or any of them could have hoped to find. The company was enamored and no one thought to hide their awe as they passed through the city with mouths agape.

Solannus trotted to Bredikai's side and together they watched the gentle swishing of Florian's robes from left to right to left to right-

"Easy there, champ, I'm sure he likes you just as much as I do," Bredikai teased the dragon and winked.

"Ludicrous," Solannus declared, lifting his head proudly into the air. And that was when he finally caught sight of their destination, perched as promised on the edge of a cliff; a titanic run-down castle with many an old tower abutting it. To no one's surprise, the castle was gleaming a glorious black. All the rooms were lit and Solannus could just make out the lights from inside the windows though he could not discern any figures within. Bredikai signalled for Lamure to keep to their side and not venture ahead. They had all the time in the world to annoy their hosts once they got to the castle whose name, Florian revealed, was the *Ire Craven*.

"Might I take this moment to state how enthralled I am with your kingdom's, er, consistency," Solannus said to the vampire. Florian had seen much in life and double that in his undeath, to the extent that there was little that could shake the stiffness of his air- but the articulate dragon's eagerness was proving new even for him.

"Death is rather consistent, one might say," spoke the vampire as the dragon replied *indeed, indeed*. Solannus could hear Bredikai giggling at his bumbling so he lagged behind while she caught up to him.

"What even are you?" the killsmith teased. "Who speaks like that?"

"You're one to talk!" the dragon hissed back. "It wouldn't kill you to aspire to a more expansive vocabulary and tone down on the swearing. One needs only hear the word *fuck* but so many times in one day."

"I do apologize for not being as worldly as you, professor, but may I ask- and pardon my petty mortal curiosity- just why it is a dragon such as your magnanimous self needs be so exhaustingly wordy?"

"You tease me, girl, but you'll want some finesse by the time our quest is out. If we ever make it to that castle, of course," Solannus said and it was a thinly veiled complaint for his arms and legs were tiring and the sense of being watched by hidden eyes was all too real. "You clearly have no estimation of what we're playing into," he whispered.

"Aye, how much longer, lads?" Murray whined from behind them. She had undertaken the duty of transporting both Fluffers and Sir Hiss-a-lot in her ribs and, for some reason, exhaustion was a thing that an undead pirate wanted to complain about. It seemed that no amount of walking was getting them any closer to the Ire Craven and they were either under some sort of enchantment or something kept pulling the castle away.

"Don't do that," Bredikai said to Solannus as they both ignored the increasing whining from behind. "Don't talk to me like I'm some inept child."

"I'm sorry, was I being rude? Oh, but I don't care anymore," Solannus huffed. "Your human sensitivities are dreadful to keep up with."

"See- *there*. That condescension. You're one scaly snob.

Maybe an attitude check is in order, Solannus."

Lamure quietly drifted behind the pair as the triplets jogged to catch up. "I say she makes him cry before we reach the castle," the wraith said and suddenly she had the triplets' undivided attention.

"Your money where your mouth is, wraith-lass!" Ashley said and searched around his bones for even a single coin.

"This be interestin' at last!" Murray chimed in.

"But we've not a shillin' to our names, you boney bandits," Lesley despaired. He was ever the sharpest of the three.

"I think I, too, left pocket and purse behind in life," Lamure admitted. "Surely we can bet with something else? Quick, they're about to peak!"

Indeed the concentration span of the company seemed fragmented and no one realized how close they had actually come to the castle. It was as though some hidden force was now expediting their trip but they had all lost interest by this point.

"Methinks that fine vampire lad be the first to crack an' end us all," Ashley declared and Murray was quick to take her brother's side. "That's us now; what say you two?"

"The dragon laddie's got a mouth on him I wager," Lesley said thoughtfully. "I say he breaks the mistress and roasts 'er."

"And I will side with Bredikai's mouth," Lamure said. "She will brandish her sword before we reach the castle. That's it then. Loser or losers will run errands for one week. Whatever they say, no questions asked. Deal?" They shook on it (sort of, since Lamure's hand simply phased through them) and the deal was struck. Meanwhile, Florian was responsible for using every bit of magic he could spare to hasten their journey and at long last his Mistress, the Necromancer Althaea, spoke to his mind and he was able to tune out the jabbering behind him.

"Just watch and walk, lads," Lamure smiled and they drifted closer to the bitching. Solannus was having his go now and he was most unamused.

"You refer to my illustrious father's remains as *bits* and dare to take issue with my condescension? The very nerve of it all. At least I had a father to speak of. But now that we are more intimate in our company I may reveal that I'd heard about you before, *Carver*. You and your questionable line. Tell me, is *he* your father?" Solannus exclaimed, nodding at Florian who was off on another mental plane.

"Fine," Bredikai snapped back, "I'll admit that literally anyone could be my father. I'm told my mother was a *tad* exuberant."

"The way bards dress is a tad exuberant. I believe the word you are looking for is *loose*."

"Oh, what, now I have dragons gossiping about me?" When Bredikai brushed her hand against the Hexia's hilt Lamure's undead heart almost leapt with joy but the excitement was short-lived. Lesley was in the lead.

"We hear things," Solannus declared. "Cease being so, so-"

"So *what*?"

"Flamboyant."

"Flam-! Excuse me?" Bredikai gasped.

"Obvious. Much too obvious. Brazen. Deluded is another choice word."

"Deluded, am I? I'm not the one who thinks his mother was a unicorn!" hollered the killsmith. "Oh, I heard you telling the triplets your little fairytales. How does that even work, Solannus? Tell me, *please*. Explain to me the physics of a ten tonne fire-drake and a one tonne fairy-mule exchanging parental heritage under the stars to make a baby Solannus. That poor, poor woman." She shivered.

Solannus' belly grew with each passing jab and Lesley was silently cheering for his champion from behind.

"Do not speak of my mother, you one-bite tooth-stain!"

Bredikai just about pulled out the Hexia to point it at Solannus' belly and Lamure was hard pressed to hide her squeals. But she was disappointed once more when the killsmith settled for finger pointing of the most middle kind.

"You started it, you steam-powered, boar-fattened chimney!"

Solannus gasped, utterly affronted. "You-! *You!*"

Ashley and Murray held onto one another and held onto the breaths they didn't need to take.

"If you cry I'm going to kill us both here and now," Bredikai said, pulling out the Hexia threateningly. Solannus bit back his trembling lip.

"And so it goes, lads," Lamure smiled as the triplets groaned.

"*You*," hissed the dragon, "I was *enslaved*, you unfeeling creature! Is that so difficult to comprehend? Heartless, *cruel* woman!"

"Now he will attack her marital status," Lamure whispered to the side.

"And is it any wonder no man will have you?!" Solannus cried. "I dare ask who would deal with such a graceless, artless wretch! Lo, but I've seen killsmiths in my day but none who have been so hopeless as you."

"I've *had* men, understand? You're so star-struck you didn't even see the eyes the vampire was making at me and, see, this is your problem Solannus: you're a snob. Like every other drake I've ever met. You're a legion of snobs, just like I've been saying. You'd do well to remember that I don't appreciate being undermined- or underestimated."

"And *I* do not appreciate being called the *f* word."

"What, *fuck*? I call everyone that."

"The *other* one."

"What's the other one?"

"Methinks we've had enough of this, lads," Ashley said to his group. "We been standin' at this here gate for more'an ten minutes."

"Don't get involved or he'll have ya for a toothpick, brother," Murray said.

"The f…. *Fat*? Oh, faaaat! Am I right?"

Lightning crackled around them as a gate with tortured gears churned upwards and suddenly the company found themselves devoid of a guiding vampire, an army of skeletons rushing inwards while ignoring them and wondering just how long it was that they had been standing at the front gate of the gargantuan Ire Craven. The wraith came out as victor of the bet but next time the triplets vowed to be more careful with their predictions. Solannus had come dangerously close to sitting on top of the killsmith and squashing her. Lamure was convinced that the lightning was Althaea's way of shutting them up and hurrying them along.

They were at the entrance of a grand raven, shining black with outstretched wings, and it bore the bulk of the castle on its back. The stone bird's open mouth served as the entrance to a fortress whose size they could not discern for it dug below and into the cliff so that it was like a blade that cut through the edge. The polished ebony structure was befitting of a necrotic stronghold and, though they could not be sure, it seemed that the eyes of the raven followed their company's movement. Through its open beak they entered. Gates and doors grew smaller the further they walked but the smallest was still large enough to accommodate Solannus' entry with ease.

"Makes sense, I suppose," Bredikai said to herself. "Literally anyone or anything can become a necromancer these days. Gotta build large." Their earlier tiff forgotten, the killsmith and the dragon walked in the lead as the remaining four and their pets followed from behind. Scores of undead souls bustled to and fro, completely ignoring the strange group or doing a very good job pretending to. If there were a few questioning brows they were not directed at the dragon so much as the living killsmith strolling around the Ire Craven with a quadruple dose of death trailing behind her. The Hexia hummed every now and again but that much was to be expected. Even Solannus seemed more at ease, his general humor lifting with the knowledge that he was no longer alone- even if he wished to be.

"Is there any particular protocol for meeting with a necromancer?" Solannus asked, and he eyed the interior with growing wonder. There were books and unholy trinkets stacked up to a ceiling he could not make out and from the looks of it the Ire Craven boasted more than ten stories in height. Intricate tapestries decorated the overburdened walls and not a few of the threaded characters were majestic dragons whose names he did not know.

"If there is then I wouldn't know it," the killsmith replied. "And don't sass me about that; I've only met a handful of necromancers before and they weren't the most gracious sort. Besides, we're about to meet *the* necromancer," Bredikai clarified. With each word her voice lowered a bit more and Solannus' neck craned closer to hear her until they were two gossiping ninnies walking and gawking at this extraordinary turn of events.

"And you know King Althaean's late wife couldn't stand her 'cause they say she found her getting up to something in the cemetery-"

"She did not!" Solannus gasped.

"Oh, she *diiiid*. Allegedly. Rumor has it King Althaean was beyond infuriated. Crazy since I know him to be a darling old soul."

"And he cast her out?"

"Ugh, you know how the patriarchy can get. They can't *stand* strong independent women who know what they want," Bredikai tutted.

"Tell me about it," the dragon whispered back. "My cousin Undallis had more than one questionable serling from different sires and she couldn't leave her cave for *years*."

"Really, it's always the children that suffer," Bredikai said, and they both shook their heads.

"Goodness, you don't suppose this Florian was the one she was-"

The two gasped each other into silence when the expressionless guildhead was suddenly before them, standing on the last step of a staircase adorned with a worn-out carpet whose color lent itself more to urine than gold.

At once the two bowed and the merry gang behind them followed suit. There was no telling of the temperament that awaited them so the killsmith and dragon bowed as long and low as they dared. Bredikai's back cracked loudly and Solannus had to help her re-form. Bits of bone fell from the triplets when they bowed and re-bowed with increasing gusto. Sir Hiss-a-Lot crawled around the necromancer's feet and the wraith sighed with embarrassment. Althaea took this moment to study the company and bear into their souls. While not altogether displeased, it would have been sinful to say that she was anywhere near dazzled by this motley arrangement and wondered once more what her brother, the great King Althaean, must have been drinking when he cooked up this scheme. They were all so very *odd* together.

"You are welcome to the Ire Craven, killsmith and company," Althaea spoke and inclined her head gracefully. Her long black attire was dull and moth-eaten in places, keeping with the general deterioration of their surroundings, but it was offset by the woman's snow-white hair and piercing green eyes that belied her age. Her dress swished at the bottom as she descended the steps, light as air. They watched the ethereal beauty- something terrifying in her own right- practically float towards them and Solannus gulped. Her black thorny crown was a delightful touch and oh-so dramatic.

"Come you in fear or despair, we will not have you leave in enmity," Althaea said. Her voice was as cool as a light autumn rain and her movements just as fluid.

"So long as we leave, necro-lass," Ashley mumbled and the triplets chuckled to themselves. In the blink of an eye the vampire Florian was behind his mistress, along with several other droll-looking undead sentinels, and not one looked as amused as the triplets.

"You are come to us with a non-hostile drake. That is no small feat," continued the necromancer. "Perhaps we may find a way to ebb the tides after all. In truth I had anticipated a greater collective but strength may be found beyond physical limitations."

"Did she just call us limited?" Solannus whispered barely opening his jaws and Bredikai poked at him to shut his yap.

"It has been too long since a dragon has graced our halls, son of Septiannus. You are as welcome as the rest of your company- if not more, for I have long awaited to meet the one who will bring an end to the Dragonfather's line," Althaea said and Solannus looked to Bredikai with dread in his eyes.

"Come," said the necromancer, "there is much to prophecy and the future is ever-shifting."

CHAPTER 4: THE AWESOME POWER OF COMMUNICATION

Bredikai begrudgingly admitted to herself that the leading Lordess of the Undead was a resource she should have agreed to consult even before the Rogue Guild. Half-assed prejudices aside, there was a telling light in the woman's crescent-shaped eyes that betrayed a lifetime of depth and experience- some of which the killsmith hoped would find its way into her company. The necromancers were proving to be so cordial and possessed of serenity that even the triplets were behaving themselves.

The company was led into a room Florian had described as being part of the Ire Craven's innermost cloister, chosen for purposes of discretion. They would be removed from inquisitive eyes and ears. There were no windows in this inner sanctum. Nothing, in fact, but shelves upon shelves of books, a score of strange armor mounted on display and more than one questionable piece of taxidermy. The deformed troglodytes were a nice touch. But claustrophobia was not an issue for the killsmith's company and they certainly didn't need to see the dark precipitation outside to know it was there, for the rumbling of the heavens was sufficient evidence of turbulent weather raging above the Craven. Lightning seemed destined to fall upon the castle itself, adding electric anxiety to an already jittery group.

When Althaea revealed that there were several drinking quarters within the Craven most appropriate for undead merry-makers, the triplets didn't need to be told twice. Lamure was hesitant to leave but Althaea assured her that, when the time came, she would sit with the wraith and they would share counsel one-on-one. Satisfied with the necromancer's word, Lamure bid her company's two leaders happy parlaying and a swift farewell. The last thing the wraith heard was Bredikai shouting at them to keep to their senses. Now only the four remained and the silence was awkward for the living half of the quartet.

"You are a more curious group than I foreshadowed," Althaea began and settled upon a velvet-covered seat larger than a normal armchair but not large enough to be called a throne. It was still ornate enough to drive the point home that this was her domain and she'd foreshadow to her undead heart's content. The woman's manner was as smooth as the wine Florian poured into ivory goblets carved into the forms of demons and Solannus looked at Bredikai with horror as she downed the drink without a second glance.

"What, I'm parched," Bredikai mumbled at the dragon and noted how even the coziest of cloisters they had passed through, including the one they were in, was large enough for the dragon to be comfortable. It actually wasn't all that bad-having a compact dragon, that is. The only thing Solannus did not have room for was to complain because their hosts had been kind enough to give him a large goblet so he, too, could enjoy a drink. They thought of everything, these necrotic hosts. Maybe life really was wasted on the living.

"We are a freak show, Mistress Althaea," Solannus said, venturing a smile that never quite made it to his face.

"We thank you for hosting us in such an…uh…" Bredikai trailed off.

"Amiable manner, my Lady," the dragon jumped in. "In truth I don't think any part of our situation is of an ordinary nature but we come before you with no ill intent. We would have been here sooner if *someone* didn't let her personal prejudices make judgment calls on behalf of the company.... You mentioned something with regards to the end of the Dragonfather's line?"

Under normal circumstances Solannus would have been appalled at his own breach of protocol but too much comfort unnerved him and he could not fully trust in his counterpart's sobriety to sustain healthy communication. Bredikai seemed far too invested in the green drink she was guzzling down like water and he thought to use this chance to get two normal sentences in before the killsmith butchered diplomacy.

Meanwhile Althaea was studying him with a pleasant ruby smile that gave away nothing. "Do not worry yourself over the comings and goings of the stars, son of Septiannus," she said, taking a sip from her own goblet. "The future is nothing more than the infinite present- and at present, you are among friends. One might even say family for I, too, hail from the killsmith's homeland. Would that I had known the part Etherdeign would play in this tale... But even my sight has its boundaries."

Bredikai had thought about keeping certain information under wraps but since the guildhead who obviously knew much more than they did- about literally everything- was in a sharing mood then who was she to judge? To not follow suit would have been an ignorant move. The killsmith obstinately stood by her decision that necromancers were not to be trusted but without proof of misconduct she had no reason to be open with her misgivings. Solannus, on the other hand, was now dipping a little too freely into the wine and letting his anxieties get the better of him. Florian sat silently.

"Solannus does the worrying for all of us, my Lady," Bredikai said to the necromancer and took a more delicate sip from her goblet. "My colorful counterpart here is the last son of the late Septiannus. I'm Bredikai Cronunham, as you know. The triplets in tow I have neither explanation nor excuse for, and the wraith is Lamure. They're not from Etherdeign but, as you mentioned, we are," she said and raised her goblet to Althaea. The others followed suit and drank to the kingdom. "My company has come together for mutual gain."

"Indeed," said Florian from his mistress's left. "And what does your company have to gain from this venture?"

Bredikai's thoughts were interrupted by several skeletons carrying more generous amounts of drink followed by light foodstuffs that looked non-lethal*ish* to consume. Althaea apologized for not having food brought out sooner. She had become forgetful regarding mortal manners, you see, for they entertained very little company from the outside world and even fewer who were still alive. Althaea urged the killsmith to continue.

"Um... Let's see; Solannus here doesn't really know what he wants but he definitely does *not* want his evil brother to ascend as Dragonfather and in that we're in agreement. As far as the triplets, I think they want to help us and die. For...for real this time. And, you know, stay dead. Lamure is still trying to figure herself out. My grandfather has a young charge whose skill in magic is proving both impressive and worrisome for his age. He seems to have struck some sort of deal with the wraith. So either the boy's going to be an asset to our guild or a liability but he's a good kid and I'll be damned if he grows up to be some sort of-" Solanus poked such a rough claw into her back Bredikai face-planted into the table. But it stopped her from finishing her rambling thoughts with the word *necromancer* and getting them hexed out of the Ire Craven.

"It appears there is still much to discover about your company," Althaea said and her ghostly smile never faltered.

"You have approached the mission in an unusual manner but one befitting a killsmith who is forced to partnership. And how comes the Carver from Etherdeign into such a situation?"

Solannus perked up, curious as to how much detail his counterpart would be divulging to the undead. Bredikai could see him breathlessly waiting for her to speak from the corner of her eye.

"His Majesty, er, your brother King Althaean, has placed upon me a special task," said the killsmith. She now knew better than to expect any outward reaction from the necromancers but Bredikai thought she caught a hint of sadness on Althaea's face at the mention of her brother. "To be blunt, my Lady, we're not loving this Borghalus character. I didn't take this business so seriously when I set out and I doubt the King wishes to induce mass panic but I'm starting to understand that there's a greater threat brewing. Solannus is helping me understand the growing severity of the situation. People have suffered enough from crazed creatures; lands have been ravaged- some beyond repair, many still bearing traumas from previous wars. It's a time for peace and surely King Althaean wishes to maintain that peace at whatever cost. That cost is us- but I guess that's implied."

"How do you intend to maintain this frail peace?" Florian asked and Bredikai set her goblet down to answer him directly.

"I'm going to aid Solannus in gathering the pieces necessary to declare a new Dragonfather. And I'm going to kill Borghalus if he stands in our way," she stated calmly. "King Althaean has promised me guild exemption in return."

"I see," the vampire responded. It wasn't the answer Bredikai had been hoping for after all she'd divulged so she awkwardly took another sip and shut her mouth.

"And you, Master Solannus."

"Yes, my Lady?"

"I take it that you are also not loving your brother, as the Carver has put it. Nor does he care for you."

Solannus put his goblet carefully on the wooden table they were seated around. It was strong and made of a dark cherrywood worn by time. He found himself staring into its rings, the smallest unfolding outward on and on until the ripples were almost as large as the entire tabletop.

"My very life seems to offend him, my Lady. In truth, I can not understand just why that should be so. If he were but a bit more level-headed and amiable, I would not think to protest his claim upon the title. But he aims to be the cruelest of dragons and his heart has turned beyond reason. He is not worthy to lead. Not after all he has done," he said and fell quiet. Bredikai had come to understand that tone and knew that a phantom sadness crawled just beneath the dragon's diplomatic words. Althaea was more intuitive than either had given her credit for as she nodded slowly and kept her emerald gaze fixed on Solannus.

"You have your mother's kind spirit," the necromancer said at last and the two immediately looked to her for an explanation. "Her fate was cruel- too cruel- even for your kin. I am sorry for your loss."

"I... Thank you, my Lady," Solannus said. He was too choked up to speak further and had just enough grace to bow his head. Bredikai looked at him suspiciously then back at Althaea. There were altogether too many questions but haranguing the guildhead with them was not worth the risk.

"Mistress Althaea-" Bredikai began but the woman interrupted her with a hand in the air.

"There is much on your mind, killsmith, and I will answer your questions as best I can. But you must take rest and stay with us a while. The dragons will not overpower us so easily and we will speak more ere you leave the Ire Craven. I would not have you cast blindly into the wild," she said and stood. With that the stoney Florian had his cue to lead them to their temporary quarters. Neither Bredikai nor Solannus cared to be placed too far apart for there was much untapped mischief in that castle. For that matter, Solannus was fortunate that the Craven even had suitable lodging for one his size but he was reminded that there were creatures larger than himself who must have been hosted by the undead in better days.

As it turned out, one room was so large that the entire company decided to share it and, much to her vexation, Bredikai could not be the only one to opt for a separate room- even if it was just next door. Such a group of drunk co-dependents.

The killsmith was given a new set of clothes, a loose shirt in black which was her preferred color anyway, form-fitting comfortable trousers so she didn't have to stroll around in burnt armor, and told to summon an assistant should she want for anything. Not wanting to run the risk of seeming ungrateful, Brediai accepted all they gave her but it took a lot of convincing and sweet talk to get her to release the Sacré Hexia for a fixer-upper.

"It's for the best, you stubborn thing! You need greater enchantments if you wish for that coppertine pick to even graze Borghalus- should the situation necessitate," the dragon pleaded with her. "Bredikai- unhand that orange monstrosity at once or so help me I shall singe you down to your pubic hairs," the dragon warned. Bredikai whimpered and groaned, eventually giving in when Solannus started puffing her way.

She felt naked without her sword, calling into question her obsessive attachment to phallic objects- or so Solannus argued- until she finally agreed to allow them to tinker with her baby. She was assured that the weapon would be returned in excellent condition with an upgraded skill-set but Bredikai didn't care much for add-ons. So long as it was returned to her with edges that could carve she was happy.

The triplets and the wraith were entirely in their (newfound) element so, with no need for sleep wearing them down, the pirates headed back out to connect with other skeletal folk and see if there was anything to be done about the curse placed on them. Lamure was given free reign to look around and research wraith-lore so as to better acquaint herself with her own situation. Whatever the weather outside, the Craven was as cold as death itself so Bredikai got the fireplace going and sat in an armchair beside it as Solannus happily gnawed away at salted meats by her side. She was lost in thought and unaware that he was observing her during his feast, wondering what she was grinding about now.

"Have it out," the dragon said and it jarred her out of her thoughts.

"Hm?"

"Your mind is elsewhere. Dare I say far from this room. What troubles you when we are fed and spoiled and protected?"

She couldn't say. It was nothing and everything; friendship unexpected with no need for repayment. A feeling of protection, as the dragon said, and want for nothing. The world was not a kind place nor had Bredikai ever known it to be so charitable. Then again, approaching genuine kindness- if one could believe in it- with suspicion and distrust would not do. She was caught in an internal debate.

"I don't know... Nothing seems out of the ordinary since I guess this is our ordinary now," she replied. "These things just rub me the wrong way."

"What things?" asked the dragon between chews.

"Think about it. We don't have anything to offer Althaea or her guild. Not a damn thing. Except hope, maybe? And last I checked people don't like their helping hands to be repaid with that."

"You are much too distrusting, Bredikai," Solannus said with a large cup held up to her. "These people have shown us extreme generosity and it is improper to repay them with scrutiny and suspicion."

"Maybe..." she said, staring into the fire once more. "But something stinks- and I've been getting a whiff of it from the moment we got here."

"It's sulfur and acids and-" sniffed the dragon, "mercury. Quite a large amount, in fact."

Bredikai was about to stand up but Solannus barred her movement and sat her right back down. He was not about to have her ruin their moment of respite to go poking around for what-have-you, with or without permission.

"You will not distrust our hosts and you will not do me the disservice of distrusting my judgment. Not tonight," he said and it was the most forceful he had ever been. The killsmith looked at him with frustration on her face but Solannus would not yield. Defeated this time around, Bredikai sat down on the carpeted floor next to him and started picking at the food. Perhaps it wasn't so wrong to take a moment to let everything sink in. The dragon smiled and passed a fruit with tentacles her way, insisting that it was the most delicious thing she would ever eat. It was a peaceful evening for the unlikely pair, filled with well-natured jibes and family gossip.

Solannus regaled the killsmith with stories from his youth, when tempers were not yet so flared and the children of Septiannus were on better terms for a brief point in time. He even threw in a funny anecdote or two about Borghalus, which he had only learned through others, long before his brother decided to become the father of evils. In turn, Bredikai spoke of her adventures in killsmithery, but she was choosey with the ones she wished for him to hear, for the sake of keeping their conversation light.

Filled and fattened from their evening, the two fell fast asleep on the floor and though there was a perfectly good bed for the killsmith, she curled up next to an uneaten haunch of a hog as Solannus mumbled in his sleep about being attacked by tentacled monster fruit.

However long the company had intended to stay, it seemed they had little choice in the matter. The Mistress Althaea seemed to have disappeared altogether and they could not get an audience with her. One week passed in a similar manner- peaceful and with the group not wanting for anything. Bredikai was given a new breastplate, lighter and thinner than what she was used to but sturdier. It shone silver and was barren of any design or insignia. This was another bit of metal too tight around the chest but she liked it and thanked the guild for outfitting her with functional materials. Another half-week passed with only a few minor incidents resulting from too much alcohol (the triplets) and not enough gold (again, the triplets) but the killsmith was growing antsy and even Solannus was second-guessing his decision to stop her from tearing the Craven apart. They were now at the end of the second week of their stay and this unexpected fantasy vacation in the kingdom of the undead needed to come to a close.

Bredikai stared at the tapestries hung around the spacious entrance where they had first made contact with Althaea. Some were worn beyond repair and she wondered why they wouldn't have replaced them with better ones telling more self-aggrandizing stories. She walked along the gallery, noting the dark figures wielding magic and fighting against all who stood in their path. She snorted when she noticed the gap in their history and shook her head.

"The Bone Wars were a series of terrible embarrassments," came the sultry voice from behind her and the killsmith almost jumped. "I can remove them from the tapestries if not from the histories," Althaea said and smiled.

"I won't pretend I haven't seen all the undead barbarians around the Craven," Bredikai said and it was the first time she heard Althaea sigh and make no attempt to hide her disappointment.

"There you are," came Solannus' exasperated voice. He had been up and down that damn castle looking for his partner. He joined them and was not shy about relating how much his joints suffered from getting lost searching for the killsmith. He noted that the killsmith was packed and ready with her newly cleaned rucksack and, for once, could not blame her for her anxiousness.

Before Bredikai could state her real business, the tired dragon turned to the necromancer and said, "Mistress Althaea, I'm afraid it is about time we take our leave. We thank you for your kindness but have trespassed on your goodwill long enough. I believe I speak for my company when I say that we have ignored our real-world problems long enough."

Bredikai crossed her arms and looked at the dragon, terribly impressed that he had the nerve to turn his thinly veiled snarkiness towards someone other than herself.

Althaea gracefully inclined her head. She bid the pair follow her back into the inner sanctum where they were seated once more.

"You must forgive my absence, Master Solannus, but a guildhead's work is never finished. I hope you did not feel that we confined you in any way," Althaea said and, out of the shadows, Florian was with them once more. Solannus, now reclaiming his sense of etiquette, was quick to perish the thought. He added all the extra pleasantries that Bredikai just couldn't bring herself to say out loud and Althaea seemed satisfied.

"My partner is right," Bredikai said and she was done dancing around formalities. Being so forceful for all of five seconds had Solannus' heart palpitating so the killsmith decided to dispense with the frivolity and continue with a sharper tongue. "If we have anything left to discuss, my Lady, now is the time. I want my company on the move this evening. Or morning. What time is it? Can't tell in this place."

Althaea looked to Florian who did a silent sweep of the room before nodding at his guildhead. Ever so quietly they could hear the sound of a few more doors closing around them and the killsmith was put on alert. Before she could reach for her non-existent sword, Althaea put up a hand and bid them calm themselves.

"I must admit I do not miss the paranoia that comes with being alive," the necromancer said and both the dragon and the killsmith looked off in embarrassment. "I am sorry to have kept you waiting but life, as they say, must go on. The Guild keeps a busy schedule and the sun neither rises nor sets with Borghalus' plans for conquest," Althaea continued and they had to admit that she made a fair argument.

"You seek the remains of Septiannus to thwart Borghalus' claim. You must know that this information will not be kept hidden from him for long. We must also consider the possibility that your finding the remains will not stop Borghalus from claiming the title regardless," the necromancer said softly and both the killsmith and the dragon were pleased to be getting to the matter at last. The woman stood and was handed a long scroll by Florian who seemed to be in two places at once, scaring the blood back into Solannus' heart. Althaea unfolded the parchment onto the table and held the corners down with thick books. To their confusion, the parchment was empty and they waited patiently for it to do... anything.

"The demon dragon's eyes and ears are long and they have a power that would be the end of us all if properly channeled," spoke Althaea. Still nothing appeared. "It is not only dragons you will face. There are many species and races in Ethra whose allegiances will be called into question; some whose loyalty can be bought...

"You will give much from yourselves should you choose to see your campaign through- and you will have to sacrifice even more should you wish to succeed. Make no mistake, killsmith, that Borghalus is the greatest evil of our time- but he is only ever a symbol; the summation of lesser evils we have not addressed as a world. Both man and dragon must either perish or survive- but they will do it together, whatever the outcome."

Bredikai and Solannus locked eyes. Althaea's words, while unsurprising, were woven rather grimly. Neither knew how to feel about her vague revelations.

"The Rogue Guild is and ever remains your best source for information. Their network of spies spans to all corners of Ethra and far surpasses ours," Althaea continued and Bredikai mouthed a silent *thank you* in the dragon's direction. "Our guild will continue to aid your quest- though I suspect trust to be an issue on your part," she finished and looked directly at the killsmith. There was no judgment in the guildhead's eyes or any other discernible emotion. It was a matter of fact stated plainly.

Solannus turned to Bredikai, silently pleading with her to not do away all goodwill in one fell swoop. The killsmith sighed and scratched her head. "My Lady, with all the gratitude and respect that I can offer, I'm not going to stand here and bullshit you. I have little reason to trust you any more than I did two weeks ago. So far as I know neither does my King but I won't speak for him. I know that he would have sent me here directly if trust wasn't an issue."

Solannus was relieved but he could tell that even being mildly diplomatic had tensed the girl up. "My company is in no position to show open aggression towards you and we're truly grateful that you've hosted us this long. Your kindness is most appreciated," Bredikai said, adding, "but I don't know you from a werecrow and your mysterious absences don't sit well with me. None of this does. I need to know where these remains are and if that's not something you can help us with then we'd best be on our way. And if our leaving poses some sort of problem for you, I'm prepared to carve my way out." That last sentence made the dragon groan and struggle to apologize but the gentle necromancer did not seem bothered in the least.

"You will need that energy for the journey that lies ahead, killsmith, ere the skies are pregnant with dragon," the woman said and there was a hint of appreciation in her voice. "The reputation of the necromancers is sullied, to be sure. As you see I have inherited a depreciated guild with very little real influence. But I am the guildhead now and strive to change my followers', shall we say, perception of the world and its politics."

"So long as you're not about to launch another series of

wars."

"I have no such plans for this decade, no," Althaea said smoothly and Solannus finally began to breathe easily. "I take no offense at your open nature, killsmith. Rather, it is refreshing to know where everyone stands. I see why my brother chose you."

"Thanks... I think," Bredikai said lamely.

"I cannot force you to accept our aid but perhaps you may trust us to help you with some of the information you seek."

"In return for...? I don't know how we could hope to repay you, my Lady."

The necromancer had such a warm smile Solannus wondered why she did not flaunt it more. But then he picked up on the ghost of sadness and wondered how deep the woman's sorrow truly ran.

"Perhaps your good word will help me to rebuild the bridge between our lands," the woman said. "I love Althaean dearly and the baseless enmity that has festered between us weighs heavily upon my heart. He grows older- far too old to hold on to bitterness. As for the one who planted the seeds of discord, may she burn-" Florian coughed before Althaea got carried away and Solannus and Bredikai exchanged a secret look.

"I ask only that you arrange a meeting with myself and my brother. Unfortunately he does not respond to me or anyone from this guild. My devoted followers have taken to joking that I have been *ghosted*. Ah, to be young and undead," she mused. "Althaean will not hear me but perhaps he will listen to one of his own. Maybe then I shall finally know peace within my soul."

Bredikai looked at the woman who was clearly pleading with her the only way she knew how. Despite her toughness and distaste for getting caught up in family drama, the killsmith felt for the woman who was obviously holding on to this world and her own complicated emotions by a very thin thread. She didn't have it in her heart to be the hand that cut that thread.

"For your many kindnesses, you have my word, my Lady."

"Thank you, killsmith."

Bredikai bowed. It was one of those moments where one expects for the beauty of the exchange to be enough to move their situation along but damned if there was a single sign of life on that beat-up parchment.

"Solannus knows well the way to his home for a dragon's heart is never far from Kharkharen," Althaea said and placed her hands on the scroll while keeping their eyes fixed on hers. "But I would advise against an unprepared return. Indeed, Kharkharen should be avoided until the last. The soul of the dragon kingdom is changing and the time will come when the followers of Borghalus will clash with those who see him for the demon he has become. That is not your battle, yet. At present you will fare better seeking the remains of Septiannus. Be warned: my informants have told me that Borghalus is already in possession of the horn."

"So there's three still out in the world," Bredikai said, rubbing her chin. "And one we have to wrangle from him."

"He will be on his guard- so much so that I believe he will not suffer himself to leave Kharkharen. He will deploy his minions in his stead. He has yet to gain full control over the land so we will be spared his personal menace for some time. But the number of his followers grows so you must move swiftly to claim the remaining three. I have seen visions of the great golden eye. My senses tell me that it is far from land and should be approached from the sea."

"A lot of ground to cover... the Sea, huh? That's gonna cramp up the triplets," Bredikai mumbled to herself. The odds were slowly stacking up against them. "Speaking of, shouldn't we see what Lamure and the ding-a-lings are up to? We haven't seen them all day."

The parchment was finally put to use when Althaea summoned tiny bone fragments to come together and move up the table. Bloodlines crawled through the leaf and delineated the inside of what looked like a tavern as the bone fragments lost their original form to shapeshift into miniatures of the wraith and triplets, right down to the wee Fluffers and Sir Hiss-a-Lot. The figures were highly detailed and moved around the picture of the tavern with ease. Bredikai and Solannus watched in amazement.

"Such charming creatures," Althaea said and she was most clearly referring to the undead parrot and snake.

"Is my Lady looking to take in pets?" Bredikai offered.

"Over my dead body," the dragon growled.

"And a dead dragon, perhaps?"

They watched as the tiny figure of the wraith floated around. Lamure had somehow managed to grip a goblet the size of her head and was waving it around, spilling the contents everywhere.

"I *love* it here!" the Lamure-figurine yelled. "This land is beaming with prophecy and potential!"

"Is that... Are they *drunk*?" Bredikai asked jealously.

"Wraith-lass! Did ya try some of this here brew?" Ashley

bellowed at her.

"Aye, my skeletal fellow. It's positively magical!" Lamure answered and they watched her guzzle more than half the content of her cup. The liquid visibly flowed through her like a white paste and disappeared around her midsection.

"It be the necrotics, lass!" Lesley said, shoving another large pint straight into her. "Made perrticularly for the likes of us!"

"Weeeeeeeee!" came the sound of Murray swinging across the bar on a rope she'd found dangling from the ceiling. No one seemed to care about the other skeleton dangling from its neck on the other end.

"We *might* consider leaving them here," Solannus said, observing the scene. "They look so… happy."

"No." Bredikai declared. "Not on my watch. No one's happy on my watch." And then a thought hit her. Even as she spoke the words she could see that Althaea had anticipated her and erased the scene from the parchment. "Can we see Borghalus through here?" Bredikai asked.

"I admit that I waited for your arrival before attempting it," Althaea answered. She looked once more to Florian, ensuring that they were secure in their own company. "Deep have I delved into the minds of others- at times far deeper than I was meant to. The journey has taken a heavy toll on my spirit. Know this: even at their weakest, dragons are deadly. They possess unknown abilities that would take the very breath from you and are not to be underestimated." Solannus nodded in agreement. Instinctually Bredikai's hand went to the Hexia but when it grasped at air she recalled that they had yet to return it to her. But the necromancers' focus was directed at the parchment now so the killsmith kept quiet and watched.

A different kind of energy was being used. Bones

crumbled and were slow to reassemble, no longer in the paste-like fashion they'd witnessed earlier. They were like dust granules haphazardly clinging together. Althaea braced herself on the table. Her veins were visible and pulsating a sickly blue. The bloodlines tracing the landscape across the parchment were a brighter shade of crimson and they depicted a rocky region where the tips of the mountains were so high they broke through the low-lying clouds. The land was bespeckled with the mouths of caves and they saw that winter had come early to Kharkharen, blanketing the wide terrain with snow. The bloodlines were recreating themselves now, aligning to form a more intimate picture of a valley fortified by sharp peaks. Little by little, figures began to form but one stood out from the others. To Bredikai's horror it continued to grow to a terrible size that, even thus scaled, could not be compared with the figures they'd seen of their company moments ago. There was no mistaking the dragon Borghalus and as his voice rose, more dragons- all smaller next to the giant that he was- gathered around him.

Bredikai didn't realize that she had been holding her breath and Solannus' terrified gaze was fixed solely on the figure of his brother. She didn't know what she had been waiting for. They had warned her- everyone had- of his size and revolting nature. Her eyes widened while her brain went through the mental process of scaling the beast in comparison to everything else. Maybe it was the optimist in her that had prevented Bredikai from aggrandizing the creature in her mind but the fact was undeniable now and she pursed her lips, wishing that she had waited to look upon him until it was unavoidable. When the details finished sorting themselves out she leaned in to study the beast and gain a better understanding of his physiology.

Borghalus was a sickly shade of white from the top of his head to the tip of his long tail. Bredikai had seen a white drake or two in her day but none who had such a vulgar pallor, where every scar and torn bit of flesh was visible and his great eyeballs were so large she almost gasped. The eyes of the beast were filled with blood and it was a thing unaccounted for, never before seen in any other serpent- until now. In that moment Bredikai understood the maladied drakes she had encountered before they made it to the Craven and she felt a new level of disgust for the beast who sought to command death.

On his enormous body Bredikai saw the odd pinkish scale here and there but they, too, looked to bear a decaying hue. She saw a gash or two around his throat and counted six horns on his head, jutting out oddly like an angled crown. They were uneven in height and cracked in places- but one did not belong to him for it was a dull black. Even so he was not worthy to bear it. His claws were shorter than she had expected them to be but their power was not to be judged by length alone. His wings were full of holes and rotting; no doubt self-inflicted wounds from the madness of imprisonment. All this and she hardly had a moment to take in his teeth...

Bredikai exhaled deeply and began mumbling to herself. "That's one big ************ *** of a ***** ******* dragon, what in the ****** **** ** ***** is that thing for?! ******* *****... ******* me," the killsmith stated and Solannus nodded knowingly.

Then she saw that the dragons around Borghalus were also red-eyed, though not at all to the same extent of saturation. They were undoubtedly turned to the mind of the white demon and shared in his lust for the kill. Borghalus was now commanding them to search far and wide and the minions took to the skies even as the demon continued to bellow orders.

"Fly, brothers and sisters! Search every hole until you find the pieces! Burn anything that stands in your path." One by one the dragons, no less than twenty in number, took flight, eager to ravage and plunge the world into chaos. But Borghalus was not done. Two remained to him, his closest in confidence and size, awaiting more personal orders. Bredikai looked at Solannus and the heartbroken expression on his face was enough for the girl to understand that the dragon knew who they were and had possibly been close to them.

"Find that wingless runt," Borghalus snarled, pressing hard on the first word. "Deliver him to Kharkharen alive." The two bowed and were off.

So stood Borghalus alone and those who watched him in the parchment were silent, utterly transfixed by his presence. It was at that moment that their watch took a more peculiar turn. The demon drake stood as if frozen. Slowly he lifted his neck and craned his head, turning his bulging gaze and sharpening his focus. Then, he turned even more until he was looking straight at them.

"You would spy on *me*, necromancer?" the figure said and laughed hideously. Bredikai's panic was on the rise but when she looked to Althaea, the woman was paralyzed. Borghalus' laughter flowed seamlessly from the miniature until it faded from the parchment and came through Althaea's own mouth. The necromancer's green eyes grew murky until they turned crimson and two serpentine slits formed in their centers. Florian was quick to react but what was left of Althaea bid him stop and keep his distance.

Solannus steadied Bredikai. It was a futile gesture as the killsmith had no weapon nor any plan as to how to deal with the possession in front of them. Harming Althaea was out of the question but the killsmith was prepared to do so if the worst befell them. She looked at the possessed woman but the serpentine eyes were fixed on the sole object of interest: Solannus.

"Come, Solannus, even you must admit that running away was a foolish bid," cackled the voice of Borghalus. "You thieved what does not belong to you- like a common brigand. And to run to the necromancers of all places!" Another condescending bout of laughter. "You are become lesser by the day, worm." He was howling now and the sound was so harsh its echoes overpowered the walls and reverberated loudly enough to draw the full attention of the Ire Craven.

Bredikai looked to Solannus for something, anything, that would shake the wit back into him but the dragon was crumbling under the hypnotic eyes of his elder. He seemed caught in a whirlpool determined to capsize his soul. Desperate for a solution, Bredikai moved swiftly in front of her partner and crossed her arms, defying the possessed.

"What's this? A killsmith…ahaha," Borghalus asked curiously. But his laughter died out at the sight of this creature and her impudent gall. "Do your parents know where you are, child?" he drawled.

"I've really had enough of chatty lizards so you'll shut your hole before I come carve it off," Bredikai said and Florian eyed her with caution.

There was a deliberate snort and the ghost of a chuckle from the demon. "And who are you, you desperate little girl?"

"Call my dragon a worm again and you'll see how I earned the name Carver of Etherdeign." The moment the words escaped her lips Bredikai kicked herself for having given away too much in the heat of the moment. Adrenaline had gotten the better of her and she had spoken without thinking.

"*Etherdeign*, is it? Surely not the Etherdeign where that sad Althaean calls himself a king. Is it possible that he is still alive?" mused the demon. "Very well. It has been long since I have visited with him," Borghalus said, still in full command of Althaea who was growing paler by the minute. Sounds of clashing weapons came from the outside. They heard metal beat against metal and the telltale sounds of a skeletal army withdrawing from all corners of the Craven to come crashing down on them. Florian was beckoning to Althaea with his mind. He knew that even Borghalus could not hold the possession forever but the dragon's power was great enough to deter his own. Suddenly there came a greater uproar from outside and Lamure flew into their midst in desperation.

"The triplets can't hold them for much longer!" she cried.

"Find my sword!" the killsmith commanded and Lamure was off without further instruction.

The possessed Althaea had control of the undead and with Florian now breaking from the mental strain Borghalus had directed at him, they needed to act fast. Bredikai ripped her necklace from her neck and held the tooth firmly in her grip. There was no more time to think. She jumped onto the table and plunged the tooth straight into Althaea's eye. The combined howls of Borghalus and the necromancer shook the room as Bredikai bore the bone into Althaea's head. She held on before pulling it out. The demon's hold was forfeit. Althaea fell to the floor where she lay convulsing and Florian ran to her aid while the ruckus grew outside their door. The sound of ambush would not yield.

"Why are they still coming?!"

"Only Althaea has the power to stop the enchantment!" cried Florian but, try as he might, there was no bringing the woman back to her wits. Bredikai tried to shake the necromancer to coherence but the woman was still powerless over herself.

"Solannus!" Bredikai yelled and the dragon shook his

head, ridding his mind of the poisoned trance.

"You'd best be doin' somethin', lads!" Murray yelled from outside. They were cracking and the sound of metal grazing for a cut intensified.

"Hold, lads, hold!" Ashley commanded.

"Is there no other way out?" Bredikai asked Florian but the vampire shook his head.

"We are in the belly of the Craven," he said, holding on to his mistress.

Bredikai looked at him cradling the moaning woman who was too lifeless, even for one so undead. "Take her and go!" she cried, for she knew a thing or two about vampires and he would have strength enough to get Althaea out at the very least. The vampire was reluctant to leave them behind but Bredikai was forceful with her decision. "Don't worry, I've got a plan. Just get her out and back to her senses!" With that the vampire melted into the shadows and took Althaea with him to a safer darkness.

The once sturdy door held fast by enchantments was now breaking and giving way from the force of the swarm. Through the broken gaps they could see the triplets fighting against an unstoppable onslaught swelling in size. But there was another who had brandished a sword and from the corner of her eye the killsmith saw that it was Lamure. The wraith had an amateur grip on the Hexia but her wild movements were doing more good than harm. She was swinging the sword in every imaginable direction and helping the triplets gain ground.

"Bredikai!" Solannus yelled and the killsmith climbed onto his back quickly.

"Alright people- get ready to latch on!" she yelled

outside but Solannus was confused as to what he was meant to do.

"You said you had a plan!" cried the dragon.

"I always say that!" yelled Bredikai, gripping Solannus' neck. "Take a deep breath and charge as fast as you can- we're about to plow through."

"Plow through to where?!"

"Just *through;* get us out of this damn castle- now move!"

Solannus had no time to question her command. A desperate adrenaline was flowing through him and he broke through the doors with spells and swords hurtling at his head. The triplets were ready and latched on to his tail as Lamure flew and tossed Bredikai her sword. A swarm of skeletons descended like ants upon the dragon even as he ran blindly without veering. Bredikai thrashed the Hexia against the onslaught as the triplets held onto the dragon's back and they sped through the castle. Few necromancers had been able to release themselves from the spell and were doing their best to ward off the attack on their guests but the majority of the Ire Craven was hot on their heels. The dragon gained speed and he could see the gate that was to be their salvation- if only from the castle prison. Solannus yelled at his company to brace for impact and broke through the gate with such force that the group plummeted outwards and lay sprawling on the ground.

Bredikai was bleeding from her hands. Quickly she crawled towards the sword that had been knocked out of her grasp. The triplets were collecting their fallen parts but it was taking Solannus longer to haul his body back to a mobile position. Just when it seemed that the horde was emptying out of the Craven, fire rained from the sky.

The killsmith scrambled to her feet. A pair of lesser dragons thundered above, targeting the castle and it was only a matter of time before their exit was spotted. Ashley had been the quickest to regroup and climb onto Solannus' back so he helped Bredikai and then his brethren. They were complete with Lamure leading the way. Solannus was in great pain from gashes running across his sides but a careful escape was no longer an option. One of the attacking drakes- long in body, grey throughout with an ovular head suffocated by twisting horns- lost no time in expelling a whirlwind of fire upon the Craven's left wing. At once the beast was joined by the other; a red tyrant who took up the assault on the right, its flame grazing the Craven lengthwise and just missing the company by a hair.

The beast's breath was so outrageous it caught a number of the skeletons shuffling out of the Craven. They perished immediately. While the grey had not yet spotted the killsmith's company, they were not so lucky with the red who was the lighter and faster of the two. The dragon boasted a greater wingspan helping it pierce through the sky towards them with unnatural speed.

With what was left of his energy Solannus ran. They swept through the undead city with fire pressing at their backs into a thick fog they hoped would disguise them. Bredikai risked a look and the last thing she saw was lightning breaking the sky above the Ire Craven. Booming explosions went off behind them, falling hard upon the grey chaos-drake and scorching it out of the clouds. The killsmith didn't doubt that Althaea had regained control over herself and as the castle faded from view so did the howling of the dragon being electrocuted in the night. When it fell, the beast's weight was enough for it to crash through the Craven and onto the castle's ground floor. What happened after that they couldn't say but there was no doubting the red predator still on their trail.

Lamure raced ahead and reported a dense forest that would give them sufficient cover. Solannus never slowed. His energy was waning and his head was badly bruised from impact- but the dragon proved to be sturdy and Bredikai was not shy about praising his fortitude. When they lost sight of the red enemy, Bredikai bid him slow down and they waited in breathless silence for a sign of life.

One by one the company carefully descended from Solannus' back and walked into a new kind of darkness where the trunks of the trees were wider than any dragon's girth and they were cautious once more. There was no sign of their attacker but the company didn't stop until they had walked deep into the folds of the wood and Bredikai thought them far enough to risk a rest. She fell on the rich soil and rubbed her legs, surveying the scene and breathing in the dank forest air. The triplets were checking Solannus' wounds and he was being fussy about the matter until the killsmith began to cackle. Something was off. Lamure had a silent guilty look about her and Bredikai's insane laughter certainly wasn't helping calm the dragon's nerves.

"Have you lost your senses?" he asked and she just sat there shaking her head. "Stop your cackling- we'll be discovered! We must press on."

"I assure you that no one in their right mind will follow us in here," the killsmith replied, wiping away the tears from her eyes. "And if that thing did, it's not going to fare any better than we are."

"Good golden grief girl, what is the matter with you?" Solannus exclaimed.

It was the guilt-ridden wraith's turn to speak and she was caught between an apology and an explanation. She said, "I think Madam Bredikai is alluding to the fact that this forest is heavily enchanted." No one really reacted as there was very little novelty from one enchanted forest to the next.

"Now, I'm no geography expert," added the killsmith with a calm sarcasm that kept them all on edge, "but you'll recall that Althaea is in the family, so to speak, and one hears things about national regions and borders even though one has not had occasion to cross them." She could tell that Solannus was too tired for her antics but Bredikai sighed and continued to smile madly. "Would you care to reveal the enchantment, Madam Lamure?"

At first they thought Lamure to be in deep thought, then her unusual silence and frozen stance devolved to stiff paralysis and none of them could snap her out of it. Just then, a voice broke through the wraith, and they would have had real trouble on their hands if this was a repeat of the Borghalus possession. Instead, the meek voice coming through was familiar; so familiar that Bredikai squinted and bent her soured face into the wraith's as if to smell out an answer.

"The Undying Wood follows the Mortlands' path-protecting the undead kingdom by ensnaring all who trespass, keeping them beyond the vacuum of time. It is ever-expanding. Mortality has no hold over the Wood, though none now know what mischief dwells within." The voice sounded like it was reading from a book for the description was as dry as it was terrifying.

"Zira?" Bredikai exclaimed.

"Aba!" the boy cried, unable to contain his excitement.

"Is that-?"

"I've been trying to get through to you for weeks! These spells are really complicated."

"I'll bet," Bredikai answered, visibly relieved to hear the boy's voice. "You alright, kid? Gramps?"

"Yes, aba. I mean, we're fine in general."

"Is not getting to the point a family trait?" Solannus muttered. "We're sitting around like toadstools here."

With the red dragon momentarily forgotten, the group focused on the voice Lamure was projecting, hoping for a good word or some real news from the world beyond the Mortlands. Solannus could not keep from fidgeting and the triplets took it upon themselves to form a strategy for when their enemy inevitably happened upon them. Lesley and Murray released the shaken pets they had been carrying in their ribs but even poor Sir Hiss-a-Lot didn't have much of the hiss left in him.

"Aba, I've been following you through Mistress Lamure," Zira said. "Just had to find the right ingredients to break through. This magic needs a lot of resources and we're running out. You've got to find those pieces, aba! More and more dragons are showing up across the countryside. The kingdom's magic isn't strong enough to keep them out. Oh, aba, can't you come back to Etherdeign?"

The desperation in the boy's voice broke Bredikai's heart but there was nothing to be done about it. "Shit. Shitshitshit," she cursed and turned to her company. "We've got to find a way out of this fucking forest."

"Don't curse in front of the child," Solannus reprimanded.

"It's fine, Master Dragon, I'm used to it," the boy replied. "I think I can help you!"

"Have you enough magical prowess to undo the forest's enchantment, young man?" the dragon asked and was immediately shut down.

"Solannus, he's *nine*," Bredikai said, leaning on her sword. "Don't get me wrong kid, you know I trust you completely but if you've got the skills to break this sort of magic then I might just consider letting *you* face Borghalus."

The boy had no idea what his aba was talking about when she said the name *Borghalus* but he noted it in his journal as a point to research and, anyway, they were no longer listening to him.

"And why must you always underestimate those trying to aid you when you yourself do not wish to be treated thus? Must you be so snide and break the boy's confidence? So blunt and discourteous! It was no mere luck that saw us through the Craven and now we've drawn my brother's minion in here with us!" Solannus whispered harshly. His attitude was something to be reckoned with. He was hurt and frazzled and shook at the very thought of a snapping twig.

"Heeey what are you getting all worked up for?" Bredikai exclaimed. "I'm just telling it like it is, not doubting his competence! You may be the eloquent one, Lord Mouth-a-Lot, but we have to be realistic and I'm not one for coddling. The boy's got to learn the ways of the world now-"

"Again with the insensitivity! Just you consider that your methods of communication are harsh enough to suck the salt out of the seas."

Bredikai's arms were up in the air and she no longer cared about dragons or being discovered or any of it. "So I'm the problem again," she snapped back. "I'm a bad aba, is that it? Then how about let's agree that you and I never have children together because I'm not going to spawn a bunch of babies that *you* turn into emotional dragonoids with anxiety."

"I would rather produce offspring with the undead than risk our children being turned into unsympathetic oafs by the likes of *you*, Madam," the dragon scoffed with a characteristic nose in the air.

"Can dragons be makin' babies with humans, lads?"

Murray asked her brothers. Lesley shrugged.

"Be mighty gruesome to behold, methinks," replied Ashley. "The boy's gone quiet. Oy! Killsmith-lass. Reckon you two scared the kid stiff."

Indeed the child's voice had gone quiet but the wraith had not moved. Solannus shoved the killsmith back towards the wraith who was still taken by the soft glow of communication but otherwise motionless.

"Zira?" Bredikai asked softly. "You there?"

Rumbling in the sky foreshadowed a heavy downpour but it felt to them that the rain would bring with it something more foul. Unknown creatures cawed in the deep and leaves shuffled their ominous green. Nothing was breathing in that forest yet everything was alive with an omnipresent energy that was enough to confuse even the Hexia into a standstill.

"Kid?" implored the killsmith once more. Before the boy could get another word in, a darker, more sinister voice broke through the she-wraith and it was arguably worse than speaking with Borghalus. It was Bredikai's turn to be frozen in place.

"What in the nine hells are you up to, girl?! Just what do you mean by going off to meddle with the likes of necromancers!"

"How did you-" Bredikai winced.

"Never you mind the hows, you be answering' to me and not the other way around! Ach-me and my poor, shamed house!" Cue the wailing. Cue the public disappointment. Bredikai hung her head in defeat.

The leader closed her throbbing eyes, pinched the bridge of her nose and exhaled. It was Solannus' turn to cackle at the girl's expense. Turning on her heels Bredikai moved towards the triplets, grabbed the closest one- who just so happened to be Lesley- and, despite his bits chipping off, hurled his skull at the dragon who would have cried from mirth if he could.

"That fucking Fitzburt ratted me out..."

"Aye, and so he did!" Old Cronunham yelled and even the skeletons chuckled and shook their skulls, recognizing the infamous grandfather from Bredikai's stories. "And just what it is you're playing at, I'd like to know! Running off by yoursel' without so much as a parchment-"

"I'm under orders from the Crown, old man," the killsmith tried to explain, "and I'm not by myself. Got a dragon with me and everything."

Solannus trotted next to the wraith and leaned in to make himself heard clearly. "I am pleased to make your acquaintance, Master Grandfather-" He was cut off instantly. Such curses had been unheard by the likes of the dragon but the triplets sighed with nostalgia for their mother and shared a group hug.

"It *really* isn't as dramatic as you're making it out to be, Gramps," the girl implored. "King Althaean-"

"Don't get me started on your damned King! Cursed be my soul if ever I vote for 'im again. Shouldn'na wasted my threads patching him up. Now you listen, you; you'd best be thinking of gathering all those pieces before you show your face 'round these parts again, understood?"

"What the hells are you wasting my time for, then?!" Bredikai crossed her arms as if her grandfather was standing in front of her but it was a useless stance. He was going to have it out with her, necrotically or otherwise.

"Sir, that is precisely what we are aiming to do,"

ventured Solannus.

"Then aim good an' proper, you brainless twits!"

"I feel now I am able to better understand your position, Madam," Solannus whispered to Bredikai and wished her luck, respectfully bowing out of the conversation. She could deal with her own family.

"See here," the old man continued, "it won't be long now 'til we're up to our necks in dragon! You've got to draw them away from the kingdoms or that'll be the end of us. People are leaving the kingdom and crippling business! Not enough magic to go 'round and the word is out."

"Word, what word?"

"That your little band be out prowling for the pieces. Rumor has it you're prancing 'round with the next Dragonfather."

"I make no such claims, thank you," the dragon hollered from the background and Bredikai rolled her eyes.

"Spineless generation, you are!" cried the old man. "This one won't take over her Guild- won't e'en register- and this one won't claim what's 'is! But I've had enough of you two. Run from your responsibilities if that's all you're good for. Stay in that forest forever. We'll be none the worse for't! But don't you be thinking of coming back, you hear?! Why I-"

Old Cronunham's voice was cut off suddenly and Lamure was back with them trying to recall what transpired in the past few minutes. The wraith had only conversed with Althaea privately the one time but the undead guildhead had warned her of possible communiqué from abroad. Her powers had truly benefited from time spent at the Craven.

In their hullabaloo Lamure had quite forgotten to mention this developing gift to the rest of her company but now they had a real demonstration on their hands. She could still hear an old man barking in the back of her mind but his magic had waned and there would be no more connections that day. Bredikai was quiet but Solannus was having his fun with her. He seemed very happy to not be the only one with crazy relations he could make no excuses for. The killsmith flipped him off- a move that had the dragon in stitches as he picked up Lesley's skull with the tips of his claws and handed him to Murray. The triplets had been enjoying the moment until the nostalgia of family caught up with them.

"Right disappointed he was," Murray began, grazing her boney fingers against Sir Hiss-a-Lot. "And supposin' we was ever to speak to Mother that way, lads."

"Would've had our balls an' your tits for dinner I wager, lass," Ashley chuckled.

"But ne'er did we let Mother down, did we? Not until now, methinks. An' we mean to make right by it," Lesley added, straightening his skull though it was now permanently off-center.

"Never?" Bredikai asked with genuine shock. "You didn't let your mother down once?"

"Not a once, lass," Ashley answered. "Reckon the light of 'er life, we was. Sailin' and plunderin' together... Wasn't a creature in all the depths could scare that woman. We gathered us a fine booty, too, an' it made her right happy. Pirate through an' through, she was. But with all that gold she was always sayin' how we was her greatest treasure."

Even Solannus stopped laughing and he scoffed at the three for always knowing how to tug at his heartstrings.

"That's... really sweet," Bredikai said and she leaned against the sword she'd plunged into the ground.

"Aye," Ashley continued, "She was as good to us as any a mother there was. Wanted to honor her, we did. That's why we set out for the sunken hoard. Greatest bounty rumored to be in the Morduanas Seas! She'd be turnin' sixty that year an' we wanted to give the old witch a present fit for a pirate queen."

"Why does that sound familiar? The hoard in the... Morduanas..." Solannus muttered. "Did you find it?"

"That we did, Scales," Lesley said. "Made a grand run of it, too. We was wantin' to surprise Mother. So we's left her at the Port Par'nell for some merry-makin' an' made off with the ship. Made 'er think she was marooned!

"You *left her there*?" asked Lamure and even her sweet voice couldn't disguise the judgmental tone.

"We're not as cruel as all that, lads," Murray chimed in. "Left the crew with 'er, too. Just in case. Told 'em we'd be back in no more'n two moons with a booty tha finest they'd e'er seen. Reckon they told her what we was up to soon as we left. Can't be trustin' pirates with nothin'. We set sail and this one here was navigatin'-"

"An' doin' well by it, sister! Considerin' the nonsense information we had to go by," Ashley declared forcefully so they didn't get any wrong ideas about his sense of direction.

"Right you are, lad, no mistake."

"You found it, right?" asked Bredikai. Soon the company found themselves seated on the ground, locked in this story they were hearing for the first time. One would have thought that two weeks cooped up in an undead castle would have been enough for such exchanges but since the triplets had been busy boozing there had been scarce opportunities to break bread together.

"Aye," Lesley said. "An' sooner'n we thought. A storm

mightier'n we'd e'er seen crept up on us, bringin' with it those cursed southern wyrms. No offense to your kin, Scales. Dragged us right through the sea! But we was raised in the waters so we knew not to fear it, lads. If it be death let my grave be beneath the waves!

"Lost the ship, we did," he continued and his siblings listened to their brother tell the fantastic tale. Lesley had the tongue for such things. "Broken through the middle! Thought we was done for 'til we was grabbed an' dragged to the shimmerin' light!"

"Grabbed?" Bredikai asked.

"Them wyrms, lass. No less'n ten of the beasts! We was surrounded an' they dragged us through the depths all the way to the shore of a cavern hidden in the belly of the sea! Thought they'd make'a meal of us right then an' there.

"Then comes the leader of the pack. *What be your business this far out, pirates?* Says he- an' we was in no position to lie. Wyrms can smell a lie, did you know? First thing you learn as a wee pirate, hah! So Ashley here tells him; he says we be after the hidden hoard an' would die fightin' for't if needs be but that we be thankin' them for savin' us regardless."

"That was nice of you," Bredikai mumbled under her breath and Solannus went to sit by her side. They did so enjoy these tales together. He bopped her with his tail and she giggled.

"For a moment they was whisperin' to themselves an' it be right confusin' when creatures don't act the way they're meant to. *Ain't you goin' to stop us?* asks Ashley, but they'd agreed that the gold be none'a their concern. Said they'd been ordered to guard it but that they be sick of takin' orders from dragons so we was welcome to it. Warned us against touchin' it, though, didn't they lads?"

"That they did, right true" Murray replied. "But that be a tall order for a pirate, let alone three," she said, holding four boney fingers up.

"So we thanks them and makes our way to the belly of the cavern," Lesley continued. "Alls you had to do was follow the light. Couldn'a missed it, lads. And what say you?"

"Gold everywhere?" Bredikai guessed with a smirk.

"Lass- when I tell you that e'en the damned cavern itself was gold-! Big enough to fit a kingdom it was- two, maybes! Ne'er in your life did you see such a thing. Gems and jewels piled on top of treasures an' gleamin' mountains of gold! But we couldn'a known that we was under its spell from the moment we walked into that accursed place," Lesley said and he looked at Ashley to take over. The latter was always better at recounting the next part of the tale for he had detached himself from the emotions of the memory whereas Lesley and Murray were still hesitant to relive the experience through their own words. So Ashley stood and resumed the tale while the company watched him with increasing curiosity.

"Can't tell you how long we was in there, lads. Murray here reckons it was the better part of a year. Lesley be thinkin' longer."

"But how?" Solannus asked softly and he was living the story through them. "You are, er, *were* humans, yes? No food, water… Humans can't last long without nourishment." At that he expected a jibe from the killsmith but she said nothing for she was also invested in the tale.

"That be the curse, Scales!" Ashley said excitedly and pointed his boney forefinger at the dragon. "You don't see yourself slippin' away. It be warm at first; golden like the fires'a the sun. Takes you over an' fills somethin' in your heart you didn't know was missin'. You stop thinkin' about the things that keep you to this life. Don't need for food nor nothin' to drink. But that warmth keeps you alive long enough to turn to poison without you feelin' the change. First your belly starts to melt away, an' your heart be pumpin' slower an' slower. Then your skin be rotted off and alls you think to do is dance 'round the golden poison until you're the cavern's slave an' you forgets the world outside. Ain't nothin' in Ethra like it, I reckon. Takes o'er your mind before you know it."

Ashley sat between his siblings. It was a nasty tale but he was happy to share it with their company and be able to recall as much as he did. He could see that they had questions but they were worried about upsetting them by prodding and the triplets, in turn, had no desire to upset Solannus.

"What be on your minds, lads?" Ashley asked, for now was the time to get their story out. "You won'ts upset us now; what's done be done an' it be no fault of yours."

"How did you escape?" Bredikai asked, feeling heavy for the siblings who were recounting their worst experience.

"Funny 'nough, 'twas wee fluffers here," Ashley replied and pat the bird on his shoulder. The little skeleton snuggled up to him and Lamure couldn't stop her '*aw*'.

"Mother's gift to me when we was scamps. This here sea-monkey's been through it all with the likes of us. Had alls but forgotten him since the shipwreck. Kept him in me pouch here, even then…" Ashley sighed and looked to his siblings who nodded at him to carry on with the story and the eldest pirate stood up once more.

"Days and nights didn't matter no more, you see. We'd become nothin' but bone an' our clothes be tattered an' torn an' there was no more reason to keep 'em on. So I takes off me coat an' I sees the pouch I'd had on me the whole time. When I opens it, a wee boney beak popped out. Frazzled the poor thing was, but he shakes it off like a proper little phoenix. 'Twas then that I be seein' what we'd become for the first time.

"Proper 'orrified, I was. Not a thing to do for it! The gold meant nothin' to me no more, an' the warmth of it died like an icy blade cuttin' to the heart of me," Ashley said pointing at his chest. "I sees these two an' if I'd had any blood left it would'a grown ice-cold, lads. Then the ground was shakin' beneath our boney feet an' I couldn't move from the shock of it all. The enemy came closer lads, poundin' like the march of a thousand fiends- maybes e'en double that! So I grabs these two for they was still under the curse an' we hid behind a pile'a the yellow poison."

He paused for dramatic effect. It had been so long since they told the story in full that he was going to savor every unclean bit of it and the horror on the dragon's face was enough to recount the memory vividly.

"*And*? Ashley!" Bredikai had sunk her fingers into Solannus' side and it was lucky he was so thick-skinned or she'd have torn into him from the tension.

"Borghalus," Solannus whispered, remembering at last what his gut had been trying to remind him of.

"Aye, lad," Ashley nodded. "An' it be his hoard what did this to us. Reckon it's power is what brought 'im to that monstrous state or maybes it's the other way 'round but I tell you that ne'er did I see a dragon so large nor so foul. He knew that somethin' be trespassin' but couldn't smell us out seein' as how we was naught but bone by the end of it.

'Know now,' says he, 'that the drake Borghalus holds power over all. I curse you to dwell in eternal grey, never again feeling the breath of life nor the salvation of death until this Borghalus releases you under light of the gold moon; for you trespass upon my hoard and I will not suffer it to be tainted by your filth. This last

mercy I grant; you are free to leave through the stoney gate, for I have no interest in dealing with bone. May the touch of the sea hold you eternally captive in your state for the disrespect you dared bring here."

"There's no such thing as a gold fucking moon," whispered Bredikai and this time Solannus groaned and shook his head with pent-up rage.

"Easy, lad," said Murray and finished the tale. "He left after that. Don't know what the beast was after but believe you me he didn't find it. We sees the corpses of the wyrms- or what was left of 'em- turnin' to foam. Made short work of 'em, he did. Then brother Ashley got 'is wits back long enough to get us through the stoney gate."

"Aye," said Lesley, "a portal, it was. Hidden way back in the cavern's tail. Took us right to Port Par'nell where we left Mother."

"Did you find her?" Lamure asked.

The triplets looked at one another and Ashley sighed. They lowered their heads and kept silent for a while.

"Near took bloody revenge on the whole port, don'tcha know!" Murray broke the silence with a sad laugh. She reflexively wiped at her skull though no tears stained it. "Better she didn't see us like this, lads. Would'a broken 'er heart." Ashley and Lesley nodded and the triplets put their skulls together in a display of affection.

They thanked the three for their story but the overall energy of the company had plummeted so they let the skeletons be and play with their pets for a while as Bredikai, Solannus and Lamure talked amongst themselves. Concerns were shared regarding Borghalus' potential to puppet the triplets from afar but what they were really wondering was one and the same: whether or not Borghalus was using his treasure hold to hide any piece or pieces he had gathered. The company now had the choice of investigating the beast's cavern or seeking further information. From what Althaea had revealed it was inevitable that their path would lead them to the sea. Then the wraith's guilt came back ten-fold and she began to apologize profusely for steering them straight into the mouth of an enchantment when they had more urgent matters to tend to. Though that had been the case, Bredikai assured the despondent wraith that they were headed in the direction of the forest regardless and any one of them could have made the call to enter it- whereupon the rest would have followed. Solannus and his poor sense of direction agreed wholeheartedly.

Since the triplets began their tale the Hexia had not stopped humming and it was proving difficult for Bredikai to keep the thing muted. She placed it between the roots of a tree and speckled some dirt on it, hoping that'd shut it up for some time. Whatever supposed upgrades the necromancers had placed on it hadn't been enough to calm it down. For the first time since their collective journey began the group found their spirits sagging, but they were stuck in that forest and the killsmith bet her blade there were far darker things to worry about in there than dragon.

CHAPTER 5: THE NATURE OF TIME AND A TIME FOR NATURE

The forest was a dreadful place but just why they should have felt that way took some time to understand. Aesthetically there was nothing wrong with it. Really, for those who share an affinity for woodlands such as wayward spirits, fairies and other floral folk, the Undying Forest would have been the perfect dwelling place. The least sturdy trunk still boasted a girth that matched Solannus at his roundest point and the trees were comfortably spread out, distanced widely enough for the company to pass through with ease. Nothing grew on the ground- no moss, no undergrowth- but the occasional root stuck out and more than once did the triplets find themselves sprawled on the ground and collecting detached bones. But there was no sky. Indeed, there was no hint of a world beyond. Only trees and a musty stillness that clung to them like mildew. Increasingly the company grew quiet and their feet dragged, feeling as though the longer they walked the farther they had still to go. Lamure argued that the enchantment was not necrotic in nature. Her feeling was that the forest lay somewhere just between life and death as a green webbed pocket taking up space between the two. Even the triplets felt their non-existent skin crawl like the tingling of a forfeited limb and these feelings were difficult to shake off.

Every now and again they would be startled by a far-off sound; perhaps the howling of some forgotten beast or the yelp of one's last fighting breath. Wings fluttered at the plenty and sometimes they came closer to the company; but never did they see anything. Nevertheless, the Hexia kept to her humming. Whatever the sounds, they were brief and quickly eaten by the tomb of the wood, snuffed out before anyone could comment.

On they walked. Bredikai noted that she felt no hunger, no fatigue, just a simple forward motion that kept her pace brisk along what may have been a path at some point. She struggled to settle on a sense of the hour and it was when she couldn't place a single minute that she decided to call her party to a halt. Wherever they stopped would be no better or worse than anywhere else. She wished to get a small fire going out of habit but there was nothing to burn so she drew a small circle into the dirt and let her sword hum in the middle as her party chose their various spots around it.

The wounds Bredikai and Solannus sustained while fleeing the Ire Craven no longer pained- but they also didn't heal as was evident by the dragon's grousing. A normal dragon would have been on the mend by now and he was still very scratched up. Bredikai poked at her own gashes, slightly worried that her wrists had been cut, then went to poke at Solannus to see if he felt anything. He shooed her away like one does a fly.

"Anyone hungry?" the killsmith asked. Pointless as it was, even Solannus was looking out of sorts though surely it wasn't hunger weighing on him.

"There's an older magic at work here," the dragon said to them. "I don't know how to put it into words. It's not a feeling; rather a *taste,* if you will; a pull that stretches from my tongue to the back of my brain." When he saw that he had lost them somewhere at *taste* he added, "Must be a dragon thing."

"I don't know about all that but something's definitely off," Bredikai said and Lamure nodded. "Those sounds we heard walking through; anyone else notice that not a single one resembled the other? I don't know what's made a home of this place but we should be ready for random diversity and random encounters of *any* kind."

Solannus pulled his limbs underneath his belly and yawned as Sir Hiss-a-Lot writhed on his back. "I thought you were a ranger. Can't you use your skills to determine a path for us?"

"Excuse me, I'm a killsmith. Literally no relation."

"So you're not a ranger, have no magical capacity whatsoever and the rest of our group is undead," he said, pointing out the obvious.

Bredikai sighed and leaned back against a tree trunk. "Whatever you're getting at please note that the other member of our company is a wingless word dispenser," she said and the dragon growled so much he shook the snake off his back.

"There, there Solannus," Lamure chuckled, "I'll venture upwards. Maybe I can see past the canopy."

They watched the wraith cautiously float above. She grew smaller and smaller until she was out of sight and nothing stirred. Suddenly a great crackle broke from above as if lightning had struck and the wraith came hurtling down through a trail of smoke. Her head was spinning and she groaned as the company huddled around her.

"You alright, lass?" Ashley asked and the wraith held her throbbing head.

"That was my mistake," Lamure wheezed as Bredikai sneezed and fanned the smoke from her face.

"What happened?" asked the killsmith. "Did you see a way out?"

"There is no way out," the wraith answered, sitting up. "This forest has neither beginning nor end. It's as I suspected;

this place is a vacuum in the world, ever-growing with each creature it ensnares- and I'm afraid we've helped it along. It's no mere sorcery," she said looking at the killsmith. "This is the very nature of the forest." They were in more severe trouble than either Bredikai or Lamure wanted to admit, caught like senseless flies in a wooden cage that knew only to expand.

"I can't say for certain but I may have glimpsed a light within the wood," Lamure said. "This path should lead us there. It's not too far to the East. At least I think that's East. Maybe it's some-"

The wraith was interrupted by the sound of screeching unlike anything they could identify. Quickly the company gathered and, with the wraith leading the way, they sped along the broken path. To their delight, Lamure's keen eye had spoken true for they were drawing closer to a faint light. The screeching seemed to desert them but they didn't care to slow down until they were in a clearing where sat an old cottage, not too small, not too large- and it looked like there was someone inside. Solannus was too large to enter so Bredikai bid the group wait outside as she held onto the Hexia and walked to the wooden door. Lamure was with her when she knocked but there came no answer. She knocked once more but still there was no answer so she nodded to the wraith to have her back and carefully opened the door.

"It's about time you made it here," said an old man whose face was all but eaten up by white hair. All that was visible were his bold black eyes but even they were shadowed by the overgrowth of his eyebrows. "Ever too early even when running late! But have a sip of this before you bleed through my floor. Come, come, child don't be so daft. I say sip but I mean for you to drink the whole thing. I should think you can't afford to be so simple when on such a quest," said the busybody and shoved a wooden cup into the killsmith's hand.

Bredikai had been standing in the doorway while the rest of her party waited for a signal. She bid the skeletons walk inside with her leading the way. "It's not a quest," said the killsmith, eying the steaming drink that looked like soupy mold. "Quests have purpose and a faint hope of succeeding. As I told King Althaean the last time I saw him: this is a prolonged suicide stroll."

"And what burden should that be upon a killsmith? One who dances on the edge of the blade for a living! Drink up, drink up, your blood is stinking up my house," fussed the crone.

"Who are you talking to?" Solannus hollered from outside until he finally found a window large enough to stick his head through. He surveyed the inside of the musty worn-down cottage and shook his head to clear his nostrils.

"There you are," the killsmith said. "Solannus, Son of Septiannus, Ye Immortal Pain in my Ass, this is..."

"Abness. Father Abness." But the fidgety hermit was looking at none of them and all of them and suddenly dressing Bredikai's wounds all at once. "Drink! We brook no malady, no disease in this house! There is always time to heal."

"I'm glad to see your wounds are not fatal, you sarcastic little witch," the dragon said.

"Thanks, Sonny," the killsmith smiled. "I've had worse but- and not that I'm panicking- this medicine looks miiighty toxic. I might vomit." She looked at the old man as she sipped on the vile drink and suddenly a fire boiled and bubbled in her chest. "Let's be clear old man: I'm drinking this because I have zero other options- not because I know or trust you."

"But I know *you*, Griffinbait," the old man said. The girl spewed out the concoction all over Solannus' face.

"Unhygienic cretin…" the dragon shook his head.

Bredikai plunged her sword into the floor, eliciting a yelp from the hairy hermit. "This world is too damn small. Bunch of fucking yappers everywhere I go. How do you know me? Why are you here? All the questions, old man! What are you doing here all alone in the middle of this awful place? I'm really starting to fucking hate trees."

Father Abness snatched the cup from her hand and instantly replaced it with another one that was full. The fumes were nauseating. "I know you," he hummed, "I know the dragon and your skeletal party. The wraith is somewhat cloudy but it will come to me, just give it time. Give me all the time- hah!"

"Are you some sort of wizard?" Lamure asked with as much politeness as she could muster..

"Not as such."

"I'll repeat: what are you doing here?" demanded Bredikai and looked around at the home that seemed to double as an alchemist's laboratory. Maybe he was a healer. Maybe he was a sorcerer caught in his own enchantment. Whatever he was, he was weird and feeding her more medicine than she cared to digest.

"I am keeping time," the old man answered, utterly unbothered as he mixed up another batch of brew. From this he took a few gratuitous sips and Bredikai was getting familiar whiffs of the Etherdeign breweries… "And time is keeping me!" the crone carried on. "Ah, but you are looking for clocks and hourglasses and mortal contraptions but, no, you shan't find any trivialities here. Time works by herself and for herself and never can you hope to catch her in an instrument."

"Keeping what time?" Lamure asked before Bredikai

could harass the riddle out of the hermit.

"All of her," Abness replied. "All of her and all that pertains to her. You would be one such creature, would you not?" he asked of the dragon. Solannus tilted his head and looked at Bredikai. She was consuming less of the drink now as it was tainted with suspicion but the old man stuck a wooden ladle in Solannus' mouth before the drake could refuse.

"Mmmm, that's not terrible!" the dragon beamed. "My compliments, Sir Father."

"None of that, none of that. It's missing something. But there's never enough time to get it right!" He mumbled to himself and rummaged around, whizzing past the triplets, flinging about roots and herbs and fancy strings. Suddenly he grabbed a large tome to squash a pest onto the grand wooden table that sat in the middle of the room and they all flinched and looked at one another. Several of his multicolored flasks fell to the floor and broke while other books came crashing down from the walls. One of his candles, still lit, rolled around on the floor and Ashley stomped on it with his foot.

"You looking to add some *thyme* to that?" Bredikai punned and Solannus snorted with laughter. She smiled at him appreciatively.

"Looks like our host has run out of *thyme*, Bredikai," added the dragon and the two shared some form of hand/claw bonding gesture as Father Abness stopped to look at them in horror.

Solannus coughed and regained his snobby demeanor. "I see you woodland folk can't appreciate a bit of humor," he mumbled. "I beg your pardon, Father, but just what is it that you've given me?"

"A brew that'll make your wings sprout!" the old man answered excitedly and sprinkled black granules of something into a small cauldron that didn't have a fire under it to warm the contents. The concoction bubbled nonetheless. Solannus was ecstatic, shaking with delight and almost bringing the cottage down from the outside.

"I jest, you silly creature," Abness huffed and the dragon's mirth was instantly deflated. "How would I know how to perform such an act? Seek a general physician."

"So cruel!" Solannus gasped.

"Forgive me, Master Dragon. Cruelty was not my intent but you proved to me your estimation of yourself. You'd do well to keep your desires at bay lest temptation lure you from your path. Drink up! Drink else you will all be crushed by time." Thus Abness handed out more drinks to the remainder of the company and even the necrotic bunch were able to down it.

Lamure went to the window to console the dragon who had had about enough of human cruelty and Bredikai walked around the table. She picked up and inspected a few of the items; a small flask filled with layers of liquid, heaps of herbs tied with string, multicolored granules- and one wondered how the old man procured them as nothing but trees seemed to grow in that forest. There was the odd book she rifled through but they were, more often than not, inscribed in a language she could not identify. You know- usual wizardy shit. But the father insisted that he was neither wizard nor sorcerer and would claim no such title.

Bredikai had no interest in stopping the triplets from poking around and with the old man reasonably occupied with undoing the consequences of the skeletons' curiosity she turned to the dragon and the wraith for a private whisper.

"This crone's abusing substances. I say we don't stick around any longer than we have to," said the killsmith. "Thoughts?"

"Indeed, he is most high," Solannus agreed. "But what is our hurry? There is no perceivable way out and our host may not be averse to aiding us with useful information."

"These wizard-types have a roundabout way of getting to the point," Lamure offered. "Best we ease it out of him."

"Fine, ease all you want, but I'm telling you we should do it quickly. Time has a tendency of working differently in places like this," Bredikai pointed out.

"And how would you know?" Solannus hissed. "When was the last time you were caught between the folds of time?!"

"I had a dream about it once," the killsmith stated proudly and the dragon rolled his eyes. "Dreamt I walked through my grandfather's old storage unit and found myself in a strange land where I could stay for years and years- and when I walked back through not a single minute had passed."

"Unending absurdities," snorted the dragon as Abness clobbered the brothers and their grubby hands in the background. Murray was playing around with brown granules and creating minor explosions on the table. "Humans and their twisted fancies. Next you'll be dreaming about dark lords and- and evil wizards and who knows what else!"

"Hey, it's a thing! It can happen!"

But Lamure had had enough of the squabbling and she floated to the hermit who held onto the pirates' skulls protectively. "Father Abness- you say you keep time. Am I to understand that you keep this forest?" she asked.

"In a manner of speaking," said the man and he tossed the skulls to the floor. "I keep her and she keeps us all safe within her breasts. We are merely lucky enough to suckle on them when she pleases. "

Bredikai looked to Solannus but the dragon was all ears.

"Ew," said Lamure. "Let us not take up too much of your time, then, since it's a precious commodity around here. We need to get out of this place, Father. The sooner the better- else we stand to forfeit Ethra to dragons."

"Your business with the dragon Borghalus is personal?" the man asked and Lamure let Bredikai take the lead.

"Well..." mused the killsmith, "I wouldn't say personal. Then again, yeah, maybe, after that episode at the Ire Craven... What does it matter? I've been hired to do a job and I'm going to do it. Besides, I should think that being overrun by dragons is personal for everyone."

"Go on then, you've found me. State your business!" Abness said, stomping an unnaturally large foot on the floor. Bredikai followed the crone as he hobbled to his armchair and she sat opposite, bidding the remainder of her company to behave and listen. The man lit the longest and most detail-heavy pipe they had ever seen and Bredikai inhaled deeply, missing the sick sweet scent of addiction.

"Mmm..." she said with a smile on her face. "Our business is dragons. Anyway, I thought you knew all about us. Don't expect me to believe you have no idea what we're doing."

"I know exactly what you're doing," puffed the man. He let out a veritable cloud into their faces and even from the window Solannus' sinuses just weren't going to catch a break. "I would like your perspective of what you're doing. Leading Borghalus' red minion into my forest was idiotic."

"If I may," Solannus interrupted from the window. His neck was cramping and he was suffocating from the smoke. "Are we correct in thinking that we will find another of my father's remains in Borghalus' treasure hold?"

Abness sent more clouds into the dragon's face and Solannus sneezed such a gale that a bit of his fire caught the granules Murray had been tampering with and exploded the table. Abness looked entirely unbothered.

"You will find… something of interest- if you keep your wits about you," spoke the hermit. "Speaking of wits, I have a special brew in mind for your skeletons," he said but Bredikai refused the offer, much to the triplets' dismay.

"Let's just leave them sober until we've settled our business, shall we?" the killsmith said, forcibly pushing goblets away. "So we're headed in the right direction- finally. Now we have to get out of this fucking forest."

"Bredikai, you're still wounded," said the wraith. "You can barely hold your sword."

"Let us pass the night here," Solannus said. "I'm sure we could use the rest- unless Father Abness is opposed to hosting us."

"You may camp outside. Stay, leave… time will pass as it does. Ruin my cottage and I shall keep the dragon as payment," Abness stated. Solannus sputtered at the audacity of being brokered like a common coin.

"Fine," replied the defeated killsmith. "We'll stay the night but this one's on you two," she said, meaning Lamure and Solannus but glaring only at the dragon. "If we find some strange shit like five years have passed once we leave then you and I are going to be having words."

Why they should be camping outside when she had spied a perfectly good spare room with a bed was beyond Bredikai's reckoning. Maybe she had been spoiled by the gratuitous hospitality of the necromancers but there wasn't a single stone nor patch of fern to rest her head against in that awful wood. The company was just behind the cottage now (all except Lamure whose sorcery-prone curiosity had won her more conversation with the old man) with a circle drawn in their group's center purely for psychological comfort. Bredikai wasn't particularly tired but the moment Solannus had his limbs tucked beneath him his neck drooped, his eyelids sagged and he was off in his serpentine dreamland. Bredikai sat with her back propped against his belly and a million unfinished thoughts running through her head. She had had no intention of dozing off but the dragon's sleep was sending soothing vibrations up and down her back. There was no telling when she drifted into slumber but so snoozed the dragon, so snoozed the killsmith.

Her dreams were disjointed and nonsensical. They felt like they stretched for days though she must have only slept for a few hours when both she and her scaly pillow were yanked out of their rest by a hollering wraith.

"Wake up, will you!" Lamure cried and finally it occurred to her to grab the Hexia and hit them awake with the hilt.

"Mm?"

"The triplets have been swooped up!" cried the wraith and Father Abness poked his head outside from the back window.

"That'll be the skyjackals. Right on time," the hermit said with an appreciative smile.

"Madam!" Lamure implored.

"I'm going to need everyone to calm down for a moment," Bredikai said. Her sleep had fogged her mind and even Solannus was too groggy to be up in arms so quickly. "Did you summon them, old man?"

"Why must I do such a thing? After all, they are always

on time!"

Bredikai rubbed her eyes and chuckled to herself. "I'm gonna kill myself," she mused. "This is how it's going to end. I'm going to kill you, and you and then carve my own fucking neck and then Lamure will spread stories of us throughout Ethra where we'll be renowned for the lunatics we are." Lamure looked off into the distance and it seemed for a moment that she was actually considering it.

"But- but Sir Hiss-a-Lot!" Solannus begged, practically on the verge of tears, "and poor Fluffers!"

"I've said it once, I've said it a thousand times: fuck Fluffers. Look, relax. It's not like they can eat them or anything. They're all bone, right?... Right?" Bredikai looked to Lamure for confirmation but the wraith could only shrug with concern.

When Solannus' eyes began welling up it was all she could do to not end them all right there. Instead, Bredikai began her breathing exercises and ordered them to gear up- not that they had anything to take other than the Hexia for the crone was not so free with his explosives.

"I'm ready. What now?" Solannus asked.

"Now," inhaled the killsmith, "we kill the bat-men."

"You have about ten seconds to regurgitate our people or I come to carve," Bredikai said to the animalesque group whose audible breathing and frothing was really stinking up the ambiance.

Her company was ridiculously outnumbered. A darkness followed the skyjackals who clung together in a pack as dense as midnight. Their yellow eyes were bulbous and pulsating at the thought of an impending feeding frenzy. They were large and humanoid in appearance; an unappealing blend of bat and man with their burnt furry skin and feral stance. Some had breasts that hung low while others bore fangs down to their saliva-stained chins. At least now they knew where all the screeching had come from. The Sacré Hexia was vibrating so much it nearly rocked Bredikai back to sleep.

"What're you waitin' for lads- cut us out!" It was the unmistakable clacking skull of Ashley, discarded by the roots of a tree. The killsmith's intention was one and the same- to cut them out, that is- but Bredikai was having a hard go of determining an approach. Such a darkness was disguising the creatures that she could hardly discern their actual number. One thing was clear: they were plenty.

The skyjackals waited for the slightest hint of aggression from their would-be prey but their slobbering and screeching added an extra tension none of them needed. Solannus was practically hopping in place.

"Will you stop that please?"

"What do I do?!" bounced the dragon. "Which one do I rip to shreds first?!"

"Easy there, killer. There's bound to be a leader. These brainless creatures always have a leader. Don't kill him."

"What, why ever not?" Solannus asked with disappointment.

"We don't know which ones have eaten our people," explained Bredikai. "You want us killing the leader and the rest flying off every which way? We'll have to end them all. Sorry

Sonny, but there's no way around it."

"But... it'll be a bloodbath!"

"What happened to ripping them to shreds?" Bredikai asked impatiently. "If it'll please your sensibilities I'll let them attack first. Would that work for your conscience?"

"Is that how you do it?" the dragon cried. "You let my kin attack you first so your conscience is free to slaughter?!"

"Is this *really* the time for the moral debate?"

"Lads! Me bones!" came another skeletal plea.

"Just a moment, Lesley, if you please," the dragon said. "Look me in the eyes, killsmith, and tell me you don't goad my kin into attacking first so you have an ethical loophole through which you slay dragons."

"Listen pal, your entire race is an ethical loophole," Bredikai declared. "Not once, *once,* have I met a dragon in full command of his sensibilities who *hasn't* been interested in making a meal out of me so you'll forgive me for pointing out that your kin hardly needs any goading."

"And what am I, an overgrown bovine?!"

Lamure groaned as the skyjackals looked at one another in confusion. Off in the distance, they heard a great explosion. The boom may or may not have come from Abness' cottage but, just then, the company could not have been less interested in the crone's fate.

"Clearly you're an exception in our present circumstance but who knows what you'd be like if you were...you know..." Bredikai said.

"Normal?! Is that it? If I was not handicapped thus?!" Solannus cried, pointing to himself for added emphasis.

"I didn't say that-"

"But that is your meaning! I would have you know that it is *your* species who is the more barbaric of the two and never has there been a provocateur in my line except for my awful brother. My father was the most just of dragons and my mother- never could you find a kinder creature in all of Ethra!

"I'm sorry, your mother the unicorn?"

It was at this moment that, just as Solannus thought to swallow the Carver whole, yet again, Bredikai was pummeled to the ground by a trio of skyjackals. They were tearing and scratching and gnawing at her every exposed limb. The unceremonious brutes had jumped her so fiercely the Hexia was knocked clean out of her grip.

Bredikai screamed and punched but the creatures were overtaking her. Solannus seemed to be enjoying the carnage for a moment but his merciful nature got the better of him in the end. He barreled into the creatures, grabbing one and then another in his jaws and flinging them against the mighty trees. The violence of his teeth was all it took for the rest of the creatures to take flight and swoop down on him like rabid birds of prey.

At present Lamure had no fighting power to speak of but as the dragon broke the skyjackals apart she glimpsed the fragments of their skeletal party and began collecting them in a neat pile by Ashley's skull. Nothing wrong with being useful and, being that they labored under the same necrotic laws, the wraith was able to handle their bones at least. Being able to touch things was a small mercy she had taken for granted in her short life, she thought.

Bredikai grabbed the wing of a skyjackal as it bit into her forearm and pulled with all her might, tearing the appendage from the creature's back. The skyjackal screamed in torment and tried to escape but the killsmith yanked it back by its other wing, grabbed its head and twisted its neck. The creature fell limp to the ground. Bredikai tried to spring to her feet but her left leg had been mangled around the knee so all she could manage was a tortured crawl to her sword. Another skyjackal grabbed her by the foot and dragged her towards him. She flipped around, kicked herself up and plunged her hands into the beast's open mouth. She pulled its face apart with her bare hands and that was the end of it. Solannus was simultaneously fighting and spitting out shredded chunks of creature from his mouth. Skyjackals tasted awful and their blood was even more sour than his mood.

"How're our lads doin'?" Ashley asked Lamure as she furiously tried to reassemble him with what parts she'd gathered.

Solannus howled as skyjackals bit into his underbelly. They latched onto him and crawled around his girth like ravenous termites. One of them was smart enough to find a barely healed gash and tear it open once more.

"They'll live. Probably," answered the wraith, tossing the mismatched bones aside. "The good news is I can touch thigs now. My necrosis must be developing."

Ashley said, "Aye, lass, an' ne'er you mind about the bones. The damned curse'll pull us together when you've got the right ones. I can hear me sister in that one's stomach, o'er yonder."

The Hexia was vibrating up a storm, eager to return to her owner. She was just within reach. Solannus and Bredikai were gaining ground but much blood had been shed. Bredikai was torn from head to foot and while her wounds did not seem fatal yet, she was steadily losing patience. As her hand reached for the Hexia's hilt, a heavy hoof came crashing down on her wrist, breaking it and rendering her right hand useless. The

Carver's agonizing scream was cut short when a clawed hand knelt to pick up the blade.

She looked up with pain-filled eyes.

"Solannus," Bredikai cried and the dragon looked at her with two skyjackals in his mouth.

"Mmph?"

"I found the leader." The skyjackal kicked Bredikai in the face and her head spun around. Her front teeth were knocked out and blood oozed from her mouth, so much so that, even as she cursed, the word came out as *'phooouuuuk'*.

They couldn't afford to lose the skyjackal leader and Solannus looked ready to torch him before the beast could hack off Bredikai's head with her own sword. Quickly the wraith floated to the creature who looked to be slightly less mindless than the ones he commanded and, acting upon pure instinct, tore into his corrupt soul with her gaze. Her eyes were glowing a hot red, injecting the dull monster with a fear that paralyzed him. The skyjackal trembled and shrank and shivered but there was little he could do except release the Hexia from his grasp. Lamure was in control of his fate now and, by extension, that of his minions.

Bredikai pulled herself back up to action as best she could and reclaimed her sword. Limping, she held the blade to the jackal's neck. The remaining rats stopped what they were doing. She bid them gather next to their leader as the bloodied Solannus slowly inched to her side. Lamure never broke her gaze.

"You alright, Sonny?" the killsmith asked.

"These things are poisonous," spat the dragon. "I can taste it in their blood. It isn't potent enough to fatally harm me but we must get you back to Abness."

"What are we to do with these creatures, Madam?" Lamure asked.

The killsmith looked at the dragon but it seemed that his appetite for slaughter was filled. The skyjackals were no longer fighting. They were still screeching and hissing, ready to take any opportunity to do away with the girl and her drake but they waited for a command from their leader. Solannus was reluctant to finish them off.

Sensing the dragon's faltering decisiveness, Bredikai said, "There's mercy, and then there's being an absolute idiot in the face of such savagery." Despite her missing teeth she managed to get her words out. She wiped the blood from her jaw and spat out more at the head skyjackals' feet. He screeched at her and spit in her face. She wiped herself again.

"It's a fine line between the two, Solannus," the killsmith said. "They made their choice. Now I trust you'll make yours. I'm heading back to the cottage."

Her pain was extreme but even amidst the messy ordeal Bredikai had a point to make and the dragon's decision would determine whether or not she was destined to undertake the rest of the campaign alone, after all. They couldn't afford mercy at every turn, even though that's how the dragon would have wanted it, and she didn't have time to be doubting his resolve. In a perfect world any sensible creature would prefer a kinder hand but such was not the world they lived in and Bredikai had neither the patience nor the inclination to explain philosophies to their attackers. So what would Solannus do? As she moved away from the shroud of darkness the skyjackals had cast her mood lightened, despite her mind-numbing pain. She was still a ways from the cottage and moving at a snail's pace. The dragon was right; the creatures were poisonous. The venom in their bites and scratches was well into her now and working its way into her bloodstream.

Just as her faith was at risk of waning, the killsmith heard a great roar and the crackling of a fiery torrent, followed shortly by tortured screeches permanently silenced. If she strained herself she could almost hear Lamure gathering the remaining bones and her skeletons coming back to life, as it were. She smiled and limped along.

"I am not a medicinal practitioner," Father Abness fussed. Bredikai's head was planted onto his floor though one could hardly see it between the man's litter and the non-medicinal junk around her.

"What's all this stone crap on the floor?" the killsmith grumbled. Her saliva was leaking out uncontrollably. Skyjackal poison was potent; so potent that she considered herself lucky to have exposed herself to many of the world's venoms in her younger days. If not for that, she would have been dead mere moments after the first bite.

Soft stomping followed by the pitter patter of six friendly foot-bones and the company was back inside the cottage and by her side. Solannus stuck his head through the open window. A frazzled Sir Hiss-a-Lot rested and shook on top of the dragon's head where he was curled up but Fluffers looked no better or worse than he always had- not that anyone cared. Lamure was quiet and there was no telling whether or not she was proud of her contributions to the skirmish or scared of her own fright potential.

"Have you seen what's outside?!" Solannus cried but his energy was deflected by a groan. Lamure floated through the cottage (most literally) to where Solannus stood and saw that a small mountain was on the rise. The stone had an odd shape that was not yet hidden and when the wraith witnessed the better part of a red head stuck mid-petrification she couldn't stop herself from gasping.

"What in the hells-"

"Do you think that old lunatic took him down?" Solannus whispered, himself in shock over the dead dragon that had been hunting them.

"I-... I haven't the faintest idea," Lamure confessed. "Certainly appears that way. Solannus we need to aid Bredikai. I think we'd do well to take this as a win for the time being and not dwell on the details."

Of course she was right, for the important thing was that their hunter was no more. Solannus could not bear to look at his deceased kin so he nodded quietly and stuck his head back through the window.

"What's with you, lass?" Lesley poked at the killsmith as the triplets gathered around their half-dead leader in concern.

If old man Abness had been in stranger situations in his days he was too distracted to make an issue of it. The skeletons were a marvel but the more pressing matter was that they were getting filth all over his cottage so he shooed them outside to his waterwell so they could clean up and look decent.

"And the bloody bird, too!" yelled the crone. Bredikai groaned from the noise.

"Fuck... that... bird." Even with her speech impaired Solannus understood her words but the leader of their company was fading fast and this was not the sort of ailment which could be cured with rest and a bunch of herbs simmering in a bacterial stew.

"What is to be done?" the dragon asked, his worry growing for his counterpart with each passing minute.

"Just on time. Come," said Abness. "I must have your bile."

"Unggg no more gore," moaned the girl. She mustered up enough energy to stick her fingers in her mouth and out came another tooth that had fallen victim to the skirmish.

"I will give whatever you need," was the last thing Bredikai heard the dragon say. The darkness overcame her like a warm acid bath. Worst. Sleep. Ever.

There was no telling how long she had been conked out. Time was ever the main talking point in that cottage but there never seemed to be a clear understanding regarding its workings. Slowly the killsmith's thoughts crawled out of the darkness and she could hear her people discussing her situation. From what she could tell she had finally been allowed on the old man's spare bed but she was too hurt to move or appreciate its comfort.

"Say she ne'er wakes up, lads. What then?" Murray asked.

"She will, when it is her time," replied the crone. "Good of you to deal with those skyrats. They were terrible to my poor herb garden. Come, which of you cares to donate teeth to your leader? I shall need four at least. Well, *you* won't do- but what about you two?"

"Aye, go on then, you silly wizard," Lesley said and the old man plucked two from the pirate's skull like weeds. He took another two from Murray just to balance it out.

"If the mixture I developed works then she will grow back her own in the years to come. She may then return yours," Abness said.

"Not like we be usin' 'em," the pirates laughed and their donations were put to work.

Solannus had popped his head in from another window, just above Bredikai's head. He had been keeping watch over the girl for the better part of the day but was getting anxious for her well-being. That and no doubt she would be in a foul temper when she woke up because they had not woken her sooner and, just like that, it would be their fault again. But it was never night, never fully day in that forest; just an endless afternoon filled with the sounds of distant creatures fighting to survive. Why they wished to continue to live he knew not; for surely they didn't have a fool's prayer of getting out of that enchantment. Bredikai would have to get up soon. He knew that she would not be fighting fit for some time but the concoction Abness brewed with the help of his bile was working wonders on the girl already. If she kept healing at this rate they could carry on without losing much more time.

The dragon was so lost in thought he almost missed the screaming just below his ears. Abness was forcibly shoving teeth into the howling girl's mouth as the pirates held her down.

"It's for your own good, you silly lass, we can'na hardly understand you!" Murray yelled at the girl who was fighting hard to chomp down on Abness's fingers.

"Bloody welcome, you are!" Lesley struggled to keep her mouth open and Ashley manned the left arm while Murray manned the right. Lamure floated to Solannus' side and both their eyes were agape as Abness pulled out a rusted needle and some thread.

"You don't suppose he's going to-"

"Goodness that's foul, utterly foul," winced the dragon and turned his head away. Both he and the wraith were thoroughly grossed out with the crude dental procedure but at least their fearless and no-longer-denture-deprived leader was awake- and with a new set of chompers, to boot. Abness was impervious to her cursing but despite the killsmith's hexes they could tell she was happy to be able to pronounce the letter *f* again- and with renewed gusto.

"Bredikai," Solannus interrupted and the girl whirled on him like one possessed. "I am relieved. You seem much improved in so short a time."

"Solannus, a word," she stated briskly. "Stay there, I'm coming outside. The rest of you monsters get away from me." The dragon signalled to the others and Abness collected them all in the main room by his armchair where they could discuss whatever the hells they wanted to discuss so long as it didn't involve sewing more bone fragments into one another.

Bredikai was so improved that instead of walking outside like a normal human being she jumped through the window Solannus put his head through and they walked together, careful not to venture too far from the cottage. Even with the pestilence of the skyjackals removed, they could feel the eyes of the forest on their backs and it was a sensation they now accepted to be the norm of the wood.

"I've seen a lot of crazy shit in this world, Solannus. Done some crazy shit, too. But I tell you what; I don't think anything else is going to live up to all this- if we make it through."

"Bredikai-"

"Thank you, Sonny," she interrupted and her words

were sincere. "You saved my life."

"You needn't thank me just yet," Solannus said. "My bile may end up killing you in some other way. We must not trust too much in this Father Abness' medicinal prowess."

"Look at you being all suspicious of strangers, good for you!" Bredikai smiled and the dragon chuckled. "But we should keep our personal gripes out of our physical ones," the killsmith added. "For my part I'm sorry that I let the topic drag on that way. And... for bringing your mother into it." She rested against a trunk and crossed her arms. Tough as she was, Bredikai never shied away from making an apology when it was due and it was likely she owed Solannus more than one.

"For my part, I apologize for partaking in it," said the dragon. "It was not the time for such a debate. And... for suggesting that you go out of your way to provoke aggression. Such a statement was beneath me and untrue."

They stood in silence for a while. Bredikai ran her tongue across her new dentures and tried to take her mind away from the disgusting nature of everything that had happened. She would have nightmares about rotting teeth for months to come.

Solannus' soft voice broke through with an admission that she had not been expecting. "Unicorn was my mother's nickname," the dragon said and looked ahead as they resumed a slow walk. Bredikai turned to him but Solannus looked everywhere except at her. "Our, ahmm," he cleared his throat, "our horns grow towards the back but mother was special, you see. She had one that jutted out just above her forehead," he smiled. "She hated it and admittedly it was an odd feature for a dragon to bear but my father would never have her think poorly of herself. *My unicorn,* he called her... She was a good soul. A strong soul. Beautiful through and through."

Suddenly Bredikai was annoyed; with herself, with her counterpart and with never having enough information to pass informed judgment. "You might have told me as much, Sonny," she said. "Now you're making me feel bad when I never meant to be hurtful. Not very fair."

"No, you're absolutely right and I bear you no ill will. I might have been more forthcoming," replied the dragon. "My past is difficult to talk about. It is not so much a matter of trust as it is my reluctance to gnaw at old wounds that have scarcely begun to heal. There is much I have blocked in my own mind."

The killsmith nodded and stared at the ground, her foot kicking at bits of exposed root. "Does this blockage tie in with your lack of wing? You must've known I'd ask about that one day."

"And one day I shall tell you, my dear little human," Solannus smiled. "You'll forgive me if today is not that day. We will both know when it is come. You have my word as a dragon, such as I am."

"Well, Sonny, you're always going to be more dragon than I am so don't beat yourself up too much. And I've got some of your bile in me so I guess that makes us family now," Bredikai smiled and winked. The dragon chuckled and was repulsed at the same time. "Hey, you don't suppose-!"

"It was quite literally three drops of spit; calm down," Solannus said before Bredikai put in her bid to become the new Dragonfather. "Still, such a foul procedure. I'm all but dried out." They both shivered with disgust and shook themselves clean of their invisible parasites.

"Change the subject, change the subject!" Bredikai icked and acked. "Alright, we need to get out of here. I never want to see another fucking tree again. That withered old loon's got to know a way."

"And what then? I propose we look into Borghalus' hoard but it will be a difficult task and we must think beyond it."

"I agree but our thinking leads to overthinking and no action," Bredikai said.

"Is this not enough action for you?" Solannus asked incredulously.

Bredikai steered them back at a comfortable pace. She was feeling fighting fit, however it had come about. "Let's just take this thing step by quicker step," she said. "I don't want to spend another hour in this place. I can feel it growing and crowding in on itself."

From the cottage came a conspicuous lack of explosions and yelling. The small mountain in the back was very much as it had been. As the pair walked back, they felt the energy of the forest balancing itself and returning to the dank stillness they had initially sensed.

"The enchantment thickens," Solannus said. "I fear we may have increased its power, shedding as much blood as we did. When we bled into the forest, it took a part of us into it."

"I understand what you're saying because that's exactly the feeling though I didn't have the words to describe it. All of this is supernatural," Bredikai said. "I think it's time we get some answers."

"Lead on, fair Killsmith of Etherdeign. I shall threaten to eat the Abness if he is not forthcoming," Solannus smiled, showing off his pearly whites.

"Sonny, why don't you just say *'I'm hungry'* and stop dancing around the point?"

When Bredikai stormed into the cottage and Solannus poked through the window with equal determination, it was to the sight of three skeletons gathered around the man's armchair, leg bones crossed and fully engaged in a story. The old goat looked far too excited for his age. The pets were curled up in Ashley's lap and Lamure was float-sitting by Abness who reclined in the dusty armchair that overwhelmed his small frame. The grand pipe was back in action and he seemed to have added new doodads and useless appendages to it. He was a smoke-blower if ever they'd seen one.

"We want answers, old man!" the killsmith declared and Solannus nodded sternly.

"Father Abness was literally just sharing the story of the forest with us," Lamure said and the wind in their sails died.

"Laaards, I miss smokin'," Murray sighed. Ashley duly plucked his sister's skull out and let it roast in the fireplace.

"I must insist you cease this silliness," Solannus said upon which Ashley pulled the flaming skull out and placed it back on his sister.

"Just havin' a wee laugh, Scales," said the pirate. "What's got you two in a right mood?"

"I think we've burdened the Father long enough," Bredikai said.

"Indeed," agreed the crone. "But you're just on time."

"Alright, I've had enough of your time for one lifetime, old man," Bredikai said. She crossed her arms and looked the hermit in his soulless eyes. "We appreciate all you've done for us. I'm not entirely sure just what that is but- thanks. We've gotta be on our way. Got dragon bits to gather and an evil brother to destroy. Now how do we get out of this forest?"

"Father Abness was just saying that there is a gatekeeper," offered Lamure. "One who asks the riddle whose answer we must provide if we are to escape the enchantment."

"Oh, how delightful," Solannus said, perking up. "I do enjoy riddles."

"I'm not sure you're going to enjoy this one," the wraith replied.

"You have but one chance to answer the riddle," puffed the crone. "Know this: to answer incorrectly means to be consumed by the Undying Wood evermore; adding to its growth, as must all who are ensnared by it. Answer correctly and the keeper will grant you swift passage to the destination of your choice. You will never find the wood again, nor will our paths cross henceforth. Make good time to the South of the raven's flight and there you will find her, the immortal guardian of the riddlepass. Find her and you will be just on time." Abness stopped as abruptly as he had started.

The group looked at each other. Bredikai swirled her tongue around her mouth and nodded. "And you know all this... how?"

"I set it up."

"Oh, fantastic," she said, toying with the hilt of her sword. "Then you would be so kind as to tell us what the riddle is."

"About that," Lamure interjected. "Father Abness does

not seem to recall."

"Nor would I tell you if I did!" huffed the old man, taking a long drag from his pipe.

"Mighty cold, that is. E'en for us piratefolk," Ashley muttered.

"And why should you get special treatment?" groused the crone. "All who enter here do so of their own free will."

"What free will, we were escaping an ambush!" Bredikai exclaimed. "In case you haven't heard a single thing we've been saying: we are trying to save the world from impending carnage. We don't have time for this, old man," she groaned. "You tell us what that riddle is and what the answer is or my friend here is going to get the lunch he deserves," she threatened and the dragon nodded sternly once more.

"You cannot eat the craftsman, killsmith; that is unseemly," said the unbothered old man. "Nor would I do you any good. But it seems that you are almost out of time and to the riddlepass you must go! I remember neither question nor answer but what I can recall is that all is simpler than you think; for you all have the answer- each and every one of you. What you must do is think of it in time!"

In the end there was little else the crone could or would do for them except chase them out the door with small pellets of explosives cast at their backsides. He cared nothing for the mountain that had sprung up behind his home, nor for the parting of company never to return. In a bustle of hair and beard he cast them out, the door was locked behind him and no longer welcoming.

"I don't suppose we should have asked him if he needed anything before we left," Lamure said as the group wafted along.

"Perhaps our greatest gift to the Father was leaving him be," said Solannus and they agreed with him on that. Though a little worse for the wear, Bredikai was indeed healing steadily. Her leg pained only slightly and her once broken wrist was broken no more. There were still slight pangs of pain that would shoot through her system every now and again but their frequency was decreasing and she could almost fully grip her sword.

The dragon and the wraith were chatting, musing over what the riddle may or may not be while the jovial skeletons were offering up answers of debatable quality. Bredikai's leg was aching now and they could afford to take a short break, so they sat for a while in the first small clearing they came across. The girl rubbed her thigh, hoping the swelling would go down in a few hours.

"Bredikai, are we sure this is the way we're meant to be going?" Lamure asked. "There isn't a raven in sight. And I wouldn't fancy running into another mob of skyjackals... or worse."

"I wouldn't either," the leader said. As they rested, Bredikai rummaged through her sack to see if there was anything she could feed to the exhausted Solannus. The drink that the old hermit had made for them had kept their hunger in check but now that they were far removed from the cottage they were beginning to feel the realities of the cold-natured wood.

"Stop fussing and just eat them- they're emergency biscuits!" the killsmith yelled.

"You eat them. I have no need for your maggoty snacks."

"What's gotten into you, huh? I'm hungry too but you're being a real grumpy dick about it."

"If I ate you it would solve both our problems," grumbled the dragon.

Bredikai walked away and tossed her last two biscuits at Solannus' head. They were happy enough to annoy each other at the best of times but the energy of their group was changing into something bitter, something more desperate, and no one knew how to quell the unraveling. They needed to get out of that damned forest before they went completely loony, Lamure thought.

Solannus spat fire in Bredikai's direction, just enough to singe the ends of her hair. As Bredikai reached for her sword, Fluffers distracted her by flying into the air. The parrot grabbed Sir Hiss-a-Lot and together they flew clumsily towards a twist of low-hanging branches. Bredikai watched as Fluffers let the small snake go and the serpent wriggled around the same few lines of branches while the bird squawked mercilessly.

"We'll wake the devils with this here racket," Ashley said but Bredikai watched the snake wriggle smoothly through the branches, in and out and across, until he ran out of steam. Fluffers was in her face now, cawing and pushing her aside. When she finally got the daft bird out of her face she looked up.

"Huh. What do you know..." Bredikai said and smiled. "Look, they found the raven."

From where she was Bredikai could see that Sir Hiss-a-Lot had been tracing the bent boughs outlining the shape of a raven. If its beak was pointed ahead then its tail surely indicated the direction they were meant to be headed.

"I don't see anything," Solannus said, squinting and angling his head every which way.

"Come stand where I'm standing," she said and moved

aside as the dragon lumbered to her place. When he was still having trouble she placed her hands around his neck and helped him crane it to the correct position.

They took a moment to quietly appreciate the subtlety of the clue and for a second their spirits were lifted, even as the skeletons shoved each other this way and that to get a good look. Bredikai beckoned for the snake to come down and she smiled at the pets being lovingly handled by her company. They headed Southwards and just as their hearts were lightened they were weighed down once more, heavily this time and more suffocating than when they had first entered the wood.

Bredikai took the lead. Her hand was on the Hexia but it was no longer vibrating or showing any sign of life. The air was thicker and mustier here. Light grew fainter and the terrain beneath their feet more swamp-like. It wasn't wet enough for them to fall through, thankfully, for Solannus' weight would have been a great problem- but it was enough of a hindrance to slow them down. A soft rain fell and the wood lent itself more to jungle. For a moment they worried about what the rain might do to the triplets but luckily their bane lay only in saltwater. It was coming down on them harder now and they were soaked to their skins. They tread on. The deeper they infiltrated the danker the atmosphere got. They were filthy from mud and precipitation.

"I'm going to need a change of clothing at some point," Bredikai said. Her clothes were pretty much rags, her armor a thing of the past, and she was exposing more skin than her vocation deemed safe.

"I had assumed killsmiths to be in possession of better armor," Solannus said and Bredikai told him how she went through breastplates and bracers and the like as though they were pure cotton. It was difficult and pricey to obtain quality metals that could withstand dragon fire and even then there was no material known to be truly unburnable.

"That is a fair point," the dragon said. "But we should outfit you with the highest grade we can procure. You will need it before the end." Just as he finished his sentence, Bredikai put a hand out and stopped them all from advancing. The killsmith bid them be still and both she and Solannus drew no breath. That was when they saw what they had walked into; the writhing of the land, the silvery slime and scales of gigantic worms slithering in and around the fell trees. They were creepers far greater in size than Solannus, dwarfing him in both length and girth. They were so great in stature that it was impossible to tell where one ended and the other began. The company could see the silhouettes of dark faeries riding on the creatures' backs. Some of the worms had legs by the hundreds, tapping and helping the creatures slide along in succession. They saw one who had slits of feathers along its back; plumes longer than Bredikai's height with aggressive patterns ebbing and flowing. At least one had the head of a bird with a great grey beak, and another a mountain cat with no mane. No two were alike and the group was surrounded.

"No sudden movements," Bredikai whispered behind her, for she could sense the triplets gripping their rusty swords. The faeries, bent-backed and so dark they blended into the shadows, rode on the worms, sometimes in twos and threes and sometimes alone. She spied spears and a few bows and arrows but no weapons were drawn. Still the Hexia made no indication of danger.

"We carry on slowly," the killsmith said and loosened the grip on her weapon though she was alert and adrenaline was pumping through her. "Keep your eyes ahead. Show no aggression."

Carefully they followed her lead. Solannus picked up his

pace just enough to catch up to Bredikai. They had perfected the art of mumbling to each other without curious ears catching on so the dragon bent his neck close to her head and they spoke without making eye contact.

"Do you think they mean to do us harm?"

"I don't think they want to be friends," the killsmith replied. "I'm betting we're almost at the riddlepass. If they wanted to attack they would have done so by now. Let's not give them a reason to."

"Agreed. As you said: if we make it out of here I have no desire to see another forest for so long as I live."

"I couldn't fucking agree more," Bredikai answered and the dragon took in a sharp breath. "What, Sonny?"

"The passage is ahead," the dragon said but he looked gaunt and was stricken with fear. Bredikai tightened the grip on her sword.

"You look like you've seen death," Bredikai said but Solannus made no answer. As they drew closer she began to make out shapes. Suddenly they heard Murray cry "Mother!" and before they could stop her the pirate was running ahead. Ashley and Lesley, possessed of the same sight, ran after their sister and soon they all followed, no longer caring for the worms or the weapons now aimed at them. Bredikai drew her sword when suddenly the skeletons came to a halt. They were at the riddlepass- just in time.

CHAPTER 6: LEAVING THE PAST BEHIND AND OTHER GARDENING TIPS

Spears, arrows and other rough old-world weapons flanked them. Bredikai moved slowly, holding on to the Hexia with her group frozen ahead. There was no telling what they were seeing at first. The skeletons had fallen to their knees in front of a phantom mother whom they had disappointed and were begging for forgiveness, all talking and wailing at once.

"Stop it, all of you," Bredikai demanded, wise to the power of illusion. "Get a hold of yourselves! It's not real." Her entreaties went unheard. "Lamure? You see something?"

"No," answered the wraith, "but I feel it. The hand of death grips my heart and I don't have the strength to pull myself away. It's tightening and squeezing the very breath from me. I... I died once. I don't want to go through it again! Bredikai?" Lamure pleaded as the spectral tears welled in her eyes but the killsmith could do nothing for her. In a growing panic the killsmith turned to the dragon who was also paralyzed.

"Sonny- what's wrong? Solannus!"

The dragon said nothing. Suddenly Bredikai's breath seized and visions saturated her mind. At first she was lost in them, grasping at every picture so she could make sense of the fragments but the closer she got the further they pulled away. Then they began to ricochet back. Echoes in the distance drew closer and the images, mismatched at first, were now clearer and beginning to tell a cohesive story. She was the triplets, she was Lamure and she was Solannus. They were all one great eye- witnessing and reliving their harshest memories.

Bredikai saw the triplets' mother about to hang from the gallows, fighting for her life just beyond their sight. She couldn't make sense of the yelling but a crowd was rallied against her- and she was alone. The pirate mother cursed at the people; swearing that her children would not desert her to such a fate. Her cries were laughed at and ignored. The woman was overpowered and bound. Her mouth was gagged for she had spat in the wrong direction. One swift kick to the box beneath her feet and she lived no more. They felt, more than saw, her heart break before her neck.

Now Bredikai was pulled into a different vision and she owed the seamless transition to the pain carrying over. She felt her blood gush out and her skin rip apart but the explosion consumed her entirely. She didn't have a single second to plead with the gods to let her live for she was young; too young and ignorant of the world to deserve such an end. But the force was strong and death inevitable. Suddenly, the helping hand of one so young and a different energy was coursing through her, preventing her passage into the beyond. Her body was gone but her spirit fought to reclaim a shape. She was now a vision of herself separated from her corporeal remains. It was the best her young savior could do but the forced denial of death warped her mind and she was left blank and shattered from the shock of it all. The vision faded but the hurt remained.

Bredikai was backed into a corner now, in a different land at a different time. She was too afraid to look upon the pale threat who had frozen her with the power of his hypnosis. The beast was grown to a grotesque stature- too large for his age and lethal to his surroundings yet still a shadow of what he was to become.

Borghalus was young- that much was clear- and Solannus a mere serling kicked to the side. There stood a female dragon facing the white demon, wounded but defiant of the death looming over her. She had already been taken and abused mercilessly by the beast and was trembling with fear for what was to come. Even then she would not break her gaze but the great watchful eye of their company knew that there was no hope for her. If she took to flight Borghalus could match her speed with ease and rip her tail from her body. Her fire was not enough to burn or wound the enemy. The heartless serpent drew closer to his prey. They couldn't make out his words but she would not fight against him even as he tore her apart. She never howled, never called for help lest the small Solannus tried to defend her. What she did beg for was for her child to flee; to run away and save his own life before it was too late. Bredikai had no control over herself and she struggled to close her eyes for Solannus' sake but it was futile. They watched as the demon mutilated his mother and ate her in front of them, piece by piece. The beast had consumed much of her before a young valiant challenger discovered them and faced Borghalus. She could not make out who the knight was but he was not enough to defy the beast alone. Now another man, older and more determined in his task, stepped in to prevent the brute's assault but he was cast aside like a leaf and his back was ravaged. The last the watchful eye saw was the broken soul of the great Dragonfather Septiannus and the vision held, frozen in time.

What emotions passed through her she couldn't say but in that moment Bredikai gripped the Hexia and slashed at the images until she cut through every last one of them. She hacked and stabbed until there was nothing left of the illusions and they fell backwards on the sodden ground, crippled from the nightmares.

Horrified, Bredikai looked to the pass. It was wooden

and large enough to let a decent-sized giant through. There was no wall behind it, nothing but the dark stretch of forest they had been passing through all along. Then, ever so gingerly, the gate creaked open. A sliver of light shone through. There were no visions now, only voices jumbled together and speaking all at once. Like pulling a thread from a ball of yarn the knot unraveled and one voice the company could discern from the others. It was Bredikai's.

Her voice was so meek they could hardly compare it with what it was now; but they felt that it was her and the killsmith remembered what she had been. Whenever the voice dared to speak a word it was silenced. Everyone was talking over the timid treble, never allowing for it to be heard. Then the illusion did something strange and they felt the hurt of being cast aside stretching over weeks and months and a lifetime. They heard outcries growing more forceful with the years and yet the voice was still ignored. It was criticised and shamed and betrayed. They felt an eagerness to help those in need, whatever the cost, only to be turned away without a care. Then their hearts sped at what dangers surrounded them and it was the meek voice now screaming for help that never came. Loneliness once feared was now coveted; sacred and impenetrable to the outside world. Death became a well-known dance; regrettable always, necessary until the bitter end. They could feel the line of ink stretch down across her face, lengthening down her nose, then over her lips. Every killdeed completed took from them a piece of faith in their world- but there was a kind heart had never truly hardened. Instead, she gave it a sword that had also been cast aside and, together, they carved a place for her voice.

Bredikai lowered the Hexia with a sad smile. Tears fell from her unblinking eyes and the illusion, now spent, could have nothing more to say.

"What does it all mean, Bredikai?" Solannus asked softly

now that they were freed from the visions and voices. The girl steadied herself and sheathed her sword.

"It means we survived," she replied gently. The rain had dulled to a drizzle and the killsmith moved the hair from her eyes, determined to see clearly once more. She was certain of herself now and in full command of her sensibilities. "Snap out of it, all of you," she said firmly. "The time for mourning's passed. We do what we can with whatever time we've got and there's nothing else in our power to control. Come to your senses or keep sulking until your regrets break you. And if that's the fate you think you deserve then ask me if I give a fuck about leaving you here." She knew it was harsh. She needed it to be harsh. There was no changing the past and poisoning their hearts with eternal longing for change was not an option. She turned around to face the weapons pointed at their backs.

"Where is the guardian who keeps the riddlepass? We've come to answer her," Bredikai declared and suddenly all weapons were at rest and every worm and rider froze in place. The breath of the wood was stopped.

At once the company had shared their all and the experience was like a dream; lasting but a moment, imprinting emotions that would last the span of their lifetimes. And like a dream woven from nightmares once borne, the deluge settled on the solemn figure of a tall woman cloaked in green, with hair the color of sunlight that brushed the very stone steps before the gate. Her eyes were pure white and in her hands she held a golden bowl from which the light of crystals poured out as steam and faded to nothingness.

The twisted faeries who had crept along the path with the company to the gate were now knights; proud and settled upon white horses with eyes as deep as the void. Their golden armor glistened as the illusion of the sun's rays burst from behind the pass. The knights held their swords high to hail the guardian but none so much as moved, nor did their beasts of burden.

"We seek to answer the immortal guardian" stated the killsmith. She put a hand on Solannus' side and when he nodded that he was alright she moved to face the ethereal woman whose golden bowl floated just a hair above her open palms.

"You are come at last, killsmith," spoke the guardian. Her voice was a melody that would have comforted the most broken of hearts but Bredikai was having none of it. Now was not the time for comforts- mystical or otherwise. "We were beginning to doubt your arrival."

"My Lady, I fear there's not enough time to go around," Bredikai replied. "If you please, we wish to enter the pass and be done with the wood."

"You have come to answer the riddle," the woman said. "And answer it you shall. But have you given to the wood as much as you have taken?"

"Have we taken something?" Bredikai asked, hoping that question wasn't the riddle they had come for.

"You have shed blood that was not yours to shed."

"They took what wasn't theirs to take," the girl said. "I did what I judged to be best."

The guardian never turned her head so that Bredikai might look her in the eyes. Her gaze was concentrated on something beyond their sight but Bredikai stood before her undaunted. "So they did and so you have," continued the guardian. "A creature of instinct knows not to go against that instinct. It is neither good- nor is it evil. It is a drop of circumstance in the ocean of time."

"In that regard I suspect we aren't much different, my

Lady," Bredikai said. "If we deprived your forest of souls then I'm sorry for it but I think we did those skyjackals a favor. Forgive me for saying this but, good or evil, I wouldn't wish this place on anyone or anything."

"Not even upon the demon Borghalus?" the woman asked without judgment, ever staring forward with her lifeless eyes.

Bredikai looked at Solannus. She took a moment to comprehend the question. Her instinct for opportunity told her that the guardian had just presented them with a worthy way to dispose of the demon. Her company was watching her carefully. The meek voice of the past was now being listened to by all and she had the responsibility of thinking before she opened her mouth.

"No, not even on him," Bredikai said at last. "When we face him the fight will be fair."

"And if your enemy is not fair?"

"Then I'm going to carve fair into him," Bredikai gritted out.

"Perhaps you will..." spoke the guardian and let her words linger. "Will you have your riddle, then?"

Bredikai looked at her party. Despite her stout-hearted answers thus far they were all a bag of nerves and even the skeletons had somehow found a way to sweat. She gestured *one moment* to the guardian who stood stonelike and unbothered.

"You all ready? We get one chance at this."

"Don't let 'er get to you, lass," said Ashley but his tone lacked confidence and he was ashamed of his own voice.

"You take our hearts with you," Lamure added, "and

they're strong." Bredikai nodded but Solannus said nothing. She breathed in and out, her hands trembled and she fidgeted on the step until the guardian's voice beckoned her attention.

"Who speaks for this company?"

"I do," she said and stepped forward to face the guardian in full. "I, Bredikai Cronunham of Etherdeign, will speak for my company."

"Do you hold their fates in your hands?"

"I do."

"And will you answer truthfully and to the best of your quality?"

"I will," Bredikai answered, not understanding what that had to do with anything.

"Then, Bredikai Cronunham of Etherdeign, answer us this: to the best of your understanding, what is time?"

Bredikai balked. She looked to her people but they were all looking at one another, stupefied and at a loss. In that moment crushing waves of disappointment were drowning her and Bredikai was powerless to swim away from the maelstrom's grasp. They had all followed her and she had led them into the mouth of an enchanted hell where they would be picked apart by time and madness if not the nameless monsters that prowled within the floral prison. Time, time, what is time? There's no beginning and no end. It's used and wasted all at once. It's enjoyed and cherished and regretted and forgotten. There is never enough time when one needs it and altogether too much when one does not know how to use it properly. It is a breaker of storms, a shaper of mountains and the songs of birds and bards alike. It's the scream of a newborn and the last breath of the elder. It's the rust on the battleworn hero's discarded armor, the smile of the apprentice who has mastered the first spell, the beginning of a story and the end of an age. It's the sunrise that comes piercing through your window however much you wish to sleep and the cool of evening when you speak your secrets to the moons. Time, what is time but the measure of a life's worth of traumas and heartbreaks, and the healing hand of kindness and friendship you're not sure you deserve? It is good and bad and the strings of circumstance woven in between. It's the gift you were given and you share with others; it is death and life entangled and everlasting. Time is all these things and more and there aren't words enough to express it, for its gift is different for everyone and none may know it the same way.

Bredikai looked to her friends and they understood that she found herself unable to speak for fear that she might damn them to this purgatory of greens and hallucinations. But Solannus was now free from his nightmare and stepped up to pat her back lightly with his claws.

"I don't think I can do this," Bredikai whispered to the dragon but he smiled and bent his neck to look her in the eyes.

"Whenever you feel ready, Bredikai. There is no rush. We trust you and we hear you," the dragon said. There could not have been a greater comfort in all of Ethra, just then. With her head soaked and her heart palpitating, Bredikai turned back to the guardian.

"Have you an answer for us, killsmith?" the pale woman asked.

"I do."

"Then tell us so that we may know: what is time?"

Bredikai paused and closed her eyes. If the gods were listening now would have been a grand moment for them to intervene but- as is ever the case- no such luck. "Time is..." she began, "... whatever we make of it." With the answer spoken, she exhaled and waited.

Behind her she could not have seen that her company, with as much hope, admiration and faith as they had in their leader, flinched as she spoke the words and Solannus trembled in place. All fell silent and the killsmith began to shrink into herself.

"You have spoken your truth, Bredikai, for the forest hears what whispers within and no mouth can speak as does the heart," said the guardian. "One heart has spoken the name of your desired destination. Go to it now with the blessing of the guardian of the Undying Wood. The memory of the forest leaves with you, though you will not be remembered by us."

With those fleeting words rose a tempest wind and the forest was caught in a tornado that lifted every last speck of muddied soil, every branch and fallen leaf to be swept away to places unknown. The company braced themselves against the wind. Then, nothing remained of the enchantment except a large wooden pass, in front of which stood a grand maiden willow, its jutting branches holding what may have once been a bowl. Where proud knights had sat on horses, holding swords high in the air, now stood twelve mighty oaks, six on one side and six on the other, each with a single branch protruding where a blade was once held.

Bredikai swept aside the hanging leaves. In the wooden basin she glimpsed a key made of crystal. She held it, laughed lightly and sank to her knees with relief. When she found the strength to look at them, Bredikai saw her company staring at her with such pride as made her uncomfortable to the point of embarrassment. Next thing she knew she was being tossed around and her name cheered.

"Alright knock it the fuck off, guys," she mumbled between the skeletal hugs, the damn parrot in her ear, the snake in her hair, a wraith dancing through her, in her and out of her, and a dragon all but purring against her back.

"You're a brainy one if e'ers I seen, lass," the eldest pirate said and stretched his bones.

"Thanks, Ashley. Guess that's it, then," she said and exhaled slowly. "Anything anyone wants to get off their chests before we leave? This is a safe space now," she smiled.

"No!" the company yelled unanimously.

"Fantastic. So we have a key and there's the pass…"

"But where does it lead?" Solannus asked, scratching his wispy beard.

"Didn't the guardian say something about one of your hearts yapping about a desired destination? Alright, who's got the loudmouthed heart?" Bredikai looked at all of them with due suspicion yet no one caved and she sighed. When Solannus' stomach grumbled she turned and her scrutiny accused the serpentine out of him. "Maybe I'm too focused on hearts when I should be concerned about loudmouthed stomachs."

"Absolutely not," huffed the dragon. "My mind was totally blank. I'm not built for this kind of pressure. And have you thought about how I'm going to get through? Much as I admire the guardian's aesthetics she might have thought to take root elsewhere," he grumbled. He wasn't wrong, for the willow that had replaced the guardian was directly in front of the pass and he didn't have a prayer of hopping over or squirming around it. There was just enough space for anything humanesque to squeeze through but there was no way Solannus could get himself in without uprooting the tree.

"Gotta appreciate her style," Bredikai said. "Anyone have a shovel handy?"

"Where are we?" Lamure asked. There was nothing

around them but green flatland far into the horizon and even she was too emotionally exhausted to go floating and prodding.

"Do you... You don't suppose we'll get cursed or anything for uprooting her?" Bredikai asked the dragon.

"*Uprooting!*"

"Don't get your scales all shriveled, we'll just plant her at the other end," the killsmith explained. "How else do you propose to get through? Come on, save us some time, just grab around the trunk and uproot her."

"Do I look like a wood giant to you?"

"Atta lad, Scales, now you're thinkin'!" Ashley cried merrily. "On with it, lads; lend Scales here a helpin' hand. Dig at the roots an' pluck 'er out."

"Everything a trial and tribulation..." fussed Solannus and kept on fussing about thorns and wood chips in his eyes all through the digging and uprooting. Lamure looked entirely too happy at not being able to touch the tree. Bredikai assured her that they would be stopping by the nearest alchemist and securing any potion that might allow her to make serious physical contact with things, if only for short intervals at a time. She also put the wraith on scare duty- which was more Lamure's current modus operandi- and got her to frighten a confession out of the one with the loud heart.

As it turned out, Lesley proved to be the most emotional of the triplets and it was his desire that had determined their destination. Bredikai couldn't bear to dwell on their shared traumas so she kept the cursing to a minimum. Solannus' stomach was the more prominent distraction but the dragon managed to uproot the tree and roll it to the other end with minimum damage. Within the hour they had the willow replanted at the other end of the oaken guards, on the opposite end facing the wooden pass.

"There. All nice and billowy," Bredikai said and handed the key to Lesley. The pirate nodded guiltily and opened the pass. As soon as the smell of saltwater assaulted their noses Bredikai sighed and welcomed back the pounding in her head. Of all the damned places he could have picked, of course he had chosen the one surrounded by saltwater. One by one she shoved them through but before the dragon passed he stood before the killsmith and searched her eyes.

"Your story..." he said and waited as if those words alone would mean something. "You called me unfair for not sharing my past yet you are equally as guilty."

"Most astute, my scaly friend," replied the killsmith. "I didn't know where to start," she sighed. "I still don't. My entire life has been a battle, Solannus, though it can't compare with what the rest of you have been through."

"Utter nonsense," declared Solannus and the killsmith was taken aback. "Grief is not something to be compared. Pain is pain and it is either there or it is not. I am at once amazed and incredulous that you should see it any other way and belittle your own struggles."

"Thank you, Sonny. I suppose each person feels their own grief most keenly. You're right; we shouldn't compare."

"I have never known someone so fearless as you, Bredikai," admitted the dragon with equal parts admiration and envy.

"Fearless?" she repeated with a smile. "My dear dragon, what in the hells gave you that impression?"

"But-"

"There isn't a day that goes by that I'm not afraid, Solannus," Bredikai laughed. The dragon now failed to understand this human whose inner workings he was just beginning to get a handle on. The killsmith saw his confusion and tried her best to explain

"I've felt fear all my life," she said. "Part of the job! Lets me know I'm still alive. I've made mistakes and been terrified for my future, my present... *death*. I'm human. But that's a part of all this, you know? I'm the one who chose to live as I do. Fearing what may or may not happen is as nonsensical as letting the hurt and shame of the past dominate our lives now. We've all got to let things go. And that's the beauty of time. Things change, people grow, circumstances develop... And *we* have a hand in determining what happens; with our choices and our relationships and the way we move past it all. A new day dawns with new doubts and new fears. It's called living, my friend. So get in there, stop stressing and let your heart lighten a little bit. We all carry the same load now."

"Perhaps you're right," said the dragon thoughtfully.

"I was right about the riddle, wasn't I?" Bredikai smiled. "The guardian asked for my understanding of time. I think the riddle was that she wasn't looking for a smart answer, just a sincere one," she said and Solannus nodded with appreciation. "Come on, you soft pile of scales, get through and let's have a few drinks. Then you can talk my head off about your miseries and we can laugh and cry and carry on. Sound good?"

"Yes," smiled the dragon, "that sounds very good, indeed." He walked through and the killsmith was left alone.

Bredikai looked around and breathed in the clean air, unsure if she believed in her own words or had spoken them to ease her friend's own heart. The experience had taken more out of her than she cared to share but it had served to prove that she would have to stay strong for the sake of her company as well as her own sanity. Perhaps it was time to be alone for a moment and reset the clock, else she'd run the risk of melting down when her people needed her the most. Her hands were still shaking. The sweat on her face was brushed by a salty wind and its chill ran a shiver through her.

As the wooden pass closed for the last time there was no one around to hear the turning of the lock. Its color dulled to a listless grey and the wood gradually ashened and was swept away into memory. The wind picked up the granules and carried them into an unknown future as the leaves of the mighty oaks and the guardian willow swayed in the sunlight.

"Ne'er thought we'd be back here lads," Lesley said to his siblings. "Seein' Mother got the better of this old soul. Reckon we'll do well to help our friends so'as we can leave this here life in peace."

Bredikai looked at the triplets but didn't say anything. Sure she had witnessed their regret but she still hadn't quite brought herself to accept that the triplets intended on this journey being their last. A pang of interest and what she dared not call concern wanted to push her to discuss the matter further but now was not the time. They had been waylaid enough.

They were standing on the far end of a dock under a sun that was no closer to losing its heating prowess than when they first set out. No one was around to spy them for it was closer to midday than morning and the islanders of Port Par'nell despised laboring in the noon heat.

"This place holds something familiar yet I'm certain I've

never been out this far," Lamure said, looking around for any hint of said familiarity.

"I don't even know what that means anymore," Bredikai said and the wraith shrugged at her as if to say *'neither do I'*. "What'd you say this place was called?"

"Port Par'*nell*," Ashley said.

"Accent on the '*nell*," Murray chirped.

"One'a ten odd islands in this chain, lads. Southernmost stretch of the Morduanas," Lesley clarified and Bredikai scrambled her brain to understand the geography of where they were.

"I guess it does make sense to approach Borghalus' hoard from here since this is where you three set out from," Bredikai said. "This water's not going to do us any good, though."

"Are we quite fit for sea-faring, do you suppose?" Solannus asked.

"Do we look fit for anything?"

"I was merely asking."

"You make a fine point, Scales," Ashley said. "We needs us a ship that's fightin' fit. These waters be pregnant with wyrms and other dark creatures."

"Ooooh, that doesn't sound safe," Solannus said, looking at the water now shifty-eyed.

"Aren't wyrms your cousin or something?"

"Yes, Bredikai," the dragon snapped. "Every single creature on Ethra with scales is my cousin. And I know them all by name and the day they were hatched and sired- just as you do every human."

"I see your point," Bredikai conceded and Lamure chuckled. "I walked into that one," muttered the killsmith.

"How are we to procure a sturdy ship?" Solannus continued but the triplets seemed pre-occupied. After the sharing of their nightmares no one had it in their hearts to talk them out of a side mission to find their mother's remains.

"I suppose we'll need one large enough to carry you," Bredikai said to the dragon. "Can't expect you to swim wherever we're headed. Just in case- you *can* swim, right?"

"In case of what? I've had little occasion to bond with water. Never been terribly interested in places where my feet can't touch the bottom."

The killsmith looked at the water, then back at her company and scratched her head. They needed a break to take everything in and a decent one this time. "Let's not think about potential drownings just yet then," she said. "You got any money? No, of course not. We don't have a brain between the six of us... Alright folks, listen up. Now this goes against my principles but there ain't no two ways about it. I propose-"

"Right you are, lass, we steals a ship!" Ashley proclaimed and held his sword in the air.

"Oy-"

"Don't you be worryin' yourselves," said Lesley. "I gots us here and I'm gon'ta get us through- just as soon as we find what's left of Mother. An' if we be touchin' the saltwater it be on our heads, not yours."

"Been too many moons since we last stole somethin', hasn't it lads?" mused Murray.

"Well don't agree with me all at once," Bredikai said, suddenly less confident about stealing anything. "If there are other options I'm open to entertaining them."

"Don't you fret your honor, lassie. We be doin' the dirty work for you an' it ain't no bother to us either way," said Ashley, flicking his boney fingers against the tip of his sword.

"Hey, I can steal a ship if pushed, alright? Bet you anything," said the killsmith and that was all they needed to hear. The company members looked at one another and were the very picture of enthusiasm- except for Solannus who didn't bother to stifle his groan. Lamure beamed and drew them all into a circle with her twirling fingers.

"Gather 'round, gather 'round and name your stakes, good folk of the Cronun-clan!"

"I think you should refrain from naming things," the dragon said.

"I'm still working on it," smiled the wraith. "Time for some good old-fashioned gambling!"

"Here we go again," the dragon sighed. The sun was in his eyes and the weather, though cooler than it had been, was still entirely too hot and humid for his draconic makeup.

"I want in this time. Name your stakes," Bredikai said.

"We can't just steal someone else's property!" Solannus argued but he was woefully outnumbered.

"Listen Sonny, under normal circumstances I wouldn't allow it either but these are not normal circumstances- as you may have gathered. We need some motivation and a bit of competition is good for company morale," Bredikai pointed out.

"You said we would have drinks," Solannus protested.

"Don't you worry your scales- I'll deliver," the killsmith smiled wickedly. "For now, since we don't have a coin to toss between us, you either offer up your services to someone with a perverse dragon fetish or get on board with the bet. Besides, this is a pirate port. I think it's safe to say we can restart our honor after we're done ransacking your brother's cursed hoard." Just thinking about curses made her chest itch and Bredikai scratched fiercely at her bosom. "Ugh, I know I *look* healed but I don't *feel* healed, you know? I feel all... dragonny and shit."

"You need some *proper* dragon medicine in you, not that foul concoction Abness put up your-"

"Hey now!" she interrupted. "I'm sure Borghalus isn't sitting there in Kharkharen waiting to heal me. I'll be fine. It's time to get us a ship!"

"I am very uncomfortable with this," Solannus emphasized.

Bredikai closed her eyes and inhaled, exhaled... One, two... "We'll return the fucking ship to it's rightful fucking owner when we're fucking done," she smiled, half crazed. "Is that alright with Your Majesty?"

"Yes, that does make me feel better about it, thank you," the dragon smiled in return.

"If you all don't mind I'll put a scheme forward," Lamure said. "Every skeleton, wraith, woman and dragon for themselves. No teams; that way we'll have better odds of actually getting a ship. Let's not forget that we need one large enough for Solannus. This is a pirate haven so keep your wits about you and endeavour to not draw too much attention to yourselves," she said and everyone burst into laughter.

"First one to procure a worthy vessel is exempt from food and beverage duty for one month. Everyone but the winner must see to providing suitably edible foodstuffs for the rest of the company, both living and undead. We have until sundown. Anything to add?" They shook their heads. The wraith really had a knack for this.

"Just so we're clear," Solannus added, "that means appropriate magical enchantments for our skeletal and wraithlike colleagues here, Madam. I have a soft spot for lamb but beef will also do nicely," he finished with a smirk at the killsmith.

"And I'm losing the bet because a dragon stomping around a pirate haven is going to go over *so well* with the locals, Master Solannus," Bredikai sassed. "I just have one thing to add. First one physically on the ship gets to pick the group name. A better one. Cronun-clan makes us sound like a hate group. No arguments, no whining. Deal?"

Everyone put their fists forward (with Lamure's going halfway through, as always) and even poor little Fluffers put the tip of his wingbone in and Sir Hiss-a-lot stuck his tongue out as far as it would go before Bredikai flicked them both off.

They broke apart and the killsmith watched her company hasten away from the dock. They ran into the harbour in all directions but Bredikai stood in place and waited. She looked to the bright blue sky, felt the wind of the sea behind her, stretched her back and crossed her arms. She waited. A crack of the knuckles, a flexing of her legs and... there it was; the inevitable screaming from various parts of the island. She smiled, walked and decided on the first bar she could find. It just so happened to be the Merry Black Dragon. She laughed to herself and strolled in for a drink.

Three excitable skeletons huddled behind a sun-bleached hovel and were engrossed in excitable conversation. They were back on familiar territory now and intent on using what knowledge they had to their advantage. Lesley had only kept memory of a few choice drinking establishments though there were so many it would have been easier to recall the non-drinking ones. Murray's experience of Port Par'nell consisted of time spent looking for a ship to steal so she knew little of the ins and outs of the island. Ashley had blocked the place out of his mind entirely.

"But the wraith-lass said each man for 'imself, lads! That be meanin' no teams," Murray pointed out.

"Come to yourself, lass, we be pirates still. We cheat an' lie an' plunder!" reminded Ashley.

"Aye, lads, an' right honorably these days. Today we do it for our comp'ny, ya hear?" Lesley cried. "Reckon we won't be gettin' far like this now. Theys already be screamin'. Shouldn't've strolled in like. An' there be saltwater everywhere…"

"Now what be goin' on in that big head'a yours, brother?" Ashley asked and they watched Lesley pace around all thoughtful and prophetic. His boney hand was on his boney chin and he was pacing in front of them with a gleam in his non-existent eye.

"Maybes I was inspired by the look of some'a the lads back in the Craven, don't you know! At that ole tavern," Lesley pondered out loud.

"Morglut's Mane? Aye," said Murray wistfully, "charmin' place. Methinks we should go back befores we die again."

"Aye, sister, but do you be rememberin' the scoundrels wrapped up and all shriveled-like? What did Mother used to call 'em?" Lesley asked.

"Mummies! Mummies they were," the she-skeleton cried.

"It might please us to visit a wee haberdashery, get outfitted an' some such," Lesley said and he was right proud of his plan. "Maybes some enchantments 'round us, just in case. Make travelin' safer an' we can gather us some infermation. What say you lowlifes?"

Murray leaned in and pecked her brother on his cheekbone and Ashley patted his brother's skull.

"Mother'd be right proud'a how smart you turned out, lad," the eldest said and they all hung their skulls for a moment.

"For Mother!" they proclaimed and with swords drawn headed deeper into town.

Though she was not used to relying on her new gifts, something from her wraithlike senses pulled Lamure into this general direction and it was such a strong sensation she allowed it to lead her along. As she drew nearer to wherever it was she was meant to be, that feeling of familiarity swelled inside and pulled her like a rope whose one end was tied around her waist and the other to an unknown source. The faster she floated the greater came the clarity and when the wraith stood in front of a colorful hovel decorated with skeletons and symbols, paper crafts and all manner of enchanted objects, she knew that her gut had not led her astray. The sign on the door writ *open* but she couldn't see anyone inside. Carefully Lamure phased through the door and the sweet perfume that smelled of pink- if pink had a smell- overcame her.

"Excuse me? Is anyone in? I'm looking for Madam Kassiah."

"Just a moment now!" hollered a voice from behind heavy drapes riddled with symbols and other ghoulish imagery. "Don't leave and don't steal nothin'!" commanded the voice and it was soon followed by flowing green and purple skirts covering a thick figure. Bells and coins jangled as a portly woman whose arms were filled with a small mountain of semi-magical crap bobbled through the drapes.

"You might give me a hand here," the woman said from behind her handful and Lamure could only chuckle at her unchanging state.

"I would if I could," replied the wraith.

A pair of mystic hazel eyes and a round nose peered just over the burden of objects whereupon the Madam known as Kassiah screamed and dropped everything in her arms. Not a single object withstood the fall. Lamure winced and blamed herself for that.

"I'm happy to see you, too," the wraith said but the look

of horror on Kassiah's face was one she was not bothering to hide.

"Unholy Lords basting in the brine below," Kassiah breathed and cast some sparkling dust around her without taking her eyes off of her visitor. "Lamure?" she asked, squinting so harshly her nostrils jutted out. "You lookin'... *lively*." At that the wraith burst into laughter and Kassiah risked a smile. Without skipping a beat she put a hand to her hip and shook her head disapprovingly. "The cards said I'd be visited by a benign spirit but you know I don't believe in that crap 'til I see it with my own damn eyes. Mm-mm-mm- girl you're gonna scare your damn parents into the grave."

"Oooh no you don't," warned the wraith. "You never saw me, I was never here."

"Then where in the hells are you?" Kassiah demanded. "Girl, do you know how much trouble you'll be in if the damn guild finds you?! Those gossipin' whores would *love* to get a hold of this. Then again, might be enough to get me back into your parents' good graces. News is news, right?"

Lamure's eyes glowed with rage. "Stop your tongue, you loose-mouthed trollop. I came to see you because I happened to be in the neighborhood," she said, trying to calm herself. "Felt your presence, you could say. My memory comes and goes but as far as everyone else is concerned I'm still studying with Master Jalix at the Sub-Sorcery Academy."

Kassiah was not having it and her other hand found its way to her other hip. "Girl don't give me that!" she snapped. "How long can a damn apprenticeship last? You think your parents are stupid? They know you haven't been nowhere near that academy for damn near a year now. Had them ravens lookin' for you and everything. Lucky for you there's dragons everywhere so they got bigger problems now. Ain't nobody got time for missin' girls turned- turned-"

"Wraith," Lamure offered. "My own fault… I think."

Kassiah mm-mm'd her friend with even more disapproval and reached for a large decanter she had stowed behind a secret lining in a shelf. The contents of the decanter looked poisonously green but if memory served Lamure at all she knew that whatever was in that vessel had been turned with liquid coloring. When Kassiah walked to turn her shop's sign around and indicate that they were closed for the day, she heard screams coming from within the town that were unlike the usual piratey howls of merriment and debauchery.

"That got somethin' to do with you?" the woman asked and pursed her lips.

Lamure sighed. "Just pour the damn drink, will you."

Solannus was like a wyrm out of water. He had parted ways with the company in full confidence that deflated about five minutes into his solitude. He reminded himself of how he had operated alone for more than half his life, of his ingenuity and his will to survive; but his wits were dulled after the experience they had in the Undying Wood.

Pirate haven or not, simply walking into the middle of town would be an illogical move. He had been lucky enough to not be spotted thus far and with the midday heat gaining on him it appeared that the piratefolk were in dire need of a nap as there was not a single soul to be gleaned on the streets. That was sure to change once he entered the heart of the town so the dragon sought a place where his presence could be hidden.

His eyes searched the area. The place was littered with small hovels and low-level establishments. Those would not do to aid his purpose. He looked further and the buildings were all relatively sub-par, until one magnificent structure caught his gaze. He trailed its pillars with his eyes from the bottom all the way to the peak. It was a pale blue building decorated with gold, terribly garish and imposing, held up by six strong pillars- three on each side of its grand entryway. At its apex was the beautiful sculpture of a maiden with a billowing turquoise dress shaped to look like waves. Clearly the building was a temple of sorts but for whom it was erected the dragon cared little. He could fit through or hide behind the structure if necessary but his ultimate goal was to find a vantage point up top where he could spy the perfect vessel.

Solannus congratulated himself on an excellent preliminary plan and tried, with all his might, to ignore the fact that the entire town had been constructed around the temple and there was no way to approach it without going through some street or another. There wasn't much else he could think to do. Standing there in plain sight on a random dock was growing more dangerous by the second. Just as he was about to make a run for it, the dragon's plan was thwarted by voices headed in his direction. Instinctively Solannus threw himself into the water and held his breath, all the while paddling so as to not drown.

He could hear a group of pirates arguing just above his head. They were yelling and cursing at one another about having spotted skeletons and ghosts.

"I tell ya we be overrun!"

"An' I be tellin' ya not to drink under noon sun, ya sea slut!"

Solannus swam carefully and hid himself in the shadow of a ship but he had held his breath for as long as he could.

Large bubbles of air floated to the surface and exploded like pustules, drawing the attention of the pirates at once. Their swords at the ready, the group gazed into the water. For another few seconds the sea seemed tranquil and they were almost relieved until a large head broke through the surface, spewing saltwater and gasping for breath.

"Wyyyyyrm! Wyrm!" exploded the cries but as Solannus clawed the side of the ship and held on for dear life his claws punctured through the hull and the vessel began to take water. Indeed the ship was too light to bear the dragon and when the drake tried desperately to gain footing by swinging his tail around he managed to tangle himself in ropes and the ship began to capsize.

To the fear-struck pirates it seemed a monstrous sea-creature had come to tear down Brown Belle, the former pride of Port Par'nell. Soon the cries of *'wyrm!'* evolved to screams of *'krakeeeeen!'* and as the dragon clung to every last bit of wood he could, he shook the water out of his ears, his eyes burning from the salt. Just then, his right hoof grazed against something and that was the end of his relationship with water.

"Kraken?!" he roared. "Krakeeeeen!"

The pirates ran and Solannus gracelessly clawed his way back onto the dock yelling about krakens and salt-monsters and soon he had outran the lot of them and straight through to the town center. Suddenly the entire town was in an uproar with half of them screaming *'kraken!'* and the other half yelling *'undead!'*. But the more the pirates screamed and emptied their abodes the harder Solannus ran and all at once the general population had either fled onto their ships and were fast making waves or boarded up into their buildings.

Solannus ran out of breath in the town center, huffing and wheezing, whereupon Bredikai calmly strolled out of the Merry Black Dragon with a large drink in hand, a very bruised eye and blood dripping from her nose to her chin. The doors to the tavern were bolted shut behind her. The dragon nodded to her, still wheezing and spitting up saltwater and he sat on the cobblestone ground to clear his lungs.

Bredikai crouched down beside him and looked off towards the screaming. The humming of late summer insects buzzed through the air. "Kraken, huh?" she asked calmly and pressed the cool goblet onto her eye.

"If I was meant for water I'd have been born a wyrm," the dragon spat out and even as the girl nodded absently they saw a small troop of pirates running for dear life. They were being chased by three mummies whose cloth bindings were kept in check by rusted fish hooks. The mummies had swords in the air but the only sounds they could really discern were muffled *'arrrgh'*s.

"Oh good golden grief," Solannus sighed and Bredikai handed him her drink without taking her eyes off the scene.

One of the fleeing pirates froze in front of the pair and when the killsmith waved a tired hello he lifted a trembling finger, pointed at Solannus who was still trying to pump water out of his ear and have his mead, too, and yelled *"wyrm!"* Then he had the audacity to faint.

"Pirates ain't what they used to be, lads," spoke the first mummy who was most clearly Ashley.

"Sad day, it is," came Murray's voice. "These youngins be lily-livered if e'er I was born," she said and Lesley shook his wrapped head with disappointment.

"There you all are. Did you hear? They're saying there's a kraken loose in the water," came the voice of Lamure upon which Bredikai gave Solannus a look of pure exasperation.

"I'm telling you something touched my leg," the dragon

said and sneezed out a puff of steam.

The wraith floated to her party and her attire looked extremely gypsy-ish. She had a friend in tow who lost no time in putting her hand to her hip and mm-mm'ing the group with extreme disappointment.

"I see you were *not* lyin'," Kassiah said to the wraith and shook her head.

"Lamure you look so… colorful," Bredikai ventured. The wraith was outfitted in shawls and skirts of every imaginable color. Her headscarf had a horrific orange animal print on it.

"How ostentatious," tutted Solannus and whispered to Bredikai. "You're not going to let her wraith around like that, are you?"

"Everyone, this is my oldest friend: Madam Kassiah," beamed the wraith. "Kassiah- this is everyone." Just as the introductions were made they heard the explosion of cannon fire coming from the dock. The entire town was turning into a madhouse and too many pirates loading up their ships simultaneously spelled more cannonballs than the group cared for.

"I was headed for that temple," Solannus said. "It's the only place large enough for me."

Bredikai looked at the rich building and felt an immediate dislike towards the establishment. Sure it was nothing compared to the grudge she now bore against forests but this ornate structure had no business hovering over a pirate haven so brazenly. It stuck out like a golden knife sat in the middle of slaughtered hams. The only sign that it bore any affinity with their location was the mass of skulls in the structure's entablature, squished in between the triglyphs and anywhere else the architect had apparently deemed appropriate.

"Come on then," Kassiah said as she ushered the company to the temple. "Domni Arno is not gonna like this, mm-mm."

"We're just going to leave that guy there?" Bredikai said regarding the fainted young pirate, but he had already been robbed clean and she saw three happy mummies decked out in new golden trinkets. Murray was squealing with delight. "Nevermind, just walk," she sighed and shoved them all towards the temple.

CHAPTER 7: WHEN IN DOUBT, THE GODDESS WILL FUND YOU

They sat quietly lined up in the first pew; three accessorized mummies, one technicolored wraith wearing half of her friend's enchanted garb, a half-drunk killsmith with a black eye and bloodied nose and a sopping wet dragon on the ground beside her. Fluffers was apparently comfortable in Ashley's satchel and he hadn't so much as squawked for the better part of an hour but Sir Hiss-a-Lot made a grand escape from his mummy and slithered around frantically trying to make sense of his surroundings. If he had been a dog Bredikai would have thrown three leashes around the hyperactive gnat.

Facing them was a short, stout soothsayer whose hand must have been glued to her hip and was as unmoving as her annoyed countenance. To the woman's left was the Domni of the Temple of Meriventi, Goddess of the Southern Gales and divine patroness to the local piratefolk. He was the be-robed and be-spectacled Arno Ervantes Justidias the Second- and he was not amused.

"A parchment was delivered unto this temple," began the Domni with a posh fraternal tone that simply wreaked of judgment, "all the way from the Coppertine Guild... In *Etherdeign*. I did not believe it and yet here you sit before me.... bleeding and dripping in my temple. It is not my way to invade one's privacy but I must tell you that the messenger emphasized urgency." With every word Bredikai felt another itch in her crotch but, she thought, it was nothing short of demonic how her grandfather operated. "I took the liberty of skimming through- just in case, if you please. Is there a *Griffinbait* among your party?" the Domni asked and the defeated Bredikai lifted her hand, mouthing the word *present.*

"I see," the man stated with thinly veiled disgust and Bredikai felt about three years old as he scrutinized her with enough disapproval to rival her grandfather. "Would you care to read it?"

"Actually I wouldn't mind if you summed it up for me, Domni."

Spectacles were cleaned and throats cleared. "It appears that your grandfather is gripped- violently gripped!- with disappointment," the Domni declared as though he were delivering a rapture, then quietly added, "difficult to imagine why. He carries on for several colorful passages regarding some of your dubious life choices but perhaps it is better to skip ahead to the less colorful parts," he said and shuffled the papers around.

"We're a sad cry from beautiful vampires," Bredikai whispered to Solannus who chuckled under his breath and was duly silenced by the Domni's withering gaze.

"Here we are," Arno continued. "He writes that his apprentice has made rather desperate attempts to reach you through your wraith but that you have been missing for some time. Several months, as it were."

Bredikai glared at Solannus, which the dragon interpreted as a strongly-worded '*I fu***** told you that fu***** time works differently in enchanted fu***** forests'*. He muted the emphatics in his head.

"He urges you to establish contact immediately," the Domni finished hastily. He readjusted his spectacles and forced a terse smile. The man's bald head shone brightly under the candlelight and he dabbed it with a handkerchief removed from the folds of his dark blue robe, rich with golden designs and heralds pleasing to the Goddess. The top of his lip sweated the most despite the general chill of the temple and Bredikai suddenly realized that the season was beginning to turn while they were having their untimely tryst in the forest.

To say that Bredikai was impressed with this diminutive man who stood before them, unafraid of their company and unequal in his disdain, was not an understatement. It also boded ill for their general reputation as a public scare group. But the Domni was no longer interested in the freakish band and he moved away to re-light some candles that had been snuffed out by the wind creeping through his imposing temple. Evenings were cooler now and a maelstrom could happen upon them without warning, bringing with it all manner of wreckage and unsightly creatures to bear upon his holy abode. He was conversing privately with the soothsayer now and while curiosity would normally have gotten the better of the company, they were just plain tired and in need of replenishment.

"What do you think, Bredikai? Should I go parlay, as it were, with our hosts?" asked the dragon.

"Shouldn't you dry off first? Can dragons catch colds?"

"They very much can and I'll catch my death soon. Look!" he said, indicating the largest fireplace they had ever seen. "What I wouldn't give to dry up beside that furnace."

"That's a big fuckin' fireplace," Bredikai nodded. "Alright, let me go *parlay, as it were,* so we can spend the night. Get us some food."

"Hold fast, now," the Ashley-mummy jumped in. "Who be winnin' the bet?"

"I was closest to a ship," Solannus declared.

"Don't mean nothin'. The kraken got to'it first!" Murray-mummy said and her argument was supported by her brothers.

"So the bet's off?" asked Bredikai.

"Indeed not," Solannus replied. "Say it is extended until one of us physically boards a vessel."

"Fine by me," Lamure said.

"Aye! More time to bring some trinkets along for the journey," said Ashley. "All this gold be bringin' the pirate out'a me."

"You even look at gold funny and I'll throw you into the sea myself, understood?" warned the killsmith.

"Easy, lass. Just waxin' nostalgic-like," Ashley said. "Wouldn't know where else to put it! This satchel here be for wee Hiss-a-Lad an' Fluffers." Indeed the snake had been shoved aside by the Domni's foot one time too many and the sad creature crawled to rest where he was appreciated.

"Where *is* Sir Hiss-a-Lot, anyway?" asked Lamure.

"In me ribs." Lesley replied.

"Goodness, can he breathe in there?" asked Solannus.

"Wee Fluffers be free to roam about," Ashley noted.

"Fuck Fluffers."

"Madam- language! This is a temple," hissed the dragon.

"Good of you to notice," Bredikai said and stood up. Something about that temple made her more uncomfortable than she needed to be but her stomach was churning. In her mind she debated whether or not it was worth the discomfort to spend the night so she put her concerns into words, as was her way. "I just might point out that you people don't seem to have a clue about how temples treat outsiders who aren't of their faith," whispered the killsmith. She wiped at her nose, disgusted with her overall state. "They're not as hospitable as you'd hope- least of all in pirate ports. So don't get too comfortable."

"*You people?*" Solannus repeated with his nostrils in the air and a quizzical brow aimed at the killsmith. "And just what do you mean by that?"

"I didn't mean *you people*," Bredikai sighed. "What I meant was, you know- *you. People.*"

"I am not a people," the dragon stated.

"I'm no longer a people," offered the wraith.

"An' we ne'er be people again!"cried Ashley.

"I think I'm having a stroke," Bredikai said. "My point, my point!" she declared, pushing away a delicate claw trying to touch her bruised eye, "is that we'd have all gotten ships and been on our way if you all hadn't been playing around."

"I beg to differ," said the dragon snootily. "These vessels are entirely too flimsy. And you promised me drink and merriment! Yet you chose, once again, to galavant by yourself and exclude us. Serves you right, these cuts and bruises. Could have done with a few more," he said, crossed his arms and turned his head away.

"You went drinking without us?" Lamure asked and she looked genuinely hurt.

"I just... needed some time to myself," Bredikai answered. She wondered, even as the words came out of her mouth, why she should be made to feel so guilty about wanting to be alone for a while but ultimately answered her own question. *You really can't choose your fucking family.*

There they were, just as she now saw them; her adopted, tightly wrapped, necrotic and wet family. She hadn't chosen them. Odds were that they would not have chosen her but some manner of twisted fortune had brought them together in this escapade and no one was getting rid of the other. Arched eyebrows and several downcast mummy-heads were enough to suggest that they were all upset and she wondered how they found the nerve after all the merriment they'd partaken in at the Ire Craven. Bredikai looked up to the face of the Goddess above them and sighed.

"I'm sorry, alright? I'll never go drinking without you again," she conceded.

"You swears it?"

"I always swear," the killsmith smiled. "I'll find blissful solitude when I'm dead and then you can all dance on my grave and make sure I still don't get a moment's peace. Deal?" The thought seemed to appease her company a little too much. They were reassured and not shy about showing it. "Now you people behave yourselves and try not to get us tossed out while I have a word with the Domni."

While the remainder of her group huddled around Solannus she heard them rush to speak at once and the dragon mumble, *"You people. I tell you this inherent speciesism is the real problem in society these days."* Bredikai made her walk of shame towards the end of the altar. In that short stretch of time she noted the opulent nature of her surroundings, how it was adorned with the richest tapestries woven from all the fine metals of the world- not the least of which was gold. Drapes hung from the high ceiling and they matched the carpeting that matched the Domni's robes: dark blues and turquoises representative of the sea and undoubtedly pleasing to the Goddess. Candles illuminated the area in scores and they, too, seemed to be cut from gold. She wondered how the Domni could get away with such a decadent setup in a pirate haven of all places. Somehow he had and this meant that he was a force to be reckoned with. She would have to play on his terms. Something stank about that place and it wasn't just a sopping wet dragon.

She walked up to Kassiah and Arno and they stopped mid-speech.

"Domni, I'm Bredikai- the leader of this company. I want to thank you for your hospitality."

"Indeed," spoke the man but though his mouth was polite, his demeanor was nothing short of disgusted with their presence. "This temple must not be soiled with those who have had dealings with the dark arts of necromancers," he carried on. His tone was even but there was no mistaking his distaste. "All who come to this island must pay homage to the Goddess and this Temple."

"R...right," Bredikai said and wondered what about them made it look like they had any money between them. "I assure you that we won't burden you for long."

"And just how long will you not be burdening us for?" asked the man.

"Say a day or two at the most?"

"Say the night and I turn on the furnace so your dragon stops dripping on my carpet."

"Done!" Bredikai said and even Kassiah felt relieved. "But I need to eat."

"I will have bread and mead sent to you. Perhaps a washcloth," the Domni added with just a pinch of sass.

"The dragon needs to eat, too."

That last bit was the straw that broke the proverbial

camel's back and the Domni sputtered and turned red with refusal. "We haven't the resources!" he cried and Kassiah folded her arms in agreement. "Is it not enough that the world is being set alight by his wicked kind! His very presence here is like a beacon to the others and no doubt we will be drowned in dragon ere you leave which, I stress with all due clarity, cannot be soon enough."

"A few bad grapes trying to spoil the wine," the killsmith chuckled fakely and from the corner of her eye she thought she saw one of the triplets climb like a mummified spider and cut a drape that floated down to settle as a quilt upon the shivering dragon.

"And, pray, what is your purpose?" questioned the man. "Do you mean to hide yourselves from the serpents on this small island? I will not stand for it."

"Domni, please," Bredikai entreated, quickly diverting his attention from the drapening. "Allow me to paint a picture. We're nothing more than a harmless company of potential do-gooders who seek shelter and your good graces for one evening. It appears to me that you *do* have the means to feed us desperate souls. I see the splendor of your temple has benefited greatly from pirate spoils-"

"Of all the-! These are all donations for the glory of the Goddess!"

"Uh-huh."

"Pray, with which guild are you registered, child?" pressed the Domni. He was closing the distance between them now, using his fat belly to impose authority. "Killsmiths and dragons, indeed! How will the name of this temple be compensated now that it is sullied through your obvious vulgarities? I venture to say that the Coppertine Guild would not wish to blemish *their* good name with a connection to *you people."*

"Alright, I hear it now and I don't like the way you said that," Bredikai said and grabbed the Domni by the folds of his robe, right under his neck. Kassiah gasped and tried to yank her off but Bredikai was a small bag of muscle growing tired of hearing her dragon sneeze. "Listen up Papa Preacher, I don't know what kind of underground operation you're running here but this isn't my tax gold at work. Now, as impressed as I am that you managed to guilt pirates into *donating* their booty out of the goodness of their charitable hearts, I could bring everything from the Meritime Guild to the South Sea Serpents Union down on your ass. I'm sure they'd love to get a cut of your *donations.* Go ahead. Call me *child* again," she threatened and flung the sputtering man away from her. Social boundaries were really taking a beating lately.

Bredikai didn't realize that her group had gathered around their little misunderstanding. The mummies took physical control of Kassiah as Lamure winced and tried to settle everyone's nerves. Solannus was draped up like a druid and still shivering but he considered that blue was a good color on him and that he should outfit himself more often.

The Domni smoothed his robes. To Bredikai's annoyance, he looked all too smug as he grinned cunningly at the killsmith. "All will be forgiven, nay, we will be rewarded handsomely for our part in recovering the princess," the man said at which point Bredikai released her instinctual grip on her sword.

Both she and the dragon said, "the *who?*"

"Ah, but Mother loved callin' me her wee pirate princess, don't you know," Murray sighed. Lamure glared so fiercely at Kassiah that she began to scare the life out of the soothsayer.

"You yapping hussy!" the wraith accused, eyes glowing

red and the fear of the undergods bearing into Kassiah's soul. The soothsayer shivered and cringed. Tears streamed down her face as one thousand terrors iced over her heart.

"Easy Lamure, easy," Bredikai soothed, inching as close to the wraith as she dared. "Release her. She's your friend... I think. We're all friends here, see?"

"Friends!" Lamure cried, breaking her connection with Kassiah's soul. "She was the Royal Prophet! Until she got herself removed from all decent society. What kind of friend leaves you behind in a place she hardly knows for an unpaid apprenticeship and never comes back?!"

"Mm-mm and whose damn fault is that?" Kassiah snapped back. She wiped her face and her hand was back on her hip. "Girl, but you about as selfish and ungrateful as I left your royal ass-"

"You lied to me!"

"The spirits guided my hand!"

Solannus let out another steamy sneeze and it was all Bredikai needed to holler "Enough!" The group fell silent but everyone glared at one another as Solannus sniffled by her side. "Fuck. Me." the killsmith exclaimed and rubbed at her face hoping to yank it off and end the nightmare.

"You," she said threateningly to the Domni. "You will host us this evening. You will turn that furnace on so that my friend here doesn't die of a cold like an absolute un-immune imbecile. You will wine us and dine us and keep your fucking mouth shut and we'll repay you with such gold as you've never dreamed. Come tomorrow you'll provide a ship for us to get to our destination. You'll do all this or I'll alert every last dragon within ten hundred leagues of the Morduanas and that'll be the crispy end of us all."

Solannus leaned in towards the Domni's head as the man trembled and yelped. "And she'll do it, too. She's crazy," he whispered ominously into the man's ear, eyes bulging and head nodding slowly.

The Domni was unaccustomed to being terrorized but the thought of golden payment- all for the glory of the Goddess, of course- was pleasing to him. Under the present circumstances he had little say left in the matter. He pressed at his robe, smoothing it until he had removed all wrinkles and traces of dust, rubbed his spectacles clean and whirled around to light the furnace.

"As for the rest of you," Bredikai turned to her company. "We're going to have a conversation regarding the differences between discretion and lying by omission so pick a spot by the furnace and cozy up." She turned from them dramatically as the first sparks of fire crackled from the pit. "Lousy fucking time to quit smoking," the killsmith grumbled.

Kassiah had thought to make her escape by shadowing the Domni but Bredikai, now settled on a pleasant puff of carpeting not too close to the furnace, had anticipated her.

"You'll be joining us, *Prophet*," she said to the woman. "Waterproof these three with the strongest charms you've got and take a seat where I can see you."

Under Lamure's watchful eye and the pointed swords of the pirates, Madam Kassiah was escorted to a cushion on the floor. Solannus huddled close to Bredikai as if her body heat was enough to take the chill from him and she patted his draped haunch all the while glowering at the Domni who was seated farthest from their company. When they were all settled and the fire steadily heated up the cavernous hall, a lethargic gargoyle pulled the first of what would be many nourishment-laden trollies to them. The cart was stacked with meats and foodstuffs gathered from all corners of Ethra. The drinks were enchanted and alcoholic so that everyone could enjoy a hot pint or five and, for Solannus, entire kegs were brought by the gargoyle attendants. They were thanked. The Domni cursed the company under his breath as he moved to say his prayers to the Goddess at the largest of his three altars. As little as his presence was desired, they could not risk his absence nor trust in his discretion.

For the first hour the party sat and ate in silence, each lost in their own thoughts and drinks. The only one whose spirits were physically lifting was the dragon's and he had finally removed the drape from over his head and set it upon his shoulders as a great blue cape. He ate as though it was his last night on Ethra and even the gargoyles were getting annoyed with his insatiable appetite.

"Slow down, you're going to upset your stomach," Bredikai said but the dragon was under the hypnotic charms of food. The Domni had excellent taste. "That's a good color on you," the killsmith said between sips and Solannus nodded happily.

"Thank you," he said with a full mouth. Any other time he would have considered talking like that be most uncouth but he was ravenous and could afford to let his manners lapse. "I was thinking much the same. A shame that we dragons have not adopted textiles into our culture. I should think we would make for very handsome creatures indeed."

"I doubt our charitable host'll let you keep it," Bredikai said and he knew she was right but it was upsetting all the same.

"Ne'er known a princess before!" Ashley declared and raised his goblet to Lamure who smiled and clanked it against her own.

"Reckon Mother ransomed a few in 'er day, before we was born," Lesley added but Murray was still put out by the fact that she was no longer the princess of the group, metaphorical or otherwise.

"I guess that's as good a way to start as any," Bredikai said and seized another refill. "So what's your story Lamure? Or should we be calling you *Your Highness* now?"

"No, please, nothing's changed," begged the wraith. She sighed. Kassiah was watching her intently but the wraith refused to make eye contact. She took a sip and swirled her cup, watching the liquid in it stir into a whirlpool.

"I apologize for not being forthcoming, Bredikai, everyone," Lamure began. "It wasn't my intention to be deceptive. As I mentioned upon our first encounter, my memories have yet to solidify. More has been coming back to me since we arrived here. I admit that I have pleaded with the boy Zira to recount our dealings but he has denied my request- repeatedly. He claims that pushing memory upon me would be akin to forcefully waking a sleepwalker and that the memories will come back of their own accord. I began to despair but his estimation is proving correct- especially since I've come into contact with one of my own. Even if it *is her*."

Candlelight flickered with a passing wind. The temple was large enough for currents to hum through long halls feeding out of the main building to rooms unknown. All were listening to the lull of the wind's echo until the soothsayer had it with her friend's guilt-laying.

"Who ever heard of a damn wraith with memory loss?" Kassiah broke through the tranquility and after the drinks she'd had even Lamure wasn't enough to scare her straight. "And your name's *Murael*. That's right. You remember that?"

Lamure stopped and stared blankly. She looked left,

then right then back at the curious faces. "Good golden grief she's right."

Finally a look of accomplishment graced Kassiah's face. "You *made* everyone call you Lamure," she stated. "Said the spirits spoke to you and gave you your true name. Pshhh."

"Alright, settle down," Bredikai ordered. "Before we get crazy again let's remember that alcohol is involved and try to give everyone a chance to speak. Agreed? Good. Since Lamure, Murael, whatever your name is; since you're still not fully aware of yourself why don't you start us off, Kassiah. You seem to have a lot of opinions."

Kassiah took another hearty sip from her goblet and held it towards Bredikai. "You look like trouble, killsmith, and I don't much care for your tone. But I'll do my part so this one stops blamin' me for her own damn troubles." Lamure began taking off her borrowed attire piece by garish piece as a form of protest and Kassiah sighed, staring into the fire. No one interrupted the soothsayer and, though no one noticed, the Domni also listened closely.

"I'm only a few years older than Murael. *Lamure...*" began the prophet. "Not many children where we're from and that's just how it's always been. Me, I've got a younger brother but this one here's an only child. It's normal for the ones close in age to grow up together, regardless of rank. And that's fine and all- but she's been jealous of my gift from the start."

"Let her speak Lamure, you'll have your turn," Bredikai warned but the glow of the wraith's eyes made Kassiah shiver nonetheless.

"Now I'm close with my brother but me and her- damn, we were like twins," Kassiah chuckled, seeing their childhood pass through her mind. "Some bonds are stronger than blood, you know? My family and I belong to the Prophets Guild whose motto is *'if you have to ask what you should already know then you should know to go elsewhere'*."

"Preposterous. That can't possibly be the motto," Solannus huffed but Bredikai shushed him with a nudge.

"It's one of the more selective guilds, bein' an important sub-sect of the United Guilds of Sorcery," Kassiah stated proudly. "Anyway, since we were pretty much attached at the hip, it really burned this one when they wouldn't have her. But that's not *my* fault; know what I mean? I can't help it if the royals can't switch their damn guilds and even if they could, her parents would never let her join the Prophets. Her family got voted to lead the whole damn kingdom and she acts like it's *my* damn fault she's a princess."

"But I had the gift!" Lamure protested. "You could have spoken in my favor!"

"Girl you didn't have no damn gift- I… I lied to you," Kassiah said and her crestfallen admission was sincere.

"What?" Lamure said but they way her voice broke they suspected that she had sensed the truth all along. Bredikai and Solannus huddled even closer together, unable to take their eyes off of the slow-impact wreck that should otherwise have been a private conversation. Finally a drama that didn't involve them.

"The- that time I predicted the plague-" Lamure said softly.

"I put a harmless curse on the court's food," Kassiah said. "Didn't count on the diarrhea lastin' that long but they stopped complainin' once they saw all the weight they lost. Should've been a dietrist, mm-mm."

"And the golden swarm passing over the sky-"

"Got a bunch of bees involved and stung my own damn

face in the process."

"And... and the ghost of the lady in the river? You can't tell me I imagined that," whispered Lamure. "She was clear as day and I commanded her with ease."

" And she mimicked your every move, right?" Kassiah asked, looking at her friend sadly. "Light charms I put on you. You were lookin' at yourself."

Lamure swallowed and stared at the carpeting. Her head hung low and she felt waves of anger and self-loathing directed at herself, though she still spared a decent part for her friend. The story was beginning to come together now but to be so humiliated in front of her company...

"Why." Lamure demanded calmly, still unable to look at any of them. Her embarrassment grew tenfold as she recalled how proud she had been of herself when finally getting simple spells right. She had wanted to develop her skills to distinguish herself among the prophets and sorcerers and surely they would have begged to have her in their guilds. It seemed to Lamure that it was all she had ever wanted; to be counted among the magical folk and use her gift to aid others. All her childhood she had dreamed of this, all her youth she had practiced- and they had all laughed away her efforts as passing fancy. She was ashamed of her childishness and angry that her company should think less of her, now that they were learning of her desperate failures.

Solannus was sitting stiffly now and both he and Bredikai crossed their hands over their broken hearts, unable to turn away from the sad exchange.

"They... You were all laughing at me. Why would you make me look like such a fool?" pleaded the undead girl and even the pirates' throats choked up.

"Girl, I... I couldn't stand your damn heart breakin' just

because those idiots didn't believe in you. I had to look out for my sister, you know? You would've done the same for me- I know you would've. I'm sorry... I shouldn't've let it go on so long."

Lamure had had enough for her feelings were now torn. She held her head in her lap as Kassiah continued softly. "Girl, I tried to get you in. Believe me, I did," the prophet said. "I stopped it soon as I could... Broke my damn heart 'cause you would've found your gift in time. I believed that. Still do. I know you got somethin' special in you... Always have. If they'd helped you along... And you should've gotten a chance either way but that ain't how the world works. So I say forget 'em 'cause it's their own damn loss for not seein' your worth!"

They fell silent. Solannus, unable to swallow past the lump in his throat, looked at his counterpart and both their lower lips were quivering. He handed part of his drape to his partner as Bredikai hissed, "I'm not crying- *you're* crying you emotional fucking dragon," and wiped the corners of her eyes.

"I... I started fallin' out of favor with the King and Queen," Kassiah continued. "They said I'd been brainwashin' you all these years, makin' you think you were somethin' you weren't; that I was responsible for turnin' the family into a laughin' stock."

Lamure scoffed and smiled dryly. "That explains why you started avoiding me."

"Thought maybe you'd let it go," Kassiah admitted. "Should've known better... When you asked me to help you, only thing I could think of was to take you to that damn Sub-Sorcery Academy. Figured Jalix wouldn't be so damn picky, seein' as how he's *still* not a guildhead. Thought you'd lose interest in that damn apprenticeship and be back in a week. I waited. And then... We never heard from you after that..."

Solannus cleared his throat but other than his gruff expulsions no one said a word. Finally the silence got the better of Ashley and he exclaimed, "Mother'a dragons, lass, what happened?! Didja e'er hear from the lass again?!" Kassiah looked at him, looked at Lamure, then drained the full content of her goblet in one gulp.

"It was like you faded into the air," Kassiah said to Ashley who was really living this story. "I was sick worried about you. Tore that academy up but they said they hadn't seen nothin' of you since they sent you to Etherdeign. And I'm thinkin' *'Etherdeign? Lamure don't know no Etherdeign from Ammondeign'*. Somethin' about you transportin' precious commodities to the King on behalf'a the necromancers. Very hush-hush. I hassled the charms off've that no good Jalix but all I could get out of him was some nonsense about dead dragon bones and too much mercury. Not like that damn fool knows mercury from coppertine even on a good day."

Bredikai was rubbing her face now and Solannus was fidgeting so vexingly she could practically feel him putting the pieces together in his mind. She smashed her elbow into the dragon's side but it hurt her more than it hurt him so she silenced him with a glare as they listened to Kassiah finish her tale.

"Your parents threatened to have my family tossed out of our guild," continued Kassiah. "You know what that would've done to them? We would've been outcasts. Those people are gettin' older and their whole life is wrapped up in the damn guild. My brother can't be takin' care of them forever- he got a family of his own. They don't have nowhere else to go.

"I got lucky. The King and Queen didn't have nothin' on me and I'd sealed Jalix up good and proper. Never did relieve them of their suspicions, though, and my own guilt was eatin' me up. In my heart I could still feel you. Can't explain it... My sight's good but not when it comes to death. Just knew you were out there somewhere; but I couldn't stay there anymore. Left that life behind... Started makin' a nice livin' here and workin' with piratefolk ain't as bad as everyone makes it out to be. The Domni said I could stay so long as I paid my rent and taxes on time. Last week I started seein' some strange visions; about dragons and red devil-eyes and a whole lotta forests... Now here you are."

"Oh, Kassi!" Lamure cried and caught her friend in a tight phantom embrace. Alcohol had helped open the emotional floodgates and everyone was shedding a tear in some form or another but the dragon's sniffling helped steady the killsmith and bring her back to the present. He told her to let them be for a moment at least but Bredikai had had enough of her heartstrings tugged at for one day.

"I don't mean to break up this beautiful reunion but I'm going to need some more information," the killsmith interrupted and Lamure released her friend. "That's like half a story. And since we're all getting to know one another yet again, I'd like to learn the rest of it whenever it comes back to you, Lamure. We're far from Etherdeign now. So let's talk about why we're here."

"Right you are, lass!" said Ashley. "We be damned lucky to be gettin' this far as it is."

"Our luck won't be holdin' much longer, I reckon," Lesley added. "Best we'd think back to gettin' us on the Domni-lad's ship."

"I'm not goin' nowhere without Mother an' I'll gut you lousy sea-rats proper if you be thinkin' anythin' of't!" Murray yelled suddenly and stormed off from the company.

"Was that my fault?" Lamure asked as she continued to

wallow in self pity.

"Don't you fret yourself, wraith-lass," Lesley said. "Methinks she still feels that ole maggot'a guilt, what was her idea to go after the gold that cursed us."

"Aye," said Ashley, "but we be agreein' to it and I tells her there be no point in kickin' an' screamin' when we alls share the blame. Come, lad, we'd best get to her 'fore she shanks somethin'." Leaving his belongings behind, Ashley walked with his snake-bellied brother to talk some sense into their sister.

Solannus was about to stop them but Bredikai put a hand on his arm and signalled for them to go. "It's a sensitive subject," she said. "Let 'em work it out and maybe we can spare ourselves some trouble for once. For fuck's sake even if they find their mother she'll be nothing but bones. Anyway, talk it out Lamure."

"What is it you wish to know, Bredikai? I will answer as best I can," Lamure said, settling back into her drink.

"For starters: just what are you the princess of?"

"I doubt my title applies in this state but I believe we are a family of informants. Is there a Spymaster Guild?"

"The damn Rogue Guild," Kassiah said, finishing her drink.

"The *Rogue Guild!*" Bredikai repeated and was practically glowing. "The information nexus of all Ethra!"

"Oh, you used a big word! Good for you, Bredikai," Solannus applauded and hiccupped.

Bredikai was no longer interested in divulging particulars in front of the Domni who seemed a little too quiet and a little too interested in their revelations. They were going to have to pay him handsomely just to keep his mouth shut- and that was if Lamure wished to keep her whereabouts veiled. But, she thought, they were meant to be making contact with Lamure's family anyway. Hopefully they wouldn't be blamed for kidnapping a royal or- even worse- killing her. The killsmith's mind was swimming with alcohol and possible outcomes and spinning and spinning when Solannus put a claw on her shoulder and she snapped out of her mental whirlpool.

He seemed to have understood her and for that she was grateful. He said, "take a break, just this evening. You've earned it. There is neither problem nor solution that can't wait one night. We have much to consider."

"Right," Bredikai said and exhaled. "You're right. I'm not loving our audience," she whispered, indicating the ever-reddening Domni whose shadow was shiftier than his eyes. "I say we bust out of here come first light, find the triplets' mother and get on our way."

"Perhaps our soothsaying friend will help us with that," Solannus suggested and the killsmith nodded at him with appreciation.

"You are one sharp lizard, you know that?" she said and raised her goblet to tap his keg.

"Thank you, I know," answered the tipsy drake. "Madam Kassiah, would you be so kind as to give us a demonstration of your gifts?"

"Mm-mm that drake's got better manners than all y'all combined. What'd you have in mind?"

"We have a person of interest we wish to locate," Solannus said. "Deceased... At least we believe that to be the case. And her name is, er... Bredikai?"

"I... Well, you know, they never mentioned, did they? Lamure?"

The wraith shrugged. "I've only ever heard them call her Mother."

"*You*," said Kassiah suddenly. "You were born under the sign of the griffin."

"Who, me?"

"Not you. *Him*," the prophet said, pointing her empty cup at the dragon.

"It's true, I was! Oh, she is very gifted," Solannus beamed.

"You're a sensitive soul; unique and born to fly among the clouds."

"Two out of three isn't bad, I suppose" the dragon muttered, choosing to not be upset about the flying bit. "Now do Bredikai!"

"Her threads are fuzzy. Let's see... " Kassiah said and closed her eyes. She mumbled some bullshit as the killsmith waited with utter skepticism. "You were born under the sign of the millennium star... Girl, how many fathers you got?"

"Alright enough-"

"No no, she is most intuitive!" laughed the dragon. He was practically sparkling at the killsmith's expense. "Bredikai is of questionable lineage and I would be most interested in learning more of her line."

"Ooooh, girl, you got a *strange* streak in you. You really go around tellin' people you're a freelance survival professional?" Kassiah said and Bredikai sighed.

"She says it so often she believes it herself," the dragon

giggled and tutted. "Now please tell us why she is this way, if you could."

Bredikai leaned back and Lamure floated to her side. Kassiah was deep into her meditation and Solannus was eating it all up, even though the prophet broke her trance to remind him that she normally charged a fair price for her services.

"Aren't you going to stop her?" asked the wraith and the killsmith sighed once more.

"What's the point? I would have told him if he'd bothered to ask but let him have his fun. Going to be disappointed, though," Bredikai added with a smirk.

"Damn," Kassiah said, pulling herself out of her trance and breathing heavily. The killsmith arched her brows and waited with an expectant smile plastered on her face.

"What? What?!" the dragon cried and waited for some grand revelation he could gawk at.

"Mm-mm, now that I see the rest of the story all I can say is you are *too* damn nice," stated the prophet and the dragon's jaw dropped to the floor. "Good to see you learned to not let people walk all over you. And you better teach this one, too," she said, indicating Lamure.

"Happy?" Bredikai chuckled but Solannus looked deflated and confused.

"I don't know what I am but happy isn't it," he said, now completely interested in changing the subject. "Madam," he said to Kassiah, "About the pirate mother-"

"Well you gotta help me out, you know! I'm not a damn necromancer. Give me a name or somethin' that belonged to her, at least."

All eyes turned to Bredikai who slammed her drink on

the carpet and squinted wickedly towards a forgotten satchel with a small skeletal beak poking out of it. Ashley had left it behind when speeding after his sister and the parrot now felt four sets of eyes trained on him.

"Fucking. Fluffers." the killsmith uttered.

The nervous bird took off and soon it was chaos as what unfolded. Candles were knocked to the floor and wax flung everywhere. Kassiah's ill-timed charms were caught by the dragon's face, sending him into a sneezing frenzy that almost caught the place on fire. Bredikai ended up slicing more than her fair share of the drapes in an attempt to shake the bird down but in the end it was the wraith's loving hand that assured Fluffers nothing bad was going to happen and he walked happily into her outstretched palms.

"You got him? Hold him tight so he doesn't get away."

"Girl don't tell me how to do my damn job," the prophet snapped back and bid the company be seated around her. She had the bird gently tucked into her lap and closed her eyes as the trance came to claim her. This time, her voice turned soft as a lullaby and it told them to close their eyes and be mindful of the shadows. "Don't speak!" Kassiah declared dramatically, "or you'll break the vision and we may never find it again."

Lamure, Solannus and Bredikai were guided by Kassiah's whispery chant. They felt a hand that was not physical but much like the pull Lamure had felt before finding her friend. The wraith knew to trust in it and the other two followed. They were visitors to this pocket of time, brought to them through a connection that had yet to reveal itself.

No less than a hundred pirates and possibly the remaining population of Port Par'nell had been roused to the edge of the city to bear witness. Several thugs could barely keep the feisty woman restrained but they held onto her as she was taken to the gallow pole by none other than the Domni of the Temple of the Goddess Meriventi. Though her mouth had been gagged they could tell that she was shouting obscenities at everyone and everything. The Domni was wiping spit from his face.

"Silence, you odious woman!" roared the man and even the pirate crowd quieted to hear his words. The thugs placed a thick noose around the woman's neck, not bothering to cover up her head.

"Merriaihna Crawberry, how do you wish to plead to the charge of attempting to steal a ship from the Temple of the Goddess?" the Domni thundered. It was clear that he was uninterested in an answer as he had not commanded the binding on her mouth to be loosened.

"See you, faithful followers, how she continues to defy the Goddess! She writhes like a serpent from the sea and would have you under the spell of her black tongue, paying no tribute to the glory of the Temple and mocking your great contributions!" the heartless man cried, fanning the flames of hatred he had incited in the crowd. Pirates lifted their swords in their air and shouted their *aye!*s. Wretched people cursed and pelted the bound woman with whatever they had in their hands, letting loose their pent-up frenzy in the comfort of a mob. Some spat at the woman's feet and the Domni smiled smugly. The remainder of his so-called questioning was brief for it was clear that the woman was to be an example of what would befall anyone who dared go against the Domni's will. She was hung shortly thereafter, her eyes kept firmly on the horizon that met the sea, waiting for the children that never returned.

As the four visitors watched, the vision passed like the sands of an hourglass were being hurried along. They saw the crowd dissipate, days melt into nights melt into days, carrion picking at the deserted corpse and other savage sights that follow a public hanging. The corpse was now bone and bleached by the harsh sun until, one day, the skull was taken down and carried away. The bones of her body were cast into the sea but a servant gargoyle took the skull with the tattered bindings still around her mouth and affixed it alongside many that decorated an already filled entablature. What they saw last was an uncountable number of skulls fixed above the entryway of the Temple of the Goddess Meriventi and life, as usual, a mere teardrop in the sea.

When they broke from the trance the group realized that the atmosphere around them had grown too quiet. There had been no cries or curses when they tore up half the temple chasing the bird and it had escaped their notice that the Domni was gone. Most likely he had left their company before they went sooth-sailing, so to speak. The triplets had not returned and no gargoyles were carrying food in or out of the hall.

"This is an ill turn of events," Solannus said. Kassiah released Fluffers and let him fly back into the comfort of Ashley's satchel.

"Where'd that murderer escape to?" The moment those words escaped Bredikai's lips, they heard the rumbling of gears and the thud of heavy doors locking them in. There were only two doors in that entire hall and they could not be broken through- nor did they have luck with the man-sized windows for, though they were plenty, every entryway was sealed tight with charms the likes of which did not respond to brute force.

"I fear I'm not at peak strength," Solannus said. "Breaking through would take the wind out of me." Even Lamure was prevented from phasing through and the Hexia was utterly useless.

"Stop," said Bredikai and put her sword back in its sheath. "He can't keep us locked up forever. Let's sit and sober up."

"But the triplets-"

"It's going to take more than the Domni to harm them. Rest now. We'll take the watch in turns. Come daybreak we make our move."

"Yes, yes," Solannus agreed. "And what exactly is our move?"

"I'll let you know in the morning," Bredikai said. "Guess that's it for the booze and food. I should've known he'd pull something."

The sounds coming from outside indicated that their triplets had been intercepted and their captors were hastening to ships, not caring for the time of day. No doubt the Domni had made the connection between the three and the woman he had hung long before they had.

"They're gonna make for that treasure, greedy sons of-."

"Don't they understand what it will do to them?" Solanus asked.

"I'm betting the Domni doesn't know or doesn't care," Bredikai said. "Not a doubt in my mind he's still around here. Sent his pirate minions instead. Fuck 'em. Let 'em curse themselves."

"But we can't just abandon our friends-"

"Nor will we," Bredikai answered. "Kassiah, see what you can do about lifting these enchantments. Solannus, Lamure, rest up. Soon as Kassiah gets us through we go after them. And we take the Domni with us."

"But how will we get there?" Solannus asked and it was a fair question for he would not have had occasion to go to Borghalus' treasure stronghold. He doubted that any other dragon had, either. He had heard of its existence and that was where his knowledge of the matter ended. "We don't know the way. The Morduanas is a gargantuan stretch of sea, from what I can recall."

Bredikai looked down at the forgotten satchel. "We're going to have to play nice," she sighed. "Fluffers," she said and the parrot poked his beak out angrily. "Come out. I'm gonna make an honest bird out of you."

By the time Kassiah spent most of her energy on the doors morning had broken and the daylight hour was fleeting. They wouldn't budge. Bredikai felt like a cotton field was growing in her mouth and as she tried to steady her breathing Solannus shoved her aside and ran to vomit into the furnace. The more he puked the higher the flames grew and even through her own hangover Lamure could tell that they were going to have a problem- they being the two living non-dragon folk in their group. But it was a solid step in the right direction as the inferno swelled and began gnawing at the fireplace, slowly gushing out towards the sides.

"Keep vomiting Solannus!" the wraith yelled and ordered them all to pile whatever they could- pillows, cushions, drapes, the works- around the furnace so the fire could spread.

"I have little choice in the matt- bleeeghhhh."

"This is why I don't take you drinking," Bredikai pointed out but she understood what the wraith had in mind. Only the doors were charmed and the fire would quickly eat away at the integrity of the structure. What with the dragon's expulsions speeding the flames along, enchantments would not be enough to stop Solannus from tearing through the walls. Such was the new plan but they would have to move quickly else the thick smoke would ensure two less survivors in their company.

The smoke was overpowering them and Bredikai struggled to breathe. Kassiah managed to churn out a bit more magic to protect herself and the killsmith but the charm had a short lifespan. When the furnace came tumbling down in flames, Solannus took this opportunity to lumber through- taking whatever was left of the chimney with him. Fire began to ripple through the temple. They could hear the Domni scream and Bredikai ran towards the man, sword in hand, eventually backing the worm into a corner from which there was no escape.

"You promised me a ship," the killsmith wheezed and she was slowly losing her merciful outlook as the bright bold sun made a mockery of her headache.

"Look at the destruction you have caused, you unthinking mongrels!" cried the Domni. "You have brought the drakes upon us to burn our island! You've betrayed your own kind, you filthy-"

Bredikai wished she had run the Domni through for it had become habit that whenever she threatened him he delivered the opposite of the expected reaction. The man was smiling evilly again and when Bredikai looked behind her she saw the remainder of her company surrounded by heavily cloaked and armed rogues-gone-rogue and no small number of pirates. They were popping up around the courtyard of the temple where the fire had forced them out, with their blades and loyalties for hire. The Domni carelessly brushed the Hexia aside and went to stand by the hired soldiers, pointing a frantic finger at the wraith and yelling "she is the one!"

"I command you to stand down!" Lamure yelled but these rogues no longer answered to the Rogue Guild, let alone a wraith. They had come on news of the missing princess Murael, not for some raggedy spectral whom they could not identify. Then, the fire eating through the temple was met with more of its kind as a dragon, dark purple with eyes the color of rubies came tearing through the skies and spraying hellfire onto them. At once the rogues' attention was drawn to the airborne terror and Bredikai brought her sword into the mix. The gluttonous Domni finally felt terror in his heart.

"Kill the dragons!" yelled the man, rushing to take cover from the fires. In his mind Solannus was the epicenter of the growing danger. What pirates remained on the island came into the heat of the scuffle now, fighting against whomever they deemed an enemy and boarding ships to aim cannon fire at the serpentine menaces. "They call to the others!" the Domni cried. Lamure followed the man's voice and found him cowering behind a pillar, unashamed of barking orders while people burned and bled around him. The wraith raced to the Domni and scared him stiff before he could run.

"Get yourselves to a ship!" Kassiah yelled to the killsmith.

"I'm not leaving without that skull!" Bredikai cried out. Forgetting the rogues and pirates distracted by dragon fire, the killsmith ran through the courtyard and around to the front of the temple with hell at her heels. Solannus ran after her but they were both spotted by the dragon above. She swooped down upon them, eyes blazing red, ready to corner them until the others came to drag Solannus back to Kharkharen. Solannus met fire with fire but it was difficult to target the creature who had the power of flight and easily dodged his assault.

Kassiah came to Lamure's side and she brought with her rope strong enough to bind the Domni. The rogues and pirates were scattering now. Kassiah was quick to hold the man with her charms, long enough to bind him. Lamure left her to do her business and flew to help her people. When she caught up with them, Bredikai signalled the gagged skull. Lamure raced to retrieve it. Bredikai had attempted the climb but she hadn't gotten far up a pillar.

Solannus waited for her to jump down onto his back when Lamure shouted her name and a blast from the enemy's mouth came hurtling at her. The killsmith jumped blindly, cursing at the purple bitch who was turning the small island into her personal bonfire.

Bredikai crash-landed onto Solannus who was still in poor condition and the fires rained upon them. With desperate agility she crawled down Solannus' back and held on to his tail. "Wait for her to come closer. Steady!" she demanded. "Fling me when I say!"

"Are you out of your mind?!" Solannus yelled.

"Now!"

Solannus closed his eys as Bredikai was flung through the air with her arms held above her head, grasping the Hexia with both hands. The dragon had not anticipated her and had no chance to shift her course. She opened her large mouth to take the pest in but the killsmith had timed her attack well and she bent her back as far as she could so the stream of heat went flying over her. The Hexia caught on the dragon's lower jaw, slicing her from the middle of her bottom lip and down her throat.

Bredikai was falling now and Solannus ran to catch her. Their enemy howled in pain and continued to spew fire into the air. The drake fell on her side and the ground quaked from the force. Blood gushed from the dragon's mouth and neck and she fought to stay alive, if only to take down the human who had carved her. Jets of fire were expelled erratically from the dragon as she twitched on the ground like a dying insect. Solannus ran to Bredikai, whom he was too late to catch, and the girl groaned from the fall, unsure of what she had broken this time.

Their enemy was out of steam now and barely able to stand but she refused to yield to death even as she gurgled out blood. Bredikai could see that the beast intended to barrel into them but she wasn't prepared to let that happen. They heard screams of more dragons on the horizon, but when the killsmith saw the frenzy in their attacker's eyes, something stirred inside her. It was a mixture of pity and whatever feeling was closest to sadness. There was no reason as to why they should have ended up this way. The drake was operating outside of her own mind and willpower. Borghalus thought nothing of sacrificing his kin. Bredikai could have taken the dragon head-on, and she would have won. The killing would have been nothing short of a mercy. But she turned away and dragged herself onto Solannus' back.

"Get us to the Domni's ship, Solannus. Don't look behind you," the killsmith said and nodded to the wraith to guide them. Solannus didn't argue. He had seen the eyes and knew his kin to be far gone so he followed Lamure and they sped towards Kassiah and the bound Domni. The prophet pointed in the direction of a ship that was just large enough to carry Solannus. Cannonballs were directed without discretion now and destroying parts of the island that had yet to burn. In the distance were telltale silhouettes of a greater host of drakes. Lamure could see them even if the others could not. Kassiah helped the killsmith toss the Domni onto Solannus' back and together they fled for the ship that would bear them away from the inferno of Port Par'nell.

"What are you doing?! Come with us!" Lamure yelled to Kassiah.

"I'll buy you some time. Girl, don't worry about me- just go!" With the very last of her energy the prophet Kassiah commanded winds. The flames of the island grew but a fog settled around the ship and masked its departure while speeding its exit. The company watched Kassiah's face disappear. The warm hues of raging fires ate up all other colors and were in turn eaten up by the smog around them. Bredikai was burned here and there but the fire never stood a chance, for she was soaked in sweat and there was nothing to be done about it until they were safely removed to the sea. She felt her ribs and they were likely unbroken but she had fallen on her left side and was heavily bruised. Bredikai tied the Domni onto a large barrel and made sure to keep his mouth gagged. She hobbled to Solannus and Lamure's side. They breathed and breathed, then breathed some more.

"That went well," Solannus said, folding his arms and sniffing out the scent of blood. When at last they heard a great explosion like, say, the sound of a temple going up in flames, it was enough for the Domni to faint.

"We might not know how to make an entrance but I think we've got our exit theatrics down," Lamure sighed, sneering at the passed out heap burdening a perfectly good keg.

"Let's get the parrot to the helm," Bredikai said. The smog was growing even heavier around them and she couldn't shake the feeling that Kassiah may have overdone the magic as they could barely make sense of the skies, let alone the seas.

"Will do, Captain!" Lamure said and Bredikai looked at her with a sinking feeling.

"Captain? *Me?* Oh you thought..." she said and scratched

her chin. "Anyone know how to sail a ship?"

"Sloppiest bunch of..." Solannus complained as his tail kept a steady hold on a rather difficult helm. "Who ever heard of a dragon steering a ship."

"You're a natural, Sonny," Bredikai said, lazing on the captain's chair she'd found below and dragged on deck. "Just man the stern and keep us full starboard!"

"What the good golden grief does that mean?" the dragon grumbled to Fluffers who now sat on his shoulder without moving. Lamure wafted to the killsmith's side.

"I'm literally just throwing ship words at him," Bredikai chuckled to the wraith. "What's the provisional situation like in the hold?"

"Enough for a few days if Solannus can stick to his diet," Lamure replied. "But I really couldn't say, considering I don't know how long this journey will last."

"About that..." said the killsmith and readjusted her position so that she wouldn't agitate her bruised left. "I want to leave the decision to you. Look, we'll head to the triplets either way but if this... If all this has soured you for our journey then I've got enough of a sense of direction to take you back home. Or the general area. You'd probably get there faster on your own but I wouldn't have you risk it by yourself. So choose your adventure, Princess."

"Why would I wish to do that?" Lamure asked with hurt

eyes. "Do you want me to leave the company?"

"No, for fuck's sake, why is everyone so sensitive? Ow," she said, shifting again. "I merely meant if you wanted to see your parents... I don't know, maybe set things right before..." Bredikai trailed off. "Look, I can't tell you how this is going to end. You might be able to endure a lot in that state but there's magic out there that's wilder and stronger. We can't even begin to guess at what it can do and you're not indestructible. Nothing lasts forever in this world, even if it is undead...."

The wraith looked around at the dissipating fog but the cloudiness of her mind was slower to clear. "In truth I don't pretend to know which is the more logical choice," she admitted. She looked across to a bit of the horizon as it began to pierce through the smog. The sounds and smells of fire had left them a while back and they were making good time with the help of the wind. But Kassiah's magic wouldn't hold much longer and they were grateful to not have a dragon in sight except for their annoyed captain.

"I miss my family..." Lamure said. "They will mourn my state. This will be difficult to explain and we haven't the time to spare. I have other commitments now- ones who need me more. And should I live to tell the tale, so to speak, I will seek to make my amends with my mother and father."

The killsmith nodded. "Your choice," she said. "I wouldn't want any of us weighed down with regret over paths not taken. Consider that they'd have a lot of information for us- if they didn't try to kill us, of course," she smiled.

"Yes... But I'm the Princess of the Rogue Guild, after all," Lamure smiled in return. "Gathering information is in my blood! That and I have your young ward in my head. I chose to mute his connection until you were ready," she chuckled and Bredikai kept her smile in place.

"That's a cunning move, Your Majesty," the killsmith said. "You never did tell us the rest of the story; how you got caught up with my grandfather and the kid. But I've put enough of it together in my head."

"He's a darling boy," Lamure said. "The rest will come back to me. I wonder... In any case, you are lucky to have such a genuine soul in your family- even though you are not related by blood."

"Eh, blood," Bredikai said, pointing to her entire situation and waving the idea away. "Kid's as close as I'm planning on getting to motherhood. It'd make me happy to see him and gramps again. It'd also be good to, you know, not die on this quest," she laughed and Lamure nodded. In a moment the wraith went to retrieve the satchel she had been carrying and presented their fearless leader with a gagged skull. Bredikai held the mother-skull in her hands for there was little that had the power to revolt her now. She sighed and placed it in her lap.

"I'm glad we could do this for them," Lamure said and Bredikai nodded, leaning back in her chair. "Thank you," added the wraith.

"For what?" asked Bredikai, wiping the skull. "We haven't been able to help you yet. If anything it's you who's been a great help to us."

"Thank you for allowing me to join you in this campaign. For giving me purpose..." Lamure said. "And showing me that I can be helpful."

"You've got as much cause to be here as any of us," said the killsmith, waving tufts of dissipating smog from her face. "As far as I'm concerned all of Ethra should be helping out but that's another complaint for another time. You think Kassiah's alright?"

"That hollering hussy? I'll be damned if she doesn't wear the fires out," Lamure huffed but Bredikai knew that the reunion had done the wraith good.

"Final decision, then. We press on together?"

"Together," answered the wraith. "Captain Solannus, Son of Septiannus!"

"Ayeee, lass," the dragon said, imitating their piratic peers as best he could.

"Our friends are in need of a hasty rescue. Please take us to the demon-dragon's hoard as swiftly as you can!"

"Aye aye!" confirmed the scaley captain and howled with determination. "Man the sails, ya unsalted swine, there be dragon booty on the horizon!"

CHAPTER 8: OF BONDAGE, BINDINGS AND BIRTHRIGHTS

Kassiah's fog took longer than expected to dissipate and by the time it had fully cleared, night surrounded the company devoid of its skeletal peers. They were grateful for Solannus' keen vision to keep them headed in the right direction- not that he knew where that was. Actually, they were entirely dependent on the undead parrot who hadn't so much as opened his beak. The moons Tuulin and Neilin were out in full, guarding the stars and a sea that was all too lifeless. One sparkled in pale grey like a ball of dulled silver and was slightly larger while the other was a soft pink- not quite as red as it would get when waning. Though the skies weren't cloudy, the stars shone poorly and the weather was turning cold.

Bredikai had ransacked what she could find from the captain's quarters but there was scarcely a decent article of clothing that hadn't been eaten through by pests and overtaken by dust. Desperate for some heat she donned an ugly red coat entirely too big and too long, reminding herself that she would somehow have to be re-outfitted as soon as possible.

Lamure floated to and fro, sometimes making small talk with the dragon, other times taking to meditation in an effort to tune her gifts. Inspiration was running low while desperation was creeping to the surface and Bredikai finally agreed to accept Zira's renewed summons. Luckily the boy had chosen a moment when her grandfather was too busy tending to guild affairs to hurl disappointments at her.

"Aba," came the expected timid voice speaking through

the wraith, "our magical resources are low. Master Cronunham believes the King will have us moved to neighboring kingdoms and... and I don't want to go to Issodeign!" the boy whined. He didn't let the trappings of his youth shine through too often but when he did Bredikai was often around (in one capacity or another) to mother him back to sense.

"They really do stink over there but I'm told I can't say things like that anymore," the killsmith said and rolled her eyes. "But I'm inclined to agree with him, kid. Staying in Etherdeign's risky... Have you spoken with Fitzburt?"

"Uncle Fitzburt comes as often as he can," the boy replied. "He says King Althaean has tripled the guard- mostly around the breweries." The dragon chuckled but Bredikai was in no laughing mood.

"That's not what he means, Solannus," she said. "With all the breweries we operate, all it takes is one puff from your people to explode the entire kingdom. The neighboring ones won't fare much better."

"Apologies, Bredikai, I hadn't thought of that," said the dragon and focused on listening.

"We're so flammable," Bredikai sighed. She rubbed her head and scratched at her scalp. "You've got to send word to Fitzburt, kid. Tell him we're doing everything we can and the safest move is to empty the kingdom. Etherdeign simply doesn't have the manpower to fight off more than one dragon at a time- and I doubt there's only one headed your way." As she said the words she doubted that the kingdom could handle even that, for the realms had not had occasion to ward off such foes for a lifetime and military prowess had laxed. She kept that thought to herself. "What's happening with the portals?"

"I don't know," answered the boy. And how could he have known? Portals were the least of anyone's concern at the best of times. But the King would have to see to them at some point for they were the fastest method of travel from point to point throughout Ethra and the company was damn near a world away.

"You stay safe and keep gramps out of trouble," Bredikai said. "Don't let him get any dumb ideas about staying and defending the Guild. Get out as soon as you can and I'll contact you through Lamure once we... once we have anything. One last thing-"

"Yes, aba."

"Tell Fitzburt that I agreed to a meeting between the King and his sister."

"But aba!-"

"No buts, kid, just make it happen," Bredikai said. "We've got too much going on on this end so I don't care how he does it, just give him the message. I gave the woman my word." When the contact broke and Lamure was no longer glowing, Bredikai leaned back in the master's chair and slouched, deep in thought. Her red coat smelled moldy and it might have been better to risk a cold, she thought.

"It's getting tense out there," the wraith said and they all knew that her worry now extended to her own people and not just their immediate well-being. "Bredikai you'd better get some sleep. We're making good time- I think. Fluffers hasn't moved all day."

"Fuck Fluffers," mumbled the killsmith. "He's starting to make me nervous. All this quiet's unnatural."

"It really is a bit too lifeless around here, isn't it," agreed the wraith thoughtfully. She had heard much of the richness of the Morduanas- as they all had- and none of the stories that came from the sea spoke of such unsettling silence. Perhaps they were unused to tranquility as they had been coasting from one skirmish to the next, she thought, and offered up her feelings to the killsmith. Bredikai stared out at the dark water. Somewhere along the way- she didn't know where or when- the tone of their journey had begun to change. Their time was turning darker and she no longer had any control over this shift that seemed to come about in the blink of an eye. She could see it only now that she was looking back. Staring into the open water, Bredikai couldn't help but want something to lunge out at them. Great or small, she cared little. It was a sad thing to wish for but would have lent her the normality she was swiftly losing control of. But the water stared back, saying nothing and keeping its secrets buried below.

"Wake me up at first light and I'll take over for Captain Creature over there," she said. Lamure nodded as the killsmith retreated to the lower quarters to have a disgusting sleep in a musty bed whereas she would rather have slept in a plague. Nevertheless, her fatigue was too much to withstand and she would have frozen on deck come the midnight hour. Now settled below, the killsmith listened for as long as she could and when there came no sound of imminent danger she let herself drift. It was a fitful sleep full of detached nightmares but they sailed through as hidden guests of the Morduanas night and Solannus hummed his serpentine songs well into the morning.

"I told you to wake me up."

"But we couldn't bear to," Solannus said. "You are at

your best when you sleep," he added and Bredikai punched him in the rear.

"Get some rest, I'll take over."

"Thank the Goddess, my tail is cramped beyond belief. Come, Fluffers, let us take some sun over here," said the dragon and it was the first time the bird moved. He turned his little beak as if considering the risk of abandoning the helm to the killsmith. Then, ignoring the woman completely, he flew to Solannus and the killsmith took over as captain of the ship.

The dragon walked carefully so as to not upset the balance of the ship. Even with the sun in full splendor they could feel the biting wind and knew that the summer season was fully spent. They had gone in at the beginning of one summer season and come out at the tail end of a second. But it was a breath of fresh air for the dragon who, as was the wont of his kind, preferred colder environments. Small tufts of clouds passed above them yet not a sound was heard from the sea save for the occasional lapping of a misguided wave and their own spurts of light chatter. The Domni was fed at regular intervals but otherwise kept locked away in the ship's hold where his menacing presence couldn't dampen their spirits further. At times they could hear him banging against the ship and hollering prayers at the Goddess to end his captors but his threats were diminishing with each passing day. A week passed in this manner, maybe even two, and the company was beginning to lose its hopeful disposition. Not knowing how long their journey was meant to last, Bredikai had taken care to ration the food and though the diet was harshest on the dragon, even Solanus had to admit that it was necessary.

But for their rotation as captain of the helm they had little activity on board. So silent were the waters that even the jittery drake was growing disappointed with not seeing a single serpentine cousin or a tentacle from a much-anticipated kraken. Once someone thought they spotted a nether-eel but it turned out to be nothing more than giant moss bobbing along with the flow of the water. Throughout the entirety of their trip thus far there was one member of the crew who had barely budged from his position- and that was Fluffers. He had found his spot by the helm where he could see far ahead to the horizon and there he stayed. Solannus was missing the ever-energetic Sir Hiss-a-Lot.

Bredikai looked at the parrot and poked it with her finger but the bird didn't so much as flinch. "Is this thing dead? Dead-er?" she asked and Lamure was at her side in a second.

"Maybe we finally broke him. Maybe we're- look, Bredikai!" Lamure said and pointed into the distance. At first the killsmith couldn't see anything for she was just a human after all and could do with a visit to the eye specialist. She squinted and strained and, with a pleasant wind sending them along, finally began to see what the wraith was pointing at.

Solannus had been sadly partitioning his meals but left the grim task to join them, tired of the rumbling of his tummy. A tremendous cloud hung lower than others around it and from its center cascaded a waterfall, feeding the sea from the heavens itself. They saw that other falls were flowing down from smaller clouds and where the waters met and mingled multilayered shades of blue swirled. It was an ethereal sight they took time to appreciate and not a single patch of grey could be seen in the sky.

"Well that's beautiful, huh?"

"Absolutely gorgeous!" Solannus declared as he shoved the killsmith aside. "But what is that there, polluting the pristine waters?" Bredikai was squinting so forcefully she gave herself a headache and surely, as they sailed closer, they tread through wreckage and the remains of logs and sails. Their ship sped forward and they saw larger pieces now, cruising through more and more debris that boded misfortune ahead. At the very least this was a return to their kind of normal.

"Look!" the dragon shouted and they followed his claw. Of course his eyesight would have more oomph to it but if they strained just enough even Lamure and Bredikai could see the makings of a solitary ship beyond turning waters, barely disguised by the shadows of the clouds. It was far enough that they couldn't distinguish much of its intricacies but one thing was for certain and that was the fact that they weren't the first ones to have made it out thus far. The Hexia didn't care to vibrate but she settled for a dull and sporadic thump which was apparently a new feature the necromancers had seen fit to outfit her with. It seemed to Bredikai that her sword could no longer decide whether they were to encounter friend or foe. Either way, the beautiful swirl they were admiring now revealed itself to be a whirlpool and it was pulling them into its belly. For the moment no one seemed too concerned except for the killsmith.

"Something draws me to that ship but I can't discern much else," Lamure said. "Shall I advance?"

"No. From this point on we stay as a unit," Bredikai decided. They were on the precipice of new mischief and already she was calculating how they would bypass the whirlpool in one piece. Suddenly Fluffers came to life anew and he squawked like his bones depended on it. His beak was determined to iterate what the dragging pool meant for the company.

"Stop screeching, we get it!" Bredikai yelled but there was no calming the bird.

"There is something beyond the whirlpool," Solannus concluded as Bredikai tried to steady the helm.

"Beyond? You mean past it."

"You know damn well I mean through it," the dragon stated. "When has anything come easily for this group? His hoard lies beneath the waves- I can feel it." The ship's course was set on fatality regardless of what they decided to do about it and it was beyond even the dragon's grip over the helm to stop it now. Had he attempted to steer off course the ship would have merely backed into the whirlpool and capsized quickly. They were in its clutches now and the time to abandon ship was nothing short of a countdown.

"Never a fucking straightforward thing," growled the killsmith. "You'd better be right about this. People get ready 'cause we're about to take a dive. Bet you can't hold your breath," Bredikai taunted the dragon with a mischievous smile. Lamure went below and scared motion back into the Domni whereupon the man screamed bloody murder and ran on deck. He was quickly re-roped by the killsmith who then took hold of the parrot before the damn thing could fly off and stuffed him into Ashley's satchel. She fortified the satchel's insides with her awful red coat, hoping the material would buffer any saltwater before it could touch the bird. She somehow managed to squish the mother-skull in with the bird.

"I do not care for bets," Solannus said, watching their leader scurry about. "As you know we have yet to conclude the previous one. However, if I *were* a betting dragon, be assured that I could hold my breath far, *far* longer than you could yours."

"Your money where your mouth is, pal."

"How could you even hope to compete with a dragon's lung power? You're a smoker!" Solannus cried.

"I quit, alright?"

"Yes, and it was sage you were burning in that filth-ridden cabin last night."

Before he could yap further Bredikai shoved the fidgeting satchel into the dragon's mouth and bid him take care with it. "If that fucking bird's touched by saltwater he'll stay that way permanently and *you* get to explain it to the trio," she warned. "Now, Big Boy Puff, let's see if you know how to keep your mouth shut."

"What about *him*?" Lamure asked, looking at the irate Domni who had shirked his fright and looked too insulted to be worried. "Think he can swim?"

"We're gonna find out," Bredikai said.

"Mnnphimnmnhugugg!" said the dragon and Bredikai rolled her eyes at him.

"What's that?" Lamure asked.

"He's got a problem with us destroying stolen property," Bredikai explained. "He means the damn ship- like we have a choice. And it's not stolen because the good Father here has gifted it to us, hasn't he?"

"You filthy little bitch-"

"That's enough out of you," Lamure glared and scared the Domni mute. Bredikai had every intention of binding the man's arms but he definitely wouldn't have survived the water so she secured the rope firmly around his belly and gave the end to Solannus so he could drag the man along. Lamure would keep her eyes on them in case the Domni decided to make an oceanic escape. Before anyone else could be tied to anything Bredikai called Lamure and Solannus aside for a quick word. The ship was creaking now and lumbering from side to side.

"Don't get taken in by the gold," the killsmith warned. "I don't know how powerful the curse is but considering Borghalus placed it I'll bet both of you will be able to touch it and that's a hard *no*. Talking about a possible fate worse than death, you hear?"

"I hear," Lamure answered and gave her captain the salute.

"And you," Bredikai said to the dragon whose mouth was too full to answer. "You're a non-traditional dragon so I'm hoping you'll spare us any gold obsession you may be possessed of. The curse likely won't affect you the same way but I would avoid touching things all the same."

"Are we not going to warn the Domni?" Lamure asked and Bredikai snorted.

"Warn him? My sweet, spectral child, how'd you think I planned on paying him?" the Killsmith asked and Solannus gasped through his barely closed mouth. Before he could argue Bredikai was on him like a shiver on timbers.

"You hush up, you old prude!" she hissed. "He'll get no less than what he deserves. Time to take that breath-" she said and the ship spun dizzyingly, quicker with each lap they completed. The belly of the vessel was screaming with age and the force of the centrifuge. Wood snapped and broke off to be claimed by the unforgiving Morduanas.

"Mmphhph!"

"Fucking improvise- now jump!"

The plan was to let the whirlpool suck them down for there seemed no other alternative to pursue- by Solannus' estimation. The dragon kept a firm grip on the be-roped Domni while Lamure deemed them secure and instead tried to keep an eye on the killsmith. Bredikai held her breath as she was pulled deeper into the whirlpool but she was being overpowered by the unending churning. In a moment of last-minute clarity Bredikai unsheathed the Hexia and Lamure, instantly wise to her plan, grabbed the sharp end of the blade, dragging their leader through the bottom of the pool. Solannus saw the wraith pull the killsmith along by her necrotic blade and was impressed with the ladies' wet wit.

Logic had demanded that Borghalus' cavern would be submerged and protected by the whirlpool and Solannus beamed at his correct estimation. To their relief there were no wyrms or other aquatic guards to prevent trespassers from uncovering its location. That being said, the cunning Fluffers who had led them this far had proven his worth and when the company found themselves on the cusp of an entryway Solannus paddled his way through and plucked Bredikai out of the dizzying dance, relieving Lamure's sore grip. Spinning around water had nauseated both the killsmith and the dragon back to life and, looking at their sickly faces, Lamure swiftly gained greater appreciation for her situation.

The Domni crawled and spit up water but he was well and bound enough to be ignored. Bredikai wrung the water from her hair and shivered but she was generally fine as was the dragon. But when Solannus carefully let the satchel from his mouth he found, to his horror, that its insides had been soaked through. Out flew one very annoyed parrot, covered in water from back to beak. Solannus was beside himself with grief for having doomed the bird to a skeletal existence and apologized to everyone and everything all at once, practically tearing up from expelling the regret in his heart.

"Heeey, easy, will you? We all knew the risks," Bredikai placated.

"B-but the poor thing- he'll never know peace in death-" he stammered but Fluffers flew to sit on his snout and rubbed his boney beak against it. Solannus fussed and wailed and continued to beg for forgiveness.

"Stop making so much noise, you two. Bet you we've got eyes on us," the killsmith said and held the Hexia in front of her. It's thumping had not stopped but she no longer had any idea what that meant.

"*Another* bet?" Lamure asked.

"No! No more bets until we settle the first one and we'll do that when we recover the triplets. Just remember what we talked about," Bredikai said and they looked at her in confusion. "About the damn *you know...* " she said with her eyebrows stretched upwards, alluding to the golden curse that surely awaited them. Stealthily they crept through an opening so large that ten of Solannus could have passed through it and there was nothing but dry stone until-

The cavern expanded before their eyes. They were in the guts of an underwater mountain, dead silent save for the occasional song of a deep-sea creature swimming somewhere above them. Ashley had told them that the very walls of the cavern were gold and he hadn't lied. In fact, it was the only indication that they were in the right place. Save for the dunes of rock and stone and the golden walls, this cavern large enough to hold a small city was completely empty. At first the sight did not register with the company. All seemed well- if only for that brief moment- and they were pleased to look around, suspicious of the natural yet barren beauty around them. What they did not realize immediately came at the expense of a sudden outburst as Solannus exclaimed, "it's been ransacked!"

There was barely a coin or two to be gleaned on the

ground and the entirety of the cavern had been drained of its riches. They were aghast as to what or whom could perform such a feat. Naught but their light footsteps echoed in that underwater kingdom and if there had been anything belonging to Septiannus in there then it, too, had been spirited away.

"We're too late," Lamure said, suddenly feeling another tug at her emotions but Bredikai was less concerned with the whereabouts of the hoard than she was with the possibility of it containing one of the pieces they were seeking. And the triplets, of course.

"Who would risk touching that stuff?" the killsmith asked but one look at the Domni and she was reminded of the lure of riches.

"That gold will be used for reparations once we are able to lift the curse," spoke a rich voice and at once they were all in a stance- even poor Fluffers. "If dragons destroy our lands then it is fitting that a dragon should pay to rebuild them."

"Show yourself!" Bredikai demanded.

"Bredikai, I feel something..." Lamure said.

"Feel it later. Stay sharp!"

Damn those rogues were good at their jobs. They plucked themselves out of the darkness and in mere seconds the group was surrounded by no less than fifty of the cloaked figures. They were garbed in all manner of dark textiles hiding sturdy armor underneath. Their sharpened weapons of choice were at the ready but this was no band of common outlaws and brigands, nor did their regal bearings bely them to be rogues-gone-rogue. Their formation alluded to their training and these sentinels of whispers had encircled the company in military fashion, breaking only to allow for the passage of the one who commanded them. A tall man adorned in silver and other telltale signs of regality walked to the forefront and, as he did so, a gasp escaped from one of Bredikai's own company.

"Papa!" Lamure cried and floated to the King. All too quickly she was aware of her appearance so instead of throwing herself into an embrace, she stopped short and knelt before her father in shame, cloaked head hanging low, eyes fixed upon the ground.

The man was stunned. For nearly five minutes he stood in silence with barely a breath to break it. Finally the King knelt and even though he couldn't make physical contact with the wraith, he made the gesture of an embrace all the same.

"Why does my daughter, the Princess of Miasmar, hang her head?" he asked kindly and when Lamure looked up they were both teary-eyed. It was moments like this where it became dangerous to leave Solannus alone so Bredikai walked to her dragon's side and placed a kind hand on his side.

"You alright there, kid?" she smiled at the choked up drake and chuckled softly when he nodded through a quivering chin.

"I didn't want you to see me like this," Lamure said to her father. "I've disappointed you and momma."

The King stood and bid his daughter do the same. He looked at the sad wraith with great affection then turned to the rest of the company. "Parenthood is not for the faint of heart," the King said and smiled. "When Kassiah's word reached us I thought it best to leave your mother home this once. She will not be pleased with either of us," he chuckled and Lamure winced. "It is enough for me that you are safe. And you have never disappointed me, my treasure."

Solannus choked back a sob. "Maybe we can ask him to adopt you," Bredikai whispered to him. Lamure was also fighting her emotions and she nodded, unable to form coherent sentences just yet.

"What exactly is your situation, beloved? Our reports did not do justice," the King said, whereupon Bredikai sighed at her mute company and stepped forward. She bowed before the King and pumped her sword against her chest as a show of respect.

"Your Majesty, I am Bredikai Cronunham. I lead our company."

"Ah, the infamous Griffinbait!" the man declared and the killsmith visibly twitched.

"Papa, we don't like to use that name," Lamure whispered.

"My apologies, Madam," the King said and bent his head to acknowledge the killsmith. "I am Manael, Guildhead of the Rogues and King of Miasmar. What brings you on this quest for the demon's hoard? Know you not that it is cursed?" Bredikai placed the inactive Hexia back in its sheath. The rogues were commanded to stand at ease.

"Actually, your Highness, we meant to warn you about that," replied the killsmith sheepishly. "You didn't touch anything, did you?"

"It is being properly handled," the King replied and Bredikai was impressed. She had a poorly hidden admiration for the rogues and their know-how.

"Your Highness, we didn't come here for the gold so much as the missing members of our company. You wouldn't happen to have come by three noisy-"

A sudden clamour of curses and three mummies wrapped up in even tighter ropes were hoisted to the forefront. When the first layers of their bindings were cut and they were free once more to move about, they instinctually- and with impressive synchronization- relieved three rogues of their weapons and stood ready to slice and dice.

"Easy, you three, battle's over," Bredikai said. Ashley turned around and it took the triplets just a tad too long to process the goings-on. Lamure waved at them and pointed to the King, all too eager to introduce him to her friends.

"Carver-lass!" Ashley cried. "Well ya might've told us you be takin' this long to get here."

"Sorry, Ashley. We're not natural sailors like you are. We were desperate without you three," Bredikai said and winked.

"An' how'd you manage, lass?" the pirate leader asked excitedly. At this, Fluffers flew onto his shoulder and puffed up as much as any skeletal parrot can. Both parties were utterly delighted to be reunited.

"He be wet to the gills!" Murray exclaimed, almost throwing Solannus back into raptures.

"We'll discuss our group's average lifespan later," Bredikai stated. "Your Majesty, we're in dire straits here. I'm afraid we're going to need more than our fair share of help if we're to stop Borghalus."

"Yes," the King said gravely, "I am aware of the growing disease. All of Ethra is aware. The islands are burning and, when last we left, the Port Par'nell was in a most unfortunate state."

"That's our bad," the killsmith mumbled under her breath and she gave Solannus a look so he could shut the Domni up before he could rant and rave against them. Lamure had anticipated the man and was keeping a skillful fright over him.

"Our lands are already under dragon fire," continued the King, "but fortune has favored us in that the demon-drake has yet to show. He sends his minions but does not care to reveal himself. Nevertheless, what he leads is no feeble number and their eyes are turned to blood. I see our reports were true and that you count a drake among your party."

All eyes turned to the dragon and Solannus plucked himself out of his feelings to face the King. He bowed his head.

"Your Majesty, I am Solannus, last son of the late Septiannus, at your service."

"Rise, Master Solannus, for we pass no hasty judgments here," said the King. "Were that all drakes had your ease of manner we might have a way through this mischief without further bloodshed."

Solannus lifted his head but was shy to look the King in his eyes. "We are not a violent species, Majesty," he began softly, "though one would be hard-put to believe that, under the circumstances. My brother has played to the fears of my kin and is using them to his advantage. His bloodlust turns them from sense and sanity now. Sadly, I am not enough to stop him. I never was," the dragon said. They fell silent and the King considered what he would do with this information. The dragon's words were a confirmation of what they had already begun to experience at the hand of Borghalus' minions and their options for retaliation were growing slim.

"That's why he's not alone, Majesty," Bredikai said and placed a hand once more on Solannus. She couldn't afford to have his confidence break. "Stop Borghalus we must and the only way I can think to do that is by honoring the Draconic tradition. We're in possession of the tooth and heart of Septiannus. Our journey's been long and I wish we had more to show for it but…"

The King held his hand in the air. He spoke kindly to the company and his words displayed a deeper admiration than they had expected or thought to deserve. The man explained that he had no intention of interrogating their methods and that his kingdom was being prepared against this international problem.

"Though I may not speak for other lands, the threat and its growing implications are known to the world and they will be heard even unto the very corners of Ethra ere we leave this place," said the King. "How the people choose to cooperate I cannot say. Borghalus may have hidden friends veiled beyond our sight, for know that he was not alone in that prison, despite what the histories say," the man revealed and this information was new to Solannus. "The King Althaean worries for Etherdeign and has reached out to others for aid. I fear it is not as simple as emptying kingdoms or removing them below ground, as we had once done."

"This isn't just a human problem, Majesty," Bredikai said. She was now gripped with added worry for her home but couldn't let anxiety win her over. There were many other kingdoms, great and small, and they would all have to hold. Etherdeign would have to hold. "From what I understand these dragons mean to do away with any species they consider unworthy. I think the time for warning's passed. We should be making a plan of action but no one seems to be doing anything-"

"And what would you have us do, Madam?" asked the King sincerely seeking an answer. "It seems whichever way one turns the path must lead to bloodshed, and that is the path most difficult to walk. You of all people know how death weighs upon the soul," the man said and Bredikai cast down her gaze.

"Your Majesty," Solannus said and the King turned to him, trying to make sense of this creature who seemed so unlike his kin. "I would not wish for Bredikai- or any of our company- to be misunderstood. There is nothing we desire more than lasting peace. That is why our company has chosen to pursue my father's remains rather than an open attack on Borghalus, such as we are. Once we have the pieces we can restore order- and it is our hope to do so before the madness spreads. We can only hope that that will be enough."

Lamure listened to the interaction with due grace. She couldn't have phrased the problem better than the killsmith or the dragon and deemed it best that her father should hear of things from the leaders of the company, lest he prevent her from continuing with them.

"Master Solannus, you speak from the heart," said the King. "I pray to the gods of our world that we are spared from open war. You must find the remaining pieces quickly and in that we may be of service to you." When the King spoke those words the light returned to the company's eyes and a glimmer of hope was restored. "My rogues have discovered the exit portal in this cavern but your road lies elsewhere. Tread through the Morduanas' Eastern pass and you will find the great eye of Septiannus. When last I heard, it was alone and unguarded, where your mother now dwells, where we must all return," the King said to Solannus. The dragon looked at him but his expression was unreadable.

The King ordered his followers to commence their exit and one by one the rogue guard filtered out towards the portal. King Manael then turned to Bredikai and spoke in hushed tones. "I dare not say more for whispers reach far, even unto the ears of the demon-drake himself. I fear that loyalties will soon hang by a thread."

"You suspect treason, Sire?" whispered Bredikai.

"Suspect everyone and everything, killsmith. My mind remains divided regarding the necromancers. Though she is kin to your king I fear Althaea may desire more from

Etherdeign than meets the eye. I pray I am wrong but we are laboring in evil times. There are few who will risk open defiance against the drakes. The majority will run and seek their own refuge when fear takes hold of their hearts. You must act before the barbarity escalates and my spies tell me that Borghalus is already in possession of the claw and horn.

"Come," the King then said, no longer whispering. "You must take my ship. There you will find a handsome gift waiting for you. May it hasten our peace and be a promise of better days." The King signaled above. Bredikai nodded, not knowing what to make of the man's words but she didn't press him for more information, taking note of the fact that some rogues chose to linger behind.

Lamure had stayed silent but when the King reached for her hand she let her own rest within his, though touch was lost to them. "My treasure," Manael said, "I cannot force your return. You are now grown and I see that you begin to understand how our choices shape us in the time we have. Your mother and I have done our best to give you the skills that would prepare you for the world but I am sorry that you must inherit it in such a state. You must forgive us our shortcomings- there is no guild for parenting," he smiled and his daughter shared the warmth of her father's unyielding kindness. "All I ask is that you stay safe and come back to us when you feel ready."

Now even Bredikai was choking up and she coughed uncomfortably. "Lamure- Murael; you have a phenomenal family. Think you've got us all a bit jealous, actually. Your Majesty, if you're in the market for adopting I think we'd all like to volunteer," the killsmith said and the older man laughed and nodded.

"You are all our children and welcome in our home."

"Just one more thing, Majesty," Bredikai said and

plucked the rope out of Solannus' claws. "Would you be kind enough to take *this* off of our hands?" she asked and yanked the bound Domni to face the King. From the look in Manael's eyes they could tell that it was not his first encounter with the decrepit man who spat at the King's feet and uttered curses too disrespectful to note. Manael made a command and two gloved rogues hastened to complete his request. The last they saw of the Domni Arno, he was being buried under a formidable dune of gold. The rogues would not obstruct him further for he was unbound now and able to leave through the portal at his own discretion. But he would have to test his greed against the power of the curse and for that none of them would apologize. The King assured the company that this was all for the glory of the Goddess.

As the last of the rogues filtered out through the portal the company bowed once more and let Lamure speak her farewells in peace. King Manael walked away- the very picture of dignity- and Lamure didn't move until he was completely through the portal. Bredikai touched her shoulder with the hilt of her blade and the wraith smiled sadly. She wiped her tears and assured the killsmith that she was alright. Solannus stood around awkwardly and tried to process everything the King had said but his head was foggy from the information and he wanted nothing more than to be out of the cavern that was stifling his sensibilities. The mummies checked their bindings and the reformed group walked back to the point where they had entered. Going through the whirlpool had been tedious enough when they worked with the current but leaving the same way was damn near an impossibility.

"Now how in the devils' names do we be gettin' us on that ship?" Murray asked and she had voiced what was on everyone's minds. Water sprayed around them. They stood at the mouth of the cave, surrounded by a whirling sea with no hope of swimming out.

"Anyone know any sea-goddesses we can pray to? *Not* Meriventi," Bredikai stated and though she had meant it in jest, her words sparked an idea in Ashley's head. The mummy took control of the situation.

"I've got me a plan, lads!" Ashley declared and everyone non-skeletal was too afraid to ask. "Brother, Sister, we're not friendless, e'en in this state! Plenty'a love in the deep, as you'll recall," he chuckled and Solannus looked at him suspiciously. "Join me now, as it pleases ya," Ashley said and, risking it all, the triplets walked into a shallow bit of water, singing words of an unknown language into the sea. They carried on without pause for a quarter hour and once they were done, they walked out, dry as a bone, grateful for Kassiah's enchantments.

Bredikai looked at the mummies and then at the water. Nothing. Once more she looked at the mummies and back at the water- still nothing. But Ashley was confident and through all the fussing and questioning he would not answer them so they all took a seat and waited for whatever, sighing and whining and trying to come up with a legitimate way to leave that awful cavern. Several hours went by and the group had grown right antsy when Lamure noted that she was seeing peculiar silhouettes in the water.

"What the-?"

Answering the pirates' secret call, the company was suddenly surrounded by the heads of a score of sirens, their beautifully chiseled faces adorned with hair of all colors and lost trinkets from the sea. For the most part they were barebreasted but their necks and arms were accessorized with corals and weeds and pearls. Their heads were like drops from the rainbow come to kiss the water, bobbing up and down as their hair danced past their shoulders. The whirling water's power meant nothing to them as they floated in place, eying the mummies. Suddenly a few of them screamed Ashley's name while others clapped with excitement, blew kisses and teasingly berated the triplets for having gone missing so long.

"Ashley, my dearest love, is that you?"

"We've missed you, handsome! What are you doing hiding your face like that?"

"Where is my beautiful Murray? How I've longed to see you, Princess!"

"Lesley, my heart, how could you leave me?"

"Don't be lookin' at me this way, lassies, I'm not the pirate I used to be," the elder mummy cried dramatically but the sirens were quick to perish the thought. Lesley came in a close second with his flurry of admirers but Murray claimed the attentions of the most beautiful ones and basked in the glory of that fact. Solannus closed Bredikai's open mouth with the back of his claw.

"I hate to be troublin' you, me briney beauties, but would you be so kind as to help my lads to that there ship? You'd be doin' this old soul a mighty favor, indeed."

"For *you*, Ashley? We'd do anything."

"He asked *me*!"

"He asked all of us!"

"No need to quarrel, me saltwater goddesses," Ashley said and the mermaids all but fainted back into the deep. "These lads here be needin' the most help," he said, indicating Bredikai and Solannus.

"I no longer understand what's happening," Bredikai said through a forced smile and pulled Lesley away before he fell into the bare bosom of one of his waterladies. When the bountiful bust danced in the killsmith's face she suddenly understood the lure of the sirens a little too well. "Are they strong enough to help Solannus?" Bredikai whispered to Lesley, unsure of this particular method.

"Aye, lass, they may be dainty to look at but don't be lettin' 'em fool you. Strong as any old drake, they are. Could tear the legs off a kraken an' the wyrm it came with. Just remember to leave 'em wantin' more else they be draggin' you down to a cozy sailor's grave."

"Were I a betting dragon, I would bet on your bust any day of the week," Solannus quietly teased the killsmith.

"Pffft, damn right you would," the killsmith mumbled back and admired her own cleavage. "Well alright then. Ladies, we are at your mercy," she smiled and bowed to the score of floating tits and the sirens they came with.

Solannus looked at the mummies, then the sirens, then the killsmith who had apparently lost her mind entirely.

"Have you lost your mind entirely?"

"Told you we was popular in the Morduanas," Ashley beamed and leaned in for a well-earned kiss to his bound face.

When a stupified rogue captain saw a new crew being dragged his way through disturbed waters he waited for no explanation before unsheathing both his swords and assuming battle positions. A handful of the guards had remained on the ship and they could have been easily dealt with but, alas, such was not the manner in which Bredikai's company dealt with obstacles. The sirens saw it fit to conjure a spray that flung the company onto the deck of their new ship but the killsmith didn't have a chance to diffuse the situation. The mummies ran past her, the dragon and the wraith, and threw the rogues overboard, kicking and cursing to the high heavens.

"Ashley!" Bredikai declared but the pirate was in full spirits, fueled by a new zest for life and altogether uninterested in explaining himself to the living.

"I captain me own ship!" he declared and commanded the rest of them to throw the remaining crew overboard. Bredikai yelled for the rogues to swim into the whirlpool and seek the portal but they were just out of earshot and already being distracted by the sirens' *floating charms*.

"They be in grand comp'ny, lass," Murray said but Bredikai sighed and shook her head.

Another fine swell of the seas and the new crew of the Tidal Titan was sent on its way along with a shower of kisses and promises of romance and return. Solannus waved at the sirens and as the beauties began their farewell song it took every last one of them to snap the dragon out of the hypnosis before he walked overboard to join the ladies. Bredikai had brought the hilt of the Hexia down on his head and it was only then that she realized how keenly it had been vibrating. When the killsmith looked back she saw the sirens heading for the rogues they'd tossed overboard and she bid them a sailor's farewell in her heart.

It took a while for the company to get their bearings for the ship was large- one befitting a king- though certainly not the largest that Lamure's father had in his armada. But it wasn't until Lamure's eyes widened and she told them to look up that they noticed the unique sail keeping the grand vessel steady. It stood apart from the rest, shimmering in leathery green and black, no doubt responsible for the ship being able to withstand the whirlpool's clutches. Solannus shuffled past them, never taking his eyes off of the mighty wing of Septiannus, fluttering in the wind and awaiting command. It was as he remembered it- and magnificent to behold. Solannus stared, deep in thought and memory. Unlike the tooth on Bredikai's necklace, the wing had not suffered itself to be weathered or worn. Though it was in stark contrast with the ship's other billowing sails the wing had a rather hypnotic effect where if one stared at it enough, it seemed to blend in with the whites and stand as one of them. The dragon smiled sadly. They were one step closer than they had been but it was the second bittersweet reunion of their day.

Now on their way and headed towards the Eastern breast of the Morduanas, Ashley decided he had had enough of his cloth confinement and, in a daring move, chose to rid himself of his bindings. Naturally, Lesley and Murray followed suit, breathing the salty air as if they had any senses left. Out popped a jittery snake, instantly overtaken by an undead parrot who had missed his company dearly.

"De-robe at your own risk," Bredikai warned.

"The risk be ours, lass," Ashley said but he didn't stop until he was back to his bones. "Had me some time to think whiles we was waitin' on you, an' I reckon' there be worse ways to live than as such. Liked what the wraith-lass's old man had to say. Good man, 'e is. Got me emotions goin' like. So we be makin' our own choices from here on out," he declared and his siblings *aye*'d the captain with upheld swords they had torn from the tossed rogues.

"We have a gift for you but I'm not sure it's what you wanted," Bredikai said. Solannus was hesitant to hand the gift-bearing satchel over but he relinquished it to the killsmith with a knowing glance. The triplets gathered around her and watched as she slowly revealed a dusty skull that was still bound at the mouth. The triplets gasped and stared at it, unmoving.

"Be this-" Ashley said with a trembling hand and Bredikai feared for their reaction.

"It was all we could salvage but yes..." she said softly. "I'm afraid she was, ah, hung... Her death was quick so... Don't ask me how I know. But we took revenge, I think- right?" she asked and Solannus shrugged. "You can thank Lamure for her quick hand," Bredikai finished lamely. Tension was rife in the air and the dragon kept waiting for the triplets to cut something. He had had enough of the day's anxieties. Bredikai was waiting the same as he was and scarcely drawing breath.

"Mother!" they cried suddenly and without forewarning the triplets danced around the skull, grabbing Bredikai by the hand and twirling around three times until the girl was dizzy. Next they danced around the confused dragon and then with the wraith. Lamure looked to Bredikai for help.

"She be lookin' just like us!" Murray declared. "Told you lads I be takin' after her the most," she added, holding her mother's skull next to her own for comparison.

"This be a happy day- mighty happy day at sea! An' you three-" Ashley said, looking at the dragon, the wraith and the killsmith, "You did us kindly, you did." His voice cracked ever so slightly and their hearts melted.

"Mighty great comp'ny," Lesley added.

"Knows it from the moment we met you!" Murray chirped. "Now, lads, I think it fittin' we finish that song we made for Mother." She placed the skull gracefully on the top rung of the helm, while Ashley went to steer. Lesley joined them to update the existing version of their shanty. While the triplets bent their focus on their gift of song, Bredikai and Lamure ventured into the belly of the Tidal Titan to see what they could make use of. Solannus passed the time with his pets.

An hour crept by with the whirlpool left behind and the Titan owned the very sea she cut through. Bredikai resurfaced with some choice textiles she was eager to try out on Solannus' head and the dragon was more than happy to let her hood him, drape him, whatever to get his mind off of his empty belly.

Just as Solannus started to complain about yellow not being his color, the triplets burst into song, thumping their bones to the rhythm and taking their parts in turn, youngest to eldest then all together.

"Mother Mer was a salty old soul,

"Hair red as fire an'a temper foul!

Golden jewels an'a furry stole-

Until she hung from the gallows pole!

What's that you say, old Mother Mer?

We're on our way to the Dragon's lair!

But you stole a ship from the preacher's own,

An' now you hang from the gallows pole!

The gods they laughed an' hearts caught fire,

While you fought your way, your crew conspired,

To take what's yours for they desired,

To have you hung from the gallows pole!"

You thought your kin was lost at sea,

They left you, those accursed three!

None now knew where they could be-

No one left to cut you free-

But we be back- your familyyyy!

An' oh-lo-loooo!

To take you down from the gallows pole!

"That was marvelous!" Solannus cheered and clapped. "Terribly grim but marvelous!" he added and insisted they reprise it. They were all in a fantastic mood, as though the weight that had been bearing down on them had lifted with the power of the wing guiding them away from the darkness. The worries and fears of tomorrow, while ever present, could be placed beside them rather than hang above their heads. Everyone was speaking, one interrupting the other, regaling each other of the parts of the story that they had missed, sharing their views and singing their emotions. They were tired now but it was a happier sort of fatigue and one devoid of the stress that had brought them to the Morduanas.

"This is great but I think we should keep the noise down before we attract undue attention to ourselves," Bredikai said but no one was in the mood for concern.

"Don't be silly, lass. There be nothin' in these here parts but your odd kraken," was Ashley's dull comfort. Solannus shot her *that look* and nodded.

"I found my father's alcohol!" Lamure yelled from below, her head appearing on deck with her body floating in

the second level. "We're going to have to test it all to see what's enchanted and what's not," she said and winked at the triplets.

"Aye! Let's drink to our health an' sail to glory!" yelled Ashley, resting his hand on his mother's skull.

"Aye aye!" the company cheered. Bredikai's geographical learning was not on par with the pirates' but her gut told her that Ashley was steering them through towards the Eastern Pass as the King had said. What no one had not mentioned was that the pass was also the long way to Kharkharen. Out of the corner of her eye she noticed Solannus whispering in Ashley's ear and decided to not demand answers just yet. Presently she was more interested in what King Manael had said regarding the great eye. The more information came their way the more puzzles twisted around them. She had not given enough credit to the notoriety of Solannus' line and, all this time she had been focused on his father, Bredikai hadn't thought to dig deeper with regards to the dragon's mother. She had clearly played a greater role in the sad story of Solannus' life and from the visions they had shared in the Undying Wood they knew why... But there had to be more to the tale and in her heart Bredikai could feel the presence of unknown stories that had culminated in the birth of her wingless friend.

Bredikai looked at Solannus and he was so happy, helping to sort between the kegs Lesley and Murray were dragging up on deck. He waved her over, shaking his claws in the air.

"Bredikai! I found you a drink that, in your words, is enough to rot the balls off a troglodyte!"

"Come join us!" Lamure beckoned with a smile. Just then, the wraith saw the concern in the killsmith's eyes and tilted her head to get a better understanding of what was going through her mind. But Bredikai would suffer no intrusion upon her worries- not just then. She smiled back and joined her company in the center of the deck, happily seated between kegs, goblets and no small amount of food they parceled up.

"So who won the bet?" she asked.

Solannus coughed and puffed up his chest. "As previously mentioned, I was the first among our party to make contact with a ship and therefore I believe it is incumbent upon me to name our company," he said with his snout in the air.

"We says *on* a ship, Scales," Lesley protested. "Twas wee Fluffers what flew on deck first."

"We never said pets were allowed to participate," Bredikai objected and the dragon went on the defensive, yelling about how poor Fluffers had been through enough and such. Just then, Sir Hiss-a-Lot gave a disgusting heave and, to their horror, out popped two golden coins. How or when the sly gnat had gotten hold of them was a mystery but the company gasped and much panic ensued. Bredikai shot up and kicked one away with her foot and Solannus tried to flick the other with the tips of his claws.

"Oh, Sir Hiss-a-lot! How could you?" the dragon begged and the snake hung his sad little head, unsure of what all the fuss was about. They took turns kicking the coins about like some sort of twisted game with only the dragon fretting over his beloved serpent.

"That silly snake be cursin' me ship!" Ashley hollered.

"*Your* ship? I floated here faster than any of you," Lamure pointed out.

"But it be *me* makin' first contact," Ashley said. "An' I be steerin' so I make the rules!"

"It belonged to *my* father!" defied the wraith. "I'm pulling rank."

"But I was so looking forward to naming our company," Solannus said and they all entreated him to reveal his idea. It was better than listening to him hypothesize about what may or may not befall his snake for there was nothing to be done about the gnat now.

"Prepare yourselves," Solannus said and held his hands in the air, "for here comes to save Ethra: *The Order of the Dragon!*"

"No, no," Bredikai said and sat back down to drink. The dragon huffed and his deflated pout was enough to rock the ship.

"Why ever not?" he pleaded.

"Sounds too wizardy."

"Oh oh- I have one!" exclaimed the wraith. "*The Dragon Force!* Yes?"

"Too...something," replied the killsmith. "Sounds like we need epic ballads to follow us wherever we go. We haven't even come across a bard in months. Months? A year? How the fuck long have we been at this... " she pondered to herself.

"Well you have a go since you don't seem to care for anything," Lamure said.

"Alright," Bredikai said with her chin in her hand. "How about *The Killsmith's Fellowship?* Has a nice ring to it, I think."

"No, indeed not; that is entirely too scholarly for the likes of us," Solannus said. "And one wants it to roll off one's tongue."

"You just don't like it because it doesn't have the word *dragon* in it," Bredikai pointed out. "And I vote against that because it makes you sound like the leader. The goal is to choose a name that sums up our quest." She made the shape of a circle with her hands to emphasize collectivity.

"True, but we have several quests."

"I thought the name was supposed to speak to the nature of our group," Lamure pointed out. "We could go for something like *The Supernaturals*."

"We're not a traveling band. *And now we present The Supernaturals performing their masterpiece 'Ode to the Dragonfather'.* No," chuckled Bredikai.

"I be likin' *The Pirates of Par'nell*-"

"No."

"*Friends of Ethra*?"

"What are we, a charity?"

"I still like *Cronun-clan*."

"Nothing good ever came out of a clan," Bredikai said. "Trust me on that."

"I have it lads: we be *The Curses of Ethra*," Lesley declared and they paused.

"Meeeeh," Bredikai said. "Explain."

Lesley leaned to rest on his right arm while he raised a cup in his left hand. "We be right cursed, as you see, an' so is the wraith-lass. Likely cursed herself- been waitin' on her to realize. Then I reckons Borghalus cursed the day Scales here was born. An' you, lass- you like to curse up somethin' fierce."

"You do enjoy emphasizing," Solannus said to the killsmith and Bredikai nodded.

"It be the one thing we've got in common."

"Oh, I don't know," Lamure said, not entirely on board. "Why not play to our strengths and pick something epic or inspirational? With such a name you draw focus to our worst attributes."

"But it be them attributes what brought us all together, lass, wouldn't't'cha say?" Lesley argued.

"That's... not entirely untrue. Bredikai help, I'm out of argument."

"If such is the criteria then the word *dragon* must be reconsidered!" Solannus cried, tapping a claw on his keg and they were back to the beginning with renewed uproar.

On and on went the debate as drinks were shared, cursed coins were tossed and two creatures of the serpentine line placated in turn. The early evening mirth rejuvenated the company and their good cheer lasted them, dragging all into a fair eve of midnight rainbows trailing across the twin moons. This unspoiled moment they agreed to enjoy, for they could not have known that they would sail a month and some days and their stocks would wane. Sadness melts into happiness, melts into sadness, and on it goes as is ever the flow of time's current. It was all they could do to cling to hope in the face of a horizon ever out of reach and a sky that grew colder with each unhindered dawn.

CHAPTER 9: IT'S ALL RELATIVE

"Can't sleep or too drunk?" Bredikai asked, settling beside Solannus. He was by the starboard side of the deck, quietly taking in the night sky. They had been sailing blindly for too long and, despite everyone's best efforts, their moods were souring. Even their conversations had turned depressing. The company was not the problem; it was the fact that their lighthearted topics naturally devolved into scrutiny of the growing darkness, killing their moods and increasing the severity of their misgivings. More than once the triplets noted how strange it was that the Morduanas was so lifeless. It was an unsettling calm they sailed through. The effort to keep their spirits up was growing exhausting and Bredikai appreciated that they had all had too much to drink and fell asleep so she could converse with Solannus in private. Enchanted drinks were a god-send.

"A bit of both but it's no bother," replied the dragon. "I've enjoyed being in the open air, under the moons."

"It's gotten cold," Bredikai said.

"This region knows only cool summers and long winters," Solannus replied, withdrawing again into his own thoughts.

Bredikai leaned against the wooden railing and made another attempt. "We're sailing awfully close to Kharkharen. I suppose that's where we were meant to go, in the end... Just like Althaea said," she pointed out but the dragon made no response. "No idea how we'll find that eye, though."

"I have already found it," Solannus said calmly and before Bredikai could comment he lifted a claw into the air and pointed at the stars. The killsmith looked at a particular cluster, spotting nothing of note at first. She angled herself to follow Solannus' claw more closely. Pale white starlight greeted her, more shine, more gleam and then; a single spot of gold, now so distinguished from the others she wondered how it had escaped her notice.

"Hmmm... We're not far from the coast- or so Ashley says. Good thing, too. Stocks are running low. We should disembark before we make a move on that eye."

"No," Solannus said. "We are too close to risk leaving it there. Borghalus will have seen it by now."

"Then why would he leave it unguarded?"

"An abundance of confidence? Underestimation of me and my cursed company? Who knows," Solannus said. "I doubt he expected me to come anywhere near Kharkharen. Perhaps it merely looks unguarded."

"That makes more sense," Bredikai mused. "Or maybe..."

"What?"

"Maybe he can't stand the thought of touching it," Bredikai offered and a shiver went down her spine from the cutting wind. "Remember what King Manael said: '*where your mother dwells*'. I saw what he did to her, Sonny. We all did. We lived it. There's more you're not telling me." The dragon never took his gaze off of the eye. He looked as though he was silently communicating with it, maybe even demanding answers of his own from the golden orb.

"Please Bredikai, do not press me for it," he said and she could hear his heart thumping at an off-beat pace. It was erratic and then tempered. So it went for the better part of a minute until the rhythm came to a calm.

"Whatever the reason for your secrecy, let's keep our wits about us," she said, understanding that no more tales would come from the dragon that evening. He could be a stubborn old goat when the subject matter didn't suit him but she had grown accustomed to his sensitivities and had more success when approaching difficult subjects gradually. "How do you propose we advance?" she asked. "Lamure can fly but likely won't be able to touch it. But she... *can* touch the Hexia! Right? Right!" she said, not waiting for an answer. "And you had the nerve to call my sword a cheap piece of shit."

"No, I called it cheap. *You* called it a piece of shit," Solannus corrected but Bredikai was pacing to and fro, her thumping loud enough to jar some incohesive mumbles out of the snoozing skeletons and the snoring wraith. Their captain had also opted to indulge in drink and it was nothing short of a miracle that the Titan was handling itself.

"Think they've had enough?" Bredikai asked, pointing to their counterparts. "Really makes you think twice about the whole *sleep when I'm dead* bit," she added and the dragon snorted. He was out of sorts and she was getting annoyed with his terse responses. Their verbal melees were starting to suffer from the dragon's increased bouts of depression and Bredikai was slowly losing her patience.

"What's with you, huh?"

"Nothing is with me," the dragon replied curtly and the killsmith began to simmer. Instead of knocking him senseless with the hilt of her sword she decided to wake up the crew. They could sleep when they were re-dead and there was no time like the present to make a move on that eye. She had had enough of the open water and even the pirates were looking like they were ready to disembark- though they'd rather throw themselves into the saltwater than admit it. Bredikai roused

Lamure whose drowsiness proved difficult to shake off until the killsmith shoved the Hexia into the wraith's hands and pointed at the sky. That got her attention.

"See that there?"

"Where?

"There."

"I don't- hmmm. That yellow stain in the sky?" squinted the ghost-princess.

"That stain happens to be my father's eye!" Solannus huffed.

"Don't mind him, he gets all defensive when you say anything regarding the *bits*."

"Ill-mannered as ever," he grumbled and Lamure looked at Bredikai, wondering what had so vexed their scaly colleague. Bredikai rolled her eyes and ignored him.

"It's the eye- just like your father said," she told the wraith. "So you're going to take the sword, cut that thing out of the sky and let it fall down to us. Which means.... that we'll have to be directly under it in order to catch it. Which means.... if it really *is* being guarded, we'll have to be ready."

"I love it when she plans out loud. It is truly a thing of beauty, watching you work, killsmith," Solannus said and even Lamure was affronted by his attitude. She had not intended to wake up in the middle of dramatics.

"You're being a tad rude," said the wraith.

"As opposed to our leader's habitual mode of existence," the dragon said and looked away. Maybe it was the nerves gaining on him or the fact that they were drawing closer to Kharkharen with each passing minute but, for once, Bredikai let him huff it out and took the helm. Lamure was at her side.

"Do you think there's something bothering him?"

"There's always something bothering him," snapped the killsmith, looking at the helm like it was an otherworldly object with that damn skull perched on its top rung. "He's utterly incapable of being happy for extended durations because he has no inner peace. They beat self-acceptance out of him when he was young," she said and then yelled, "but now he's just *choosing* to be a spoiled, dramatic dick." Solannus voiced no answer but the dragon had learned a thing or two about how to communicate with his human so he replied by lifting a choice claw at her.

Lamure was sorry she had mentioned it. Sure all their nerves were beginning to wind tighter by the day but, so far as she was concerned, that was no reason to snap at each other. And she would be the last creature on Ethra to make that point to either of them so she opted to wake the triplets instead. They needed pirate expertise to navigate them as closely to their unknown coordinates as possible.

The pirates were not light sleepers and the wraith had to bang together several enchanted goblets by their heads to get them out of their funk. Once they were awake, Bredikai alerted them to their plan and relinquished the helm to Ashley. She took the Hexia back to wipe it on the baggy rogue-clothing she had acquired from the hold and Lamure waited for her to cool down. She felt Solannus staring at her.

"More sassiness and obscene gestures, Master Dragon?" Bredikai asked. "You're saltier than the seas these days."

"I have come to a decision," Solannus said, choosing to ignore the jab. "Once we have the eye I will lead you to my former hold. You need proper clothing and armor if we're to continue as a company."

Bredikai stopped her sword-shining just long enough to

make the pause uncomfortable for the wraith as well as their skeletal voyeurs. "And what gave you the idea that we wouldn't be continuing together? Is this what all your bitchiness is about?" She demanded an answer but he was hesitant to give her one. When he stood around and fidgeted, looking everywhere but at his group, Bredikai knew that she had called him out successfully.

"The way things stand…"

"Borhalus is going to kill us. Yes, I'm aware," Bredikai said as a matter-of-fact and waited for him to say something new for a change.

"I can't ask any more from you. From any of you… " Solannus confessed.

"I know."

The dragon looked at her in confusion. If she was making a point then it went over his head and the rest of the company shrugged in turn. They had little to offer when death was the subject of conversation.

"I don't follow," Solannus said at last.

Bredikai wiped the hilt and Lamure held out her hands but still the killsmith would not give up the sword. The wraith waited awkwardly.

"I know you can't ask any more from me and it'd be mighty selfish if you did," Bredikai said calmly. "I might just tell you to fuck off, actually. That's why I'm not going to put you in a position where you have to ask. And I don't believe I have. I made a promise; to you, to my King and to myself. And this is exactly the point I've been trying to make; freedom of choice. I'm a grown woman and almost exactly where I set out to be. I'm a killsmith and that's a job I take very seriously, Solannus. It's my life. It's all I have to my own name. There are no kingdoms waiting for me when this is over... No children to continue my line. I came to terms with that long ago..." she said and Solannus was unsure of what to make of her statement.

"Please Bredikai- do not pretend that you do this out of the kindness of your heart-" he ventured but she stopped him.

"I've never made such a claim," she said defiantly. "From seeing this mission through I stand to gain my professional freedom and the world of Ethra is relieved of a poison that threatens to turn our lives for the worse. I told you before; I'm not a charity. For all I know we're the evil that needs to be stamped out and Borghalus the unforeseen savior of the world. Let history judge me if it can remember me- I couldn't give a fuck right now. But I know I'm where I need to be and that I'll never let a loud-mouthed serpent- or anyone- silence me again. Are you, Solannus?

"Am I what?" he asked defensively.

"Are you where you need to be?" He was quiet but now his silence triggered her anger. "Oh spare me the soul-searching, will you. If you have to think about it that long then maybe you should be the one to bow out."

"Perhaps I just might!" Solannus cried.

"Bet you you don't have the balls. Or the sense of direction!"

"Bet you whatever I've got it's bigger than yours and you can't tell a sextant from a quadrant!"

"Lads!" hollered Ashley from the helm. All the squabbling had put him in a foul mood that was already annoyed at being woken up from a delightful dream filled with sirens and floating chests of the boxum kind. It was a delightful surprise to the triplets that, while they did not *need* to sleep, they could choose to do so all the same. Having been yammered out of his reverie, Ashley was uninterested in quarreling. "Hold on to your bets tils we can all join you. We be close now. Are you ready, wraith-lass?"

Bredikai shoved the Hexia carelessly at Lamure but every time the wraith was physically able to hold something she was grateful for it.

"We're not done with this conversation," Bredikai said to the drake but they turned to watch the wraith in action. Lamure was slow to ascend at first for her experience lay primarily in horizontal floating. The more she climbed the greater speed she gained. The pale blue glow of her spectral self grew smaller until she was about as big as the yellow dot she meant to carve out.

Little did the group realize that they were holding their breaths, watching the small blue dot twitter and flutter around a yellow one like a deranged moth. Even Solannus' eyes weren't enough to distinguish the details. Then they saw the yellow dot quiver.

"By me Mother, she's done it lads!" Lesley yelled as the golden speck slowly dropped from the sky, growing to the size of a fine orb as it drew closer. Bredikai held her arms out and the remainder of the group followed suit.

"Bet you deck-dogs a keg I catches it first!" Ashley said and everyone, including Solannus, took that bet with much enthusiasm. But the eye was not yet within reach and the group was pushing and shoving to the point where Lamure's cries fell on deaf ears. Suddenly, the awaited remnant was gripped between long brown talons and swept away from their grasp. At once, the gut of a second creature hammered into them and it was large, with enough momentum to knock them all down- even the dragon.

Stunned, Bredikai reached for her sword but it was never around when she needed it most and Lamure made swiftly to bear it to her. Quickly they regrouped in the center of the deck as a yellow wyvern, now joined by a third, all sick with frenzy and blood-red eyes, crawled onto the deck while the first sought to escape with the great eye of Septiannus. Bredikai called out and Lamure raced to plunge the pulsing Hexia into the fleeing wyvern's tail. The wraith flew with all her might and managed to cut the tail off in a single stroke. The creature howled as the lump fell on deck nearly crushing the killsmith. The ship rocked from the impact but luckily nothing had been punctured. The wyvern was intent on escaping with or without its tail and it wobbled around while its wings pulled it ahead.

One of the creatures on deck was circling Solannus as the dragon protected his perimeter with deep growls. The yellow beast salivated in return and they paced around one another menacingly. The last wyvern was being dealt with by Lesley and Murray but it's crimson focus was fixed on Bredikai.

"Ashley!" the killsmith yelled and the pirate understood her command. Like a spider he lunged and crawled from sail to sail until he was grappling with the tailless monster who would not relinquish the eye. The pirate was getting in a few clean slices and the poisoned blood dripped onto Bredikai's shoulder before she could dodge it. The killsmith screamed in pain. She was waiting beneath them to catch the eye but Ashley seemed unable to match the serpent's feline flexibility. The wyvern had Ashley's ribcage in its mouth now but it had not accounted for the necrotic nature of the skeleton and it was impossible for even its spiked mouth to break through the pirate's bones. It couldn't even close it's jaws.

Bredikai grabbed the Hexia from Lamure and made for Ashley but the other wyvern was cunning and cast the others aside like cloth. It took flight quickly and swooped down to tear at the killsmith, ripping her flesh, tearing at her left shoulder and bearing down on her. The pain was mind-numbing and Bredikai barely had the lung power left to howl. The skeletons were kept away by the force of the creature's tail. Bredikai used what was left of her energy to turn around with her ravaged back pressed against the wooden deck. The rabid wyvern towered over her and as it went in for the kill, mouth agape and salivating poison, Lesley and Murray took hold of its long neck momentarily stalling it. The beast twisted and pulled and made every attempt to fling them off when Bredikai stuck the Hexia deep into its belly, twisting her blade to ensure the kill. The contents of the beast's stomach spilled onto her and she rolled out from under it before the beast could crush her with its deadweight.

Bredikai stumbled to her feet before stomach acids could drown her but she was not entirely successful in her escape. Bloodied and broken, there was not a thing Lamure could do for her as the killsmith fell back on her knees.

"Get the eye!" she yelled, tossing the Hexia to Lamure. The wraith flew to the struggling Ashley but it was no use as the wyvern flung the pirate from his mouth, straight into the wraith whom he could no longer pass through. Lamure lost her hold on the sword and the creature was out of sight faster than they could act.

Solannus had been gnawed all around his neck but he had managed to overtake his adversary and now stood on the beast's wing as the ferocious neck still darted forward to catch a piece of dragon between its jaws.

"You may not wish to see this," he said but as the company drew closer they felt something raw and animal, a blind frenzy for the kill- and it was emblazoned in the wyvern's eyes. The creature had had its heart twisted and there was nothing more to say about it. Solannus grabbed the beast's head and a decent portion of its neck in his mouth, ripping it out as one plucks out a tooth. He spat out his kill and walked away from the carcass to Bredikai's side. She was gasping for air and shaking from the quick-acting poison. The company gathered around her and Lesley put himself at her side to prop her head up. Bredikai was swelling and turning blue, clawing at her neck for want of air.

"What do we do?!" Lamure pleaded.

"Got to clean out the wounds, lass! Dress 'em out as best we can," Ashley said and Murray sped below with the wraith to find anything of use. Solannus, close to forfeiting what was left of his nerves to a growing panic, paced around frantically. When she began to choke he could only think to puncture a small hole in her neck to let out the excess blood clotting her throat. She breathed slightly easier for the moment. The dragon was in pieces.

"Uggghhh fucking... he only... sent three... How... insulting..." Bredikai gurgled out and began to wretch. Solannus did his best to shut her up and keep her focused on breathing. To their surprise, Sir Hiss-a-Lot was most useful as a tourniquet around her neck and his contributions were appreciated by all. Even Fluffers was busy flying out what little supply he could carry from below deck. Murray was back quickly with more bindings and off-putting potions and Ashley ran down to gather anything else. Quickly they cleaned and disinfected the girl, with Solannus licking at any open wounds he could find. His saliva helped to numb the pain and worked as a mild anti-venom; for dragons are cousins to wyverns and face no such peril from their poison.

They kept a close watch on Bredikai for the next few hours. It was a fact that the great eye was gone beyond their reach. No doubt it was being whisked away to the claws of

Borghalus but they thought themselves lucky to have retained the wing which had gone unnoticed by the warped creatures.

Bredikai trembled and wailed when the poison pulsed through her and Lesley and Murray used all their strength to keep her from throwing herself overboard into the cold saltwater. She was burning up. They were at it for the better part of an hour, feeding her whatever herbs and enchanted potion they could identify. Look as they might, there was nothing in the Titan's inventory to act as a proper antivenom but they had patched the girl up as best they could and she was relieved of most of the burning, though it passed through her in turns as if she was being subjected to an infernal spray.

"This will not keep her for long" said the dragon. He had not stopped pacing for a moment and they wondered how much more rocking the ship could handle before giving out. "We have enough to slow the spread of the poison but nothing short of dragon medicine can stop it from killing her."

"Ugggghhh," moaned the girl, draping herself over Lesley who was most dedicated to his role as caregiver. "I feel like you're blowing fire up my ass," she croaked and drooped over the skeleton.

"Lay her down on her side," Solannus directed. "You three, hold tightly to the wing." The triplets obeyed him without question and gave the ropes attached to the wing of Septiannus a little more manpower. "I will hasten us to shore," the dragon said and it was no longer a question of stopping or not stopping. They were meant for Kharkharen, to the only safehold he could think to lead them. "From the shore we must travel quickly to my hold. I pray it has not been discovered."

With that the triplets held to the ropes and planted their feet firmly on deck. The dragon stood back and inhaled as deeply as his lungs would allow. Outwards he expelled a stream of fire that put an immense amount of pressure on his father's wing-turned-sail and thrust the ship forward. He repeated the expulsion ten, perhaps even twenty times, until the Tidal Titan cut through the sea like a blade through soft butter.

As they propelled through, Bredikai lay face down on the deck with Sir Hiss-a-lot suffocating her neck and Fluffers tapping a foot every now and again to check that she was still alive.

"Bredikai," Lamure said softly. "How are you feeling?"

"Like a volcano's roasting me from my ass to my face," came the muffled reply. But the wraith figured that if she was well enough to complain then the medicines were doing something at least and she coaxed the girl up to take more. Bredikai slowly sat up, still woozy from whatever they had been forcing down her throat, but she managed to stay up long enough to look at the living fuel source a-blowing them towards salvation.

"Look!" Lamure yelled, "I can see land! Just keep puffing!"

Solannus kept at it but he was getting dizzy and ready to pass out for even a dragon has physical limits.

The groggy killsmith winced and waved one arm at the dragon. "What's your plan for stopping?" she croaked at which point Solannus stopped puffing and pursed his lips. Not only did the Tidal Titan not slow down, it gained speed as the wind picked up and the ship pierced across what remained of the Morduanas.

"We didn't think this through," Lamure said.

"Name one thing we've thought through until now," said the groggy killsmith. She couldn't raise her voice but the point was made loud and clear. "Brace for impact, folks."

With the skeletons being thus cursed, jumping ship was not an option. In any case, Bredikai didn't have the energy to jump or swim to shore and she threatened to kill Solannus if he so much as thought to abandon them. So the company braced themselves and closed their eyes as the monstrous vessel shot through shallow water and began to skid on its surface like some sort of nautical pebble until, on the third skip, it flung itself onto the shore. Sand exploded around them and they finally, *finally* skid to a stop.

"Everyone alive?" Bredikai wheezed from beneath a pile of kegs. Whatever she was sure was broken she couldn't feel at this point. She was a battered stump surviving out of sheer spite.

"No," came the answer and she knew that her company was well. Solannus had been flung farthest and the skeletons could be found all across the grassy weeds dotting the shoreline. Luckily no one was wet, the dead remained undead and the living lived to mock the cold hand once more.

With Bredikai essentially paralyzed, Solannus lost no time in taking the lead and he bid all able crew to de-wing what was left of the Tidal Titan. They ransacked from the ship only what they could carry; the last of the medicines, a keg or two of the best drink, the pirate-mother's skull and a few other choice knick-knacks. The pets had priority over Ashley's satchel. The group was to board Solannus so that he could navigate them quickly to his secret sanctuary and they would make the journey hidden beneath the wing while holding it above their heads. They had made it to the shores of Kharkharen, indeed, but they were still in the outskirts, removed from the epicenter of the mountainous region. Solannus could trust in neither darkness nor uninhabited shores. With dawn fast approaching they would need to hurry along but the able undead kept plucking from the vessel whatever they thought might be of use. Solannus' insistence that he was not a pack mule went ignored.

The dragon's hold was no easy distance. The journey took them the better part of two days, whereupon they were feeding the killsmith mere droplets of what medicines remained. They stopped at regular intervals for fear of being spotted by winged terrors. Trees were sparse but, even so, both Bredikai and Solannus had been abused by one too many wood, utterly refusing to take shelter under a sparse canopy. In his mind Solannus thought they owed their stealth to the great wing they moved under, and it helped his heart to imagine that a piece of his father was speeding them to salvation.

The dragon's humble hold was located within the shadowed crevice of a dormant (Solannus assured them) ice volcano, the road winding upwards and getting steeper with each step. A few times even Solannus lost his footing, skidding against the steep snow. The skeletons helped steady their friend and so continued a hellish climb.

Solannus had chosen this cave because of its inconvenient placement. The mouth of the cave was high enough to afford a fair vantage point to keep track of comings and goings but it was difficult to detect from afar and one of many hundreds of similar holes that bore through the volcano. Not even his father had known of this hideout and Solannus had squirrelled into his cave what little possessions he had acquired over the years. He was glad for whatever he could do for his company and wracked with guilt for Bredikai's state as Lesley repositioned her so that she could vomit freely. The girl could only bear to lie on her stomach for her back was spent but traveling with constant pressure on her belly meant for unending nausea.

Through their whisper-laden journey the wind grew icy and at one point the company was forced to travel through a light snowfall that, fortunately, only turned into a blizzard once the dragon had delivered them to his petty paradise. Solannus lay down, exhausted, and the triplets helped Bredikai descend. She limped around to stretch her legs and considered herself lucky to have foregone the initial paralysis. It was dark at first but Solannus had always made use of a fireplace when he could and he had carved out a decent hole that would provide sufficient light and heat. He was also excessively delighted to have guests in his cave, no matter how he may have sworn to never return.

"Anyone else hot? No, of course not," Bredikai groaned and stripped down as Lesley stared.

"You'll freeze to death," Solannus said. "Put something warm on."

"Just let me catch my breath," replied the killsmith and limped around darker corners where smaller caves rested like private rooms. Solannus brought over a cloth he draped on her shoulders and paid no mind to her refusal. The company sat down around the dragon-made fireplace and took a moment to orient themselves as Bredikai waddled to them and took her place farthest from the heat.

"Not a golden coin in sight," she announced, biting back the pain. "Solannus, you rebel."

"It is hardly rebellion," the dragon said. "I couldn't afford to keep gold as it would attract my kin and I needed to be removed from prying eyes."

The killsmith shook every now and again but insisted that she was feeling better. The pirates warned her to not be fooled for such was the way with wyvern poison and no doubt enough of it was still swimming in her body to warrant better medicines. Solannus told them to rest as he busied himself with strange concoctions and they were cozy in their own spaces now, appreciative of the dragon's hospitality.

"Reckon at times I miss livin', lass," Ashley said to the killsmith, and it was the first time he admitted such sentiment. "Poison or rot, sickness or death; I'd trade places with ya- if I could."

"I miss my home," Lamure sighed, following suit. "Don't misunderstand, I'm seeing more of the world than I ever dreamt, but there's hardly promise of return. This Borghalus business... I feel it gnawing at my heart... Maybe it's because we're in Kharkharen after all, but he is a greater reality to me now and I admit that that was not the case when we first met," she said, looking into the fire. She reached out to touch it and laughed sadly as her hand went through the flame without disturbing its tendrils.

"I miss my father," Solannus joined in while blending choice liquids together. Sir Hiss-a-Lot had been removed from Bredikai's throat and was now acting as the dragon's support system. "He knew how to approach any situation- *any*- with a clear head. He would know what we are meant to do... What do you miss, Bredikai?" he asked the shivering killsmith.

Bredikai thought about that. She had had no father or mother to speak of and no siblings she was aware of. Living a nomadic life had not afforded much attachment with regards to location and, while she held Etherdeign in her heart and loved her Grandfather and Zira, she couldn't quite say that she missed anyone or anything in particular. Surely she would have the chance to see them again and, in that sense, she was the luckiest of her company.

"Bredikai?"

"Hmm? Oh, I don't know. I guess I'm more detached than you all," she said and when they judged her she rolled her eyes at them. "Don't be so melodramatic, you guys. Sure there are things... Like waking up to a quiet dawn not knowing where the road will take me. Sometimes it's to new adventures, sometimes it's a breath of familiar air. New lands, new kingdoms... I never know and that's the beauty of it. But I'm living that now so it wouldn't be fair to say I miss what I'm still experiencing. I guess you could say I love my life the way that it is and the thought of giving it up... Well, that's just not going to work for me, you see. That's how I ended up on this campaign." She scratched at her sore throat but was careful not to poke at the hole Solannus had put through her. It had scabbed over nicely but she could feel the uncleanliness of the poison just beneath the surface.

"That's right," Lamure said. "You alluded to that back on the ship. I hope my father didn't expect to have the Titan returned," she added as an afterthought and Bredikai smiled.

"Yep," continued Bredikai, "the King of Etherdeign himself promised me that he'd grant me amnesty from guild registration- which is great because I think I passed the due date before we reached the Morduanas."

"So you're truly not helping me out of the kindness of your heart?" the dragon teased, uncorking a particularly rancid mixture that was sure to do the trick.

Bredikai chuckled, knowing that Solannus was laboring under no such illusions and merely poking fun at her. "Let's face it, I'm not the pinnacle of altruism. It'd be a fine world if people like me didn't have to go around killing things but where there's good there's always bad. Good thing, too, or I'd be out of the job!"

"You said it, lass," Murray said. "But the world ne'er be turnin' how we be expectin' it to." Her brothers agreed with that sentiment.

Solannus looked at the killsmith as a shiver shot

through her. She grabbed one of the random bottles they had brought from the ship and downed the entire thing without care.

"Have you ever regretted a kill?" the dragon asked. Bredikai wiped her mouth and gagged. Solannus plucked the bottle out of her hand and replaced it with the first round of what horrendous concoctions she couldn't guess at.

"To be honest I don't think about it anymore," she said, closing her nose off to the stench. "I made a promise to myself when I became a killsmith that I would never abuse my rights. I'm not a lawmaker; I see shit go down and fix the problem if I can- for spoils. It's never much but it's always been enough to meet my needs."

"Drink. Ah-ah, the *whole* thing, thank you," said the dragon. "Not a student of philosophy, I see."

"Actually you'd be surprised!" Bredikai smiled. She drank the entire foul mixture in a single gulp and her smile was no more. A tear slid down her cheek and her lip quivered but the dragon was merciless in his liquid assault, quickly replenishing her cup with the next round. "Every hrmmachh," she continued and tried to stop herself from gagging, "every kingdom has its own variation of the rules but the one thing they have in common is that they make you enroll in courses- one of them being philosophy- before you become a licensed killsmith. There's some random knowledge for you all."

"We be goin' through somethin' of the kind, too," Ashley said and Bredikai almost regurgitated her medicine.

"Excuse me?"

"Surely not the finer grammatical rules of the international tongue," Solannus said and they all laughed.

"You jest, lads, but it be normal for pirate children to

get some form'a education on ships, seein' as hows we aren't landed enough for proper schoolin'," Ashley pointed out and they looked at one another with impressed surprise. "Mother saw to us learnin' geography an' basic creature features... Art'a combat an' the like. We was ne'er too keen on parlayin', though, were we lads?"

"But you've killed, all the same," Bredikai said.

"Aye, an' there ain't no other way to say it, lass- but don't nobody be goin' into piracy for the charity!" the eldest pirate exclaimed. "We killed an' robbed an' plundered our fair share."

"But we avoided the landfolk much as we could," Lesley interjected. "Pirates be killin' other pirates for the most part an' that be for gain, not for sport."

"Gave 'em proper sea burials when we could," Murray concluded.

"If you ask me, this company is entirely too comfortable with death," tutted the dragon disapprovingly.

"That's why we never ask you," the killsmith said and they shared another laugh before growing sullen. As host, it was up to Solannus to keep his guests' spirits alight and for their particular mood he had the perfect remedy.

"But we are forgetting something!" he declared with a claw in the air. "This young lady has turned thirty and I believe that means that drinks are in order!"

"So it does, Scales!" beamed Ashley and the skeletons were swiftly on the job.

"Look at all the greys on my head. I only had two when we met, Sonny," Bredikai said. "We don't need to make a big thing out of this," she smiled but was overruled.

"Nonsense, nonsense," said the dragon. "You have

exceeded the due limit for guild registration before fulfilling your quest which, correct me if I'm wrong, means that you have likely obtained outlaw status. To Bredikai, our leader, the Killsmith of Etherdeign, Denier of Guilds, Bane of Griffins and other winged creatures!" he said and asked them to raise the goblets the triplets distributed. Solannus no longer looked darkly upon the kegs he had been made to haul all the way up the damned volcano.

"Is this a toast or a roast?"

"I shall dance the line in between," the dragon said and smiled mischievously.

"To Bredikai!" the group cheered.

Much to her dismay the dragon forbade her from drinking any more alcohol but was happy to replenish her medicine as long as she could stomach it. He insisted.

"Many happy returns and pray you live to see your thirty-first!" Solannus said and he was so jovial that they were all taken in by his good humor. "Now, if you please- I bequeath a fitting gift upon our maladied leader," he said and scurried about. Not finding what he was after, he disappeared deep into the cave as the group watched him in amusement and curiosity. Bredikai took this opportunity to spike her medicine with alcohol and, despite Lamure's fussing, she lived to tell the tale.

When Solannus returned it was with difficulty for he held various pieces of armor in his arms and had to do a delicate balancing act so as to not drop everything. The light was flickering and while it was lovely for the purposes of general ambiance, it made Bredikai pause and make certain that what she thought she saw was really before her. To her astonishment she was presented with the finest pieces of armor she had ever seen and though it was not whole, what pieces remained- the helm, the breastplate, one gauntlet, and some other odd bits- were now neatly laid out in front of her. It was a stunning coppertine, cleaned and polished by loving hands, not bright enough for the tone to be offensive, yet deep and pure like the last light of a setting day. Speechless, Bredikai leaned forward on her knees to trace her fingers against the gleaming breastplate that was devoid of its fauld and tasset, then the single gauntlet, all the way down to the greaves and back up again. The breastplate was not bare and upon closer inspection she found the pattern engraved into the noble metal. The get-up had clearly belonged to a knight of the highest order but to which kingdom it hailed she couldn't make out. Surely coppertine was the product of Etherdeign but it was not the only kingdom in the world to make use of the metal. The engravings were unlike anything she had seen in the wide world. What had happened to the former owner of this armor Bredikai could only wonder.

"Did... did you..?"

"No," Solannus said quickly, banishing the notion of such violence. "Ah, I inherited it, you could say. Rinn was his name. Sir Reginnald- but he went by Rinn. You would have liked him, I think." His voice grew soft and he turned to refill her medicine, tutting at her for spoiling the previous one with alcohol.

"Oh?" said Bredikai, letting her fingers rest on the cool metallic surface. "And what was so special about this Rinn?" Lamure floated towards the armor and was intrigued to find that her touch did not pass through. To the best of her ability she searched the tone of the armor but it bore only the slightest necrotic touch. To the wraith it seemed that what necrosis lay upon the metal had embedded itself long after the armor had been produced, but it was strange that the power would hold. Coppertine was a most stubborn metal and did not fare well with necrotic charms. The Hexia was a prime example of this. When she fell back into their conversation Lamure heard the dragon sigh and it was wistful, reaching back to a time best left unbothered.

"In my youth he was my dearest and only friend. More like an older brother, you could say," the dragon said and smiled. "The one I should have had." It was another expression veiling sadness but Bredikai wasn't going to let him off with half-assed explanations this time. While the skeletons and wraith continued to study the beauty of the metal marvel before them, Bredikai pressed for the details Solannus was averse to sharing.

"Human? Looks human," the killsmith said. "I don't recognize the sigil. Odd for a knight to bear a dragon on his chest. Where did you say he was from?"

"I don't recall that I ever knew," Solannus replied. "Perhaps I have blocked it from memory. My father would know those details. It was Rinn whom he entrusted with Borghalus' imprisonment in exile, you see."

"I... I see..." Bredikai said but her voice betrayed surprise and her eyes shot open with suspicion. She didn't even notice herself drinking the awful medicine anymore.

"So your father *did* actually choose to imprison and exile Borghalus rather than... you know. Even after he.. ah..." said Lamure and they all knew the incident to which she was referring.

"Indeed," replied the dragon but with all eyes on him now he didn't have a prayer of escape. He sighed and the company waited patiently. "My father could not bring himself to suffer his son's death, let alone be the one to bring it about. Despite everything... he chose imprisonment in exile. And Rinn would come and go, checking to make certain the prison held, bringing us news and in the meanwhile learning of our ways and teaching us of yours. You could say we grew up together as he was young- much younger than you are now, Bredikai, when he came to us."

Bredikai and Lamure exchanged glances as the killsmith coaxed more drink into the dragon. He glared at her but took the keg anyway and sighed once more before resuming his tale.

"Rinn would play with me for hours on end, whenever he came back home. But this was many years ago when I was a serling and before Borghalus committed his crimes. Father let Rinn go off on adventures when he wished. It would not do well for a human to be cooped up in Kharkharen. Oh, but he would tell me the most incredible stories about giants and harpies and sea-wolves and other evils he had defeated in combat. I was so taken in by them. Truly I wished to become a knight if ever I could have been anything other than half a dragon. Mother adored him. Father respected him like a son. When we played he would always pretend to be an ill-natured creature so I could be the hero that gallantly slayed him. I could barely puff out enough to light a candle. I did manage to singe his barely-formed beard off once. He was so proud of that stupid beard," Solannus chuckled softly.

Bredikai smiled at her friend. "Seems like a fine man. And what happened to Sir Reginnald?"

Solannus took a long sip and thought back to memories he had long since locked away. "After the... the incident, all of Kharkharen lay in shock. It was too terrible, you see, and Rinn felt the shock most keenly. In time he seemed to come less and less... I could tell he was growing older and indeed I was a serling no more; certainly too old to be entertaining fantasies of becoming a knight. I began to notice that a shadow had settled on his brow but I thought it to be my imagination getting the better of me for my brother's terror was locked away, his evils never to resurface. I do not understand much about human physiology but it seemed to me that a gloom was cast upon Rinn's heart; the grip of a phantom claw ever tightening and robbing him of his good nature. He still smiled and laughed when we were together but it was strained and I sensed… *something*. Something off."

"Like what?" asked Bredikai. "I'm a human. I feel like I can help out here."

"That's precisely it; I don't know," Solannus said sincerely. "He began to withdraw from our company and swiftly grew frail. He became irritable. It seemed to me that he was aging far more quickly than was his due, like a parasite was gnawing at him and bleeding his lifeforce out. Father would not speak of it. Rinn's visits became infrequent but when he did come they- he and my father- would spend longer hours together, away from all eyes and ears, uninterrupted and muddled by whispers. Then, one day, he was gone."

"Gone like how? Like he died in Kharkharen?" Bredikai asked, nervous tension stretched across her face. Lamure was on the edge of her seat and the triplets couldn't even divert their attention back to their drinks.

"Like I never saw him again," Solannus said. "Father summoned me one evening and he looked run-through. Even through your human eyes you would have been able to tell how drained he was."

"You know you say *human* like it's some sort of disease or like a, uh, urinary infection or something. Every damn time."

"Old habit."

"Anyway, what happened then?" asked Lamure.

"As I said, father summoned me and gave me what remained of Rinn's possessions. His armor was the greatest treasure among them. He told me that Rinn would have wanted me, the bravest of his squires, to keep it and honor his memory. It was covered in blood and from my father's severity I dared not ask what transpired between them. I never saw Rinn again and mourned him through the long years of my youth. I missed him dearly but father never spoke his name from that day on. And to be honest… I never quite forgave him for it." Solannus cleared the lump in his throat. "Something was broken in our relationship from that point on."

The triplets quickly refilled everyone's drinks and remained quiet, as they often did when such stories were passed around. Though it seemed that they always had some silly air about them, their pirate instincts had trained them all their life to listen and acquire as much information as they could. Solannus was the only dragon they had ever known but his pain was one they had all shared, even before forests and visions bonded them.

"That's quite the story," Bredikai said and mentally banned herself from commenting anything that might upset Solannus further. Then, of course, curiosity got the better of her. "I suppose it's safe to assume at this point that Rinn's no longer with us. I'm sorry for your loss, Sonny…" she said and he nodded. "You've always spoken so highly of your father…" she paused. "Any thoughts on the sigil? It's like the guy really wanted to be a dragon. Look, it's a human head on a dragon's body. Huh. He and you should have switched bodies."

"I've often wondered if I would, were I given such a chance," the dragon admitted.

"I would switch bodies with you for a day just so you could hear what a fucking elitist you sound like every time you say *human*," Bredikai teased to lighten his burdens and Solannus' laughter rang through the cave, warming the atmosphere with its reverberation.

"No, you're not putting enough exasperation in your voice," he said. "Just imagine trying to convey reason to the most nonsensical and tiresome of species-"

"I can't get Mother's skull out'a this accursed helmet!" Ashley barked and both the dragon and his companion exploded into laughter. Lamure shook her head.

"You be makin' fun of us, lads, but I was top of me class when Mother was alive," Murray said and they were hard pressed to not laugh at her proud declaration. "Not like these here gold-gluts. That there be the symbol of Eberen an' no mistake," the pirate stated and crossed her arms, utterly satisfied with her education.

"The what now?"

Lesley and Ashley leaned in closer as Solannus tried to dig the skull out with his claw.

"An' so it be!" stated the eldest skeleton and he took a moment to bask in his sister's glory. "Good on ya, lass."

"Eberen," continued Murray, "Great God, 'e was! Call 'im the beginnin' of all humans an' dragons. An' yous thinkin' us simple."

"Literally never heard of him. Is this someone you knew?" Bredikai said to the dragon. "Look who I'm asking."

"Ridiculous," Solannus huffed with his claw now wedged in between the skull and the helmet. The experience was really beginning to annoy him but Lamure was happy to find that she could help, tugging at the helmet with all her might.

"Scales here must now about 'im, at the very least," Lesley said, trying the gauntlet on for size.

When he felt the killsmith and the wraith staring

at him, Solannus gave up and just let his claw's fate be determined by the wraith. "It's one of those ridiculous creation myths that elders pass on to the young. Rinn used to tell me about how man and dragon were born of the same god, this Eberen character, who also created Ethra and the suns and moons, and whatnot. I assure you that Rinn himself bore no relation to a god- so don't get excited," he stated.

"Well, what's this god's story?" Bredikai asked but the only one interested in telling it was Murray. The pirate-lass stood as they all got comfortable once more and, with her goblet in her hand and wild gestures to the air, began her tale.

"Mother used to tell it all beautiful-like but I'll do me best," she said and cleared her non-existent throat. For a moment they were afraid that she was going to do voices and they'd have no chance of understanding her but thankfully she limited herself to just gestures and promised to keep her articulation clean. Solannus raised a keg for that alone. So began Murray's tale of Eberen and the forming of Ethra.

"Eberen created Ethra when all other gods had tired- for his spirit was fiery an' he had an energy much different from his kin. Many worlds had been created an' the gods wished to rest, havin' spent much of themselves to shape the darkness in their image. But Eberen was a lifeforce who seldom tired, an' he'd shaped no world of his own as yet. Always he'd had the others' stoppin' an' stayin' his hand. He longed for a land unlike any other, one bearin' the calms an' storms of his soul. So he set out to shape Ethra alone, ignorin' the words of wisdom from the other gods. They thought Eberen too unpredictable to shape a world but were happy to see him leave, for his protests had grown an' he was disruptin' the peace they so coveted. His misguided energy was too much for the gods to handle in their state so they urged him to stay away so long as he would.

"For a time Ethra was Eberen's paradise. He was alone to

create and unmake as he pleased. An age passed with the god shapin' his world but in his mind he could still hear the others sneerin' at his amateur hand. Eberen felt them watch an' judge his deeds which were ne'er good enough to outdo the great fantasies they'd created. But the fire in Eberen's soul burned brightest among the gods, so he gave in to his own vanity an' sought to make himself creatures greater than any his kin had shaped, strong as the gods themselves an' mighty to behold. Thus came about the first children of Eberen an' the gods watched with judgment in their eyes.

"The god toiled an' bent his children to his will but, try as he might, the creatures fell short of his vision an' Eberen could hear the heavens laugh at his failure. Angry at these simple designs, he wiped the first children from Ethra without a thought.

"The second children fared no better an' lasted shorter than an age by our reckonin', for they were too large and dumb for Ethra to carry. They almost broke the world apart with their weight an' understood nothin' of their creator. Great laughter filled the heavens again an' Eberen was quick to wipe his creations out. So ended the second children, without a thought.

"One day when he could stand the laughin' no longer, a vision came to Eberen from his own heart. He began to shape creatures within himself, watchin' as they grew an' took unimaginable forms. Eberen fed them from his soul, givin' different gifts to each creature who took 'em greedily for their own. Soon these beasts began warrin' against one another, one destroyin' the other, to then be devoured in turn. His soul was ravaged but this energy be pleasin' to Eberen; for the creature that remained would be the perfect design, worthy of his favor an' life on Ethra. Monstrous form whirled inside the god an' for ages he watched the fightin' like a stranger in his own soul. In time the bloodshed lessened but the war wasn't over, for two were left fightin' an' Eberen kept a close eye.

"They say the first was a great winged serpent made of fire an' greed- but within him lay a stout heart, disciplined an' proud. The second was a human made of water an' powerlust- but within him lay a tender heart, relentless and cunnin'. Eberen waited as the two battled, neither side provin' stronger than the other. While he waited he busied himself with the makin' of other things, like the moons an' Sun an' nearby stars, but he was grown tired after an age an' decided it was time to choose a winner. Eberen entertained himself by pickin' a side to favor. Sometimes it was the serpent, an' it's said that from him came the fires of volcanoes an' the blood of Ethra. Other times he favored the human, an' it's said that from him came the seas an' bottomless oceans. On an' on the god would turn his favor from one to the other, but neither was enough to claim sole victory. What Eberen didn't realize was that his creatures grew strong with his gifts an' his favor- stronger than their creator intended. The endless battle raged an' soon became too much for Eberen's soul to contain.

"Even the god's tireless energy was now spent an' he could no longer trust to his own strength to hold his children. Fearin' that his end was near, Eberen tore his children from himself an' fled from Ethra in shame, leavin' the creatures to suffer their fates alone. As punishment for his recklessness the other gods wouldn't do away with the creatures. They let 'em live as a reminder of Eberen's failure an' that he may ne'er forget the monstrosities he'd created.

"As for the children: they were awful to look at; nothin' like the humans an' dragons you see in Ethra now. Mindless an' left without a guidin' hand, they stopped fightin' an' learned of sadness There was an empty calm in Ethra an' the creatures retreated to far corners to shape their surroundings as pleased them most. No one knows which one felt it first but, in time, they grew lonely in their separate worlds. They sought one another an' knew comfort when they were together once more. Their battle was ended. Now eager to return to their maker, the creatures cried an' sent their wordless prayers to Eberen- but the god had abandoned 'em to retreat in shame. Such howlin' an' desperate tears reached the heavens that even the other gods- those who'd rejoiced in Eberen's failure- found their hearts moved. They took to populatin' Ethra with creatures both beautiful an' terrible to behold but the children wanted to behold their own kind an' in that the gods failed. In vain they tried to recreate the original two but they weren't enough to match the wild visions of Eberen's soul.

"They say that as punishment Eberen was brought to look upon his creations an' he, too, was moved to deep pity when he heard their cries. He had left his soul in Ethra an' it was callin' out for him, beggin' like wounded animals do. Unable to suffer the grief he'd caused his children Eberen broke himself in two. With what was left of his energy, he fashioned his one half as a great winged serpent an' the other half as a human, that his children may never be alone again. It's said that the split caused great quakes throughout Ethra; bent the skies an' tore open the lands 'til the oceans filled 'em an' great mountains rose. So the children of Eberen multiplied an' shaped the world, plentiful enough that they claimed much of the land. But the species grew distant over the ages 'til they'd all but forgotten that they were come from the same soul. Through the ages other gods an' lesser gods would leave their mark upon Ethra- but they cared only for their own creations, leavin' the children of Eberen to their own affairs. There are none who remember Eberen now and he is no more. Even the gods choose to forget his name. But the children live on, never alone, each keepin' a piece of Eberen's soul in their hearts."

Murray bowed and waited for her due applause.

"Fuck me, Murray, that was a beautiful story," Bredikai said with total awe and they all burst into applause- all except for Solannus. They were mentally drained in the best sense and it was almost like they had been transported to another world entirely, so moving was the tale the she-skeleton had regaled them with.

"And that's all it is: a story. *Obviously*," said the dragon, breaking through their mythology with a swift metaphorical punch to the gut.

"What's wrong with *you*?" the killsmith asked. "I don't look half as offended at the idea that we might be distantly related- and I've made a living through my thinning of the herd, if you please," Bredikai smiled evilly and raised her glass to him.

"Right she is, Scales, an' I'm almost offended for ya, lass," Ashley chimed in. "What bein' formerly human an' all... Why is that offensive to you, lad?"

"It *doesn't* offend me," Solannus sighed, struggling to clarify his sentiment. "We were discussing it mere moments ago, weren't we? You all know very well I would much rather be human than such a sorry dragon."

"Oh well that's just sad," Bredikai said, gathering up the pieces of her new armor. She tried on the breastplate for size and Solannus held his claw up so she could pluck the helmet from it and remove the skull. He delicately fitted the killsmith into her inherited breastplate but his irritation got the better of him as he pulled and tugged a little harsher than was necessary and the killsmith winced. "I think that story speaks a lot to our inter-speciel relations," Bredikai added, yelping with every indelicate prod.

"Just drop the subject, please."

"I most certainly will not. Come on Solannus, why don't you want to be related to me?" she whined.

"Aye!?" demanded the skeletons simultaneously. Lamure simply sat and sipped.

"*Because!*" the dragon said forcefully, pulling so tightly on the breastplate Bredikai could barely breathe. "Because it would mean that all these wars, all this fighting and bloodshed and frayed goodwill throughout the centuries- it's all been for nothing! Utterly pointless. I would not have us go to war with Borghalus if it was in my power to prevent it."

"I'm sorry," Bredikai countered sarcastically, pulling away from his rough hand. "Was it supposed to have a point? Does innate hatred ever have a logic to it or a foothold in reality? Does war ever amount to anything but misery?"

"What I mean is-"

"I know what you mean, Solannus," she interrupted. "Your heart's in the right place and that's something I haven't doubted from the moment I met you. But- and excuse me for being so blunt-" she said with a finger in his chest and Lamure slowly pulled the triplets out of the crossfire, "you're the worst kind of dreamer that I've met in a long time."

"That's the last gift I give you," Solannus huffed, grabbing the gauntlet with half of Lesley's arm still in it.

"Please allow me to give you the gift of reality in return," Bredikai said and held her goblet out to the side to be refilled with anything- she cared not what. "You and I can sit here and discuss the philosophies of war and politics until we've melted our brains but it's not going to stop the likes of Borghalus from tearing Ethra apart, stone by stone, until he reshapes it in the image he deems worthy- much like the god-father our friend here mentioned. And that image does *not* include us," she said, pointing at herself and all former humans. "But I don't have it in my heart to hate Borghalus, you see. He has a sense of purpose and, deluded as it may be, it's the one thing I can't hold against anyone.

"So here's something you didn't know about me- seeing as how we're all in a giving mood today: I spent a lot of my life feeding off of anger. You could say I let it get the better of me for longer than I care to admit. I was lost and screaming to be heard and searching for something to hold on to. Hatred became my support and that's a kind of poison that works faster and deeper than anything a serpent can inflict. I had been screaming for so long that, by the time I stopped, I had to learn how to listen all over again. I aim to live better now and the gods, or fortune, or whatever you want to call it, saw it fit to place us on a shared path. Borghalus I understand. He's busy screaming. It's you who begins to make less sense."

"Me? How so? I have been nothing but forthcoming!" cried the dragon and when his grip loosened on the gauntlet Lesley crept forward and reclaimed his arm.

"So you tell yourself but do you even recognize what you're trying to do?" the killsmith asked, growing more accusatory with every sentence. "And do you have the conviction to see it through? Your brother's committed to a course. I set mine the moment I left Etherdeign. What about you? You won't entertain the idea of becoming Dragonfather- though you'd be a fucking noble one; won't even see yourself as a true dragon... And that makes me genuinely sad, Solannus," she said sincerely. Her voice softened but her words lost nothing of their bite. "What am I supposed to make of you? How do I know where your heart will stand when we're looking into the demon's eyes and he breaks into our minds, chipping away at everything we know to be real? It doesn't take a soothsayer to guess what happened to Rinn... You won't bring yourself to say it but you're smarter than that. I think we all know what came from too much exposure to your brother's wickedness. So I'm going to kill that wickedness before it spreads. There's no other way and if you have second thoughts and try to stop me- I'll kill you." Bredikai spoke the words so calmly she hardly recognized her own voice but her severity was beyond doubt.

"Look at me," she said and made sure that the dragon

looked straight into her eyes. "I will kill you, Solannus. Your father took the merciful path and look where it's lead us. This is no longer a question of empathy. How do I know you won't leave me and run when it comes time to kill your brother?"

The triplets looked to Lamure and quietly pleaded with her to step in. At first the wraith thought about intervening but, upon due consideration, she decided that these two had long been destined for this brutally honest exchange. She whispered to the triplets as much, helping them to understand that it was better for them to clear the air now before it was too late. Borghalus' hand would come down hardest on Solannus and this was all Bredikai knew to do to stiffen his heart. In truth the killsmith knew no other way to prepare the dragon and it was not her intent to bully him so much as to force him to face reality. He had a tendency of avoiding difficulties and it was a dangerous habit to be flouting now that they were dancing on the edge of the blade.

"I am hurt that you think me so weak," Solannus said and their hearts broke for him but if Lamure had learned anything about the killsmith she wouldn't allow him to cower into an escape.

"No, Solannus, it hurts *me* that you think so little of yourself; that deep down in your heart you feel he deserves to live and you don't," Bredikai replied. "But there's little time to heal what's left of your self-worth and I can't do it for you. Lucky for you I don't much care for your brother's desired massacre. There's always going to be rotten ones like him. Would that we lived in a world where there were valid reasons to fight- and that's assuming that valid reasons even exist! But we don't so we're gonna work with what we've got. Now I don't know what Borghalus' problem is but at this point you can bet that I don't fucking care. If he could be reasoned with we wouldn't be here having this conversation. Maybe there *is* a better way to do things. If there is then I haven't figured it out and I don't want you fooling yourself any longer. We're going to face him and that's that."

They were waiting; waiting for the dragon to explode into rage or tears or some other drastic display of emotion. Lamure would not have been surprised if Solannus screamed them out of his cave, skeletons and all, into the wilds of Kharkharen. Instead the dragon tilted his head and refilled the killsmith's drink, politely handing it to her and watching her watch him.

"In that we are agreed, Bredikai," he said at last and the company calmed. "We will have to face him- you are right. I have tried to do things diplomatically, amicably, without harming others as they took from me all I held dear. A piece of my soul dies every time my hand is forced into violence. That is my character and I will not change it- not even for you. I do dream of a better world and I will not fault myself for it. But I know in my heart that merely sidestepping Borghalus is an impossibility. To me, he represents all that is going wrong with this world- all the badness we are allowing to prevail while goodness suffers and withers away. My brother is an extremist consumed with hatred towards those he is not willing to understand. He will not stop while he breathes. But, as you said before, maybe *we* are in the wrong. Maybe Mistress Althaea was right and I am the end of the line..."

"I wouldn't get too hung up on it," Bredikai said. "Let's worry about the uprising before we start worrying about the downfall. Sound fair?" Solannus smiled but it was a crescent of emotional exhaustion. He hung his head low. Brediai walked to his chest and gave him as big a hug as she could though her arms were not enough to stretch across his belly.

"Thank you for my gift," the killsmith said and Solannus patted her on her unharmed shoulder. "I don't know about gods or knights or anyone else but I'll cherish this all my life."

They sat for a few more hours after that, watching the fire and exchanging shorter stories, keeping their moods temperate, making up what they couldn't remember and exaggerating the rest for entertainment purposes. The alcohol had been enough to see them through the twisted celebration and, though Bredikai was gripped with the shakes every half hour or so, Solannus' vile brews eased her suffering until they were all lulled into a cozy sleep. Solannus kept the first watch for he had much on his mind and sleep evaded him. Icy winds spat snow into the cave and swept the clouds over both moons. Very little stirred across the land but the occasional night beast would dare to howl, putting an end to its unfortunate prey. Even the animals had grown scarce- not that they were ever plentiful around Kharkharen- but they were still in the outskirts where winter creatures should not have been uncommon...

Solannus watched the wind whip clouds around. A flake of snow fell on top of his snout and melted upon contact. The blizzard was dying down but he had enough supply to keep the fire going even if another one bore down on them. Now that he shared in Bredikai's newfound hatred of forests the dragon took no small delight in burning wood. He smiled to himself, looking at the killsmith every now and then. He was grateful for her sporadic shivering for it meant that she was still alive and that his medicine was proving potent enough to do *something.* He watched the midnight world a little longer until his keen ears picked up the sound of strife and suffering in the great distance. They had come to Kharkharen but never more could he bring himself to call it home.

CHAPTER 10: THE MOUNTAINS OF KHARKHAREN

Solannus was the last to sleep and the first to rise and it was the least rested he had been since they had first embarked on their journey, especially when compared to their time with the necromancers. His cave did little for his nerves and Kharkharen was much changed in too short a time. The very air had grown pungent, it seemed to him, and it was unfamiliar enough to sap what little emotional strength he had left for the next part of their mission. As far as he and the company knew they were three for three regarding his father's remains but Solannus was beginning to lose faith in the authority they would hold, even if acquired in total. He let that thought linger until it faded of its own accord.

The dragon walked to the mouth of his cave and looked upon the horizon, watching the lazy sun rise and shine onto the snow-capped lands. Not a single mountain was bare and where grasslands had lain the ground was blanketed with frost. The land had yet to ice over completely but it would not take long for winter to hold all of Kharkharen captive. Solannus filled his lungs with fresh chill, grateful to be away from the heat.

Bredikai was the next to rise. She was intensely drowsy from the mixture of medicines and alcohol she'd consumed but she was made of stiffer stuff and even the dragon was impressed with the small human's fortitude.

"I live to fight another day," she greeted the dragon with a groggy smile and surveyed the outside.

"I begin to think you might not even need a shield to face Borghalus," the dragon joked. "But I have one for you, in any case. I'm afraid I'm running low on swords."

"Don't worry about it," the killsmith yawned and shivered. Her stomach acids were eating through her so she leaned against Solannus to steady herself. "I wouldn't have taken another sword, anyway. The Hexia and I have had our fortunes tied for the longest time. Wouldn't feel right trading the old girl in." As she spoke and their hungover company began to awaken, Bredikai's attention fixed upon something in the air, moving away from Kharkharen almost beyond their sight. There was another one thing, and then another, until she spied a trail of dragons as small as ravens flying erratically.

"Now where are they off to?" she mumbled to Solannus.

"I smell blood," replied the dragon. His instinct urged him to hasty action and without a further thought he let out a grand call, making their presence known to the exodus. To the killsmith's horror a few of the dragons turned and made for their safe haven.

"What are you doing?! For all we know they're Borghalus' minions!"

"They are hurt Bredikai- I can smell it from here! Now make way," he said and had no sooner finished his sentence and pulled her out of the way when a battered trio of dragons ranging in size, color and grandiosity flung themselves into the cave.

The slowest dragon to enter was the most heavily wounded and he didn't land so much as fall in, skidding across the cold stone. An agonizing groan let them know that the creature was suffering most heinously and Solannus rushed to his side without invitation. He was bleeding from his side and his jugular appeared torn. His breathing was ragged but it was evening out, though he couldn't yet stand or sit. The triplets, now fully awake, drew their swords and Lamure looked to Bredikai but it seemed the drakes were too hurt to worry about their presence.

"Solannus," spoke the strained voice. "Is that you, boy?"

"Mergalus!" cried the dragon and looked at the others. "Torgen, Valtiga! What's happened to you?" There was blood to spare in the cavern and their great wounds accounted for the drakes' erratic flight pattern. Bredikai watched their interaction without a move but she could tell that the first two were now aware of their company and unsure of their next move.

"Our last desperate attempt to escape Borghalus," said the dragon Mergalus. Suddenly they heard a greater clamber from the outside of the volcano- the sound of claws digging into the stone and clinging to the mountain's side. Others had taken note of the refuge and were now determined to enter any hole they could find. The company listened for a while until the shuffling and piercing sounds subsided and the very volcano became a hive for the wounded in exile.

"Please, put your weapons down! They won't harm you," Solannus begged his group and Bredikai gave the order for the triplets to stand down. Upon second glance the drakes were in such a sad state that, for an amoral killsmith, they would have spelled an easy slaughter and a bounty of spoils. Full-grown dragons were still dangerous even in their worst condition though Bredikai noted that, as tense as the situation was, the Hexia didn't budge. Now the dragons' attention had been drawn to the other creatures in the cave- especially to the killsmith- and they were prepared to defend themselves, even though their growls were interrupted by pangs of pain. The killsmith took note of one important detail that would affect the outcome of this meeting greatly and that was the color of the serpents' eyes. They were all golden and she was relieved.

"My friends, please," Solannus pleaded with his brethren, "you are among friendly company here."

"Solannus," said the smaller dragon that was still twice Solannus' size. He was the one that had been referred to as Valtiga and he shone in crimson like a flame in the darkness, with a battered wing and torn scales. "We gave you up for lost!" Valtiga cried. "Yet here you are in strange company. With a *killsmith*- one who hunts our kin for sport!"

"I do no such thing!" Bredikai snapped and put her sword away. "Lords on high, I'm misunderstood."

"Easy, easy... Bredikai here is the leader of our company," Solannus said and hoped his introduction would be enough to appease everyone. "She does not hunt us for sport and has traveled with me thus far. I have no reason to question her loyalty. We are united in our quest to stop Borghalus."

"Borghalus commands greater numbers each day," said the ailing Mergalus and as his breathing steadied he was able to gather himself to a less vulnerable position. He now sat on his limbs the way they'd seen Solannus do many times, like a giant feline with limbs tucked beneath his body. "He has bent the minds of our own against us and means to wipe out all he deems a threat to our race."

"But how can he do this?" Solannus demanded. It was not shock that caused his outburst but the harsh reality that his greatest fears were coming to pass and he was not yet ready to witness the carnage. In his heart he now understood that this was but a fragment of what Bredikai had been preparing him for and he wished he had lent greater heed to her blunt assessments. He pushed the thought away. "Even his powers cannot be enough to take control of all minds."

"It is not minds he possesses, child, but hearts,"

Mergalus replied. "Hearts he commands through fear. All who allow for him to get a foothold must risk the invasion of his powers. Where his inherent magic fails his brute strength flourishes though I could not say which is the more dangerous."

"He is not Dragonfather yet- what authority allows for this madness to transpire?!"

"His cruel nature turned for the worse during his long imprisonment, Solannus. A greater power moves through him now and he will not suffer dissension. Neither will his minions," Mergalus said and Bredikai crept closer to see his wounds. "Those of us who would not serve under him and those whose hearts he could not possess are as you see. There are more, Solannus- far more than have entered this mountain; more who are afraid to go against him for fear of what may happen."

"Never in our history has dragon turned upon dragon," said the one called Torgen. She was younger than Solannus- if her voice was any indication of age- and a dark blue in color. Her horns had been torn off and the tip of her tail severed clean but it was the least of her worries for she bled heavily from her back and could barely suffer to move her wings. Their flight to safety had been hard on her. "Borghalus has set a dangerous precedent- one that too many are keen to follow. Much has changed since you ran, brother Solannus, but we do not fault you for it. To forfeit Kharkharen is our only hope for survival. You would do well to follow suit," the young dragon concluded.

Solannus turned to Bredikai who was taking their words in, then to the ailing elder bereft of hope. "He will be stopped, Mergalus. This I swear to you," he said but the elder met his determination with tired eyes.

"How can you stop such a blinding force who has forfeited all reason?" Mergalus asked. His voice was gurgling from what bile welled up in his belly and his body was too bruised for him to make sudden movements. "Forgive me, my boy, but you are small," he said, "much too small to undertake such a task. Even if it was possible, we could not ask you to slay your own brother. It is not our way."

Seeing Solannus' head hang low Bredikai thought it time to step into the conversation and offer her own thoughts, else the dragons would surely have been content to ignore her altogether. Killsmiths were least popular among dragons but Bredikai wasn't about to let that stand in her way.

"We possess half of the items necessary to proclaim a new Dragonfather," she spoke up and the dragons all flinched at her voice. "If we can reclaim the one that was taken from us we'll have the majority. Believe me when I say that none of this has come easy," she said.

For the first time since they had entered that cave Mergalus acknowledged the killsmith in full and his scrutiny lost no time in sizing her up. The girl shivered every few minutes or so and when he got a better hold on her scent Mergalus could smell trace amounts of wyvern poison still flowing through her veins. She would not last the week in that condition and from the look in her eye he presumed that she was aware of it. Mergalus took note of the tooth of Septiannus proudly hanging around the killsmith's neck and nodded solemnly at her. "Do you think that to be enough, human?" he asked when his analysis was complete.

"Eh? What does that mean, Solannus?"

"He means that our efforts count for nothing... That collecting the remains will only ensure that we become Borghalus' next target," Solannus explained. "He will kill us and claim the title."

"Borghalus cares nothing for titles," Mergalus said. "He

merely pretends to honor our traditions to bring what remains of the swarm to his side. He has already usurped much of the control over Kharkharen but when he claims the pieces his authority will be unquestioned."

"Doesn't look like it's being questioned all that much now," Bredikai mumbled to herself and coughed violently. Specks of blood caked her lower lip but she wiped them away, unconcerned. Lamure bid the triplets venture around the cave for extra medicines and Solannus told them what to look for. He could still smell the poison in her and, in such close proximity, knew the others could as well. Certainly the killsmith had the appearance of one who was healing and his medicines had done well to stave off her internal pain but the venom was still working its way through her, resisting the cures Solannus strove to conjure.

The elder dragon Mergalus shifted and groaned. Whether it was his group or the killsmith who was in a greater state of decay was uncertain but they were a company of rotting shells in that cave and their conversation was doing nothing to ease tensions. Skeletons and wraiths- and a killsmith to boot! What wicked sorcery had driven the son of Septiannus into such awful company, Mergalus thought, and his pity for the dragon who was still a child in his eyes grew tenfold. His old heart ached for what they had become and he wished for it to stop beating before he could see more of their future.

"Forgive us, Solannus. Forgive us, son," he said with his voice level and barely above a whisper. "You know the love we bore for Septiannus. You have his heart and your mother's endless kindness. Though she was not our kin, she became the best of us. She deserved her fate no more than you do yours. This we have always known among us. Forgive us, my boy. We failed you once and we must fail you again. You have not the strength to face Borghalus and you would summon your death were you to claim the throne," he said. "He is become something more terrible than I can relate. Understand that you are not enough to stop him. None of us are."

Solannus turned away and cleared his throat. He nodded at the ground and waited awkwardly, cursing himself for allowing his foolishness and childish expectations to dangle hope in front of his company. He was too ashamed to look at any of them but Bredikai's heart broke for her friend and the words spoken may have drained the dragon's spirit but they meant nothing to the killsmith. Not now when they were so far along the path. She would not suffer to have her friend's dignity trampled by the mere suggestion of size and phantom terrors for, in her mind, Borghalus had yet to take shape in full. She vowed at that moment to prepare herself for the moment of their first meeting with the demon and that, if nothing else, she wouldn't allow him to break her mind.

"My friend here is worth ten of Borghalus- even without the wings, even if he didn't have a spark of fire in his belly," Bredikai said and the other drakes scoffed at her naive bravado, thinking her too far removed to grasp the severity of Mergalus' words.

"It's alright Bredikai," Solannus said, "they speak the truth."

"Well I'm not having it," she declared. Mergalus looked at her with extreme doubt and prejudice but the killsmith had been triggered and would allow for no more despair. "Stop belittling yourself- I won't stand for it anymore, do you hear?" To their surprise the girl then whirled on Mergalus and Solannus feared for what her words may provoke. "All his life he's been undermined- and look what it's turned him into. You don't talk to him or me or anyone in my company that way," she demanded. "And that goes for you two, as well. Fucking sad dragons everywhere I look," she grumbled and, as expected, her words angered Torgen and Valtiga in a timely fashion. Mergalus bid them stand down while he met the girl's defiance head on.

"I do not know what has brought you together in company, killsmith, but you do Solannus a disservice by giving him false hope and resign him to death. Killsmiths are not ones to meddle in our affairs. If you care for him and for the well-being of your company, you will walk away from this and leave us to sort out our own."

"So now this has nothing to do with the rest of us? That's just great," the girl grumbled and Solannus tried his best to calm her temper but even he knew that his efforts were futile. "I think you're all a bunch of idiots if you think this problem is yours alone. No, Solannus, hold on. I'm going to have my say whether he wants to hear it or not," she said and the dragon sighed with resignation. The girl was determined to be destroyed by whatever dragon she could find.

"You are choosing to take Mergalus' words the wrong way-" Solannus ventured to say but stopping a killsmith on the warpath was like sending a fart into the wind and hoping it stayed in one piece.

"Am I now?" Bredikai snorted and turned to him. Her shivering was growing more frequent and Ashley had stuck his skull out once or twice to interject with some sort of medicine, opting instead to wait for the tides to ebb before risking his bones. As far as he was concerned she could have a right go at them and, though the killsmith didn't know it, they were all cheering her on from the shadows.

"Do you know what people see when they look at me, Solannus?" Bredikai asked. "You don't know or you won't say? Well, you don't have to because it's the same look you had in your eyes when we first crossed paths; the same way your elder here is looking at me now."

"Perhaps we see what you will not," Mergalus said and the killsmith paused. She looked at the elder dragon and the corner of her mouth lifted.

"I haven't carved my way out of ridicule and belittlement and underestimation to stand here and have our efforts counted for nothing," she said and for a fraction of a second Solannus thought he saw the gleam of red in her eyes. He blinked rapidly and it was gone so quickly he told himself that he had imagined it. "I don't know why my sense of worth should be so offensive to everyone," Bredikai said calmly. "Goodness knows I've questioned it my entire life. But I make no apologies for it. My King trusted me. *I* trust me. And that's just going to have to be good enough for you people." They stood around like stone, each figure more obstinate than the other with no intention of backing down.

"*You people*," whispered Ashley from the safety of the sidelines and his siblings shook their heads.

"You know what I meant!" Bredikai hollered behind her then turned back to reprimand Solannus. "Now stop letting them in your head with their ghost stories. Have some confidence. You might not have wings but damn sure you've got a backbone in there somewhere." She shivered and shook and continued to hurl curses at everything.

Before Solannus could open his mouth Mergalus put up a hand and bid the youth be silent. "Had you considered, child," he spoke to the killsmith, "that the king you mention had his reasons for sending you first into the mouth of death?"

"Of course I've considered it, how dumb do I look?" Bredikai retorted and groaned from the bile swelling up in her throat. "Yet here I stand." She smiled just as the nausea overcame her and fell on her knees with her insides expelled to the ground. She coughed and wretched so violently that there was nothing left in her stomach to release. Then, like nothing happened, Bredikai wiped her mouth, stood back up and crossed her arms.

"Ever unusual is the human mindset," Mergalus said. His face betrayed mild revulsion but he twisted his head in an attempt to better understand the girl. "And you speak for your species, do you?"

"Not... as such," replied the girl calmly. "I speak for myself and this company and that's usually enough."

"It is often too much," Solannus mumbled but was overheard.

"I'm sensing dissension among the ranks," Bredikai said. "Come now, this isn't the Solannus I've been travelling with for five years."

"It's only just passed the twelvemonth," the dragon noted, confused.

"Feels like a fucking decade is what it feels like," Bredikai bit back. "Now you get a grip and get it good because we're going to take that demon down or die trying and then you can proclaim your damn pets the new Dragonfathers for all I care. Fucking Fluffers is going to outlive us all, anyway," she cried and the bird squawked dreadfully on cue. "Listen to me: Borghalus isn't anything more than a crazed serpent and I've had my fair share of serpents for a lifetime. No offense," she added half-heartedly.

"None taken. I think."

"I may have spoken too quickly," Mergalus interrupted and his hoarse voice betrayed a mixture of awe and genuine amusement. "If your approach is to sass Borghalus to death, he might have a true fight on his hands. No offense," he mimicked and at that the killsmith smiled, happy to sense the elder dragon's feelings begrudgingly shift in her favor.

"Absolutely none taken, Master Mergalus. I pride myself on my *special* bond with unreasonable reptiles," she said and winked at him.

"Indeed," the elder chuckled, looking at Solannus.

"Words fail," Solannus sighed and for once he was glad to have witnesses for if ever he sought to retell this story he feared there would be none to truly appreciate the madness. At last the triplets thought it safe to come forward, their arms full of Solannus' remaining medicinal stock and other foul blends of questionable healing prowess. There was one small keg Lamure insisted she had good feelings about and when the dragon saw it he thanked the wraith and felt the weight lift from his shoulders. He had torn the cavern apart in search of the *special medicine* that would surely relieve Bredikai or her *problems-wyvernesque* but come up empty. Now that it was found and brought forward the rancid smell saturated the cave and the killsmith didn't know if she had the stomach for it.

At first the dragons Torgen and Valtiga were most vocal about not permitting a killsmith to partake in dragon medicine (now dubbed *dragonaid* by a self-congratulatory wraith who finally got to name something) and for half an hour they went back and forth with the girl. Somehow- and the *how* part was anyone's guess- the debate slowly shifted to the point where the dragons were now zealous about Bredikai taking the medication for her own good while the killsmith was the one to utterly refuse.

"Perhaps it is from loss of blood that my heart begins to change… but my hope rekindles ever so slightly with this strange assortment," Mergalus said to Solannus, watching Torgen chase the killsmith around with the keg of dragonaid. The triplets were chasing Valtiga in turn, hollering at the dragon to stop so they could check for anything that needed amputating. "You are better than I hoped to find you, my boy. One wants for positivity in times such as these."

Solannus smiled, tending to the elder carefully and checking the bindings they had secured around him. The triplets had done a fine job and his bleeding had been stopped by an odious salve they managed to brew up with what disparate ingredients Solannus had lying around. Sir Hiss-a-Lot was having the time of his life around his big cousins who seemed to enjoy the tiny creature and his endless wriggling. The snake was on Mergalus' body now, doing his best to check for any cuts or gashes the company may have overlooked. Thankfully dragons were quick to heal, unlike the killsmith whom Solannus continued to worry for.

Solannus laughed when he saw that Torgen had backed the killsmith into a corner and was threatening to shove the entire keg down her throat when Lamure broke the moment with an unexpected outcry. All stopped what they were doing and their eyes followed the wraith as she floated to the killsmith.

"Bredikai," Lamure said and her voice cracked as she searched carefully for her next words. From the look on her spectral face there was no question that the news she was about to deliver was ill and Bredikai could feel her heart racing.

"What's wrong?"

"I have received word that- that King Althaean has been taken... by dragon fire," Lamure said and her own ears were desperate to understand her mouth. "It was Borghalus himself. He... he has moved on Etherdeign and is accompanied by a host of minions."

"W-what?!" Bredikai said, shaking and shuddering, and it was no longer from the poison alone.

"The King... he's perished, Bredikai," the wraith let out

in desperation. "Your kingdom is under attack and burning."

"Who tells you this?" Bredikai demanded quietly at first. She was in shock but her heart was beating madly, her head was pounding the alarm, and she was being overwhelmed on every level. "Who speaks to you?!" she cried and all who heard her stood in shock.

"Mistress Althaea! She has seen it," sputtered the wraith and searched deep within her thoughts. "She leads an undead army and marches to fight for Etherdeign."

No words came out of Bredikai's mouth. Everyone in the cave was startled into a standstill. The dragons felt for the killsmith and for a great kingdom's blood being on their hands. Instinct drove Bredikai to brandish her sword but she hardly knew why and Torgen flinched backwards. No one expected Bredikai to make an aggressive move, nor did she intend to. She had acted reflexively out of frustration and a year of pent-up rage directed at the one fiend she was locked in on yet always unable to confront.

"I'm... I'm so sorry, Torgen," she said and her shaking hand dropped the Hexia to the ground. "All this way... I've come all this way- for nothing! I-I... should have stayed to... I'm sorry everyone, I didn't mean- didn't want to-" she said and suddenly screamed until the entirety of her anger reverberated through the mountain. She fell to her knees, feeling the final twist of the wyvern poison gripping her now and her hands went numb. She rubbed them as one does when they have been exposed to a piercing cold. It seemed to the others that the killsmith was gone mad before their eyes as she grabbed at her own head and sunk her fingers into her skull. The scene was difficult to watch but Lamure prevented the triplets from intervening. Best their leader dealt with her internal strife now than do something stupid and get herself killed before they even had a chance of stopping the evil.

Solannus went to her slowly. With great care he plucked the girl from the floor. He nudged her face with a claw and commanded her to come to her senses. "Stop this at once," he dictated calmly. "That's the poison trying to overpower you. Borghalus commands the wyverns now. You're only making it easier for him. Breathe. Breathe!"

Bredikai's eyes bulged but she held Solannus' gaze as if under his spell. She did as told; in and out and in and out...

"Hit me," she said.

"What?!"

"Hit me now!" Solannus did as he was told but fortunately he was so caught off guard that he used but a fraction of his strength. Even with such a light blow the girl was knocked back into a corner and landed on her ass. She stood up and shook herself while the dragons watched in horror.

"Thanks. I'm not dead yet," she said, stating the obvious. "Lamure, tell Althaea I'm on my way. I have no choice. I'm sorry, Sonny-."

"Bredikai, you needn't explain," he replied. "We're coming with you."

"Aye, we be fightin' fit, lass, an' nigh indestructible, to boot!" Ashley roared and his siblings followed suit with blades in the air.

"No," she said. There was no time for sadness. The time to mourn Althaean would come but she had to think more methodically than she had done until now if there was any hope for Etherdeign. "We can't risk losing Solannus. We can't risk it, Sonny. This is turning into a war and we haven't even been through the battle yet," she said and begged his understanding.

"Never you mind me," the dragon said and took the keg from Torgen. "I have committed to a path and I shall see it through. We know where Borghalus is and he will not leave before he has burned the world down. I sense he does this to draw us to him. I won't abandon you, Bredikai- and we will not abandon Etherdeign."

Bredikai looked at him solemnly and respected his choice. If she argued against his coming then she would be the biggest hypocrite in that cave and damned if she allowed for Borghalus to manipulate them from afar. But their approach also had logistical problems to consider.

"How are we going to get there? Even if we all flew somehow, it would take weeks!" she said.

"Need a portal's what we need," Lesley said. Bredikai paused for a moment. Surely the portal outside Etherdeign was destroyed when she and Solannus had battled their first enemy, but they had encountered the triplets in that same shitty forest. In fact, she had noted how far the triplets had been from the Morduanas...

"I-I'm sorry Bredikai," Solannus said, following her train of thought. "There were many portals scattered throughout Kharkharen but I destroyed what I could before I fled. I could not risk being followed."

"But wait," the killsmith said, thinking out loud. "There *were* portals, correct?"

"In a manner of speaking. I do not know what remains of them but rubble."

"That's a start," the girl said. "There has to be one that's functional. Borghalus will have used it to get to that area so quickly."

"And what if he has had it destroyed for fear of others

using it?" Solannus asked.

"We've got to take the chance. And if they are all broken we've got enough smarts to fix one so long as all the stones and runes are there. Who's gonna steal them, right? Not like anyone's strolling through Kharkharen these days," she carried on. "Now how do we get it to spit us out near Etherdeign? The closest one was the one we destroyed, so far as I know."

"Reckon the necromancer-lass could get an exit goin' for us," Ashley suggested.

"That's good thinkin', brother!" Murray said. "We gets us one goin' on this end an' she lets us out another."

"Zira will know how to piece one together," Bredikai said. She dared not think of what may have happened to him or her grandfather and wouldn't allow herself to dwell on the worst. "Reach him Lamure! Make sure they're safe and learn whatever you can. Solannus, where's the portal Borghalus would have used?"

"I... Let me think."

"Brother Mergalus," Valtiga spoke up. "You know which one it would be." Mergalus closed his eyes and considered their options despairingly.

"In the heart of the land," the elder answered grimly. "He will have used the one in the canyon of Dulhein. But he will not have left Kharkharen empty. Though the number of escapees increases, many are still being imprisoned while his minions patrol the kingdom. He will not have risked the entirety of his supporters for the fall of one small kingdom. It would be safer to assume that the bulk of his supporters remains in Kharkharen."

She needed to think. Bredikai gave the order for them to prepare for departure, hoping that Althaea could hold off total destruction until they got to Etherdeign. Everyone was rushing around the cave now while the killsmith stood at the mouth of the cave trying to form a clearer strategy. Her shaking had intensified since the news of Althaean's death and, ignore it as she might, its potency was gaining on her. Solannus came up behind her and took her away from the dark reverie.

"Here, drink this. Don't smell it- I said do *not* smell it!"

"Why are you trying to poison me now?"

"Ridiculous, just drink the damn thing," he said and it was as close to swearing as she had heard him get.

"But it's got blood and bits swimming in it!- I can smell it from here and ooomonjgjfunngk!" Solannus forcefed the medication into the girl and pulled her to his chest so she couldn't think to spit it out. For good measure he held her pressed into his underbelly long enough that she almost suffocated- and that was just for all the fussing.

Bredikai forced the nasty dragonaid down and it was akin to setting oneself on fire. The medication was working through her in unimaginable ways. At first she felt her bowels loosen and was about to excuse herself when the sensation was suddenly pulled and redirected to her hands, then just behind the ears and in her knees and, finally, on her back. While her scars remained, the residual pain was subsiding with great speed and Bredikai felt herself to be possessed of newfound energy.

The mind-numbing hot flashes were fading and, though she didn't know how she knew, Bredikai was convinced that she now had the fortitude to withstand extreme temperatures with little protection against outside exposure. She had control of every nerve ending, every hair on her head, and it seemed to her that she could run into the very epicenter of Kharkharen and back, breaking only a mild sweat.

"You gave me something illegal," she said to the dragon but Solannus was already busy with feeding the rest of the gross mixture to the other dragons, with the greatest and last amount to Mergalus who needed it most due to his advanced age. Odd that while the dragons appeared to be healing quickly, their reactions to the medication were not quite so... hyperactive as the killsmith's.

"Gotta get my armor on, all the armor on," Bredikai said, spinning around the cave while the triplets hurried to catch up with her and outfit the remaining pieces. Luckily she had worn most of the armor already. The breastplate was squashing her breasts and no matter how she tugged at her cleavage the piece was still not a great fit. But so much was to be expected. After all, the armor had belonged to someone else and she would treat it with the respect it was due. Solannus guided Ashley to the shield and its size was almost on par with the girl's. It, too, bore the sigil of Eberen in black against a coppertine background; a dragon with the head of a human. Bredikai was fortunate that she could haul it around, what with the new life coursing through her system, but Solannus warned her that these side-effects were not to be trusted to last and that he was no human healer. The killsmith spun the shield, threw it into the air and caught it with perfect ease as if she had been tossing one of the triplets' skulls.

"Should we be concerned about this?" Lamure whispered to the dragon as the girl's armor was checked and she began pacing wildly, talking to herself and making plans that she ruled out, reconsidered and ruled out once more. There were plans aplenty and she only needed one to work.

"I am not entirely sure this was the best course of action," Solannus admitted to the wraith. "But the poison has been neutralized- of that we may be certain. She smells better."

Ashley walked over to them, followed by his siblings. "She's doin' me skull in, Scales. Best we sends her off to war now while she's still got it in her, I reckon." Bredikai rushed to them with the power of a stampede and, they guessed, a bloodlust that could rival the demon-drake's own.

"Alright," Bredikai declared enthusiastically, "seeing as how we're all on the mend it's time to have that talk. See who we can count on to fight with us. But not here. Master Mergalus, how many dragons do you suppose have followed you into this mountain?"

"Not many," answered the elder and shifted to a more comfortable position. "Ten, perhaps twelve at best. That includes those whom you see here."

"Still better odds than a moment ago," Bredikai said. "Grab whatever's necessary and summon your people. We meet on the slopes immediately."

Mergalus nodded his head and at his bidding both Torgen and Valtiga howled outside the cave. The force of their breath was so strong it seemed the volcano rumbled and Bredikai looked up in concern. An explosion was the last thing they needed right then. The dragons took to flight, cautiously descending to the skirts of the mountain. But when Mergalus made to stand, they understood that his wounds had been dire indeed and that his healing would take more time than they had to give. The dragonaid medicine was the most potent known to dragons but it was not a potion of miracles- such a thing was not known to exist- and Mergalus was in no state to fight.

"I will not allow it," Solannus declared. "You will stay here where it is safe until you are healed completely. We will come back for you."

"You do not command me, young one."

"Then you'll have to get through both of us," Bredikai said. "Stop being stubborn, old man. You've been more help to us than you can possibly know. And I suspect we'll need you for the days ahead so you'd better heal up."

Next came a teary moment of separation as the triplets brought forth their parrot and asked a mighty favor of the elder dragon. They were confused, the remainder of the group- for what harm could possibly come to the cursed bird, they thought. But Ashley would not suffer the little one to come to ruin, possibility or not, and Solannus now wished the same security for his own little one. Mergalus was happy for the company and accepted responsibility of Fluffers and Sir Hiss-a-Lot. The sounds coming from Ashley indicated that the separation was hardest on him but he stiffened his backbone and the triplets bowed to the elder dragon. They left the cave and began their descent.

Mergalus was disappointed that he could not be of aid in battle but he was in no position to argue, especially with what little faith he had in their campaign. Bredikai took the wing of Septiannus and laid it on Mergalus' back as a sort of leathery blanket. There was no sense in taking it beyond the cave. In fact, she would have done well to leave the tooth behind as well but she had grown fond of having it dangle around her neck; like she had her own connection with the Dragonfather and he had helped guide her hand when Borghalus possessed Althaea. So she kept it and Solannus made no argument.

With that Bredikai bid Mergalus a respectful farewell and left Solannus to exchange his final words in peace. She walked out of the mouth and was about to make her way down but her feet stalled. She wondered what they would discuss when she was out of earshot and for a moment she thought to spy on them. But Solannus would smell her out with ease so she turned to her path and sped down the mountain as fast as the icy winter gales.

"I have let my anxieties get the better of me, child," Mergalus said when the girl was gone and her scent had cleared. "Know that it is not your heart I doubt."

"I know, Mergalus," Solannus said. "You have always sought to open my eyes. At my worst you did not send me away. Please trust me to repay your many kindnesses over the years with what little I can do."

"Kindness need never expect repayment, my boy," the elder said and watched the little snake console the skeletal bird. He drew the creatures next to him with a delicate claw and they curled up beneath his neck. "I regret that the consequences of older days have caught up with us at last. I am ashamed for what we have allowed to fester but you must forgive your father. He lost much in life; he could not bear to end his own son. I dare ask that you find it in your heart to forgive Borghalus as well- though I know it to be an impossibility."

"I fear Borghalus was lost long before my father imprisoned him," Solannus replied. "He is rotten from within. Always was... He has claimed more than the dragons of Kharkharen already."

"You speak of his dealings with the humans... And Sir Reginnald," Mergalus said and Solannus looked off into the horizon. His throat was tightening. "I see you have given his armor to the girl. Was that wise? I do not wish to place my doubts on your shoulders but a killsmith is not a knight, my boy. They are reckless. Unpredictable... They will go to any lengths to complete a killdeed. How ready are you to watch your friends die?"

When Solannus looked at the elder there were clouds hanging over his eyes and his chin quivered with an anger he refused to give into. "How can one be ready for such a thing?" he asked and his voice broke. "Was I ready for my mother to die? Was I ready when my father cast my brother into a stone prison and his heart forever broken? Was I ready when my only friend in the world was broken and taken from me?" When Mergalus did not answer Solannus swallowed the lump in his throat and bit back his rage.

"Father killed him, did he not? Tell me, Mergalus, for there is nothing that has happened that has escaped your watchful eye."

The elder Mergalus sighed and turned his head away but he would fear this conversation no longer for, medicine or no, he was nearing the end of his days. "Borghalus broke his mind, my boy. Reginnald begged your father to end his suffering. It was an act of mercy."

"So what are you saying?" Solannus cried, no longer caring about being overheard and unaware of the familiar scent that had crept back towards the mouth of the cave. "Slaying Rinn was an act of mercy on par with sparing a kin-killer because that kin-killer was his son?! Rinn was no less a brother to me than- ... No, this hypocrisy isn't to be borne. It is injustice of the highest order-!"

"It is mercy, child, don't you understand? It is either there or it is not. You are not the one to judge how it comes about," Mergalus said, softening his voice against the younger dragon's growing outrage.

"And I suppose the great Septiannus was."

"Do not speak his name in vain, boy, if you did not understand your own father," the elder said with hurt defiance. "He was the greatest leader of our time! He only ever followed the path to which he was absolutely committed. He made his mistakes. Bore the responsibilities. Allowed himself to grow vulnerable- but not in the manner for which you would blame him; for which your brother blames him still. He opened his heart and you will not fault him for it. There is not a creature so perfect that it does not make mistakes every day of its life! Septiannus made his peace long ago and suffered himself to go through the hells so that his sons grew to be better- to act better and lead better-"

"I was a mistake! Borghalus has every right to wish me dead-"

"If you believe that to be true then it is not your birth but your life that has been a mistake," Mergalus said, regaining his insurmountable tone. "Humans have never been my favorite of the species but I would suggest taking the little human's example and reconsider my self estimation before marching off to face Borghalus. We are not all meant to lead but with this mindset you are barely fit to follow. Is there not a one among you worthy of becoming the Dragonfather?!" cried the elder and though it wounded him deeply to be harsh, it was the truth that Solannus had needed to hear. Mergalus heard a faint growl from outside but made no allusions to it and Solannus was too preoccupied with his own turmoil to notice. The scent was fading now, rushing back downwards no doubt- and so much the better. Solannus bowed his head angrily and stormed out of the cave. His rage, mostly directed at himself, helped speed his step and he hardly realized that he had made it to the bottom where seven dragons (including Torgen and Valtiga), all in various stages of grief and ailment, awaited.

"You alright? What's wrong with you?" Bredikai whispered to him.

"Nothing. I am in the throes of internal strife so kindly back off," he said curtly.

"Have your meltdown later," she said. "You need to talk to these dragons and convince them to join us." She was right. The dragons were hurt and confused and now they were mixed in with a bunch of skeletons and a ghost-woman and a killsmith. Torgen and Valtiga were too frazzled in their own rights to make convincing arguments. Their tensions were elevating and it would take a fellow dragon to steer this group towards their cause.

"Solannus, has Mergalus healed?" asked one of the drakes, eying the company suspiciously.

"Why do you turn us from our path? Kharkharen is lost to the evils of your brother!" cried another.

"My brothers and sisters," Solannus said before they could bombard him with more questions. "I turn to you for aid. Borghalus has attacked the Kingdom of Etherdeign and burns it to the ground as we speak. My company and I have traveled for over a year to collect my father's remains. No doubt word of our campaign has reached your ears."

"So it has," replied a long orange drake whose eyes looked fierce. His energy was strong despite his wounds and he looked at Solannus with intensity. "How have you fared, young one?"

"We have the tooth and the wing is with Mergalus," Bredikai said, stepping to her dragon's side. "We were almost in possession of the eye but it was taken from us by Borghalus' wyverns. It's safe to assume he controls them now. Solannus is in possession of the heart."

"Then it is true- you stole the heart of Septiannus! But where is it?" demanded the oldest dragon in the group. He was Arctor, a creature of spectacular breeding, born to rich hues of browns, golds and a crown of dark yellow horns that decorated his large head. He was the very picture of nobility and took great pride in his line. His words were calculated and his mind methodical. Nevertheless, for all the sharpness of his eyes, he could see no sign of the heart.

"It is hidden," answered Solannus. "Deep within a mountain where none may reach it but myself. I will not risk disclosing its location until Borghalus is stopped."

"So we have the three, you see," Bredikai concluded. The drake Arctor looked at her but chose to speak with the dragon instead.

"Solannus, this is not a matter of majority rule," Arctor said. "You must have them all or they count for nothing! Not that there is a dragon large enough to command Borghalus' submission. He will bow to no one's title and kill anything that stands in his way."

"And I couldn't agree with you more," Bredikai intervened, choosing to not be ignored. She planted her shield into the snow and rested her right arm on top of it. Solannus was grateful that she chose to step in and help him out for he had no answers that would please the elder drake, or the others. Bredikai put a hand on his side and it drew some whispered judgment from the crowd. "We've already had these conversations and I'm about done with the magical bits of Dragonfathers past," the killsmith said. "If Borghalus' madness has advanced this much then the remains are useless anyway. He must be killed. End of story."

"Unsurprising and unimaginative that a killsmith would just suggest murder when there are other alternatives," said one of the dragons as the others chuckled. But Arctor did not comment, fixing his scrutiny upon the killsmith and the dragon.

"I'm sorry, should we just combine our strength to restrain him, then?" Bredikai said innocently and looked at them with an unreadable expression. "We could all hold him down maybe. You look like a strong one… Slightly bruised but maybe you're man enough for the job, so to speak. Or even better- we can just *give* Borghalus the bits we've collected and spare him the trouble of hunting us down. Fuck it- let him have my kingdom. King's dead anyway. We could just wait for him to come back to Kharkharen. I'll try to stand still while he torches me in the face."

"Bredikai, calm down-"

"I will *not* calm down. You all should be ashamed of yourselves," the killsmith said and pointed at the dragons rudely. "My King was a friend to Septiannus and wouldn't have needed convincing if this was the other way around."

"And who was your king, killsmith?" Arctor asked.

"Althaean of Etherdeign," Bredikai answered, lifting her chin and daring the dragon to breathe a word against the man they'd all held so dear. "We received word not one hour ago that he was killed in battle- against Borghalus himself," she said and the dragons ceased their chatter. "I respect your hesitation in slaying your kin. If there's another way to do this then please tell us and we'll do everything in our power to stop this war. But... I beg you to follow us to Etherdeign. I may not be the same species as you but in my heart I know that Septiannus wouldn't have thought twice about helping those in need- especially the friends he honored," she finished sadly. The dragons shifted around uncomfortably, no longer making light of the situation or looking at the killsmith directly. They made no answer. It was Arctor alone who turned his head to survey his company and, suddenly, a wave of shame came over him, that they should live to see the day when they needed a killsmith to speak to them of honor.

"Indeed he would not," the dragon said at last and both Bredikai and Solannus felt their hearts race with hope. Arctor was a proud creature, so elitist in fact that the others could not hide their shock when he was the first and only one to agree with the killsmith. Even Bredikai had expected him to pose the fiercest opposition but it appeared that she had been too hasty in her judgment. "Nor do I need to think more on the matter," the drake stated firmly. "I will fight with you for Etherdeign. My decision is made."

"Arctor? What are you saying, brother?" asked a red drake who was long in the snout and had scarcely stopped bleeding. "You would follow this human into death?"

"Brothers and sisters, don't you see that it is death that follows *us?*" Arctor asked his people. "I would think twice about fraying relations with anyone, be they human or otherwise, when we are cast out of land and home. We flee from Kharkharen to spare our lives but in doing so have committed ourselves to a perilous exile. The road is long and cruel for refugees without a destination. Did you consider what we would do once we had fled far enough? What we would eat or drink? Did you consider that Borghalus would view this as the ultimate betrayal and send our own to poach us from the shadows? You lie to yourselves if you think that we have cheated death. Perhaps I, too, chose denial over reason. But I am free from the spell and see that Kharkharen is lost to us while Borghalus lives. Look around you," he said and there was a new sadness in the dragon's voice. "Look at the death that has overtaken our home."

It was then that Solannus finally understood the reason for his unsettling feelings and how his home had changed, and the pungency of the air that had bombarded his senses from the moment he returned to Kharkharen. New mountains had sprung where the land had once borne fertile soils and lush grasslands. Trees and forests had been swept aside to make way for stone. Mountains filled the landscape in scores; some reaching high, some keeping low. Many were grand but the most haunting ones were small and their numbers were too great to ignore. They were the remnants of deceased dragons now petrified and lost. All this time they had been standing in the middle of a graveyard.

"He is changing the very face of Ethra and it is not only dragon blood that feeds the ground," Arctor said. "One way or another this war will come to an end and should we live to see that end I will not have it said that dragons turned their backs on those who needed them. I trust Etherdeign will return the favor by not abandoning us to the wild," he said to the killsmith.

"You have my word."

"Swear it."

"I... I swear it," Bredikai said. "As heir apparent to the Coppertine Guild, I, Bredikai Cronunham, give you my word that no dragon will be turned away or refused aid from Etherdeign, should they need it. This is my oath for so long as I should live."

The host of dragons was now grappling with Arctor's sad words, turning to one another to make certain that they were all in this together. For the most part their favor seemed to veer towards aiding Etherdeign but they remained in conversation among their own.

"Humans have never been favorites among us dragons..." Arctor said, drawing closer to the killsmith and a nerve-wracked Solannus.

"Yeah, that particular phrasing keeps getting tossed around and I'm starting to read into it a little too much," the killsmith replied, venturing a thankful smile.

"Much too exasperating to deal with," the drake sighed and his snobbish nature was unparalleled. "But every generation or so there comes one who carries a bit of that- that *fire* inside. You will forgive my brethren, killsmith, for they are young- perhaps too young to remember that it was the King Althaean of Etherdeign who entrusted his only son to Septiannus, to live among us in Kharkharen. Such was the strength of the bond they shared and we will do our part to honor it. Reginnald was loved and lives on for those of us who remember him. Do not shame that memory," he said, leaning into the girl's face. Bredikai nodded without blinking. She didn't need to look at Solannus to know that he had heard Arctor's words just as clearly. She had also heard his sharp intake of breath and it absolved him of her suspicion that he had known the truth of his friend's lineage.

"I will fight with you," Arctor said and nodded back towards his brethren, committing them to the battle with the strength of his fortitude. "And so will they."

CHAPTER 11: THE KILLSMITH OF ETHERDEIGN

A power raw and animal was flowing through the killsmith. Solannus had to warn her to not get carried away. The dragonaid hadn't bequeathed her enough power to take down a drake barehanded per se, but Bredikai's strength was on the rise and her agility no less than twice what it had been. They were barely approaching the midday hour but they could not afford to wait for nightfall while Etherdeign burned at the hands of Borghalus, who was no doubt relishing his easy conquest. The skeletons were sent ahead of the company into the folds of Kharkharen and the canyon known as Dulhein to see what they could make of the portal. They were light of foot and could easily disguise themselves as a harmless pile of bones should they encounter any patrols. Solannus discussed serpentine technicalities with his kin while Bredikai strategized with Lamure.

"Have you had any more contact with Althaea?"

"She is holding them off as best she can but the magic of the necromancers is proving weak compared to the brute force Borghalus commands," answered Lamure, staring through Bredikai while she reported on the images in her mind. "Althaea has managed to keep them at arm's length for now. This will give us some time but her numbers are not enough and she fears for what may descend upon the Ire Craven when Borghalus is finished with Etherdeign. We must hasten to her. She will open an exit on our word," concluded the exhausted wraith. These mental tasks and communications were draining and energy was not in endless supply. Indeed the whole of Ethra could wield but little magic at a time and enchantments were growing weaker with the years, only a sad phantom of their former potency.

Lamure worried that Bredikai would be freezing on that slope with the cold coppertine armor tightened to her form and winter's hand touching them at every chance but the latter was merely jittery and eager to pounce on the first enemy they encountered. So much for their time in Kharkharen, thought the wraith. Without realizing, Lamure sat on the closest rock she could find, resting herself and wondering why she should feel so fatigued. Perhaps it was her mortal habits creeping up on her psyche but she needed a moment to steady herself if she was going to be of any more help.

"I'm sorry Lamure- I've asked too much of you," Bredikai said. She knelt before her friend who smiled through the exhaustion, wanting above anything to be of service. "I have just one more request..." Bredikai closed her eyes and inhaled deeply. "I need you to establish contact with Ten'Mei, the Gr-... the Griffinlord," she said and shuddered. Pieces of her armor scraped against one another from her disgust-filled twitching.

"Tell him that... *Griffinbait* summons him to honor his oath to Etherdeign immediately and that King Althaean is dead." The wraith looked at Bredikai like she'd turned into a killer pigeon but the killsmith was tired just making the request. "I can't get into it now," she said. "Let's just say he owes me. I mean *big*. They won't be far from Etherdeign this season."

Lamure nodded and promised to reward herself with the infamous story if they survived. "Couldn't we convince others to join us?" she asked. "Etherdeign has more than one neighboring kingdom, if memory serves me. They could reach-"

"I'm afraid there's no time left," Bredikai said. "Word will have gotten out and if the kingdoms value their lives they won't need convincing to stand and fight. Whether they rush to our aid or move below ground is on them now- I just hope they don't turn our people away and that enough have evacuated in time. Contact Ten'Mei and go meet the triplets. We need that portal working *now*."

Lamure heeded the command and sped off somewhere quiet where her concentration would not be broken. Her skills had developed to their advantage but they were still little to boast of and thus far she had never tried to contact someone whom she had not met. Bredikai joined the dragons and told them of her updated plan. When she conveyed the part about the griffins and how they were not to be harmed, Solannus looked at her like she had taken the dragonaid rectally and it had traveled up to explode in her brain. Bredikai assured him that they could save some storytelling for after the battle and hoped that they would live to exchange many more.

Arctor had no interest in tall tales from humans or other tedious creatures but he had to admit that he was intrigued; if only to get his mind off of their impending doom. To turn back on his word was not even close to being in the realm of possibility for the dragon but that did not mean that Arctor expected to live past the battle for Etherdeign. Nor did he labor under any delusions for the rest of his company but hope, however small, had set a spark in his heart and they would have to try.

The killsmith's company had been correct in thinking that Borghalus' minions would be recognizable by their bloodied eyes when Arctor confirmed their observation. The golden gaze of dragons that had persevered through ages of evolution the demon-drake had, somehow, undone in half a lifetime. His achievements thus far were incredible in the most sadistic sense.

"We'll need two of you to transport Solannus," Bredikai said. "We won't get far on foot. We fly into the Dulhein portal as soon as Lamure sends word."

No sooner had the killsmith spoken than they saw the wraith speed off past the nearby mountains and deep into enemy land. She faded quickly from sight. The canyon, Lamure was told, was not far but it was a deep dive beyond a stretch of flat land under open sky where anyone and anything could be easily detected. Speedy flight was their only choice.

"Master Arctor, if you'd be kind enough to bear me as your burden, I would be grateful," Bredikai smiled and bowed.

"I suppose there is nothing to be done for it," the drake said but Bredikai knew his snobby attitude was meant for the sake of keeping up a reputation rather than any real reluctance. The drake cleared his throat and looked bored- really keeping that exasperation alive- but the killsmith would say anything to keep their spirits up at this point.

"If it'll help us bond better, there's a chance I'm part dragon now- thanks to Solannus here," Bredikai said and nudged her counterpart. They could do with a chuckle, she thought.

"I beg your pardon," Arctor huffed.

"We're blood brothers, in a sense," the killsmith said as Solannus flicked her arm away. "Stop growling Sonny. This might be the last story I get to tell so you'd better believe I'm gonna regale them with every last disgusting detail," she said and now the host of dragons was very interested in the company's prior dealings. The sound of hearts pounding was palpable and they needed some sort of conversation to take the edge off of the collective anxiety. Arctor sensed what the girl was intending but he took it upon himself to fly to a higher level, risking a call to others who might join them.

"Just how vile is this story?" asked the red dragon whose name Bredikai had not learned.

"There's blood and bile and teeth and holes," replied the killsmith and suddenly she was surrounded by a group of very curious drakes who attempted to feign disinterest- poorly.

Half an hour passed without so much as a hint from Lamure and Bredikai was growing weary of keeping her worries bottled up for the sake of the others. The dragons were conversing among themselves and she could feel their resolve folding. She had only gotten through the first part of her story before they were too revolted to hear more and she was too distracted to delve into any other topic that might hold their interest.

Arctor would not budge from his position above them. He was growing hoarse from the calls he sent into the sky but his efforts, while commendable, were proving pointless. No others heeded the elder's call. Bredikai couldn't find it in her heart to blame them. Now that she was seeing the drakes clearly and had a moment to reflect on the death they were standing in, they were a dismal group who had had their spirit bled from them. Now she was asking them to follow her into a storm and question the rain later- and no one could promise fair weather past the dawn.

Solannus hadn't spoken in all that half hour. He sort of lingered about, lost in his own world of misgivings. Seeing him dawdle was keeping Bredikai on edge. There was something about his air that told her he was second-guessing himself again and that was all they needed before marching off. This time, instead of bullying him back to reality, she chose to sit by his side and put thoughts into words.

"There's something that's been bothering me all this time," the killsmith began. Solannus looked up to Arctor roaring above them. Still no answer came. "There's got to be a reason why Borghalus is the way that he is."

"Does evil need a reason?" Solannus asked though he wasn't really needing to be answered. "I have never known him to be anything other than cruel. If he has changed it has only been in the degree of his malice. Isolation does things to an already bent mind."

"I'm sorry but that doesn't sit well with me," Bredikai said, tracing the sigil on her shield. "I think, now that we know more about him, that Rinn's presence in Kharkharen may have been part of the problem. But that can't be all. I feel something in my gut and, you know, my perception of dragons has somewhat changed in our time together."

"*Somewhat?*"

"Look," Bredikai ventured again, "in my experience there's little evil without impetus in the world and lords know I've never come across such a thing. There's usually a driving force behind the madness. Some *grand delusion*," she said theatrically, twirling her hand in the air. "Know what I mean? I want to know what his is."

"Young lady, are you trying to enlighten me on the nature of evil or dragons?" Solannus asked irately.

Bredikai shrugged and stretched her arms against her shield. "Maybe both," she said and glanced up at Arctor. "All I'm saying is that, more often than not, there are reasons why people are bad. Look at the rest of your kin," she said and nodded to the soul-sucked drakes. "On average they're of no better or worse character than any other species I've encountered. So what makes Borghalus so fucking special?"

"Business must have been terrible for you," the dragon snorted.

"I said on average. The *really* bad ones I most definitely killed," Bredikai countered. "I'm sorry but I did. My point is that there's got to be more to him than superficial hatred."

"I wouldn't know now, would I?" Solannus snapped and stood on all fours, meaning to walk away though he could not bring himself to move. "He wasn't a particularly over-sharing sort of older brother. I should think that would have been clear from, say, everything I've told you about him. How would an answer benefit us, anyway?"

"Damn, what crawled up your behind? I was just thinking out loud."

"Well, I'd never thought I'd say this but: stop thinking so much," the dragon replied. "My nerves are shot as it is."

"You're being mighty lippy considering I'm probably going to die trying to save all of us. The hell's your problem, if I may ask?" Bredikai asked, now standing up with a hand at her hip. If that power move had worked for Kassiah it would work for her.

"Never you mind."

"What never I mind? I mind, Solannus."

That Arctor had not taken a break from sounding the call to arms was really grating on Solannus' ears but he would not be the one to dissuade an elder. For his part, Solannus had long since given up hope of drawing others to their cause and he felt himself losing the battle against his own fears.

"No one has asked you to sacrifice yourself and I won't

have your death hanging over me, too!" cried the dragon angrily. Solannus quieted himself quickly but his fear had escaped him. "Borghalus will not risk killing me for I am the only one who knows of the heart's location but you-... Look what he did to your king! He will think nothing of destroying you and I can't- There is nothing left of my heart to break, Bredikai," he said, silently begging her to understand his feelings.

"Is that why you've been snarling at me?" the killsmith asked, rubbing at her eyes and face. "You think I'm doing this just for you? I thought I made myself clear on the issue."

"What does it matter?" the dragon snarled. "Althaean is dead, your guild exemption is likely a faded dream and there is not a hole in Ethra we can crawl into, nor a treasure hoard we may bury ourselves in to escape our ruin."

"Huh," Bredikai said and it wasn't the sarcastic retort he had expected. He glared at the girl who remained unnaturally calm, as if they had been discussing local gossip during afternoon tea. "Maybe that's what this is all about," she stated. "Maybe it's just plain old greed and it's all of Ethra's gold he's after."

"That is decidedly not the case," Solannus grumbled and sat back down.

"You don't know that for sure. Have you seen the exchange rates between the metals lately? Bet you anything all this gold-hoarding's cramped up the economy."

"I assure you that Borghalus cares nothing for the financial sector," Solannus replied and rolled his eyes.

"If you say so," Bredikai shrugged. "We might've held onto a bit of his treasure, though. Cursed or not, we don't have a coin to our name. The triplets should've taken some. It's not like they can get more cursed, right?"

Solannus rolled his eyes once more and tightened his mouth in frustration. "You will have to ask them," he said tersely. "Better yet, you may confer with Borghalus regarding the particulars of his curse; the rules, regulations and such."

"See that kind of mouthiness right there might have something to do with all this. I feel like poor attitudes and foul dispositions run in your family," Bredikai pointed out.

"Ridiculous. Your ill manners and crude tongue have wreaked havoc upon my noble breeding," Solannus said and the girl chuckled at his huffiness. Despite his inner snob Solannus could not hold a candle to Arctor's old-school elitism. By comparison the younger dragon was the very picture of humility.

"At least you're standing up for yourself now," Bredikai smiled. "Small price to pay for a bit of backbone, I think." Solannus looked down at her not knowing what he expected to see but she simply smiled at him with tired eyes. Hopefully the crash from the dragonaid high would not deprive her severely.

"I am sorry, Bredikai," he said. "I shouldn't be taking my frustrations out on you."

"Look, I get it. I'm always scared when I face dragons. Really," she said when he looked at her in disbelief. "I never know if I'm going to make it out alive and one of these days my luck will run out and I'll burn until I'm nothing. *Puff* and it'll be like I never existed!" the killsmith chuckled and Solannus scoffed at what he perceived to be sheer recklessness.

"That is too grim. I was expecting an epic speech before we made off to battle."

"Nah, I'm out of speeches," the girl said. "Tell you what, though; it's nice to do something of value while we have the strength to do it. And there's no one I'd rather do it with," she said and nudged him with her behind.

"Me neither, you morbid little witch," he said and returned her smile.

They sat only a minute more and Bredikai stood, stretched her back, picked up her shield and donned her helmet. The headgear was beautifully crafted, with deep engravings carved all over its chromatic dome and black trimmings to encircle it. But the attachment to the lower half of the face in the shape of an open dragon's mouth was the real crowning glory. Four horns jutted out from the top; one to each side- left and right- one placed in front and the final in the back. Her gleaming get-up shone under the winter sun and Bredikai looked to be the physical manifestation of the good golden grief the dragon was always going on about. Except she was better for she was coppertine! Slight bias.

"Do I look threatening?" she asked and the sunlight bounced off of her into everyone's faces. So much for a stealthy dash to Dulhein.

"Madam, at the right angle, you could burn holes through my eyes," Solannus replied, approving the get-up and his own dexterity for molding the girl into it.

"Works for me. Now get up, you overgrown pouch; it's time," Bredikai declared.

"Lamure speaks to you?!"

"Not but I can't stand waiting any longer. If something's gone wrong we need to be there to fix it. Time to move out!" Bredikai hollered and it was not a moment too soon for the group morale had all but plummeted. Arctor glared fiercely at his kin and landed beside them, desperately seeking to veil his own disappointments. Without further debate Solannus helped Bredikai climb onto the elder's back. Next, Torgen and Valtiga hooked into Solannus from the stumps on his back where wings should have grown, apologizing for any hurt they caused by digging into his flesh. But the dragon felt nothing, for they were just that- stumps of excess flesh- with no nerves to damage. The dragons' claws sunk in like metal hooks and at once they were up in the air. Pure adrenaline sped them away.

The experience was as magical as it was terrifying. At any given moment Bredikai felt that the wind would upset her balance and the weight of her armor would knock her off of Arctor's back. She held on to whatever horn or scale was closest- for no one teaches proper dragon-riding etiquette anymore. Arctor felt pieces of her armor digging into him in the oddest places and he was hard put to not shake the tick off his back. She was making him itch terribly. On the other hand, Solannus was breathtaken and whatever shame or embarrassment he may have felt towards the two drakes bearing his burden had been left on the slopes of the volcano. He wished wholeheartedly that he could shout his elation, that he could share his heart with Bredikai and the others. He was flying and it meant more than the world to him. A tear or two may have escaped his eyes and he couldn't put his feelings into words- but he didn't have to. When the killsmith saw the dragon's wonderstruck face her heart leapt for her friend and she shared in the purity of his happiness.

If ever there was a moment to be frozen in time and kept forever, Bredikai wished it could be then. She perceived nothing of the outside world. None of it existed beyond their flight. She closed her eyes and imprinted the image in her mind. Then, a blaring thought intruded and it was the voice of Lamure reaching out to her, bidding them to make haste for the task was done and Althaea could not hold the exit open for long. They were within reach, gradually putting the flat land behind them with the edge of the canyon just ahead. Arctor was beginning his descent when a pillar of fire barred their way and stopped him in the air.

The dragon's halt was so abrupt Bredikai almost fell off. She screamed and was barely hanging on with her gauntleted arm. Two serpentine behemoths came at them from above and Arctor yelled for her to hold on tightly. The killsmith tried to claw her way back into position but Arctor's flight path was evasive now, twisting and turning to dodge the streams of fire. Her fingers were bleeding against his scales.

A great black beast with eyes the size of bowls gushing blood was coming at them, roaring between expulsions and commanding their death- but the fire was not meant for Solannus whom Borghalus needed very much alive.

Bredikai was struggling to hold on. She yelled for the two carrying Solannus to make for the portal while the four that remained of their group went after the black beast. The second foe was quick to intercept them, ferocious in dark green and of larger bearing. It was four against two now and they were caught in the literal crossfire with only the portal for escape.

"Go through!" Bredikai yelled to the company awaiting them and they obeyed. "To the portal!" she cried behind her and hoped the dragons could hear her screeching. But the clash of the beasts thundered through the air. The force of serpentine bodies meeting bodies was so strong it sent them all reeling into the canyon.

Arctor was the first to land and Bredikai fell off instantly. Neither entered the portal for Solannus and his carriers were not far behind. The moment they touched the ground Bredikai bid them stay on task and go through. She saw the remaining four dragons slash and tear into their enemies. They were attempting to make the descent now but were headed to the portal at too great a speed.

'She can't hold it any longer!' came Lamure's voice in her

head and Bredikai forced them all through as the portal began to collapse.

"Get through!" cried one of the four and with that the dragons hurled themselves through the crumbling entryway. They were spat out the other side almost instantaneously and as their exit began caving in on itself, out came a dragon, and another, and then another. The group looked to one another for confirmation, catching their breath and counting their numbers over and over again. But they had sacrificed one already; the red drake whose name Bredikai had never learned, and no amount of counting would bring him back. Solannus came to the killsmith's side as the girl tried to process their location. The triplets followed him, as did Lamure, and the company was now together in the middle of a familiar scorched field. Not enough of the meadow had grown back and Bredikai knew at once that she had been there before.

At first she was disoriented from their flight, but when the killsmith turned around she was met with the gasps of her company and the shamed whisperings of the dragons around her. Only she and Solannus did not turn away from the sight. Billowing clouds of smoke and great fumes of destruction were visual obstacles veiling the totality of the scene before them. Etherdeign stood but a short distance ahead and they were just outside the kingdom, a mere breath away from death's harvest.

There was no correct way to react to the unfolding fate of Etherdeign. Despite defenses both magical and otherwise, everything was burning. They could hear people running from the fire like mad beasts, the royal guard everywhere yet nowhere when needed, all just animals loosened in a frenzy. A gang of dragons was terrorizing the skies. Without a word Bredikai began running towards the chaos. The weight of her armor meant nothing to her and she thought herself to be gaining ground but their enemies still looked about as big as wasps from where she was. Just then, she was plucked up from her sprint and found herself on Solannus' back. They charged forward together while the skeletons matched their pace. Being this close to so much necromancy gave them even greater speed and soon they out-ran the dragon in a flurry or garbled battlecries. Lamure sped ahead to find Althaea and, with one last look, Arctor led his group into the sky.

They were alone now, the killsmith and the dragon; out of the others' earshot and panting towards the kingdom's walls. The castle Etheria burned light into her enemies' eyes and she seemed unassailable even at her most desperate hour. Beams of red and hot orange streaked in lines from the sky onto the city of Riverlong while catapults and heavy ballistas lethargically reciprocated. The contraptions were bulky- too heavy to operate quickly- and needed much magic if they were to pose a decent threat to the drakes who were quick to move out of range. But the beasts had not recognized the breweries yet. Though the city burned, it was not lost beyond recognition. Bredikai knew that luck had spared them for the time being.

Solannus' legs were cramping and his breathing grew ragged but it was the energy of the charge and the human explosive on his back that sped him on.

"Make straight for Borghalus," the killsmith said and Solannus dared not refuse her, though he could not spy his brother. Bredikai looked into the sky illuminated with infernal torrents and screams that disappeared into the heavens. Of the dragons she could discern, no one stood out as a unique menace, and she began to think that the demon may have appeased his appetite for the day, moving on to destroy other kingdoms. It was a selfish, evil hope- one she was ashamed to have let into her heart.

And then they saw him. Despite the burst of adrenaline Solannus skid to a stop and time froze for the pair once more.

Whereas the silhouettes of the other drakes had appeared to be like wasps, there now descended a shadow large enough to mask the visage of the sun. Only the light from Etheria challenged his descent and he was a pale tarantula creeping down from the clouds. His sickly limbs were piercing through and he was enshrouded in a throne of fire and ash. The creature seemed to be in no great hurry as he descended slowly to sit on top of the castle. He was not bothered by any swords and spears that came his way and there was not an arrow that could touch his evil comfort. They saw his wicked smile as he surveyed the destruction caused by his minions, watching the great battle for Etherdeign as if it were a tawdry sporting event he deigned to oversee. The necromancers and other wielders of magic were so engrossed in their own battles against his minions that not a shred of harm came the beast's way and Borghalus took in his devastation with great satisfaction.

"Fuuuck me," Bredikai breathed, unhooking the bottom half of her helmet. Solannus said nothing. He never took his eyes off of his brother and barely breathed but his heartbeat was wild and difficult to ignore. "That thing's gotten even bigger since we last saw him," Bredikai said, inhaling and exhaling rapidly. She put a hand over her mouth then rubbed her chin. Borghalus was larger, paler and more menacing than the figure they'd seen on Althaea's parchment. The only thing overshadowing the whiteness of his scales was the rot that steadily crept around his gigantic form but he looked to be in peak condition nonetheless. This was no dumb brute. They could see the hunger in his eyes and Bredikai knew that he was biding his time, making sport of the carnage before he ended Etherdeign and all who remained in it. He was reveling in the blood and scorched death around him and its melody was so pleasing to the creature that he would not intrude upon it lest he disrupt its harmony.

"We have to draw him out," Bredikai said and Solannus

snapped out of his paralysis. "I can't fight him from where he's sitting. We have to get him away from his minions."

As she spoke, dragons collided in the air. Their enemies were not all strong enough or possessed with sufficient fortitude to withstand the magic of the necromancers but they had other dark weapons with which to retaliate. Bredikai saw one clearly gifted with venom and its bile was acidic enough to melt through stone. There was another whose teeth had outgrown its bite and when it closed its mouth they jutted out like crude spikes. One had a tail with spikes bigger than the ones on its head. Borghalus they knew to be capable of possession in the very least and whatever attributes the others had over him, the demon-drake still remained the grandest and most malicious. When they got a better look at his face they saw that one of the demon's eyes was different from the other. Instinctually Bredikai reached for the tooth around her neck and knew it to be responsible for boring through the necromancer's face when she had been held captive by the demon's possession.

"Fight him?! Look at him, Bredikai! This was a mistake-" Solannus rasped and he was shaking his head. Bredikai descended from his back. She walked to face him and searched his eyes. They were both terrified and there was no sense in hiding it.

"You can walk away, Solannus," the girl said softly and meant it with every bit of sincerity she had left. "I won't hold it against you. We're not getting out of this alive."

"No... It is already too late," he said and the girl's heart stiffened with unparalleled coldness.

Bredikai felt her hairs stand on end. When she turned, Borghalus was looking straight at them. They could see his body shake with laughter but it was cut short by some different energy falling from the skies. Screeches pierced their ears in tones higher than the dragons' roars. Borghalus turned his angry gaze towards this unexpected menace. His minions were momentarily startled and searched the clouds for answers. To Solannus' eyes the newcomers looked like locusts at first- a wave of pestilence come to rain down upon them. But the swarm grew both in number and size and from this vantage point the pair saw the legion of creatures who had come to fight for Etherdeign at a moment's call.

They were half bird and half beast, their constitution pure muscle with talons strong enough to tear through dragon scales. In size they were but half of a standard drake but the griffins were more agile and cunning in their maneuvers. Dragons were not so flexible in comparison nor were they as quick to move. Against such creatures as griffins was when their large bodies worked against them and in the air they were matched in prowess.

Bredikai closed her eyes and sent a silent thank-you for their coming, letting out the breath that was suffocating her chest. Even she was surprised at the force the Griffinlord sent.

"Magnificent," Solannus said, watching the noble creatures attack red-eyed dragons in groups of tens and twenties. This was an unwelcome surprise for Borghalus whose wicked smile turned into a snarl. He was now prepared to scorch the pests out of the skies and cared not for the minions he would surely sacrifice in the process.

"We've got to get him away from there!" Bredikai cried but Solannus had a different idea.

"No. He will not be goaded," Solannus replied. "We go meet him head on. If we fail to kill him we may at least wound him and give the others a chance to finish the task."

"But he'll break the kingdom apart!"

"Bredikai," Solannus said severely, "whether we win or

lose Etherdeign as you knew it is forfeit. Look around you," he said and she swallowed back a lump. Her eyes stung and she clung so fiercely to her sword that her knuckles ground into her gauntlet.

The killsmith jumped on Solannus' back as the two charged into Riverlong, straight towards Etheria upon which sat a great white evil basking in the splendor of carnage. Now they were at the beginning of Etheria's long courtyard and there was some distance between them but the beast had taken no notice of them as he was more interested in scorching the griffins to ash. Solannus knew that it was on him to draw the demon's attention now. Bredikai leapt off and held her ground as Solannus took in the largest breath his lungs would allow. When he roared the killsmith felt the ground shake beneath her. She held her hands over helmet as Solannus' expulsion reverberated around her skull. His roar was so loud she thought her head would explode and it carried on for longer than she had expected.

Through the incredible chaos in and above Etherdeign, past the sounds of battle of dragon against dragon, griffins against serpents, necromancers and skeletons and everything else fighting in the madness, Borghalus stopped and turned his head around. They watched as his spine stiffened and his eyes surveyed the battlefield. From out of the bowels of the mayhem he had heard that familiar voice and his gaze trailed over the broken bodies, piercing through the smoke until...

The demon-drake smiled in that cruel manner they had become accustomed to and locked eyes with Solannus. No matter the distance between them they now saw one another and Borghalus took to flight to meet his brother.

"Get behind me," Solannus said, watching the white terror head towards them, unhindered by spells and other obstacles that lay in his path. He went through them with ease. All eyes, both friend and foe alike, turned to the demon advancing on the killsmith and the dragon.

"I'm staying right here," Bredikai said. The drake flew down. His shadow was so large it eclipsed the castle. Borghalus landed gracefully and stood across from the pair leaving roughly two medium-sized dragons worth of space between them. The sun was slowly deserting Etherdeign but it was not yet night; just a foul stretch of poisoned evening pregnant with smoke. What slight wind blew was stagnant and carried with it the stench of the burned. The three stood speechless in that barren place, the two eying the one and the one surveying them with due disgust. Tensions were mounting yet no one made a move until, in some strange leap of faith, Bredikai fell back into the ways of old and sent the Hexia flying towards Borghalus. The dragon didn't blink. The blade spun gracefully and landed like a small spike in front of the demon, its tip planted firmly in the cobblestone ground. With a cruel smile the dragon acknowledged the blade, the company that came with it and the supposed end to the charade he had endured.

"If it isn't the runt and his troglodyte keeper," Borghalus said smoothly and sat on his hind legs with his front neatly poised against his chest. "You have kept me waiting. Such unbecoming behavior..." he chuckled. He was like a statue, smooth and solid, aware of his breathtaking presence and the aura he commanded. He was so sure of himself and unthreatened by them, in fact, that the malicious smile twisting deep into the sides of his face never faltered. His one barren socket bore in it the golden eye of Septiannus and it was smaller than his bloodied own. But one would be mistaken in thinking that it made the beast look foolish to have one eye smaller and different than the other. If anything it made Borghalus more grotesque and one was never amiss as to which eye to look upon.

"I was beginning to wonder that you had drowned in the

Morduanas," said the demon, still amusing himself. "Gold does wonders for the soul. But you didn't touch it, I hope? One really hates to leave one's possessions unguarded," he chortled and his giant breast jostled around. "No, I sense even you are not so dull. I must admit, Solannus, I am rather impressed you've chosen to face your end head on. Good show, young man. Entirely pointless, of course…" he added and sighed, looking off towards non-existent rainbows. "But we shall have a chat first, little one, for you have information to give me and I the mercy to listen. Perhaps you would be kind enough to ask your human to take her flimsy arts elsewhere and give us due privacy."

Borghalus waited for an answer. When Solannus said nothing, Bredikai suddenly burst into laughter. He looked at her because clearly she had lost her mind and wanted their demise to be quick. The killsmith took her helmet off, planted her shield into the ground and put her hand over it like it was a cane. "Finally!" she cried as her laughter died down. "*Finally* the kind of dragon I'm used to. Oafish. Arrogant. And entirely detached from reality. See, Solannus, *this one* I understand. We speak the same language."

"It's not the time for this, Bredikai-" Solannus murmured.

"Are you kidding? " she cried and looked back at the amused demon. "This is the *perfect* time. This is, in fact, the only time," she said, turning deathly serious mid-sentence. "You owe this land a king you fucking snake- but I'll settle for your death as justice done." She wasn't laughing anymore but her voice remained steady. There were no sounds from their surroundings, or maybe their perception had lapsed. Either way, neither the dragon nor the killsmith could afford to turn around and survey the silence.

Borghalus snorted at the girl and ignored her, choosing

instead to provoke Solannus. "You are quiet, little brother. Are you not happy to see me? I am most insulted if that is the case," he said with false hurt and mimicked Solannus' frozen face. When the smaller dragon did not reply the demon's laughter rang across the broken courtyard and over the turned up stones bathed in blood. "Come, come, you must have something to say to me after all this time," he entreated.

"There is nothing I would say to you or of you that has not already been said, Borghalus," Solannus replied softly and the white demon was taken by roaring laughter once more.

"It speaks at last!" Borghalus said and pointed a claw. "Now that your tongue has loosened, perhaps you will tell me where you have hidden my father's heart. Honestly, Solannus, you surprised me with your thieving but *treason* against your kin… that is a bold move, indeed."

"Are you gonna let him talk to you like that?" Bredikai said to him but Solannus made no reply.

"He has no choice, killsmith. Do you, cur? Even a worm knows death when he sees it," replied the beast. "Tell me the location of the heart and I will keep our reunion brief and your deaths merciful."

"I do not know where its destiny lies but wherever it falls it will be beyond your reach," Solannus said with frail determination. "For while I live, never will there be another Dragonfather in Kharkharen."

"Strong promises from such a crude wretch," spat the serpent and his mirth turned to instant rage. "Worthless, deficient waste of a dragon! Shameful enough that you are a thief and a traitor, but you are also a liar and a poor one at that. Where is the heart?!" Borghalus' temper was swift to rise but his threatening bark was not enough to draw an answer from the smaller drake and Bredikai was motivated to speak, if only to rile the beast into a disadvantage.

"Solannus lied to me, too, you know," the killsmith said calmly, picking at something in her teeth. Her blood was pulsing thick and strong and the adrenaline she had hitherto felt was coming back to her now- but she kept her strength hidden. Her quick thinking reminded her that Borghalus couldn't risk killing the only creature who knew the location of the heart. His weakness had been staring them in the face this whole time. Surely the beast knew that the pieces he lacked had been discovered and he did not worry about recovering them. It was an easy enough task for one who commanded great numbers. But despite the rumors, the wild hunts and searches across Ethra's deepest corners, Borghalus had been unable to discover the location of the heart and without it his usurpation would be incomplete. He could continue to torture and kill as he pleased but whatever cruelty he unleashed, there would always be drakes to defy his rule. Bredikai chose not to dwell on what that meant for her own safety.

Indeed Borghalus had not worried about Solannus' demise before. Rather, he had encouraged the hunt. In the beginning he had been confident that he would not need the little rat to uncover the location. But over time his desperation grew and, as reports flooded in, telling of all the remains without a hint of the heart, Borghalus called off the order to destroy Solannus on sight. The pest would have to disclose the secret and the killsmith was somehow involved in the mystery.

Bredikai paced in front of Solannus without taking her eyes off their enemy. Borghalus was watching her intently now and trying to break into her mind. She could feel his eye invading her thoughts and calling her to meet him in that subconscious realm- but he could not get close enough and his fury was on the rise. The more the gnat yapped, the greater his distraction grew.

"Solannus does have an annoying habit of fibbing or lying by omission, you could say," the killsmith carried on like one without a care in the world. "I'll give you an example: despite the anguish of his darkest memory he still couldn't bring himself to tell me that *you* had caused his mother's death. Took a soul-sucking forest and a bunch of enchantments to traumatize that shit out of him. Yes, Sir…" she drawled and stretched her fingers. "All that messy business just so my friend here could relive the greatest trauma of his life; where you had your way with that poor woman and tore her apart- no better than a ravenous animal," she said.

A wave of noxious gasses floated between them and if there was a battle raging around them they cared nothing for it. It seemed now that there were only the three and they were locked inside a bubble ready to burst from within. They were impenetrable from the outside and Bredikai sensed that this was a touch by Althaea's hand. She took a few steps forward and the beast's eye faltered into suspicion. "Just like an animal…" she repeated softly. "And even then he couldn't put it into words. But I will. You're a kin-killer, Borghalus; the most abominable of creatures ever to blight this world. I tell you all this because you don't need to break into my mind looking for shards to scrape against me. I invite you in. Come and take a look around but don't you stop looking into my eyes. I want you to endeavor to understand the misery you've brought upon so many."

Borghalus' belly rumbled but the girl stood her ground. He was snarling at her but still vying to keep his arrogant demeanor at the forefront. He could have ended her then but he didn't need his wretched younger brother doing anything foolish- like attempting to protect the girl and getting killed in the crossfire before he could extract the necessary information. She was carving into him with her words and permitting him to enter her mind, this pathetic pint of a creature.

"Who *are* you, killsmith?" Borghalus asked, lowering his evil eye. "None of this concerns you. Why have you inserted yourself into our narrative? You wear that pathetic Reginnald's armor but you are not of his line. Do you even understand the sigil you bear? Certainly not, else you would know that it is Eberen himself who gives me this power! The gods were never enough to do away with his strength. He is the father who will claim his son- the one who should have had rightful dominion. But this means nothing to a little human- one whose very blood is tainted. Mmm, yes... I sense you are not long for this world."

"Does my health concern you, demon?"

Borghalus lifted his nose into the air and sneered at the girl. "I am merely trying to understand why a killsmith would risk her limited life for this waste of breath. Entertaining as your antics are, what know you of the slights of the past? Of this fell mistake and the bitch who bore him? For she was no kin of mine- that much should be clear."

"She was innocent!"

"False drake come to sully our line!" Borghalus barked and Bredikai knew she had dealt him the first blow. He was pacing now, albeit slowly, with his eye ever pointed in their direction. "There was no one to protect my father from her- and he would not hear me, the best of his heirs! Think you that I was the only one who saw what he had become? The once great Septiannus now a frail creature devoid of his senses and his strength! He let emotion overrule his duties. He spent my mother with his selfishness and polluted our family with his stupidity. You dare summon these overgrown snakes to aid you, these deserters of Kharkharen, when it was they who laughed behind his back and cursed his name, mocking the once proud Dragonfather for what he had become! And the whore who brought it all about..." he carried on, salivating from the force of rage coming out of his mouth. "Her whelp was destined to be a deformed cripple. Nature spat on them as I predicted it would. I performed an act of mercy when I took her life. Pity that I was prevented from following through with her spawn," he spat and Bredikai could feel Solannus sinking into the wasteland of his heart. In her bid to wound the demon before them she was sacrificing Solannus- but there was nothing to be done for it now.

"It is *too* much to bear," Borghalus cried and sat back in place. "It was a grand deception and weakness of character that spent this family. I broke no laws when I ended her life for she was no dragon born of Kharkharen! Now do you understand what he is, girl?" barked the drake, looking at Solannus the worm, the embodiment of his twisted rage.

"He knew what she was and loved her still," Solannus said, unable to look Bredikai in the face. "You still deny the purity of what they had; that it was *your* actions that broke our father's spirit- but I have never taken you for a fool, Borghalus. Even you cannot be so blind."

"Their connection was an abomination- as are *you*, cripple," Borghalus replied and there was no laughter left when he delivered his revelations. "How dare you stand among us, you crooked thing? You who are no more a dragon than the nonsensical child who speaks on your behalf. We are the most majestic of Eberen's children! What is love but our sacred duty to cull the weak? To protect our line for the sake of our own preservation, ere lesser beings mean to subdue us by spreading across Ethra like a disease! But you are right to stand there, for there never was nor will be a place among you with true dragons. No," he growled and his tone was the closest to hurt that they would ever discern. "I will suffer your company no more for even my patience has its limits. You will tell me the location of the heart and perhaps *then* you will finally have the decency to die."

Silence settled upon the three. Though Borghalus' chest bobbed up and down with anger it made no sound despite the demon's size.

"Huh," Bredikai said. From the corner of her eye she could see the glimmer of unshed tears in Solannus' eyes and knew that he was about to break. There was nothing more that Borghalus needed to say. She, too, was hurt, making short work of piecing together what the demon was alluding to and what she had suspected for some time. And no matter what little sense the hows and whys made to Bredikai, Solannus made no denials nor did he fight back. He was avoiding her gaze and she was happy to avoid him in return. But the demon-serpent's tongue had lit a fire in her own belly and though she did not let on, Bredikai was also at her breaking point. "Guess I was wrong..." she said, mostly to herself. "Doesn't really mean anything at this point, does it..."

"You are a strange one, killsmith."

"Am I?"

"You have been fed half-truths yet you still speak to defend this liar. But you stand lesser than the length of my tongue and twice as dull. The absurd ignorance you veil with sarcasm and guile will not save you. You understand this much. I can sense it."

"I'm not buying it," Bredikai said, toying with her helmet.

"What is your meaning, parasite?"

"I mean I've spent a lot of time thinking about why you are the way that you are," the killsmith replied. "Damn near melted Solannus' brain looking at it from every possible angle with the information that was given. Then it occured to me: why the fuck do I care? None of it matters... So he's half human. So fucking what? I remind you dragons that that's not the insult you think it is. I get it now... and I realize we've met before."

"Have we, now? Do enlighten me with your last breath."

"We have," Bredikai said and walked back to Solannus. She smiled at her friend and placed a hand on his neck. The gesture alone got Borghalus riled up but he was listening to her make sense of herself.

"Oh, maybe not me and you in the literal sense but you, Sir, are every puffed up tyrant who's built up a death scenario, desperately seeking a title to deify his delusions. You've forfeited all sense. Tortured and bled those you deemed weaker. Beasts like you are always underestimating what's in front of your faces. You tell yourself that you're better, that the gods designed you to *be* better- but the truth is you're a superficial lump looking for something to drive you, to give your existence meaning so you can justify your misguided bloodlust. And when you sit and simmer in dark corners you begin to understand just how worthless you are in the grand scheme of things. Where no one can hear the voice of your self-doubt, you realize that you've known it all along. You are *nothing*, Borghalus," she said and stood upright. She felt strange now in her own skin, more powerful and concentrated, her heart pounding to the bitter end.

"You're an insect trying to take down a forest," she said. "You eliminate those who would expose you for the empty shell that you are. You've gone to a place where neither reason nor rhyme can find you and tell yourself that the world you've created in your mind is the only way for a world to be. And it's at that moment you became the very opposite of how you would see yourself: a dumb beast frothing at the mouth, ready to pick apart anything that challenges your fragile self-worth... And the truly sad part is that you're too far gone to notice.

"So, you see, we've met before. I've come across a hundred of you in my short lifetime and I'll likely see a hundred more if I live past today. But believe me when I say that you're nothing special. Slightly bigger than what I'm used to, I'll grant you. You're all the same in the end... And there's no reasoning with the rot that sits at the bottom of the fucking barrel."

Borghalus pretended at unconvincing laughter. With the flick of a rotten claw he sent the Hexia whirling into the air, never taking his broken gaze off of the killsmith. As the shimmering blade pulsed it cut the air and through the deathly silence of their making they could just hear the metal weaving its way back home. Bredikai waited until the moment was right, her eyes stinging from the Hexia's turning reflection. With her right hand held up she plucked her sword from its descent and held it against her chest.

"Then we are come to it, killsmith, and neither of us will have to endure one another's company much longer!" roared the drake and unleashed a whirlwind of flame. Bredikai swiftly donned her helmet and braced herself against her shield, digging it further into the ground. If not the heat, the sheer force of the flame was bearing down on her and she was being pushed backwards. With all her might she held on and pushed forward. Solannus charged past the fire and went headfirst into Borghalus. He stopped just short of impact for he was too small to make a meaningful dent in the beast so he sunk his teeth in Borghalus' foot where the creature was soft and Borghalus howled, his fire interrupted.

The great enemy was not hurt so much as vexed, for the wound Solannus inflicted was a mere puncture to him. He shook his leg and flung Solannus aside and the dragon fell heavily upon the ground. With Borghalus' attention turned from her Bredikai had a new opportunity to attack and the surge of strength bolted her forward. She swung the Hexia, now pulsing with extraordinary force, down on the beast's leg just above where Solannus had bitten and carved through for as long as she could drag her sword. The Hexia had never been sharper, its strike never truer, belying the simple appearance of the blade. Borghalus was so lacking in color that the gushing blood shone bright red in stark contrast to his outward guise. The dragon aimed to kick her with his wounded leg now split and exposing folds upon folds of muscle but she was too small and evasive for him to catch. In her haste to get clear Bredikai slipped in the pools of the demon's blood and when the beast tried to crush her, she flung herself away and into her shield. When her helmet knocked into her she spat blood out of her mouth and rushed to stand. Her ribs were in pain and her breastplate was caving in on her left side. She touched it and winced but it was not enough to impede her counterattack.

Solannus quickly regained composure and took the chance to jump onto Borghalus' tail. He crept up the demon's spine to gnaw viciously at his back. Leaving no room for thought, he tore holes into the Borghalus' right wing then began clawing deep cuts into the back of his neck. Borghalus shook himself wildly but he spewed fire as he strove to fling Solannus off. Bredikai did her best to run through the crossfire but one forceful expulsion landed directly on her shield and she was knocked down. Her shield was charred and losing its constitution. In a more desperate attempt she ran past the beast, ducking and dodging his flailing tail. She had to take the risk and attack from where he couldn't face her directly so she jumped onto his tail and ran upwards. Solannus sunk every one of his teeth into his brother's back and was holding on through the frenzied movements but he simply was not making enough damage. He blew fire into the wounds he'd torn open and it pained the beast greatly but not enough to stop his thrashing.

Bredikai used the spikes on Borghalus' tail to gain ground and steady her footing, stabbing the beast's back with the Hexia to help move her forward. She had almost got up a decent way when the beast shook so wildly Solannus was thrown off and Bredikai fell back down the tail. With little chance for a second ascent Bredikai carved through his tail and, with great difficulty, she just about severed the end off before she was thrown and crashed in Solannus' side.

Borghalus' rage was at a level of blinding madness as he surveyed the severed tip of his tail now hanging on by one mangey piece of flesh. To their utter horror, Bredikai and Solannus saw the creature bite off the dangling tip and consume it in one gulp. He was bleeding heavily from his leg, his back and from what remained of his tail but, still, these wounds were not enough. Bredikai could barely move and she backed into Solannus, trying to move him from the oncoming inferno, but he would not budge. He was wounded and groaned from her touch.

In their skirmish they had moved around the courtyard but were still not where Bredikai needed them to be and Borghalus was coming at them now with enough firepower to melt even Solannus' dragonhide. Then, just as the great mouth was about to unleash final doom upon them, there came three voices so familiar she hardly needed to see them to know them. The bubble of isolation had broken from around them and the deafening cries of battle came thundering back like a tempest. The hearts and hopes of every fighting creature were with them now and they were not meant to be defeated so quickly.

"Cut 'is wicked head off, lads!" Ashley yelled and with a grand "*aye!*" the triplets flew on great dragons of bone straight into Borghalus from the flanks. Ashley was on one while Lesley and Murray sat together on another and they barreled into the demon like battering rams. The stench of mercury filled the air as Bredikai desperately tried to shake life back into Solannus. He was struggling to come to his senses and could barely hear what the killsmith was saying to him. He was bleeding from his belly but it was the force of his fall that had ruptured his insides.

Borghalus took to the air and met the undead dragons with full strength. He was shaken from the impact of the collision but they had a fraction of a living dragon's constitution and the demon was making short work of pulling their bones apart. With the triplets thrown to the ground Borghalus flew low and plucked Lesley and Murray like they were flowers. The skeletons slashed at his claws and fingers but he crushed their bones beneath his feet and what dust remained he kicked onto a paralyzed Ashley. Lamure gave a heart-wrenching outcry.

The wraith was in front of him now, facing the demon with what was uninhibited rage. She drew the dragon's gaze, her eyes on fire, and bore into the bent serpent's mind. Borghalus stopped dead in the air, flapping his tattered wings like a bird of prey, frozen by the wraith's hold. Althaea was with them instantly, bloodied but otherwise alright, summoning all necromancers who remained to entrap the creature. Few could rush to her side for the demon-drake's minions were powerful and kept the magic-wielders and griffins engaged. Arctor had had his left wing torn in half and he was bleeding from all sides. But he was still in the fight and landed by the killsmith's side, shielding them from any outside force. There was no sign of Torgen or Valtiga.

"Sonny you have to get up!" Bredikai yelled. "Arctor, we need to cause more damage- we've gotta move!" she cried and pointed towards the nearest brewery she could see. Arctor followed the killsmith's hand. He took to the air out of

Borghalus' line of sight. Solannus, shocked by the skeletons' fate, nodded blankly but understood what she had in mind. Lamure was losing her hold. As Borghalus' smile grew they saw both the wraith and Althaea shake. They were beginning to shrink under his mental oppression.

"Solannus!" Bredikai yelled, just as Lamure could hold the demon no longer and Borghalus pulled himself out of the necrotic enchantments. "Time to fly," Bredikai said to Solannus and hopped on his back. The dragon bit away the pain and roared to get his blood pumping. They charged into the city as the demon sped after them. Faster and faster Bredikai could hear the pulsing of Solannus' heart and they were just past the breweries with Borghalus not far behind. They were clearing through when the killsmith cried, "Burn them, Arctor- do it now!" The dragon swooped from above to let loose an inferno as Borghalus flew through the breweries.

The first explosion was enough to throw Bredikai off Solannus' back but he swiftly took her in his mouth, shielding her from the oncoming tornados and Etherdeign was consumed once more by flames. The explosions grew in number; higher and louder, decimating the city and engulfing everything they touched. Dark clouds overtook so much of the atmosphere that Solannus could hardly stop himself from coughing and had to spit Bredikai out. The dragon moaned and fell on his side and Bredikai shielded herself as best she could.

They opened their eyes to silence and a rising blackness that blended into the night. Nothing stirred for a moment and Bredikai exhaled, hoping the tremendous feat had been enough to break the beast. But when the smoke began to clear and Bredikai could see behind them, the demon Borghalus was crawling out from the ashes, wounded heavily but not enough to die. The killsmith felt her heart sink. What was left of her hope deserted her and she turned to the frail Solannus whose energy was entirely spent. Bredikai crawled and rested her back against the untorn part of his belly. He was breathing heavily and she moved up and down with the rhythm, chuckling at their useless state.

"I guess this is where we die," the killsmith said and smiled defeatedly. "Can't say we didn't try, right?" She spat out more blood and wheezed from the fumes. Not even the beast creeping towards them was enough to scare them now for they had done all they could and were depleted in both mind and body.

"No, Bredikai," Solannus said, groaning through the words and the blood spilling from his mouth. "Not you. This is where *I* die... Do not argue," he said, stopping her interruption as the wounded demon slithered towards them. "He must not get the heart- and I can stop it."

"Then give it to him, Solannus," Bredikai pleaded with the dragon. She winced and crawled over to look him in the eyes, "Let him have it and we'll live to fight another day!" she entreated but Solannus smiled drowsily and would not hear her.

"You know where it is..." he said calmly. "Where they both are. And you know to aim for mine. He must not claim it," he whispered and Bredikai shook her head violently but the dragon would not be overruled. "Stop this nonsense at once, killsmith. You have a killdeed to complete. Now lay down. You will know when to strike."

"You're out of your fucking mind," the killsmith said angrily. "I won't do it, Solannus! No- you're, you're delirious from the pain," she protested, her hands shaking and unable to handle the Hexia properly.

"Bredikai, listen to me," said the dragon, "I have lived more this year with you and our company than I have in my entire life. I ran, I sailed... I flew! This part of our story is over," he whispered and smiled. "I am fulfilled… I have to let go now- and you must do the same. Strike true and break the cycle of cruelty. You gave me your word, killsmith." Something sharp caught in her throat but Bredikai was out of time. If she wished to follow through she had to go with Solannus' plan so she lay by her friend's side as if unconscious and Borghalus' head hung over them, a pale veil over the shadows.

"Enough games, boy, my mercy is not infinite," came the beast's gravelly voice and Bredikai listened, completely still. Borghalus plunged his claws into Solannus' tail, nailing him down to prevent escape. But Solannus did not cry or scream. He lifted his head to look at his brother while their blood spilled into the ground.

"I invite you into my thoughts, brother," Solannus spoke softly. "There you will find what you are looking for; but you must walk the path for the heart is in the mountain. Know that I never meant you such grief," he said but both warning and warmth went ignored. Borghalus gazed deep into Solannus' eyes. At first the younger dragon gasped from the coldness of the intrusion but he let it crawl through him uninterrupted. Down dark paths he drew Borghalus in, dangling the promise of a heart in front of the beast. Through crags and crevices he called to his brother until a mighty peak shone in the darkness. The creature followed, his veins pulsing from the thrill of exposing the treasure. And just when he saw his bloodied prize, a small voice fluttered from the world outside.

"Now, Bredikai."

Bredikai grabbed the Hexia with both hands and took a last breath. She closed her eyes and plunged her sword deep into Solannus as two monstrous howls seized through the air. The ground began to quake violently beneath them as fissures of stone tore through the body of Solannus. Like the first fires of a long-held eruption, great spikes flew out from where the dragon lay bleeding and Borghalus was not quick to move. He was still caught in Solannus' mind and his claws were deeply embedded in the dragon's tail, impeding his escape. Stone was rumbling through Solannus' body now, swiftly and strong enough to tighten around the demon.

 Bredikai screamed and lost hold of her sword as it stuck into Solannus and was swallowed by stone. The killsmith rolled away and hobbled to her feet. As she ran, a great crevice broke the earth, separating her from the dragon and drowning Borghalus' cries. Borghalus roared with insanity even as the mountain grew past his height and imprisoned him. But the great enemy was worn and out of fire, unable to make sense of this new entrapment. A sharpened spike arose from where Bredikai struck, consuming the Hexia and what remained of Solannus. The great mountain continued to spring forth, tearing upwards and consuming Borghalus whole. The bottom was expanding in size even as Bredikai ran but the mountain cared nothing for the ground crumbling around it. Bredikai could not afford to stop. The stone now expanded forcefully into the air, growing taller and mightier than the demon had been. Ruptures deepened in the ground and the earth was breaking apart beneath her feet. The killsmith was losing her agility and it was becoming difficult to avoid the huge gaps that threatened to drag her into their clutches.

 Rushing to the girl's aid, Arctor swept by as Ashley hurled the killsmith onto the dragon's back and they flew away from the quaking earth. A small swarm of griffins intercepted what remained of the demon's minions as the blood-fueled drakes tried in vain to tear open the mountain. Soon what was left of the enemy was spent on the battlefield and those who did not die that day fled far into the night, beyond the borders of Etherdeign.

 Bredikai had neither spirit nor energy left. The ink on her face would lengthen no more and it ran long and deep with the history of feats accomplished. Her eyes were clouded and couldn't focus on the land they flew over. She remembered nothing from that point on except that she would have given anything to lie unawakened. The dragon Solannus as they knew him was no more, and the last deed of the killsmith of Etherdeign stood as a testament to that end; mighty enough to touch the heart of Eberen himself.

Killdeed complete.

EPILOGUE: A KINGDOM WITHOUT A KING

"Please, you must leave her to rest, it's only been a few hours-"

"What did your father 'ave to say about all this, then? That's what I thought. Ach-me! I ought to tell him *and* your mother about what the hells you've all been up to. I've a right mind to send them a parchment young lady- and I'd do it, too, if I didn't think he already knew!"

"Will you *please* stop hollering above my head," Bredikai groaned, struggling to open her eyes. Every piece of her ached and when she saw the stone slab she was laying on she understood why. "Really? No one thought to move me to a bed?" she asked incredulously as Zira gave her something called a special blend though it was really just warmed up Coppus Ale. "Ugh this tastes like shit," she grumbled, drinking it anyway. "Don't we have anything colder?" The boy looked around innocently enough but was swept aside by an ever-disappointed grandfather who was looking dirtied and ashy but otherwise fit as a horse.

"*Colder...*" the old man repeated with fake sweetness. "The wee heiress wants something colder, does she? Perhaps you should've thought about that before you set the whole rotten kingdom ablaze!" he hollered and Bredikai flinched from his shrill complaining. Looking up, she realized that it was barely dawn but light was coming from fires yet to be put out. That was going to take some time. "Perhaps you'd like to explain why there be dragons laying about in the bloody kingdom- and necromancers!"

"I think it's self-explanatory," Bredikai stated curtly and sighed. Zira helped her sit up properly and she gave him a hug, thanking the boy for all he'd done to help them.

"Let the girl breathe, Uncle Roray," came a voice. "She looks worse than the breweries." It was Fitzburt and the man exchanged a flirty hello and wink with Lamure who, if she didn't know better, blushed in return. Bredikai looked at them through squinted eyes and tried to re-orient herself.

"How many years have I been out?" she asked suspiciously.

"As I was saying," interjected the wraith, "you've only just had a few hours of rest. Lay back down." But Bredikai refused and looked around her. There was much movement even in these short hours and creatures foreign to Etherdeign were everywhere, dutifully coming and going about their business of reparation. No one was left jobless or without an errand to run. She breathed a sigh of relief when Fitzburt informed her that most of the civil population had safely emptied the kingdom before the battle but they had not gotten far and soon found themselves returning. While lives had been lost, Etherdeign would surely recover in a few years' time.

"Have the, uh... have the griffins left?" Bredikai asked her cousin.

"Yes, they have," the captain replied with a smile. "But Lord Ten'Mei has asked me to deliver a message. He expects a visit from you at your earliest convenience. He would like to have words... Many, in fact," he smirked and Bredikai groaned, wondering how long she could delay that event.

"And what about Althaea; is she still here? I'm seeing some of her people," she said. Truly there were a few necromancers around, as could be seen from the glow of enchantments flowing through the air. There was also no small number of skeletons walking about but her heart sank knowing that they were not from her company. Lamure saw into the girl's heart and understood what her thoughts dwelled on.

"Mistress Althaea has returned to the Ire Craven," the wraith explained. "Indeed many still fear retaliation from Borghalus' minions but I think it unlikely to happen so soon- if at all." She took a moment to remember the rest of the goings-on and wished to deliver her words delicately to their former leader. "Master Arctor is still with us but he means to make the long journey back to Kharkharen. He wishes to check on Mergalus and assess the state of their land. Ashley intends to go with him. He wishes to be left to his thoughts for a while…"

"I see," Bredikai said tight-lipped. She began removing what was left of her armor. When she had fallen unconscious they chose to leave her as is for there was no telling how deep her wounds ran and they didn't want to disrupt her body further while she lay in a seemingly critical state. They had bandaged what was exposed. With the breastplate now removed Bredikai felt around her ribs and checked for other fractures. "I'm sorry, gramps," she whispered and didn't know what else to say. Old Cronunham scoffed and folded his arms. For some odd reason he still had his apron on and when he sighed she could see his large belly move up and down from underneath it. "I didn't know what else to do…"

"Ach," replied the old man, waving off the apology. Smiling was not in his character so one had to listen closely to discern any compliment. "Don't know that anyone could've done better..." he said and cleared his throat to indicate that that sentiment was to be forgotten immediately. "And you'll have time to explain it to everyone. Don't even think about leaving this kingdom until every last bit of it's back in working order, d'ya hear? Best start with the breweries," he ordered with a fat finger to the face. Grandpa Cronunham turned and walked back to what remained of his poor guild with the boy sheepishly at his heels. Bredikai watched them leave and gave a short wave to Zira when he could sneak a look behind.

Carefully Bredikai stood up and linked her arm through her cousin's so he could help her walk. Lamure was at her right as Bredikai hobbled and cursed and Fitzburt was moving faster than necessary. They stopped at a point in Etheria's broken courtyard where they could get a clear look at Riverlong and the general state of Etherdeign- or what was left of them. No stone was where it should be. Half the castle had been crushed under Borghalus' weight- not that it mattered anymore, since they were devoid of a king...

"Oh mercy, they didn't elect you king, did they?!" Bredikai asked her cousin, terrified of his answer. His reply was an instant relief. Fitzburt clarified that he was still very much a captain of the guard (one of the few remaining) and that, in fact, no one was volunteering to take over the kingdom as yet; what with all its current problems. There was even talk of rebuilding below ground but nerves were frayed and everyone was saying everything at the moment. They had a decent enough system in place that meant Etherdeign could survive without a king or queen for some time.

Lamure stood next to Bredikai as they surveyed the wreckage being scavenged by Althaea's people. With whatever magic was left to them they cast spells and high grade enchantments upon the dead and Bredikai grimaced knowing she had no excuse for what was happening.

"When I told you that the necromancers would be of aid to you, this was not what I had in mind," Fitzburt said and everyone pursed their lips. "We realize this poses a potential problem, do we not?" the man asked as they watched the resurrecting battlefield with mild concern.

"Eeyyup," Bredikai answered. She rolled her tongue around her mouth and grazed it against the new teeth coming in above the ones Lesley and Murray had donated to her. "And there go the bone dragons..." she mumbled, watching them fly off. "Well this is just what you want to see right now, isn't it..."

Fitzburt turned to say something but was called away by a group of soldiers most concerned about the sporadic reanimation of the fallen. He winked at Lamure and left the ladies, all the while wondering how they thought he'd be able to deal with the situation.

Bredikai assured Lamure that she was fit to walk and they carefully paced out of the courtyard. The wraith did not need to ask where they were headed and she floated beside her friend silently until they were at the foot of a terrific mountain whose shadow was not devoid of warmth. It stood majestically, watching over Etherdeign; a pillar of warning to those who meant the kingdom and its people harm and a symbol of hope for those who had witnessed what transpired. They were the only two there for no one had dared come close.

Bredikai trailed her swollen hand against the stone and, overwhelmed by the grief she had yet to accept, began to cry. She sank to her knees, laying her forehead against the rock. In her mind she told herself that she could hear the beating of a heart deep within the mountain but it was too much to hope for given the circumstances.

"How did we get here, Sonny?" she asked and Lamure had to look away else she'd fall to pieces worse than her friend.

"You're safe now. I promised you'd be safe in Etherdeign. No one can hurt you anymore," Bredikai said, wiping her eyes against the back of her hand. Slowly she braced herself against the stone and used it to help her stand.

Lamure looked at the broken woman. The former leader of their company was miserable, almost green in pallor and desolate in spirit. Her eyes were filmy and disoriented. Bredikai cast the rest of her grief aside for when she could wallow in it in solitude but there was something else amiss, something in her eyes that lingered on a problem unrelated to the loss of her dearest friend. Lamure could not place it but it felt to her like a growing vexation the woman had no intention of verbalizing.

"We should get you back," the wraith said softly. "Your color looks off. You alright?"

"Hah," Bredikai chuckled sadly and sniffed. "No."

"You want to talk about it?"

Bredikai looked at her reflection on a bit of smooth surface. Her mind was everywhere and her thoughts were nowhere. "We all did what we had to do," she said. "I know that. And the shock will pass, as it always does. But the pain... Poor Lesley and Murray... They deserved a better end. And Solannus... I don't- I don't know if I did the *right* thing, you know? I don't know anything anymore..." she said and let the words linger around them.

"Life chose to test Solannus heavily," Lamure replied. "Heavier than most. But I think the friendship you two shared was the greatest gift you could have given each other. Death doesn't have the power to undo such bonds. Trust me," she smiled kindly, "you will always have it."

Bredikai nodded and smiled through her heartache. They turned and started walking into the city with no particular destination in mind. It felt good to be able to stretch her legs and Lamure was intent on lightening their hearts else they risked the both of them collapsing into sobbing heaps.

"You got a lot out of Borghalus," Lamure said. "I think he spoke to you more than he's spoken with anyone in his life. Actually, I'm surprised you were able to get such a rise out of him."

"Fucking lizard," Bredikai spat at his name and the wraith smiled to see her regaining her form. "They're all a bunch of fucking yappers- the ones like him, I mean. And so sensitive. Everyone with their daddy issues. I wanted to know what lay beneath the surface and sure enough all I had to do was carve it out."

"Listen, Bredikai, about Solannus' mother... When I looked into Borghalus' mind I saw more than I was expecting to and-"

"Let's not think about it now," Bredikai said and the wraith nodded with understanding. "I know what I heard but I need to make sense of it in my own mind first and it looks like I'm going to be here a while. But you- you should go home and see your parents," she said. But when Bredikai saw the wraith look off towards the castle with that strange spectral blush her eyebrows shot up and she chuckled genuinely. "Or maybe we need you around here for a while?" she asked.

"Oh I wouldn't dream of leaving you here to handle all this by yourself," the wraith said. "You're going to need every bit of help."

"Uh-huh," the killsmith said with a crooked half-smile, not believing a word of it.

"And of course there's much to discuss," Lamure said, more seriously now. "In my heart I doubt that Borghalus' minions will take this lightly. I'm afraid we've caused them more than a few problems- not the least of which being that the Dragonfather's line is broken. Septiannus' remains are scattered; at least half are locked in that mountain. The eye, the horn, the claw, the bone... The wing, of course... and the heart. Say, Solannus never did reveal the location of the heart, did he?" the wraith asked sincerely.

"He didn't have to," Bredikai answered cryptically, looking away and fiddling with the tooth around her neck. "I'm going to hope that Mergalus is protecting the wing. Arctor will know what to do about it. Borghalus had the eye and horn. He was bluffing about the claw, though. I think that thing's still out there. Not that it matters... Althaea was right about everything."

"The necromancers have been good to us, Bredikai. I fear you are still hesitant with your trust but we would not be here without Mistress Althaea. This alliance is not something we should cast aside." The woman nodded quietly, turning her thoughts to the Hexia she had left plunged in her beloved friend's body. "However Borghalus' minions choose to proceed, all of Ethra will have turned against them by now," Lamure added. "My father's network will have seen to it."

"Ah, the Rogues... You're a fearsome bunch."

"Never too late," smiled the wraith. "Now that you're free, maybe it's time to look into something beyond killsmithing."

Bredikai's lip curved despite her poor mood. "I think killsmithing is done with me at this point," she said. "You know, I always thought it would be nice to open up a little tavern. That would take my mind off things for a while... If I know Etherdeign, we should have at least one functional brewery by the end of the day," she mused.

"That's a fantastic idea," Lamure beamed. "I won't lie- it would be good to stay settled in one place for a while. I think we've all had enough travel for the foreseeable future."

"We all…" Bredikai repeated sadly. "Who's left?"

Lamure didn't answer. Out of habit of company she had said the words. She looked away in sorrow. Solannus was surely beyond her reach and not a single grain of Lesley or Murray remained. There was nothing she could recover from them; and she had tried. It warmed her heart that they felt no pain and didn't have to live a cursed half-life anymore. They would not abandon Ashley to solitude- Ashley who by all accounts should have joined his siblings in the beyond, now that Borghalus was ended. Curious how these curses worked.

The walk was doing them both good and rays of early sunlight gained in potency when they had the ill luck of falling upon the coppertine castle. So began the re-blinding of Etherdeign and even the undead were complaining about the heat. When the wraith grew quiet an idea came to Bredikai.

"We should dedicate our tavern to the triplets. I know Ashley would like that. He'll come back to us when he's ready. I'm gonna miss those crazy fucks…" she sighed. "Zira could enchant the drinks so we could have both living and undead customers. There's a lot of both running around these days, and it'll get the boy off of gramps' ass for a while. What do you think?"

"I think it's perfect," Lamure said, now wiping at her own face and smiling through the tears. There was a sparkle or two and the spectral sentiment was gone.

"I know just the place for it," Bredikai said. "There was a poor excuse for a forest where we found them. It was where I first met Solannus, too… Just outside of Etherdeign. I'd say we could push the kingdom to pay and fix that damn portal but maybe we could convince your father to finance us instead."

"I think that could be arranged."

Bredikai smiled. "I could see you as a tavern-wraith."

"Me?"

"Why not?" the woman asked, taking in the morning fumes. She coughed and almost hacked up a lung but the citizens of Etherdeign, who were now returning by the dozen, were utterly disinterested in putting out any more fires. They were tired, frazzled and far more invested in discussing the unholy resurrection with a group of very annoyed necromancers. Some returnees were poking at skeletons and the skeletons were poking back.

"Break the mold," Bredikai continued. "See? It's a new age full of hope and we seem to have sidestepped death yet again. Permanent death, anyway."

"If you're going to open up a tavern you need to apply to the Brewers Guild for permits," came Zira's voice and Lamure asked Bredikai to remind her to sever their connection somehow.

"Good golden grief these guilds don't let up, do they?" said the wraith.

"Why do you think I damn near forfeited my life to get out of one?"

"You *could* have become an elected royal, you know," Lamure offered. "Before all this, I mean... Or you could have started your own killsmithing guild and reigned supreme."

"The thought never even crossed my mind. Huh," the woman shrugged and they chuckled at the thought.

The pair walked and floated away from the castle, heading deep into Riverlong. It was a beautiful morning and, as crisp as the weather should have been on that winter day, the mind-numbing heat was inspiring unparalleled levels of motivation in the populace to rebuild and re-enchant. That and they desperately needed shit to stop burning. Locals were passing out from the swelter and getting too comfortable with skeletons doing their bidding.

As the undead continued to rise around them and the familiar sound of skin melting off and confusion grew, Bredikai sighed and played with the tooth around her neck. A new Etherdeign was sprouting around them and it would be a better one so long as there was nothing to endanger the fabric of their peace.

"All this busyness..." Lamure observed. "Pretty exciting to be part of something new."

"Sure is."

"And we absolutely must consider returning with Arctor, if only to check on Mergalus and tie up loose ends. Make certain Ashley doesn't do anything drastic. Then I'll go with you to see the gr-... er, Lord Ten'Mei, of course," the wraith rambled on, checking things off in her head one by one.

"Sounds like a plan."

"In fact, there is much too much to discuss. If you have the energy, I think I might be ready for our first post-battle drink. Surely your grandfather can spare some more from his stock," she continued excitedly.

"I am beyond ready- and he has no choice," Bredikai said.

Lamure paused as they looked everywhere but the mass resurrection taking place. "Fantastic, yes..." she said and kept her smile plastered on. "And maybe- after you've knocked back a few dozen, of course- you'll be interested in discussing the fact that you are turning into a dragon," she pointed out and watched the former killsmith frown angrily and grind her teeth to dust.

"Not even close to being interested," Bredikai gritted out. She closed her eyes and sighed at her own stupidity. "Of all the fucking things...." she grumbled and Lamure couldn't help but chuckle at her friend's newfound torment.

The sun continued its noble ascent. As light brushed against the marred face of the land, Bredikai looked back to the mountain piercing through her kingdom. It was so tall the summit was shielded by the clouds and there was no telling how far it would continue to grow. She saw Arctor perched on the face overlooking their direction. He was surveying the world beyond Etherdeign, keeping a watchful eye. The elder roared and she likened it to his call upon the slopes of Solannus' sanctuary but the tone was changed and no longer conveyed desperation. Indeed, this was a call of another kind; a summons to those who had lost their home and their way. And then, there were dragons breaking through the clouds. More and more they fell like stars cast out of the heavens, battered and bleeding from their forced exile. Arctor roared again and the drakes descended upon the mighty mountain of their refuge. The elder's call guided them as they flew through the tendrils of sunlight, disrupting the golden beams with their crimson-stained exodus. One by one the mountain welcomed them to their new home.

ABOUT THE AUTHOR

D. Ertug

D. Ertug is a 37 year old dragon who hails from Northern Cyprus. She was raised in New York City. She received her bachelor's degree, double-majoring in Communications and Philosophy from the university formerly known as Virginia Wesleyan College. She then took her edumacated self to Japan where she spent close to a decade teaching English in the beautiful Fukui Prefecture. Upon returning to the Mediterranean, she opened a small tattoo shop where she continues to lovingly inflict body art on anyone who utters the word "tattoo". She, along with the three cultures simultaneously swimming in her head, are lovers of fantasy and literature. Now she is sharing the craziness born from that love with the world.

Made in the USA
Middletown, DE
28 September 2024